A DISTANT SHORE

Peter Yeldham's extensive writing career began with short stories and radio scripts. He spent twenty years in England, becoming a leading screenwriter for films and television, and also wrote plays for the theatre, including the highly successful comedies *Birds on the Wing* and *Fringe Benefits*, which ran for two years in Paris. Returning to Australia he won numerous awards for his television screenplays, among them *1915*, *Captain James Cook*, *The Alien Years*, *All the Rivers Run*, *The Timeless Land* and *The Heroes*. His adaptation of Bryce Courtenay's novel *Jessica* won a Logie Award for best mini-series. He is the author of nine novels, including *A Bitter Harvest*, *The Currency Lads*, *Against the Tide*, *Land of Dreams*, *The Murrumbidgee Kid* and *Barbed Wire and Roses*.

For more information please visit
peteryeldham.com

PETER YELDHAM

A DISTANT SHORE

MICHAEL JOSEPH
an imprint of
PENGUIN BOOKS

MICHAEL JOSEPH

Published by the Penguin Group
Penguin Group (Australia)
250 Camberwell Road, Camberwell, Victoria 3124, Australia
(a division of Pearson Australia Group Pty Ltd)
Penguin Group (USA) Inc.
375 Hudson Street, New York, New York 10014, USA
Penguin Group (Canada)
90 Eglinton Avenue East, Suite 700, Toronto, Canada ON M4P 2Y3
(a division of Pearson Penguin Canada Inc.)
Penguin Books Ltd
80 Strand, London WC2R 0RL England
Penguin Ireland
25 St Stephen's Green, Dublin 2, Ireland
(a division of Penguin Books Ltd)
Penguin Books India Pvt Ltd
11 Community Centre, Panchsheel Park, New Delhi - 110 017, India
Penguin Group (NZ)
67 Apollo Drive, Mairangi Bay, Auckland 1310, New Zealand
(a division of Pearson New Zealand Ltd)
Penguin Books (South Africa) (Pty) Ltd
24 Sturdee Avenue, Rosebank, Johannesburg 2196, South Africa

Penguin Books Ltd, Registered Offices: 80 Strand, London, WC2R 0RL, England

First published by Penguin Group (Australia), 2009

1 3 5 7 9 10 8 6 4 2

Cover design by Marina Messiha © Penguin Group (Australia)
Text design by Cathy Larsen © Penguin Group (Australia)
Cover photographs: Sunset © Richard Cummins/Corbis;
Pacific Ocean sunset from boat © Jupiter Images
Typeset in 11.5/17pt ITC Legacy Serif by Post Pre-press Group, Brisbane, Queensland
Printed and bound in Australia by McPherson's Printing Group, Maryborough, Victoria

National Library of Australia
Cataloguing-in-Publication data:

Yeldham, Peter.
A distant shore / Peter Yeldham

9781921518089

A823.3

penguin.com.au

For my brother Dick

School teacher, soldier, salesman, farmer

Prologue

I was nineteen the first time I saw Katerina. It was during the hot summer of 1968; she was seventeen years old. I doubt if she even noticed me, for this was at a crowded New Year's Eve party, and my reticence kept it a distant admiration. Besides, she was in love with someone else.

We were the new generation called baby boomers, and had been told we were the heirs to an exciting age. It felt more like an unstable and turbulent age: an American president we admired was assassinated; his brother, who might have been president, was shot on a public podium; there were riots, revolutions and the murder of peacemakers like Martin Luther King Jr. Russian tanks crushed rebellion in Prague, the French tested nuclear weapons in the Pacific, the Cold War was a threatening shroud we lived under, and the race to build the biggest bombs made us uneasy about the men whose fingers on atomic triggers had the capacity to destroy us.

It was little wonder we marched in protest. Katerina and I were allied in dissent against the Vietnam War, and in time our camaraderie forged a close friendship. I knew it could never be more than that, although when I left Australia it was she who came to the wharf at Woolloomooloo to say an emotional goodbye and wish me luck. She was married by then so youthful dreams were in vain, but my abiding memory was her slim figure, her dress ruffled by the breeze as she stood waving, before the cargo ship – the cheapest passage I could afford – edged into the harbour and turned northward from Australia towards the rest of the world.

It was the last time I saw her for thirty years.

By then she had created headlines, been vilified by the media and savagely traduced by radio luminaries on their chat shows. Then she was brought to trial in a closed court, in the name of national security. But regardless of the prohibited reportage from the courtroom, details did emerge. I'm told that despite her probable loss of freedom she appeared calm. It was unnecessary to add she looked beautiful; she had always been that.

It is on the public record that she pleaded guilty. Legend has it the judge asked if she had anything to say before he passed sentence.

She replied she would like to quote something.

He wanted assurance that it was brief, and thus would not take up the court's valuable time.

She promised it was brief, and in the empty court she spoke in a voice that only His Honour, the prosecutor and a few officials could hear: ' "All human beings are born free and equal in dignity, and should act towards each other in a spirit of brotherhood." Article One of the United Nations Declaration of Human Rights, that has been forgotten lately in this country.'

It was rumoured the judge frowned, and expressed himself forcibly when sentencing. The media was allowed to report only that the accused had been sent to prison for four years. It seemed unbelievably severe, without impartiality or mercy. When I heard, I thought surely there would be outrage.

But this was Australia in 2002, I was reminded. A very different place to the one I'd left years earlier. A far harsher country. Rigid new security laws, the interception of the Norwegian ship *Tampa*, claims of children thrown overboard and the Pacific Solution – it was an Australia I would not easily recognise. It was a time when fear ruled, and the safeguards of Magna Carta and *habeas corpus* were endangered. An unhappy and troubled time, when we lost integrity, and felt like strangers to ourselves.

As for the sentence, I was told most people were satisfied she had been dealt with so firmly. Opinion polls all declared that justice had been done.

PART 1

Kate

Chapter 1

OCTOBER 2001

The wooden fishing boat was overcrowded and had no name. In time it would be called SIEV X, the initials standing for Suspected Illegal Entry Vessel and the X denoting its unknown origin. The passengers on board, the majority of them women and children, were frightened, for the boat was not what they had been promised. They had been assured it was a seaworthy craft, one that would take them to an Australian island where relatives and friends would be waiting to welcome them. They were prepared to pay whatever they could afford and take any risk to be reconciled with their families, until they saw the vessel.

It was dilapidated, rotting in places, and appeared unsafe for a voyage anywhere, let alone a thousand-kilometre journey across the Java Sea to Christmas Island. Realising the danger, most of the passengers were trying to disembark and reclaim the precious money paid for their passage, but a squad of armed police summoned by the smuggler, Abu Quassey, was preventing them.

Bewildered children began to cry, unnerved by the anxiety of their parents. There was a scuffle as a husband pushed his way to where Quassey stood protected by a bodyguard, demanding the right to take his family off the boat. The bodyguard produced a pistol. Passengers scattered as Quassey used the butt of the weapon to hit the complainant savagely to the temple. There were screams, then a cowed silence as the man collapsed with blood streaming from his head.

The clamour to be set ashore resumed among the terrified parents. A young mother with three small daughters approached the police, begging them to help her leave the ship. Her daughters, pretty girls between the ages of six and nine and wearing colourful batik dresses with matching white ribbons in their hair, all watched while their mother was forced back at gunpoint and told this was impossible; there could be no refunds, nor could anyone disembark because the local authorities had lost patience and decreed these homeless people could not remain in Indonesia any longer.

Included among the nationalities on board were Afghani men and women in flight from the Taliban, and Iranian fugitives escaping religious persecution. But the majority were Iraqi wives with children, attempting to reach Australia to join their husbands who had fled from Saddam Hussein. The men had come on earlier boats to places like Christmas Island or Ashmore Reef, and after interrogation in detention centres had been granted temporary protection visas. But a rash of new legislation had imposed different conditions on the visas: from now on they would find it almost impossible to become citizens, and if they did manage to stay in this country they would not be allowed family reunions. The reality that this was in effect a lifetime ban against ever seeing their wives and children again took time to absorb; it seemed so inhuman.

It was not something the wives or children knew about. After long separation they had escaped from Iraq, selling their homes to buy fares and forged papers that would take them on a perilous journey across Pakistan to Jakarta. Their first goal was to reach the Australian embassy and apply for the right to join their husbands or relatives. Some were already classified genuine political refugees by the United Nations, but at the visa application centre on the Plaza Abda this did not seem to count. There they pleaded for safe asylum, lodged their applications as directed, then waited in hope. They heard nothing.

In some cases a few years passed without a reply. Stranded in Indonesia, disliked by the locals and called illegals, they were refused entitlement to work or access to medical care. Their children were prohibited from attending school. The families lived by banding together, renting derelict buildings, sometimes as many as forty or fifty people occupying a few dilapidated rooms, getting a few hours rest each day by sleeping in shifts. What money they still had was rapidly diminishing. They felt utterly rejected by the rest of the world, wondering if anyone knew or cared of their plight, and correctly suspecting in their misery that no one did.

So when Abu Quassey – an Egyptian smuggler who operated with impunity in the region – circulated news around the marketplaces that he had a boat capable of taking them to Australian territory on Christmas Island, those who still had money gladly accepted his offer. Any cost, any risk, seemed preferable to what they had been enduring, living in limbo without prospect of a future. It was how most of them felt until they saw the flimsy transport, and then at gunpoint they were prevented from disembarking.

The boat had barely left the Sumatran coast before it was perilously low in the water, and one of the bilge pumps failed. The crew forced male passengers to help keep it afloat by bailing. The women tried to find space for their children to rest, and sought protective shade from the harsh afternoon sun. As it grew dark the air became oppressive. A humid breeze brought no relief. The diesel engine kept a steady rhythmic beat, but the ocean swell grew turbulent and towards midnight waves started to wash over the deck. Some passengers cursed, others prayed; all were dripping wet from the increasing spray and the sweat of their own bodies. There was a total of four hundred and twenty-one people on board, and most of them were unaware that there were only sixty life jackets.

Kate drove home feeling tired and discouraged. It had been a frustrating day, ever since she reached the Villawood Detention Centre in Sydney's west that morning to be met by the sign she knew from previous visits:

PROPERTY OF THE COMMONWEALTH OF AUSTRALIA.

There was a rumour the sign had once contained the word 'Welcome', but Kate assumed this was just a sick joke. Welcome was not something she had ever experienced there, and after a ninety-minute wait in the heat before being admitted to the visitors' processing area, she then had to undergo the slow security check through access gates protected by a razor-wire fence. The procedure was always rigid, but the mood of those on duty could vary, and today the guards seemed more aggressive than usual. Despite being a frequent visitor she had to fill in the same form each time and prove her identity, and was then abruptly ordered to leave her car keys, her licence and mobile phone – all of them forbidden items that would be returned when she left. Handbags and other personal objects had to remain in the car. Anything in the way of gifts brought in for detainees had to be listed, then handed over to be placed on a conveyor belt and X-rayed. It was a long, slow process endured by a queue of refugee advocates, caseworkers, lawyers and volunteer visitors, all trying to conceal resentment at the confrontational manner of the guards, for it would only increase their hostility.

A band was attached to Kate's wrist before she passed through the metal detector. It did not trigger the alarm, for she was carrying only a telephone card for her client and packets of biscuits for the children. A loud announcement on the public address system drowned the next order from a female guard, but Kate knew what was required; she held out her hand to be imprinted with a coded stamp, then queued to go through the final locked checkpoint. It was hard to believe this place had once been a cheerful migrant hostel.

In the compound with its few plastic tables and sparse number of chairs, she met with a Burmese mother and her two daughters who had been detained for over a year. A petite attractive woman, she was plainly afraid of being deported back to Burma, where her husband had been imprisoned and then executed by the military junta. Kate had to break the distressing news that they'd exhausted every avenue for a stay of expulsion. A last appeal to the Immigration Minister to grant a bridging visa on humanitarian grounds had been turned down. He gave no reason for the decision to send them back, nor under the new regulations was he required to do so.

The children cried and their mother did her best to calm them, while she tried haltingly to express her thanks for the efforts made on her behalf. But despite this instinctive courtesy, it was her scared and dismayed face that stayed with Kate long after she left.

The remainder of the day did not improve. There had been two hearings before a single arbitrator at the Refugee Review Tribunal, both cases dismissed with little hope of an appeal. All afternoon their small office had been crowded with people anxiously seeking help. The work was becoming more stressful as the public attitude to refugees turned increasingly hostile. There had been previous tides of opinion against people seeking asylum – Kate could remember the antipathy to the fleets of escaping Vietnamese after Saigon fell, and later resentment against dissident Chinese who fled after the massacre in Tiananmen Square – but this time the xenophobia came with a far broader impact. The startling electoral success of the One Nation political party had unearthed an ugly ant-heap of racism.

It had always been there – Kate knew this from her own childhood – but now it seemed to be allowed to openly flourish. The equivocation of censure by the government and the lack of an official curb on broadcasters freely voicing their racially prejudiced sentiments had rapidly created a climate of intolerance that bred hate and fear. 'Boat people' became an expression of odium and denunciation. No matter that they had escaped from terror, torture and threats of death – they were regarded as trespassers, unwanted, and, if they managed to arrive at all, detained and treated like prisoners. The prime minister proclaimed that he would decide who came to live here, and the electorate cheered and voted for this siege mentality.

It was with a feeling of respite from the trauma of the day that Kate drove across the Gothic-style bridge and turned into the peaceful familiarity of her street where she had lived for the past twenty-five years. The house was built on a block of sloping land that had once been chaotic with wild blackberry bushes and lantana. It was a very different setting now with the shrubs they had planted flourishing in a riot of spring colour. Hibiscus and waratahs blended with a display of wisteria and bougainvillea, while towering over the house and garage were red gums that had been saplings when they moved in, now stately landmarks.

Kate was just a month away from her fiftieth birthday, but looked younger. Slim and above-average height, an olive skin was almost the only legacy of her Greek origin. She had dark-blue eyes that often caused comment, which Kate met by explaining these had been inherited from her mother, so the question of where they derived from should be addressed to her. The eyes were offset by silky black hair that she'd worn long when young, but was now neatly cut so it framed her oval face. A face, Joshua had once said, that could launch at least a thousand ships. Joshua and his silver tongue, she thought, in a sudden slip of memory.

She had found this house by chance. Her car at the time, an old Kingswood, had broken down, and she'd walked up the driveway to ask if she could use the phone. On first impression it had appeared like a derelict bungalow with a FOR SALE sign. Two cars were parked outside, and as she approached a couple had hastily emerged from the house, followed by a discomfited estate agent. Kate was close enough to hear them say it was a shocking dump, an absolute tip, and no wonder it'd been on the market for ages. As they drove off, the agent, without any real expectation, invited Kate to inspect the premises. When she asked if she could use the phone to get road service, his sigh made her laugh sympathetically and agree to a quick look around while waiting for the breakdown truck.

The interior was shabby and in appalling disrepair. But Kate had taken one look at the surprisingly generous-sized rooms with their high ceilings and, despite crumbling plaster cornices, broken bathroom tiles and a smell of damp rot, had fallen in love with it. Despite also a surveyor's report that warned the drains were blocked, the electric wiring was dangerous and the roof was an invitation to disaster the next time it rained.

They had risked what seemed like a mammoth mortgage in those days. It had been a struggle, but gradually the district with its leafy proximity to the city had become a target for developers. Friends said they should leave, estate agents made offers, but Kate determinedly held out against temptation. In time as their neighbours sold, took profits and moved to coastal retreats, the original homes were all demolished until theirs was the only one remaining. Old and ramshackle to some newcomers but a cherished relic to her. She prized its abundant foliage that almost hid it from the neat rows of compact villas that had become the up-market neighbourhood.

Leave here? Kate thought, as she settled herself with a glass of wine, not bloody likely. She secretly knew, of course, that she couldn't really afford it any longer, but preferred not to think too deeply about the state of her finances.

She switched on the evening news. High on the agenda was a debate about retaliation against those who had attacked New York and Washington a month earlier. The world was still in shock from the constant television replays of the unthinkable; two planes filled with passengers crashing into the twin towers of the World Trade Center.

Informed opinion declared a war was certain; Osama bin Laden and Al Qaeda were the logical targets, but there was talk of an invasion to enforce regime change in Iraq. American, British and Australian leaders were united in declaring they had positive proof Saddam Hussein possessed weapons of mass destruction. Intelligence sources added their authentication about the threat of chemical warfare: missiles that could deliver poison gas and potent killing agents like anthrax. Even the likelihood of a nuclear strike was mooted; in the rush to overturn Hussein nothing was ruled out.

These subjects, together with a federal election heading into the final weeks, were the main topics of debate on the television screens of Australia that October night.

In the darkness on board SIEV X the terrified women tried to shelter their children from the wind and unceasing torrential rain. They yearned for the dawn, but when it came it brought an even greater foreboding; a vast empty ocean without a trace of land and, far more ominously, the certain prospect of worse to come. The sea was a churning vista of unruly whitecaps and threatening waves were sweeping across the overcrowded deck. Within an hour the temperature had climbed to a blistering 40°C. One man holding his infant son tried to bribe the captain to turn about and head for Java Head, but was berated as a coward by others who offered the crew a bonus to continue sailing south. They felt certain they were almost in sight of Christmas Island. It could only be another hour or two. We must go on, they insisted. We've waited years for this chance, and there will never be another.

Children became seasick and fretful with sunburn. Their mothers tried vainly to comfort them. Though it was not one of their own legends, the name Christmas Island had a magical sound. Santa Claus Island, one of the women who had been a teacher told them. She promised it would have a sandy beach, palm trees and houses. Their fathers would all be gathered there to greet them. And afterwards they would travel on a fine boat to Australia, where there would be homes to live in, jobs for their parents and schools for them to attend.

A fairytale, some thought sadly, but if God was kind they might yet live happily ever after. They weren't asking for much. Just a refuge, a place in which to be free. In Australia there could be no despot as dangerous and malevolent as Saddam, and no place like Abu Ghraib, where many of their relatives and friends had been tortured or hanged for dissent or imaginary crimes against the regime.

The afternoon passed slowly. The sea grew wilder. Rain became more ferocious. Despite the turbulence some passengers managed to sleep. The teacher did her best to engage a group of children with more stories. Then at four o'clock the engine abruptly stopped. In a moment of shock that followed, the captain shouted a warning that the boat was taking water, but there was barely time to imagine what this might mean before the SIEV X rolled violently and then capsized amid screams of terror, mindless chaos and death.

In Australia twenty-four hours later the media reported rumours of a fishing boat missing in the Java Sea, and later confirmed that wreckage had been sighted and some survivors already picked up. The news received scant coverage because of a busy weekend of sport with the impending Melbourne Cup, and the start of a new cricket season. In addition the federal election mood was intensifying, with both parties claiming their ability to govern the country in this frightening new era of global terrorism.

Kate woke early on the Monday morning. High in one of the red gums a kookaburra greeted the day. She took meat scraps from the refrigerator out to the lawn and watched the bird swoop for his expected offering. Then she brought a tray with her own breakfast to the side verandah and listened to the radio. More election news, after which the bulletin switched to the missing fishing boat. It was now confirmed forty people had been rescued, but full details were not yet available. The weather report predicted a hot day, with it already five degrees above normal. It would be even hotter in western Sydney, Kate thought; the detention centre was a long way from the coast and any prospect of a sea breeze.

She showered and dressed in cotton trousers and shirt, comfortable summertime wear, rinsed the dishes and locked the house. As she drove out of the garage there were more election promises on the car radio, but no further reports of the fishing boat survivors. Kate switched to the CD player, chose a disc by Pavarotti and heard the blissful opening chords of 'Celeste Aida'.

Stopping at the gate to adjust her seatbelt, she frowned at the sight of a figure walking in the middle of the road towards her. Not walking, she corrected herself: marching, as though he was still in army uniform. Although aware he was in her way, he prevented her from driving until he went past. She did not like Victor Henderson, who told people he preferred to answer to his service title. She did not like *Captain* Henderson, AMF Retired, who was notorious in the neighbourhood for airing grievances and complained frequently to the local council about her gum trees growing too tall and shedding leaves on his property.

She did her best to ignore him, but was conscious that whenever she was in the garden he stopped his twice-daily walk to gaze at the house. Though not really at the house; he gazed at her. Stood there, fingers combing his military moustache. No nod of greeting, just a stare before moving on. It began to anger Kate, who tried to tell herself not to be stupid. She had some very congenial neighbours – surely she should keep one hostile one in perspective? After all, he was staring, not stalking. She could hardly seek a restraining order against a stare.

It was with surprise she realised he was approaching the car. He paused beside her open window.

'Nice morning, isn't it.' They were the first civil words he'd spoken to her in months. She could hardly believe he was actually smiling.

'Yes, it is,' she answered. If this was conciliation she should at least contribute, and meet the unexpected olive branch halfway. But before she could say anything further, he continued.

'Not so nice for those boat people,' he said, the smile still in place. 'Some must've drowned, I reckon. Teach 'em a lesson, won't it?'

'*I beg your pardon?*'

'Well, that's my opinion. Boat people . . . they'd overrun us, those wogs, given half a chance. Serve the greasy buggers right.'

His smile was what appalled her. Not trusting herself to reply, she turned Pavarotti up to full volume. As he took a step backwards reacting angrily to the blast of sound, she drove off without a word.

The office was open when Kate arrived, and Roger was already at his desk trying to manage two calls while a third phone line was ringing.

'Hi, Dodger,' she murmured, kissing the bald spot on the crown of his head. He smiled with relief and spoke to one of his callers.

'Kate's here. She'll handle your enquiry,' he said, and for the next hour they had no chance to exchange another word as the phones rang incessantly.

It was another typical day; soon clients would be arriving. By lunchtime there'd be a queue into the street. The owner of the shop downstairs would complain again. The line of their patient petitioners was an annoyance, blocking the entrance to his premises, he claimed. Other shop owners in the street would support him. It was becoming a problem.

For months the workload had been increasing; their days now began earlier and ended later. They knew the firm needed two additional lawyers, but Roger could not afford them. He could only afford Kate because, as he said when offering her the job, the people he represented were often unable to pay but he didn't feel able to turn anyone away.

'Put at its simplest, Kate,' he'd said quietly, 'I work with a very disadvantaged group. They don't have much money, and I run the place on the smell of an oily rag. They're either refugees themselves – with a family they had to leave behind who are now trying to get visas – or else the family have managed to get here but are being held and treated like criminals in a detention centre. They're not the most popular people on the planet at the moment, and most of the work is pro bono. As for Legal Aid' – he shrugged at the idea – 'there's not much of that about. I'm a one-man band, but I need help. I need someone who knows how to run a law office, which is you, and someone who's able to live on what meagre sum I can afford to pay, which I can only hope you might consider.'

She had met Roger Montgomery, or Roger the Dodger, as he'd always been, years ago when she first worked as a young clerk in his father's law firm where he'd been a junior partner. In those days it was a fine legal practice with offices on the top floor of a gracious sandstone heritage building in Macquarie Street, with a view across the Botanic Gardens to the harbour. In the rush to modernise, the sandstone structure had been replaced by a modern tower of glass and steel, while the law firm, after his father's death, became the subject of a bitter family battle. Roger resigned from it in disgust. The firm still existed but was barely recognisable; a decade of mergers had converted it into an international behemoth, with a list of partners now too long to fit on the letterhead.

Three years away from his sixtieth birthday, Roger was a rumpled and overweight figure despite weekly visits to the gym; a man with enquiring grey eyes and thinning sandy hair. Even as a young lawyer he had been deeply committed, and now more than ever he was seriously concerned about the direction the country was heading in.

'Kids in detention is an obscenity,' he said, when first trying to recruit her. 'The Minister reckons we must have some safeguards. Okay, I'll go along with that, but putting children behind razor wire is immoral and plain crazy. One day they'll grow up to be disturbed adults, or become our enemies queuing up to be suicide bombers.'

'Where's the office?' she'd asked him.

'In Chippendale.' His prompt reply had revealed his eagerness.

'Near the university?'

'No, the less salubrious part. It's a fairly grotty room over a sandwich shop.'

'Sounds irresistible,' she'd said, laughing.

'I can offer you lunch if you'd like to see it.'

'Would that be a sandwich from downstairs?'

'They're very tasty,' Roger had promised.

~

Driving home that afternoon she fondly recalled her first visit to the office. They'd eaten sandwiches while she watched him cope with the flood of human heartbreak, and there had never been a real doubt in her mind that she wouldn't work there. In fact, she began the next day. She knew the problems he faced; his cases were complex and protracted. Costs were high because of the need for interpreters and translators; in prolonged hearings they were often required on stand-by, and the returns from clients rarely ever matched this outlay.

Expenses and a token salary she'd said would be adequate; she had some savings and a small annuity – enough to live on. He'd been surprised but had accepted gratefully, and she'd gone to see her bank manager and made private arrangements to augment this modest amount. Had she been able to afford it, she would have worked for nothing.

Surprising to think it was over ten years ago now, she realised. Somehow, she and Roger had managed to deal with the scores of cases brought to them until recently, but things had begun to change. The last few years had seen the introduction of much tougher immigration laws, as well as the opening of new detention centres and a growing ruthlessness by the federal government upon discovering border protection was an election winner.

The rest of the Pavarotti disc from that morning accompanied part of Kate's journey home. When it ended with a reprise of 'Nessun Dorma', she switched on the radio. The six o'clock news was in progress. There was an announcement they were crossing back to the ABC's correspondent in Java for a further report.

'This is Warren Riley with the latest on our main story. The death toll from the fishing boat tragedy has now been confirmed as three hundred and sixty-five people dead, one hundred and forty-two of whom were children . . .'

'Oh Christ,' Kate exclaimed, and pulled in to the side of the road because her hands were trembling. She sat there listening in horror.

'A further one hundred and forty-six were women. It is estimated most of those on board the overcrowded vessel were from Iraq, and the United Nations has verified many had already been assessed as bona fide refugees who had spent years in Indonesia unable to find a country willing to accept them. One survivor we spoke to, Aamar Zaheer, said he was classified in this category more than three years ago.'

'I wait there for so long,' an accented voice said in an interview, 'but no country will help. What can I do . . . I take my wife and baby on this boat, pay the last of our money . . . to find a place to live.'

The correspondent took up the story again. 'Mr Zaheer's wife drowned, but he managed to stay afloat for over twelve hours while somehow holding his baby daughter safely all this time. After a night in the sea they were picked up by another fishing boat, and the child is now being cared for in an Indonesian hospital. There are more reports asserting that many of the passengers, alarmed at the overcrowding and state of the vessel, were prevented from leaving it at gunpoint by local police. A spokesman for the Bandar Lampung police has denied all knowledge of such involvement. This is Warren Riley reporting from Java.'

Kate switched off the radio. It was several minutes before she felt able to drive home.

There was more news during the following days, and harrowing stories of entire families drowned. A political storm erupted between the government and the opposition, with each party trying to claim the moral high ground in a disturbing exhibition of vote chasing and what appeared a callous disregard for the tragic loss of so many lives.

'The equivalent of a jumbo jet full of people have been drowned in this catastrophic event,' one commentator charged, 'and it is appalling to hear both political leaders publicly blaming the other. It is political expediency at its worst, an unedifying spectacle that must make people ashamed at the way each side is exploiting this tragedy. This is a sad week for all those children, and a dishonourable one in the Australian parliament.'

At the end of the week, after a series of distressing stories, came a photograph in the *Sydney Morning Herald* that seemed to encapsulate the heartbreak. Three young sisters between the ages of six and nine, shy and beautiful children wearing colourful dresses and each with white ribbons in their hair, had all drowned, together with their mother. The photograph was one supplied by their grief-stricken father who had been waiting for them in Australia.

'All dead', he was quoted as saying. 'My three children and my wife, all my family are now dead. The immigration department gave me a temporary protection visa after I flee from Saddam Hussein because his police try to kill me. They gave me a visa, but no access to English lessons. No permanent place, no family reunion. If I stay in your country I'm told I can never again be with my wife and my daughters, so they take the risk to come here to be with me. And now they are dead . . . and I cry alone. I have no one left.'

Kate slept badly that night. She kept having nightmares in which she saw the three drowned girls floating to the surface. The dye from their bright dresses was staining the water the colour of blood, while she was restrained by friends from diving into the sea in a desperate effort to retrieve their bodies. She woke agitated and shivering.

By now she knew from the newspaper stories that the children's mother had sold the family apartment in Baghdad to pay a neighbour to smuggle them out of the country. They had left with only the clothes they were wearing and whatever they could fit beneath their dresses. No personal belongings for fear of being stopped by a police patrol. After crossing the border she and her daughters travelled by train to Pakistan, then to Jakarta where they applied for visas to join her husband in Australia. She filled in forms and was advised the matter would be considered. It seemed nobody had thought to tell her that for people on temporary protection visas in Australia a family reunion was no longer possible. It was also apparent from a report that this mother had begged to be allowed to disembark from the boat, but had been prevented by the police.

Kate finally accepted further sleep was out of the question. She felt thirsty, and pouring herself a glass of water she took it out to the side verandah. It was a still, warm night. There was a sky full of stars, and she could see the distant glow of the city's lights emanating from a thousand brightly lit and empty offices. In one of the trees behind her house a night bird was softly calling.

It was so peaceful. Impossible to imagine the terror of those final moments, the sea sweeping everyone overboard. She knew there were nearly one hundred and fifty children, but in her mind she could only see the three little Iraqi girls.

What kind of a world was it, where people like her unpleasant military neighbour could gain some perverse satisfaction from the death of those three children? And what sort of life would they have had here, she wondered, if the boat had managed to reach Christmas Island? Years in a detention centre? Years of ill-treatment and abuse? Or would they have been reunited with their father who was now grieving so deeply? She wanted to believe they might have been given a chance to belong here, like she now belonged. But she had come at a far kinder time, and under different circumstances.

And yet . . . it had not always been easy.

Growing up had been full of cruelty at first: the malicious names, the bullying and constant scorn. The fear she had experienced in the school playground, trying to hide from the other kids in the eleven o'clock break, where freed from the teacher's gaze they could vent their intolerance.

Hey . . . wog! Yeah, you!

Don't try to run away – we mean you!

Yeah . . . how did you get here?

Yeah, how?

And why did you come?

What was wrong with your own country?

When are you gonna go back there?

Soon, we hope. We don't want yer here!

Or far worse, the remembered trauma of lunchtime.

What's that horrible muck you got in yer schoolbag?

Jeeze, it stinks.

Crikey, what a pong.

We thought somebody had let off a fart.

Phew!

Crumbs, how can you eat smelly foreign stuff like that?

No, she didn't want to think about those days.

Contemplate instead that photo, look at the youngest of the sisters. I was six years old, the same age as her, Kate thought. Rather awed by the sea, by its immensity, the way it extended to the horizon and so far beyond . . . awed and a bit frightened of it at times, like she must have been. And almost sailing across the same stretch of ocean.

But mine, Kate thought, had been a very different journey.

PART 2

1957–1970

Chapter 2

On the day the letter came, Sofia seemed uncertain whether to be pleased or not. Her moods were inclined to vary, depending on all manner of things. She could, for instance, become upset at being called Mama by her daughter. She always said she felt more like an elder sister, because after all, she was still youthful, only twenty-three, and being called Sofia sounded nicer than being labelled a mother. Especially when they had company, as they were having tonight. Gregorios, who worked on the docks and was nicknamed Tarzan because of his muscles, was coming to dinner, and six-year-old Katerina already knew that she'd be sent to bed early because Tarzan would be staying the night.

But the letter was unusual – and far more interesting than worrying about yet another of her mother's boyfriends. It was the only letter they'd received for almost a year, and she wondered if it was from her father. 'What is it, Mama? Who sent it? Was it Papa?'

'Just be quiet. Let me read it first, without so many questions.'

'But who is it from?'

'The bank. Now please, Katerina!'

Katerina sat and watched her mother frowning over the letter. They'd never had one from the bank before. They'd hardly ever had a letter at all, except the two her father had sent in the years since he left Nicosia – and each less than a page.

'Is it bad news, Mama?'

'Of course not, darling. Your father has sent the money at last.'

'For us?'

'For our fares. We have to go to the bank to be identified and then we can collect it.'

'Why do we have to be identified?'

'I don't know who you take after, my sweet, but it isn't me. And I don't think it's your papa. I had an uncle who asked a lot of questions. Probably you take after him.' She smiled then, and Katerina, who could never resist her mother's smile, felt happier. Everyone said Sofia was beautiful, especially when she smiled. 'We have to be identified so they give the money to the right people.'

'And after that we can go to Australia?' When her mother nodded, Katerina hugged her. 'But that's good news, Mama. Can we go to Australia tomorrow?'

'No, darling. Tomorrow we go to the bank.'

'Then, Mama, we can go to Australia the next day.'

'I think it might take a bit longer than that. And for heaven's sake, try to remember to call me Sofia, especially tonight when Gregorios comes to dinner.'

They had not left the next day, or the next month. There had been no chance of a berth in a passenger ship from Limassol, the island's main port, for many people were fleeing Cyprus that year. When her father sent the money to the bank he had not anticipated this lack of shipping, and it was insufficient to get them all the way to Athens, where vessels for Australia and the Pacific left regularly. In the end they had to take cheap deck space on a cargo vessel to Beirut and begin their journey to Australia from there.

It was the following June before these arrangements were complete. By then the idyllic island of Cyprus had become a dangerous place. The leading political figure, Archbishop Makarios, coordinated outbreaks of violence in protest against British rule. While the authorities denounced him as a terrorist priest, he and the guerrilla force EOKA orchestrated civil disorder. To Katerina, it sometimes seemed as if there was no place safe from this ferocity. Asleep in the small house she and her mother shared with three other families, they woke in panic one night when the post office a hundred metres away was blown to pieces. A week later her primary school was destroyed by fire. There were shootings in the street, crowd rampages, brutal reprisals by the police and constant bombings.

Meanwhile Sofia, her capricious young mother, seemed unconcerned and, oblivious to the concern of others, spent much of her time with Tarzan when he had time off from the docks. She had been known to have several other such friends since her husband went to seek a better future in Australia, pledging to save money so he could send for his wife and child. Sofia felt certain her little daughter knew nothing of these liaisons, but Katerina had learnt to add up her mother's lovers on her fingers. Even now she could recall they had filled all the fingers of one hand.

She disliked most of them, but Gregorios seemed different. He sometimes bought her chocolate and was always friendly. When the money came for their fares he made it his business to help. It was he who organised their transport to Beirut and free accommodation at the house of his cousin who lived there. And, like a miracle, he even obtained reservations for a cabin on a passenger ship bound for Sydney – the *Ottoman Star*, leaving Beirut at the end of the month.

'Not just tickets,' Sofia said gleefully, 'he's managed to get us our own two-berth cabin!'

Life was good; it seemed nothing could go wrong. But who could predict on the night voyage to Beirut they should encounter a violent storm? Those unfortunates being carried as deck cargo bore the full force of it. Towering seas reared so high it seemed they must drown the ship. Torrential rain drenched them. Katerina remembered being buffeted by the waves, and desperately clinging to a stanchion as she was almost swept overboard. Her mother screamed to the crew for help, but in the turmoil no one heard. All night the ship rose and plunged, and she was repeatedly sick. At dawn the next day, when the freighter limped into the calm of Beirut harbour, Katerina cried at the tranquil beauty of it, but her real tears were those of sheer relief at still being alive.

There was no one to meet the ship, and they could not afford a taxi. All they had was the address on a scrap of paper. Bedraggled and burdened by their luggage, they arrived on the doorstep of the cousin's tiny house, to be met by the perplexed gaze of the cousin's wife.

Who were they? What did they want?

Gregorios sent us, Sofia said.

Did he, the cousin's wife replied. Did he indeed? Well, there had been no letter about them. Gregorios was fond of sending people without bothering to ask. She had never met her husband's relative, but he was clearly a person who took liberties. They certainly couldn't stay here. She attempted to close the door, but anticipating this, Sofia moved her suitcase to prevent her, and sat firmly on it.

When the husband reached home he encountered two very angry women and a frightened child. He tried to broker a peace, claiming his cousin Gregorios must have sent a letter but clearly it had gone astray. Under the circumstances, he declared, it was only fair and reasonable to offer them a few days' refuge. Sofia was on the point of accepting with gratitude when the cousin's wife continued to object. It would not do, she said angrily. She had not met this wretched cousin and hoped never to meet him, and she certainly did not care for the way he sent them total strangers like these Cypriots to look after.

'We're not Cypriots!' Sofia shouted. 'We emigrated to Cyprus when my daughter was born because there was no work in Athens. We're Greeks.'

'I don't care if you're Albanians or martians,' the cousin's wife shouted back, 'you're not staying in my house!'

Because of the child, she said, they could occupy the shed in the backyard for a few days, but could not come into their home or use the family bathroom facilities. They must wash at the tap in the yard and use the outside toilet. That was the best she could offer, and they could take it or leave it.

Sofia nodded her thanks, but when they were finally left alone in the shed she complained bitterly. 'Bloody men,' she said, referring to her helpful boyfriend with the muscles, 'it's always the same. Every promise comes with a handshake covered in shit.' Thank God, she told her small daughter, soon they would be aboard the ocean liner. Just the two of them, a nice double cabin, free of Cypriot promises and bloody Lebanese women; they would be on their way to a better life.

~

Kate tried going back to bed, but sleep continued to elude her. She could hear the early traffic on the road that curved down towards the bridge, and felt a chill as the south wind rustled the trees outside her bedroom window. She remembered the straw mattress on the concrete floor in Beirut.

A few days in the uncomfortable shed had become a week, for the ship was behind schedule. They ran out of money, because every spare drachma had been sent from Cyprus to pay for their cabin. If it had not been for Gregorios's considerate cousin, she wondered what would have happened to them. He called each day on his way home from work, surreptitiously leaving a loaf of bread and a few pieces of fruit outside the shed, tapping on the wall to alert them before hurrying to the front door of his house. It became clear his wife knew nothing of this furtive kindness.

On the last day Kate had found a scrap of paper and drew a picture of two people standing on a ship with little speech bubbles from their mouths like cartoon characters. In each bubble she wrote the word *Efharisto*. She hoped he knew Greek and would realise this was meant to be their way of saying thank you.

The thought of her childish drawing evoked a brief smile as she sat up in bed. There had been little else to smile about on that last day, she recalled. It had been over an hour's walk to the quayside where the ship was docked. They were both tired when they climbed the gangway, and she'd rested wearily on her small suitcase while her mother handed their papers to an officer.

If only, Kate thought . . . The memories now began to disturb her, and the possibility of sleep a lost battle.

If only Tarzan had been as nice as he pretended.

If only her mother had not been fascinated by him and therefore so gullible . . . how different all their lives might have been.

It was pointless remaining in bed; Kate sighed and reached for her dressing-gown, wrapped herself against the unexpectedly cool morning and went out to the kitchen. She switched on the kettle to make a cup of tea, and tried not to think about the voyage on the *Ottoman Star*.

There had, of course, been no two-berth cabin awaiting them. When her mother began to argue loudly with the deck officer he called for some assistance. The purser who arrived was a good looking and smartly dressed young man who promptly saluted them both and even bowed to her mother. Ignoring this, Sofia shouted at him she'd been robbed; money had been sent, and this second-rate shipping company was trying to cheat her.

Kate could still remember the politeness of the purser. He had left with another courteous bow and returned with documents. Money had indeed been sent, he said, and here was a receipt for it. However, it was payment for bunks in dormitory accommodation on E deck, not a private cabin. He deeply regretted her position, but it seemed the villain in the case was this Cypriot fellow Gregorios. The man had obviously betrayed her, stealing the rest of the money she'd entrusted to him. If there was the possibility of a vacant cabin he would have been more than happy for Madame Vassos to occupy it, but sadly the ship was full. For her own sake and that of her charming daughter she must please remain calm, because the captain was a difficult man whose word on board was law, and he reserved the right to reject any passenger whom he felt might create trouble.

'Please, Madame,' he implored her, 'you have been victimised, but not by us. It would be a tragedy if you antagonise the captain, a man who is prone to temper, and we are made to sail without you.'

Katerina's mother began to respond to this charm. Sofia's blue eyes softened; she gazed at him pensively, then nodded agreement and bestowed her appreciation with a dazzling smile. The purser smiled in return, the sort of smile she had seen other men give her mother, declaring that he would be delighted to personally escort them below. He ordered a seaman to carry their suitcases.

The cheap accommodation on E deck, formerly a cargo hold, was a vast space filled with improvised bunks and even some hammocks. It was crowded with men, women and children who turned to stare at them as they arrived with an escort and followed by the seaman carrying their luggage. Sofia was appalled at the primitive conditions under which they would have to travel.

'So many people,' she said in dismay, 'and no privacy.'

The purser was swift to express his regret. The ship was packed with migrants, he explained; in fact it was grossly overcrowded, he added in an apologetic murmur to Sofia, because the Australian government had at last opened its doors more widely to people from Malta, Italy and Greece, as well as places like Yugoslavia. Everyone wanted to go to this new land, where there was work for all and the sun was reputed to be warmer.

He selected a pair of bunks adjacent to a porthole, dispossessing an elderly Egyptian couple by insisting there had been a mistake and these had been previously reserved for this young lady and her daughter. The pair, after angrily protesting, had gone to seek an alternative berth with enough bad grace to make Katerina feel uncomfortable. She could see most of the other passengers staring at them, disapproving of what had happened. Hoping for a welcoming face, she was disappointed. The majority were Lebanese; there were also Arabs and others whom she imagined must be Yugoslavs, but no one who seemed disposed to be the least bit friendly.

Meanwhile she could hear the purser promising her mother he'd do his utmost to make her journey as pleasant as possible. It was very sad she had been so unjustly defrauded, he sympathised. He fully understood how she must feel, because this accommodation was really not suitable for someone like her.

In fact . . . he paused, his effusion replaced with a thoughtful frown. His voice dropped, but Katerina could still hear him. Actually there might be an alternative, he murmured, but that could be best discussed at another time. Perhaps when the ship sailed, after dinner tonight when her sweet young daughter was put to bed? Was it possible she would care to join him for a drink to discuss it then?

On the second night out, Sofia moved into the purser's bed. By then Katerina knew his name was Michel Doumani, a Christian Lebanese who had attended university in Beirut and spoke fluent English, Greek and Arabic. Nothing else was said between mother and daughter, but each night she lay in the upper bunk trying to stay awake for her mother's return. Inevitably she fell asleep, and by morning Sofia was there as if she had come to bed so late that nobody in the dormitory accommodation knew what time it had been, and while they speculated on a possible – and considering her looks – highly likely flirtation, it was not until the ship left the Mediterranean and was headed southward that anyone found out the truth.

The wind was fierce in the Atlantic. It was a longer voyage to Australia via South Africa but some shipping lines found it an advantage, able to carry cargo and passengers to Capetown and the

Canary Islands. By the time they reached Teneriffe most people in the dormitory accommodation had learnt where Sofia spent her nights. A woman had been out at dawn to observe and sketch the sunrise, and instead had observed Sofia locked in a fierce embrace with Michel the purser. They were inside his cabin, the door was ajar, and he was wearing only a towel around his waist. A very small towel, the woman insisted, eager to give intimate details of his physical attributes.

It was a juicy morsel of gossip that swiftly spread, for many of them had not forgotten or forgiven Sofia for taking the elderly Egyptian couple's prime berth. However, while it satisfied their speculation it was hardly the stuff of scandal. This kind of thing often happened at sea; it was nothing unusual, just a passing shipboard affair. A lonely wife, a handsome young officer. Some of the women even envied Sofia.

But after Durban where they took on supplies and more passengers before heading east across the Indian Ocean, word spread of a new development. It was whispered that Sofia and the purser had had a row, and she'd transferred allegiance; rumour reported that her nightly nesting was now in the bunk of the chief engineer. There was also a reported sighting of her leaving the cabin of the second officer at dawn. This was true opprobrium at last; indecent immorality, and her with a young daughter! The news rapidly swept E deck. That was when six-year-old Katerina first heard her mother called a whore.

Until then there'd been no overt hostility. But this turn of events was too salacious to remain clandestine, and Sofia Vassos was too obvious a target. It became shipboard news of daily interest; boredom was replaced by hearsay and hilarity. Before long they were laying odds on whether she'd make it to the captain's cabin before the ship reached the Sydney Heads. It was inevitable the children in the hold would soon hear of it from their parents, and that was when Katerina's own nightmare began.

In the communal shower two big girls jostled her. 'Your mum's a tart,' one said.

'Opens her legs for them officers,' the other taunted.

When their victim appeared bewildered, the first girl flopped down on the slatted shower-room floor and spread her legs wide to illustrate. She moved her hips vigorously up and down.

'Like this,' she called out, 'that's what your tart of a mum does, every night.'

'I don't know what you're talking about!' Katerina shouted, close to tears as she tried to escape her tormentors.

'Of course you do. She fucks all the crew.'

'She does,' the second confirmed gleefully. 'They reckon she's gonna keep going till she fucks the captain.'

Katerina didn't understand what some words meant, but she knew the gestures implied her mother was involved in something awful. She tried to ignore them, hastily drying herself and dressing, but the girls were bullies and far from finished. When she ran from the showers they followed, cornering her and chanting a crude song they'd improvised.

'She's a whore, a dirty whore,
One bloke won't do, she wants more,
Everyone goes tut-tut-tut,
She's nothing but a lousy slut.'

It was a cruel verse that most of the children on E deck soon learnt, and took pleasure in chanting at her whenever they found her alone. If the adults heard it, they chose not to intervene. Relishing the gossip as an item that enlivened each day, they otherwise cold-shouldered Sofia and ignored the persecution of her daughter.

Katerina began to think the voyage would never end. It became unbearable. She hated the ship; unable to escape from it she experienced a profound depression, and grew homesick for Cyprus and the friends left there. She dared not look down at the waves because the sight conjured irrational thoughts, like wondering how long it would take to drown.

She was even starting to become frightened of what kind of life lay ahead of them. When she thought of her father she was unsure what kind of welcome they'd receive. It was difficult to remember him, although she knew what he looked like from the photo she kept in her suitcase. In this he was dressed in a double-breasted suit and tie, gazing unsmilingly at the camera. He had a neat black moustache, dark eyes and jet-black hair that was shiny with oil and firmly brushed. He looked rather serious, she thought, even quite stern, as if not pleased at having to pose for the photograph. She often studied it, trying to recall things he had said to her, even the way his voice had sounded: was it soft or loud? Was it kind?

Despite her efforts he remained a shadowy figure in her mind, one who had rarely been at home before she was put to bed at night. Each day he was gone from early morning until long after dark, working as the chef in a restaurant whose Turkish owner had promised him a half share. According to her mother he'd been too easily tricked by the slimy Turk who'd underpaid him for years on this false promise, then abruptly sold the business and vanished without a word of warning to a sleazy suburb in Ankara.

Katerina had just one clear and sickening recollection after this; the night she heard them arguing violently when they had thought her asleep: her mother yelling he was stupid, brainless, a pathetic apology of a man; his voice low but sounding full of rage, telling her to stop, to shut her mouth – and when she didn't, when she just kept calling him even worse names, came the sound. The dull thud of a fist hitting flesh, her mother's smothered shriek, more punches followed by the crash of a body, a mirror smashing, furniture being broken and agonised cries of pain. Sounds that still haunted her, but not as much as the sight of her mother the next day, both eyes and her nose swollen beyond recognition, her face and body black with bruises. There were other injuries that had to be treated in the local hospital: a broken wrist, two ribs, all of which she insisted were caused by a fall.

It was soon after this that her father had withdrawn their savings from the bank, leaving half with them, and had gone to search for a new life in Australia. He had been away for over two years, his letters brief and infrequent. Before the money arrived Katerina had begun to imagine she would never see him again. In her thoughts he became a stranger. Despite the photo of him she carried, the faces of her mother's successive men friends in Nicosia were more familiar.

As the shipboard teasing grew worse she started to roam the vessel in an attempt to find refuge. She became clever at avoiding questions from the crew when trespassing on the upper decks, or in the many places where passengers were forbidden. Eventually, at the stern of the ship where warning signs restricted all access, she found a lifeboat whose covers were loose. No one was in the vicinity so she wriggled her way into it, hiding beneath the canvas. She stayed there the whole day, missing both lunch and dinner, and only venturing out when it became dark. She managed to reach E deck, and thankful for once her mother was elsewhere, she tiptoed towards her bunk without being noticed, and fell into it, pulling the blankets over her head. The relief of not being chased and tormented that day almost made up for the hunger she felt from lack of food.

'Where were you yesterday?' Sofia asked the next morning.

'Around,' was her muttered rejoinder.

'That's hardly a satisfactory answer. I looked all over the ship and couldn't find you.'

'Why did you want to find me?' Katerina asked brusquely.

'Don't be stupid. You were missing at lunchtime, and also at dinner. So where were you? What's going on, Katerina?'

'Nothing's going on, Mama. I wasn't the slightest bit hungry,' she said with a rebellious shrug.

She felt truculent and under no obligation to tell the truth to her mother, who was so careless of her behaviour and seemed indifferent to the gossip that was becoming even more squalid. Less than a week out from South Africa with half the voyage still ahead, the children were now claiming Sofia spent her nights with several other officers who took her to bed, one after another. And did she know, the lascivious older girls asked, that her mummy put on a nude show at nights for the crew, and would Katerina like to hear exactly what things she did for them? When they proceeded to explain, she fled from them in tears, and tried to obliterate the lurid pictures in her mind.

The lifeboat became her sanctuary. It was not easy to hide there. First she had to surreptitiously steal slices of bread from the queue at breakfast time, enough to last her for the day. Then fill the water bottle she'd found, and after that make her way up to the higher deck without being stopped and questioned. Once safely hidden she sweltered all day beneath the canvas, but having successfully gained access did not dare leave there until under the cover of darkness.

The days were long. It was rare that she could sleep; mostly she attempted to pass the time in simple ways. Estimating how many miles to go before they reached Sydney, which she'd been told was on the east coast of Australia. If it was still 6000 miles, which she had heard one of the passengers say, then how fast was the boat going, and how many more weeks would it take? Unable to solve these mathematical enigmas she turned instead to wondering what would happen when her father and mother met. Would they like each other again, or not? And if not, why were they going all this way across the world to such a distant place to meet him?

She had tried to ask her mother this in Nicosia after the money arrived, but the answer had been puzzling.

'Will we be good friends again, your papa and I? What a peculiar question, Katerina. You are an odd creature sometimes.'

'But will you? Or will there be shouting and fights, like before?'

'Shouting and fights?' Her mother had shaken her head. 'Don't be ridiculous.'

'Mama, I heard you —'

'If we had an occasional argument, so does every married couple.'

'But he hit you —'

'Now stop making up silly stories.'

'You had to go to hospital.'

'That was the night I had a fall. You were asleep when I tripped and fell and cut my face.'

'I wasn't asleep. I heard what happened.'

In a rare display of affection, Sofia had picked her up and

hugged her. 'My darling, whatever you think might've happened is now over and forgotten. It's the past. We're going to join him in Australia because' – she gave a faint shrug as she held Katerina on her knee – 'because there's no choice for me. And no chance. Not in Cyprus. Or even in Greece. A woman either remains with the father of her children, or she's considered to have failed in her duty. Do you understand?'

'No,' she'd said.

She didn't understand then or for a long time afterwards. Understanding was complicated when one was hiding day after day in the blistering heat of a lifeboat, praying the journey would end before her mother shamed her again. But the next humiliation did not occur on board the ship. That happened when they reached their destination.

He was a small, almost solitary, figure on the dockside as the ship was ushered in by a tugboat and secured to its moorings at a wharf with the strange name of Woolloomooloo. In the bustle of arrival Katerina was able to study her father as his gaze tried to search the crowds lining the decks, unable to see her tiny figure amid the jostle of passengers eager to catch their first glimpse of the city.

Her relief was unrestrained for at last this was the end of the voyage. She had stayed on deck all night to watch the dark outline of the coast as they approached, marvelling at the sky full of stars that were so huge, so much bigger and brighter than she had ever seen, until their luminosity began to fade with the dawn. Soon afterwards she saw the sun start to rise across a calm sea as they turned towards the giant portals of the harbour, and this daylight glimpse confirmed that her ordeal was finally over.

The harbour itself was a revelation. As the sun lit the shadowed coves to the south it revealed small white beaches and marinas full of anchored yachts. Above these bays were terraced hillsides with rows of fine houses. On the opposite shore there was a different panorama: bushland and small inlets, from one of which a ferry emerged. On the cliffs above this were more splendid homes, while in the distance ahead of them appeared a majestic bridge. Six-year-old Katerina had seen many harbours since leaving Nicosia, but never one to match this.

After docking, there was a long delay as customs and immigration officials came aboard. She ran to the stern where she could climb on the deck rail unimpeded and thereby wave to her father, but he was no longer on the wharf. People were being marshalled back; a voice was shouting they must be patient, official procedures would take some time. Those waiting were advised to go to one of the cafés and have breakfast or coffee. It all sounded quite easygoing and friendly, and Katerina wondered if she would like it here.

By the time the formalities were completed it was mid-morning. She could see lines of traffic in the city streets, and a much larger welcoming crowd was now filling the quay. Her father was again back there among them; she could see him. She wanted to shout and signal to attract his attention, but he was stern and unsmiling, just as he appeared in her photograph. In fact he seemed exactly like the photo; his hair and moustache looked just the same, even his clothes . . .

'Good God, I swear he's wearing the same mouldy old suit,' her mother said as she joined Katerina at the rail.

They both looked down at him, and there was the strangest moment. He was scanning the line of passengers on deck, and the way the movement of his head stopped so abruptly made Katerina realise he'd seen them at last. Or at least had seen her mother, who was easier to distinguish than anyone else. Taller and prettier. But he didn't wave or blow a kiss; he did none of the things expected of couples after a long separation. He just stared up at her, and in much the same icy manner Sofia gazed down at him. Katerina wanted to climb on the rail and call a greeting, but waited for her mother to smile or wave first. She did neither; instead she shook her head and gave what sounded like a sigh.

'Mama . . . it's Papa.'

'I can see that,' she answered. 'I know who it is.'

Katerina looked at her, puzzled. 'Aren't you going to wave?'

Sofia seemed to hesitate before raising her arm in a bare gesture of acknowledgement. There was no response from her father.

'Wave properly,' Katerina begged.

'Take a good look at him,' her mother said, and the bitterness was palpable. 'He's the one who ought to be waving, but he won't. I'm sorry, my love, but nothing changes. Nothing will ever change.'

'But Mama . . .' Katerina was confused, close to tears. These were her parents. Why did they behave like strangers or worse, like enemies who hated each other?

'You go down and meet him.' Her mother handed her a slip of paper. 'That's a permit to leave the ship.'

'You mean on my own? What about you?'

'There's a lot to do. Arranging for luggage, goodbyes to be said. Go darling,' she insisted, and without waiting for an answer she hurried towards the companionway that led to the officers' cabins. That was when Katerina looked up and saw the purser, Michel Doumani. He was on the deck above them, waiting for her mother. She tried to fathom what this meant, struggling with the possibility that the gossip she'd been told about other men had been false. Just lies, invented by her tormentors and believed by all the people on E deck; lies that had given them something to gossip about, and that had caused her such unhappiness.

She knew they had been untrue when she saw her mother reach the purser, and the way they held each other so tightly. She realised there had been no one else. No other officers, no naked shows for the crew, nothing was true except what was so evident now. It had been Michel the whole voyage. Katerina knew it when she saw how they embraced as if no one in the world mattered but themselves.

She looked down at her father on the dock and knew that he was seeing it too. And her young mind tried to grasp the realisation that he was meant to see it.

Chapter 3

Four months after her arrival, when it was November in Australia, Katerina received a birthday letter from her mother. It came from Athens, with an array of colourful Greek stamps that seemed expressly chosen to dazzle, bearing pictures of the Acropolis, the pillars of the Parthenon, and the brilliance of Omonia Square at night. An envelope, it would seem, selected so her daughter could take it to school and impress her friends.

The difficulty with that, Kate could vividly remember, was at the time she had no friends. She was also perceptive enough to realise that if she had tried to impress the other kids with the flamboyant envelope, they would have sneered and found a way to belittle the alien stamps.

She had spent three unsettled months at the local primary, where her lack of English and her name had brought her the sobriquet of 'another bloody wog' or simply 'the dago'. The lunch she brought to school was so derided as foreign muck in the playground that she had begged her father to make her Vegemite sandwiches. He in turn described this local fare as a peculiar-tasting extract with nothing whatever to recommend it. Even at her young age she could tell he was not adapting to Australia and its ways, so between his dislike of the country and her classmates' aversion to her, Katerina was left both confused and desperately unhappy.

Each afternoon she escaped from the school as soon as the bell rang. Today she walked slowly home to the side-street café in Dee Why, where they lived in a small flat above the premises. It had been one of the very worst days. The teacher, Miss Abercrombie, had kept picking on her, pointing out the difficulty of learning anything if she couldn't speak English properly and making the situation worse by asking her what language she had spoken before she came to Australia. When she had replied Greek, Miss Abercrombie had raised bushy eyebrows and said it was unlikely she'd have much chance to speak it here. Katerina, who thought her English was improving, felt the teacher was prejudiced. Prejudice was a word she'd heard from her father, who found it a constant of his everyday life. As her class had all sniggered agreement with the teacher, and made remarks about it in the playground afterwards while holding their noses as she tried to eat her lunch, she considered them prejudiced as well. It was a miserable seventh birthday, and all the way home she worked herself up into a state of high resentment against her mother for bringing her here, and then so unfairly abandoning her.

When the postman had called at the café, Andreas Vassos was on the phone being forced to listen to a harangue from his boss, a property developer who was complaining about recent takings, and threatening that if things didn't improve during the next summer holidays changes would have to be made. It was a frequent grumble and Andreas knew what it meant; this man not only owned the café but also the freehold of several adjacent shops, and had ambitious plans for expansion one day.

After putting down the phone he moodily sorted through the mail. When he saw the Athenian postmark and familiar handwriting he felt such an onset of rage he almost ripped it up. But today was Katerina's birthday, as well as her name day. A big event in her young life, or it would have been if they were back in Cyprus or – even better – still in Greece, where name days were a special event. Of course things could never be the same here; he had tried but failed to make her realise that.

He was quite unable to cope with Katerina's unhappiness. He could barely cope with his own. After it happened he did not know what to say to her, this bewildered child. Two years apart had made them virtual strangers, and his wife's shock desertion of them both, infuriating for him, had been a violent rebuff too difficult for her to absorb – coming as it did just when she thought her parents were to be reconciled.

Their bus journey to the northern beach suburb took less than an hour, but had seemed interminable. Katerina had not cried; while her lips trembled and her face was stretched tight with misery there were no tears. But neither had she spoken after he returned from his confrontation on the ship with Sofia, after the bruising encounter when he'd shouted at his wife, not caring what kind of spectacle he was making of himself, refusing to go ashore until she explained what was happening, although by then he knew. He'd guessed it from the moment when she stared down at him from the deck of the ship, and known it for certain when she openly embraced the young officer. But while aware of what Sofia was going to say, he felt at least he was entitled to hear her say it.

Five minutes, he thought, five short minutes – that's how long it took to end a life together. Not even angry words, just her measured statement there was another man, and even if there hadn't been, their marriage was always an awful blunder. Seeing him again, she said, had made her realise there was no love, no affection, no hope of a future. And because her own future was going to be uncertain and their daughter needed a settled existence and security, Andreas should take her.

He looked again at the gaudy stamps and Sofia's handwriting on the envelope and wished he could burn it. The gas range on which he cooked the endless mixed grills his customers demanded would dispose of it, and he could wash the ashes down the sink. Time would heal his daughter's grief and lessen the memory of her mother, whereas this letter . . . he sighed, dismissed the thought, and carefully placed it on the nearest formica table.

He had seen how reluctantly she'd set out for school that morning, indeed every morning; he knew her feelings because he'd been called the same names and was aware what it was like to be considered different. So when late that afternoon she came into the café looking downcast, he realised it had been another bad day. He said nothing, just handed her the envelope. He saw her glance at the stamps, glimpsed her look of surprise and sudden elation, then watched her run upstairs to read it.

No matter how much he resented his wife for the wreckage of their marriage, Andreas had a rare moment of appreciation that she'd at least bothered to write, and the fortunate timing of its arrival had brightened this day. He was glad he'd resisted the temptation to burn the letter, although he hoped this was not a precursor of regular communication between them.

~

Inside the envelope was a card with drawings of Greek antiquities on the front, and filled with her mother's cramped writing on the back. A fifty drachma bank note was pinned to it.

My dearest Katerina,

I think of you every day, and hope you are well and settling down to a new life. We have been here in Athens for two months now, and Michel has left the Ottoman Star and found work with a shipping company at Piraeus. We have a room nearby, and are looking for a small flat. I can't give you an address yet because we will soon move, and anyway – perhaps you are still angry and do not wish to write to me.

My darling, try not to stay angry for too long. I'm truly sorry for what I did, but some day when you're older I'll try to explain. Look after your papa. Try to make him smile more often; he needs to smile sometimes. Tell him when I find a job and have money saved I will repay him for the ticket, which is only fair. It might even make him smile, but you'd better not tell him that.

Enjoy your birthday and I hope you have made some good friends and will have a nice party with them.

Much love, Mama

Friends? she thought. A party? Even aged seven she knew her mother was playing make believe, pretending she was happy in her new country and everything would be fine. But how could it be fine when she was always being told to go back where she came from? It seemed to her you could only be happy in Australia if you were born here.

'Athens,' her father said at dinner that night. 'Did she give an address?'

'No, Papa.'

'No address? So you cannot reply to her.'

'She is going to move soon. And she thinks I might be angry and not want to write.'

'Or else,' he observed, after a moment of silent contemplation, 'perhaps she was worried you might give me the address and *I'd* write.' Telling her how unhappy you are, and what a deceitful treacherous slut she is, he wanted to say aloud but managed to restrain himself. A faithless wife, a disreputable and feckless mother. He felt as if he could vilify her for at least five minutes in English without duplicating a single word. Five minutes in English, but easily twice as long in Greek.

Instead he asked Katerina if she liked the moussaka he'd cooked especially for her, and said that afterwards there was a small cake for them to share – with seven candles.

The following week at her school there was a celebration to mark the end of the year, and the start of the long summer holiday. There were sports displays and parades, and the youngest class was lined up to meet a visiting Santa Claus, a jovial but rather bibulous local actor hired for the occasion. He was suitably disguised with predictable white whiskers and red robes, and despite the faint trace of whisky breath, was popular with the children in Katerina's class. This appeal was considerably enhanced by a small sack containing boiled lollies, caramels, liquorice allsorts and even chocolates.

'One to each of you,' he told them. 'You can all line up for a lucky dip before I leave. But first, come up one at a time and tell me your secret wish for the big day.'

They were called to be interviewed in alphabetical order, so with the surname Vassos, Katerina was last in the queue. Balancing her on his knee, he asked her what she wished for Christmas. When she shyly whispered that she wanted her mama to be joined again with her papa it seemed to confuse Santa and the yuletide cheer he was trying to promote.

'Where is your mum?' Santa asked. 'I mean, your mama.'

'She's in Athens,' Katerina said, and seeing him puzzled by her answer she tried to help by adding, 'it's in Greece.'

'I know, my dear.' Santa smiled kindly at the small worried face. 'And is your papa also in Greece?'

'No,' she told him, 'he's in Dee Why.'

'They're a long way apart, aren't they . . . Is she on a holiday?'

Katerina shook her head. It was becoming difficult to explain, but she had to try. 'No. She's with . . . Michel . . . a man on the ship.'

'Well, never mind,' Santa said briskly, 'I'm sure they'll be back together soon. Is that your Christmas wish? For them to be reconciled?'

She looked at him blankly. She had no idea what 'reconciled' meant. But he seemed nice, and was asking her more questions than the other children, so she tried her best to explain.

'I wish they don't hate each other,' she said. 'And my papa don't hit mama any more.'

That was when Santa decided that wherever these embattled parents might be, he personally was in difficult territory. So he hastily changed the subject to ask when her birthday was.

'Last week,' she told him.

'Last week! Well, aren't you a lucky girl? Did you hear that, children?' he called to the rest of the class, 'this young lady has just had a birthday. What's your name, pet?'

'Katerina,' she mumbled, wishing she could get off his knee and hide from this sudden unwelcome focus of attention.

'Kata-what?' he asked, leaning down to hear her better.

'Reena,' one of the boys called out loudly, and the rest of the class laughed.

'It's a wog name,' another called out to yet more laughter.

'It's a very nice name!' Santa said, all of a sudden sounding rather angry and not like a real Father Christmas at all. 'And I don't think that's a pleasant or polite way to speak about a classmate. Since it was Katerina's birthday so recently, I'll tell you what I'm going to do. I'm going to give her the lollies in my sack as a present.'

'What, all of 'em?' a voice cried out in dismay.

'All of them,' was his prompt and firm reply.

The class erupted in protest. They'd each been promised one in a lucky dip, so why was she being given the lot instead? The whole sack full! It was some sort of favouritism. There must be heaps of lollies in there and it just wasn't fair.

'It's perfectly fair,' they were told, as the actor remembered the role he should be playing and reverted to character. 'Santa's job is to decide who should get presents. I've made up my mind that Katerina is to have these because she's come all the way from the other side of the world to live here, and you should do your best to make her welcome. Make her feel glad she chose to come to our country.'

He looked around the class as he lifted Katerina from his knee, leant down to kiss her cheek and handed her the contents of the sack. 'And if she likes you, then perhaps she'll share her present with you. But not, I should imagine, if you call her names or treat her unkindly.'

That afternoon, setting the tables for his customers who liked to eat early, Andreas heard shrill voices outside the café window and, fearing trouble, he looked out. A small circle of children were clustered around his daughter. On the point of shouting at them to leave her alone, for he instantly assumed they were making fun of her, he managed to stop as he realised this was not a hostile gathering. Quite the opposite, for in the centre was Katerina, dispensing sweets to them all. He stood back from the window to prevent being seen, watching in amazement.

'What happened?' he asked when she finally came inside, and the others had departed with farewell shouts and cheerful waves.

'Some friends,' she said, manifestly excited, and breathlessly giving him an account of what had happened.

'Friends today, but maybe only while you give them caramels and chocolates,' he warned her, but she ran upstairs, unwilling to let anything dampen her joy. In her bedroom she elatedly relived the event.

She knew not all the kids who walked her home and shared the lollies would be her friends. But some would. A girl called Melanie had said she hoped they could meet up in the holidays, and that she'd ask her mother if she could invite her around. A boy called Jimmy wanted to know whether she liked swimming, and when she admitted she'd never tried, he promised to teach her.

As recently as breakfast that morning she'd been thankful the ordeal of school would be over for six weeks. Now she looked forward to late January when it would resume. In later years she would often remember that particular day, when a man dressed up as Santa Claus helped change her life.

Chapter 4

Each birthday the cards came, always with a Greek banknote Katerina could exchange at the local Commonwealth Bank for a few Australian pounds. In 1966, the year decimal currency was introduced, this became Australian dollars. But in the intervening years far more than the currency had changed. Her name had been abbreviated to Kate. She no longer lacked friends. She not only spoke English fluently without trace of an accent, but was near the top of her class in third form.

Some things remained the same. They still lived in a cramped flat over the café. While her father was now manager in addition to his real job as chef, it was a purely titular promotion with no extra salary, and the owner still harassed him with complaints about profits and threats of redeveloping the site. But business was flourishing, so Andreas no longer feared for the future.

It was during Kate's formative years that the seaside town of Dee Why began to undergo a huge transformation, as old beach houses were torn down and apartment blocks began to proliferate. What had been a quiet holiday and weekend retreat was becoming a commuter suburb with supermarkets and a shopping mall. And the arrival of permanent residents saw the café adopt its own minor conversion. A hopeful new name, *The Corinthian*, was painted on the window, and the ubiquitous cuisine of all Greek restaurants in Australia – the mixed grill – was now supplemented with more adventurous fare: kabobs, spit-roasted lamb, souvlakis, taramasalata and the occasional appearance of *retsina* wine.

A modest rise in takings meant they were able to afford part-time waitresses for the summer holidays and weekends. One of these, a Spanish girl in her early twenties named Isabella, had begun to stay overnight with Andreas. This usually coincided with times when his daughter was sleeping away from home, and since Kate now had a circle of school friends, this was frequent.

On her fifteenth birthday her father broke the news that Isabella would be moving in permanently. He also gave her a surprisingly bulky airmail envelope from Athens delivered that morning. When Kate took it up to the privacy of her room, she realised this was not the usual card, but a letter comprising many closely written pages.

My very dear Kate,

It still seems strange to call you this, but I do understand why you have altered your name, and I'm sure you and your father would know best about such matters. You are growing up there, and you must do what is easiest for you to belong comfortably in Australia.

It is over eight years since we saw each other, and you are on the threshold of your adult life, so there are many things I need to tell you. Things I have delayed until now. Firstly, about Michel. Although I still feel very ashamed of the moment when I had to choose – whether to step off the ship and start life again with your father or remain on board and sail back to the Mediterranean for a new life with Michel – there could only ever be one choice. A selfish choice, but the truth is from the moment we met I knew I would end up with him. Your papa and I, this is difficult to explain, but we never really loved each other. And please believe, I am not talking of that violent night you overheard: we were already not the least bit in love long before then.

We should not have married. It happened because our families in the Greek town where we grew up were such close friends – and even from our school days they were forever arranging to match us. At seventeen I was young – far too young – but it seemed as if everyone would be pleased, all our relatives took it for granted – even the local priest smiled on us as if he knew we were destined for each other, and so we were flattered and foolishly agreed.

On my wedding night I knew it had been a mistake. No fault of your father's – please believe that, but if you fall in love as I'm sure you will some day, you will know the difference between simply making love to a man and being in love. There is, believe me, a world of difference.

Yes, it was a mistake, but not entirely – for how could any event be a mistake that produced you? It was wrong, let's put it that way, for we were incompatible. It became more obvious, this incompatibility, when we left Greece and went to Cyprus, because I was lonely there. And that meant I took other lovers – but I hasten to add this was not when Andreas was here; it was after he left us and went to Australia.

Such behaviour is ended. Michel and I are very happy, so there is no need for me to search elsewhere for a chance of happiness. (I assure you I never found it, not until that first moment I met him on board the Ottoman Star.)

He has a really good desk job in one of the Greek shipping lines, and I have a new job this past year in the office of an architect. My employer is a great fan of the wonderful Danish architect Joern Utzon who has designed the Sydney Opera House, but we were sorry he had so much trouble with the politicians over the cost of it. The pictures of it in our newspapers look magical. My architect says the Dane is a genius, and politicians are idiots and should be kept away from great enterprises. He is envious of Utzon's design. He even envies you, because I told him you live in that city, and might attend a concert there when it is finally opened. Some day, with luck, I would love to visit it, especially if I could visit it in company with you. One day, perhaps. If that seems unlikely, we can but dream.

Darling, I have to ask you not to show this letter to your father. It is very personal, and written entirely for you. It is something I have been plucking up the courage to write for several years, a confessional that I owe you from long ago when I had to choose between two men and two very different ways of life – and in selfishly seeking happiness for myself I treated you shamefully. The hardest thing I ever did in my life was to abandon you. I can never forgive myself for that, but perhaps one day you can find it possible to absolve me. Enough, my dear daughter with your new name. Please write when you can. Same address as last year, but please keep it to yourself. It saves me from unwelcome letters.

Fondest love,

Sofia (Mama)

Kate knew her father would be curious, but he showed no sign of interest until the next morning at breakfast. And then it was a rather clumsy attempt at interrogation.

'So . . . the usual birthday card, was it?'

'No, Papa, a letter – for a change.'

'I wondered. Such a thick envelope. It must've been a long letter full of news,' he said with a glance at her, and added, 'for a change.'

'Yes.'

'Still living in Athens?'

'Still there.'

'And him?' Kate knew he meant Michel Doumani. 'He's also still there, is he?'

'Yes, Papa. No real alterations in her life. Except she has a new job, working for an architect.'

'Hmph.' He sipped his coffee. 'Funny sort of job for someone like her. What does she know about such things?'

'She works in his office. Not on a building site.'

He shrugged at this, and after a moment said, 'So the sailor . . . he can't earn enough to support her?'

'I don't think it's like that,' she replied, trying to stifle a growing resentment at this probing. 'I got the impression he has a good job, and that Mama works because she wants to. But I don't know – after all, does it really matter to either of us?'

'What else did she say?'

'Not much.'

'A big letter for not much.'

'She asked about school and my friends – things like that.'

'Stupid to ask such questions, when you can't write back and tell her.' His eyes above the rim of his cup were intently studying her as he drank the last of his coffee. It was a trap she had almost stepped into.

'Well . . .' She rose to gather the breakfast dishes. 'I can't, can I? The things she asked are called *rhetorical* questions. Ones that aren't meant to be answered. We learnt that word in English class.'

'Then she still doesn't give her address, eh?'

'No,' Kate said, feeling uneasy and wishing she had not been placed in this position by either parent.

'I don't believe you, Kate. I can always tell when you lie.'

'Papa, I'm late for school, so can we please forget about it? Even if she did give it to me some day, you know you don't want her address.'

'Of course I don't want it. The last thing in the world I'd wish to do is write to her. But I don't like it when you tell me lies.'

Kate went to school upset. After eight years, the animosity between her parents remained. Both of them still bitter enemies, making her their unwilling battleground. It did not get better as time passed; absurdly it seemed to have become more entrenched. She was relieved he hadn't asked to see the letter, or she would've had to lie again and say she'd burnt it. For the moment it was safe in her satchel, but in the end she might have to get rid of it like she had some others in the past. Which was stupid and unfair, for this letter was one she wanted to keep. She wondered if life would be easier when Isabella came to share her father's bed, and hoped their relationship would last. She felt certain it would make her life less stressful.

Dear Mama, she wrote back,

You ask me to keep secrets but Papa knows I'm telling lies. I'm not able to understand why you still hate each other after so long. I have friends at school whose parents are divorced, but they're not always angry like this. Why does the ill-feeling persist? I don't hate either of you, but nor do I want to be part of a conspiracy and forced to tell lies. I could say to you it's easiest for me if you don't write any more, but I love hearing from you, especially the last letter, so there is only one way to solve what has become a truly difficult situation.

Ever since you sent me the first money for my birthday I started to save, and now have a small account at the Commonwealth Bank. Also, I earn from helping in the café after school, peeling potatoes to make chips for the mixed grill. Have you ever heard of this meal? I very much doubt it. When people in Australia go to a Greek café they like to order a mixed grill, which is an assortment of steak, chops and sausages – with chips – so that's our main dish on the menu.

Papa doesn't like cooking mixed grills, but that's what many customers expect. He also complains about all the potatoes we have to peel because they want lots of chips, and he asked Isabella, the Spanish girl who now lives here, to do this, but she got cross and said she didn't come to live with him to peel spuds (spuds is the name for potatoes) so he pays me for this boring job, and I put what I earn in my bank.

I'm telling you all this to explain I've saved enough money to rent a mailbox at the local post office, and that's where you can send letters from now on. I have my own key to the box and nobody knows about it except you and me, so I'll check each month in the hope you'll write more often. Please do.

Love,
Kate
PO Box 2571
Dee Why 2099

My dearest Kate,

My first letter to Number 2571. What a clever schemer you are! A post office box, and your own key. Of course I will write often – I'll try to write every month, for it would be such a waste to have our postal box and not make use of it. Enclosed is a cheque which you can put in your savings account, and it will help pay for the box! What fun. I love the thought that we share a secret like this.

Fondest love,
Mama

It was strange, Kate thought, how being secretive did make it fun. And how sometimes she felt so close to this woman who had walked out of her life – had indeed deserted her, as Sofia herself admitted – and caused her such unhappiness. Now that they could keep in frequent touch Kate wrote regularly during the following year. It was akin to a release after so much of her childhood spent with an often distant and taciturn father; this was suddenly like discovering a new companion to whom she could confide almost anything.

Her replies to the succession of birthday cards had been polite but rather stilted exchanges; now she found so much to say about her daily existence, about school and her friends as well as life above the café with her father and Isabella, and even the onset of boys – one a pimply sixteen-year-old who professed himself in love with her but whom she spent her time trying to avoid, and another the captain of the adjacent boys' school whom she liked tremendously, but had to admit he hardly even spared her a second glance.

Life, her mother wrote back,

is a bitch sometimes. But when I was sixteen I was already as good as promised to your father, so cheer up, my darling. You at least will have the freedom to find the right guy and make your own choices. And thank you for the photographs. My heart leapt at the sight of you. Such a transformation. Last year in that school photo you looked sweet but gawky. But now in such a short space of time the duckling has become a swan and you look almost grown-up and so lovely. I'm impressed, astonished and proud. The captain of the boys' school is clearly extremely short-sighted or else blinded by his own self-importance.

Kate liked the comment. She decided that saving up for a Box Brownie camera to take the photos had been worth it. In later letters she sent cuttings from newspapers showing the progress of the Opera House since Joern Utzon's shock resignation and abrupt departure to Denmark.

Everyone wishes he was still here to oversee the final stages of his masterpiece, but after the battering he had from politicians we hear he's vowed never to return to Australia. Such a shame, because after all the fuss about the cost everyone seems very proud of it. So we should be. The roof looks magnificent, like a wonderful sailing ship with its canvas hoisted. They say it looks fantastic from a plane. It's certainly a great sight from ferries on the harbour. Our class went on an outing to the art gallery in Sydney, and we travelled by ferry from Manly so we passed right alongside it. Seeing it from so close it was hard to imagine that the original building before this one on Bennelong Point was a tram shed.

She often sent snippets of news from local papers. Sofia liked this; she said it kept her up to date with what was happening in Australia, for it was impossible to find any news of such a faraway country in the Greek papers. In the next letter Kate included front-page pictures of the largest street protest so far against Australia's involvement in the Vietnam war.

Just imagine you can see me somewhere in the middle of this huge crowd, Mama. I'm one of about 80 000. The police said it was only 30 000, and the organisers estimated at least 120 000, so take an average and you will probably get the answer. I'm wearing a T-shirt that says 'U.S. go home' and we're all chanting: 'Hey, hey, LBJ – how many kids have you killed today?' I was in another protest last week when lots of us laid down in the middle of the road to demonstrate against the visit by a bunch of American politicians.

Me and some of my friends from school went to it, along with a boy named Freddy who only joined in because he says he's keen on me. But I'm not keen on him, because he was too scared to lie down on the roadway like the rest of us, especially when the Premier was quoted as saying 'Run over the bastards'.

Instead we managed to stop the motorcade for about ten minutes, then the police moved in to arrest us. My girlfriends and I got away, but they grabbed Freddy because he was wearing this T-shirt with the words 'FUCK THE WAR' on it. The cops said it was obscene, and Freddy told them that the war was the obscenity and they were a bunch of Nazi thugs for supporting it. They gave him a belting before locking him in the clink all night, and next day he was lucky to get off with a fine.

Now he expects me to hop into bed with him because he's a local hero. I've already told him to find himself a local heroine if she'll have him, because as far as I'm concerned he's a local drongo. (That's an Aussie expression meaning a fairly stupid person. There are other names for it including a galah, a dummy, a dickhead or a birdbrain. In the case of a girl drongo, she's a dumb Dora.)

So you see I'm keeping extremely busy, improving my knowledge of the vernacular and demonstrating against the war. I also now have to help wait on tables in the café. There was a serious falling out with Isabella and she's left Papa – gone off with a jazz musician. He said he didn't want any more complications in his life, and he insists I do her job as there will be no more impractical attachments.

In between times I came top in class. We're about to start the long summer holidays, then we go back for our final year at school and sit for the leaving certificate at the end of 1968. And then . . . who knows!

Much love,

Kate

My dearest Rebel,

It all sounds exciting and very alarming. I'm worried at the thought of you being provoked into calling a policeman one of those funny names, and getting a belting and then being locked up. So please be careful and not too adventurous. I know you and your friends are saving the world, but I'm sure your father must be alarmed at these activities. Or – dare I guess – perhaps he doesn't know.

Congratulations on coming top of your class. That makes me feel full of pride. I approve also of your rejection of Freddy the drongo. Do take your time, choose wisely, and don't be like me and rush into the first pair of arms held open for you. There will be other Freddies, nicer ones I'm sure, perhaps even braver ones who will lie down on the road with you. (What on earth am I saying, for goodness sake? You don't need any more encouragement!)

Enjoy your summer vacation, and take more of your nice photos to send me. Happy New Year, and may 1968 be a good one for you. I hope things are not too grim at home, and the more I think about it the more I'm certain that Andreas is blissfully ignorant of your valiant attempts to end the Vietnam War.

Fondest love,

Mama

P.S. I do feel sorry about him and Isabella. He doesn't have much luck with his romantic life, does he.

Dear Mama,

Of course you're right. Why wouldn't you be! Papa doesn't have the slightest idea about the anti-war demos – which I hasten to add is not a Greek word; it's short for demonstrations. Everything here gets abbreviated and reduced to one or two syllables. That's what happened to my name. Kat-er-in-a, that's four syllables if you say it slowly. Or even if you say it quickly. It never had a chance.

I would have written sooner, but I've been flat out waitressing in the holiday period. Papa seems resigned about the loss of Isabella (whose name was condensed to Bel), and is slightly cheered by a change of menu. There are so many more Europeans living in this district now, and so we serve more Greek food. Less mixed grills, and he is cooking up a storm feeling more at home with kabobs, couscous and gorgeous things made with fetta cheese.

Must go. Tables to be set.

Much love,

Kate

P.S. I wasn't going to say anything yet but I haven't only been busy working in the café. I've met someone. His name is Joshua. I'm not entirely sure yet if I like him or not . . . but I think I do. More when I find out for certain!

Chapter 5

A fairly obvious beach ambush, she thought with quiet amusement, the first day she met Joshua Maitland. It was a scorching day that promised to fulfil predictions of a torrid summer, and The Corinthian Café was unpleasantly airless and crowded by holidaymakers. A lone ceiling fan spun ineffectually, while fumes from the chargrill and clouds of cigarette smoke blended into a pungent haze. Andreas was in a foul mood because newcomers kept leaving the screen door open; flies were crawling over his face and arms while he swiped at them with a spatula to protect the food. Kate was upset because she had planned to see the new Paul Newman film with school friends, but one of the part-time waitresses had not turned up, and with such a large crowd, she had no option but to assist.

By two o'clock she had helped with the washing up, and decided to spend what remained of the day on the beach. She went upstairs to her bedroom in the tiny flat and changed into a costume. Not the bikini that she'd saved up to buy; it was hidden in the bottom drawer where it would no longer offend her father. One glimpse of it when she'd changed into it and proudly showed him had shocked and scandalised him. So today was a more modest two piece with a towelling robe, and a beach bag on her arm containing a book to read. At least that was the plan. She had no intention of being picked up by anyone like Joshua.

She must have passed him on the beach but was unaware of it. The surf patrol was more of a distraction, whistling at her as she came near them. Carrying on, Joshua told her later, like a bunch of randy roosters on sighting a new chick. It was what made him wake up, for he was drowsing on the sand, anticipating a dismal summer when he woke to see this slender nymph going past, looking like a vision of a goddess on the beach.

She was unexpectedly beguiled by the thought of being a slender nymph, let alone a vision of a goddess!

Until seeing her, he said, it had promised to be a dreary summer holiday. This year most of his former school mates and their families had migrated to fresh playgrounds; Palm Beach was everyone's new fashionable favourite, although a few with rich parents had gone north to Queensland and the Mecca of Surfers Paradise with its high apartment blocks and sexy meter maids in bikinis.

Surfers, he told her, was where his best friend Toby Robinson had gone – travelling by flying boat, would she believe – Toby, his parents and Toby's sister Noelene, who had just turned eighteen and was already a photographic model. He really missed Toby; the beach was not the same without him – or without Noelene, he added, though making that sound like an afterthought.

This exodus of friends was why he'd been dozing on the sand feeling bored, until alerted by the sudden chiacking of the surf patrol. Their rowdy overtures had brought him a first glimpse of her – though his was a silent tribute, he insisted – pure admiration of her silhouetted figure that was tanned like honey, and of course the rest of her: the shapely legs, her flowing dark hair, the startling blue eyes and a face that could launch at least a thousand ships.

But all of this, including her laughter at his flowery but rousing verbosity had come later, after he had succeeded in picking her up. She had walked resolutely past the surf club hutch where they held court between rescues and shark watching, and found a deserted spot at the far end of the beach. She spread her beach towel and was comfortably settled with a book when she became aware of a distant figure making a gradual approach, and bent her head as if to concentrate on reading while her peripheral vision gauged his progress.

She'd faced and dealt with beach ambushes before. He strolled on the wet sand letting the waves ripple over his bare feet, giving an impression he was absorbed and oblivious of her. His entire attention seemed focused on picking up shells, and just when she felt certain he was about to meander past, he had gone through the charade of visibly noticing her. This had been done by a casual glance, a puzzled frown of trying to identify her, then a second look – one of possible recognition this time. After that came a nod followed by his voice.

'Hi there.' He'd accompanied it with a flicked wave of his arm, adding it was a nice warm day, then expressing regret for the chorus of larrikin invitations she'd received from the lifesavers.

Quite a performance, she thought, nodding by way of reply but not audibly responding. Reserving her opinion, even though she had already formed the impression he'd had plenty of previous practice at this kind of thing.

'It's completely wrong,' he said, pausing near where she lay, 'the way those surf-club drongos try to own the beach. As though it's their private kingdom, and any good-looking girl is fair game.'

'They come in handy.' This time she'd felt obliged to reply, while not missing the accolade paid to her appearance. 'At least they do when people are caught in a rip and liable to drown.'

'That's true,' he agreed, 'we need them in moments like that. But it doesn't happen very often, and the rest of the time they're a blot on the landscape. Or should that be on the seascape?'

'Perhaps "a blot on the horizon" would cover it.'

The moment it was said she knew it sounded like an invitation. He hadn't needed another, had simply smiled agreement, spread his towel and sat down. My mistake, she thought, but wondered if that were true. Her mistake, or her intention? They were the only two people on this part of the beach; he was unlikely to move, and she had no intention of doing so.

She was aware of an easy youthful charm. He had thick curly dark hair and bright brown eyes. Slim and suntanned, with a good physique. If pressed she would have declared him good looking. She sought refuge in the page of her novel, trying to find the last line she'd read before being distracted.

'Good book?' he asked, after a moment.

'Hard to tell. I haven't got very far.' She'd looked up to find he was smiling.

'Don't you find it difficult, reading on the beach?'

'Not particularly.'

'Windy days . . . Sand gets in the pages.'

She'd thought it time to reinforce her pose by turning a page, but before she could do this he'd spoken again. 'They're an arrogant mob.'

'Who are?'

'The lifesavers.'

'Don't let their juvenile antics spoil your day.' She was tiring of the subject, but he persisted as if not noticing.

'It's hard to believe my father was a leading light in the surf club when he was my age. A champion swimmer in those days, in fact a bit of an all-round athlete – tennis, golf, the lot – and apparently a magnet for all the girls around here, my poor old dad.'

'Is he dead?'

'My father? No, he's a dentist in the western suburbs who hates his job.'

'Oh. The way you spoke of him, I thought . . . Why does he hate his job?'

'How would you feel, gazing into people's mouths and drilling infected teeth every day for the past twenty years?'

'Well, if you put it like that . . . !'

'And to make it worse, his practice has changed a lot since he first started. Most of his patients these days are New Australians.'

Kate bristled. 'Is that a problem?'

'It is for him. He's very anti-immigration, and a bit of a racist.'

She wondered if that warranted a reply and resolved to ignore it. She glanced down at her book and turned an unread page instead. He showed no sign of moving, picking up handfuls of soft sand and letting it sift slowly through his fingers, so she gave up the pretence and shut the book.

'No good after all?' he asked, his cheerful mock-innocence so transparent it was beginning to irritate her.

'No chance to find out,' she retorted.

'Sorry,' he said with a shrug, accompanied by another amiable smile. He seemed to have an endless quantity of such smiles. 'Then I'd best leave you to it.' He rose, picked up his towel and flicked the sand from it. 'But before I go, if I tell you my name, will you tell me yours?' Without waiting for an answer he continued, 'I'm Joshua Maitland.'

'Katerina Vassos,' she told him after a brief hesitation.

'Katerina?'

'Yes. Katerina Vassos,' she repeated more firmly. 'It's Greek.'

'Oh,' he said.

'But I'm called Kate at school,' she told him. 'Friends advised it. Apparently it avoids me being branded one of your father's unwelcome New Australians.'

'That's bloody ridiculous.'

'Of course it is,' she replied heatedly, 'and so is your dad and a lot of other people like him with their siege mentality. The so-called dinkum Aussies, the ones who like to call us reffos, wogs and dagoes.'

'Forget my father,' Joshua said, 'he's a Neanderthal.'

'If he is, there's plenty of them in this country.'

'Forget him. Besides, the last thing you need is a dentist.'

'What?' She was momentarily confused by the digression.

'You don't need him. Apart from assets too numerous to mention, like lovely eyes and a wonderfully cute nose, you have a truly great set of pearly whites. It's a privilege to look at them.'

She started to laugh, unable to help it.

'Anyway,' he said, 'I like the name Katerina. If your family's Greek, so what? You sound like you were born here.'

'Is that meant to be an accolade?'

'You mean you weren't born here?'

'No, I was born in Cyprus. I came here when I was six.'

'How long ago were you six?'

'Eleven years ago,' she replied.

'That makes you seventeen. Sweet seventeen,' he added.

If you insist, Kate thought, and deciding she might as well take part in this banter asked him, 'So how long ago were you six?'

'A bit longer than that. I'll be nineteen in March.'

74

'Well, have a happy birthday – in March.'

'Thank you. When's yours?'

'Just gone. November 26th. That's why I'm called Katerina.'

'What do you mean?'

'The 26th is my birthday – as well as my name day.'

'Name day? What's that? Is it a Greek thing?'

She nodded. 'Greek and lots of European countries. We all have name days as well as birthdays. It's like having two special days each year. Only mine are on the same day, so you could say I missed out.'

'On what?'

'On getting presents, and being fussed over.'

'That happens to Greek kids twice a year?'

'If they're lucky. I was unlucky.'

'Name day,' he repeated, looking interested. 'I've never heard of that before.'

'You live and learn,' she replied.

'I'd like to,' he replied. 'Will you improve my knowledge and tell me about it?' Before she could answer this he added, 'I don't mean now, because I know how much you want to get back to reading your book. But perhaps the next time we meet?' He gave a grin in response to her raised eyebrow. 'I mean is that okay? Would it be in order with you – the idea of us meeting again?'

She feigned indecision for a moment. 'When?' she'd asked.

'How about tomorrow,' he'd said.

It was on the following Sunday, the hottest day of a blistering summer, that Joshua prevailed on her to take him seriously. Below the beach house, he said persuasively, where his grandparents had once installed a wine cellar and a games room, that was the perfect place: it was spacious, bone dry, protected from the sun and far cooler than anywhere else. They'd be alone and perfectly safe down there, he pledged, the oldies were spending the day with friends in Manly and not expected back until nightfall . . . so, that being the case, and thinking about how much they now meant to each other, how did she feel about it?

She felt, when she thought of it in later years, that she had been curiously naïve and far too easily seduced. A pushover! Pushed over by his charm, looks and, perhaps more than anything else, the ability to make her laugh. As well as his declaration that he'd been thinking about her and nothing else since their first meeting.

It was, as he'd promised, decidedly cooler below the house. What he had not mentioned was a sofa. It was almost hidden towards the rear of what had once been a family games room, amid a debris of discarded childhood relics: a play pen, an open cupboard containing a koala and other soft toys, a rocking horse and a dusty ping-pong table folded away in a corner. While most of this miscellany was under a thick layer of dust, the sofa was protected by an old tarpaulin that Joshua removed. She felt nervously excited as he undressed her, then removed his own clothes. They lay on the sofa and embraced. In the past week since meeting they'd kissed many times, but never quite like this. The intensity of it swept away her last reticence. She found herself starting to tremble as he entered her. She expected pain but he had fondled and teased her into lubricity, and was surprisingly gentle.

'All right?' he whispered.

She nodded, not willing to trust her voice. The feel of their naked bodies wrapped so tightly together was both alarming and thrilling.

'Not hurting?'

When she shook her head he started to move with slow steady thrusts and her body began to arch and tremor in response. The tremor became a rhythm, it felt euphoric and unreal. She stopped being afraid that his grandparents might return sooner than expected and catch them. She even ceased worrying that this might just be a summer romance, over and forgotten when she went back to school. Or worse, when his friend Toby – and especially Toby's sister, the model – returned from their surfing paradise, that she might find herself discarded, dumped, just a wog girl for a holiday quickie whose time was up. Instead her mind was full of what was occurring, how his hands were exploring her body, fondling her breasts, moving to grip her buttocks and draw her so tightly against him she could feel the pulsating rhythm of his heart. Or was it her own heart that was beating so violently?

She could hardly believe the feeling of ecstasy and undreamt of pleasure: the delirium that friends declared never happened the first time was unquestionably happening to her. And to him. Although she doubted this was his first time. He was so assured, it couldn't be. Had he done it here in this place before? With who? How many times? But it was only a faint shadow in her mind; nothing could spoil her bliss as their fervour grew.

She felt his rising passion, his excitement as he ejaculated. She cried out wildly in Greek as she too climaxed, declaring that she loved him and wanted it to last forever. She repeated it again less stridently until the delight finally ebbed, when she lay still and exhausted, feeling an immense happiness. And some surprise, for she rarely spoke Greek now, and to the best of her knowledge had never used those words before.

Later, when they were upstairs in the house and sharing a

shower, while he was soaping her and beginning to excite her again, he asked about the cries she'd uttered in such a frenzy.

'Sounded Greek to me,' he said with the same engaging grin. 'What did it mean?'

'Just that it was nice,' she said, all of a sudden feeling shy.

'Is this even nicer?' he asked, as the hot water engulfed them and his hand explored her intimately. She gave herself willingly to him again, so aroused she completely forgot about his grandparents who might return at any time to find them making noisy love in the shower recess.

But it was another half hour before they did arrive – and by then she and Joshua were dried, dressed and sitting innocently on the spacious verandah with its view down towards the sea.

'This is Kate,' he told them. 'I invited her for afternoon tea, and we went downstairs and had a game of table tennis.'

Kate could remember it vividly. She recalled the thoughtful gaze of his grandmother, a well-dressed matriarch with a corona of coiffured silver hair and astonishingly alert eyes, more like those of a young woman than one in her sixties, however stylish. It was the assessment of these eyes that expressed a hint of scepticism, increasing Kate's concern that Joshua, so eager to be slyly smart and amusing, might have misjudged his grandmother's perception.

They were an oddly matched couple, Aaron and Rosetta Morris. He was short, thick set and burnt the colour of a walnut by the sun; as unprepossessing as his wife was graceful. She was almost a head taller, her skin pale and flawless. She wore a brightly coloured calf-length summer dress with an easy elegance, while he, incongruous in the heat, was squeezed into a tight business suit, rigid collar and lace-up boots. In contrast to his modish wife the clothes made him appear stiff and outdated, but he was the first to respond and extend her a welcome.

'Pleased to meet you, Kate,' he said, surprising her by formally shaking hands while asking if it was short for Katherine.

'Katerina,' she told him.

'Much nicer,' he replied. 'But I suspect too much of a mouthful for our locals. We have a fetish to reduce names to the minimum. Almost everyone and everything gets abbreviated in this country.' As if he had done his social duty he went and stretched out on a cane chaise longue, one of several on the verandah, declaring it far too hot a day to have been visiting friends. 'Should've spent the day downstairs in the cool. Like these young folk.'

His wife gave a fleeting smile, then turned to Kate. 'You must be thirsty after your table tennis,' she said, and Kate was instantly tongue-tied, alarmed she might be asked who'd won and aware of the eyes still analysing her. She felt certain Mrs Morris would remember the derelict table that looked as if it hadn't been used for years. Probably she would be aware there were no longer any bats or ping-pong balls . . . she desperately wished Joshua had not made his flippant and unnecessary comment.

'I know I'm thirsty,' Joshua said, too late to rescue her.

'Then how about a nice cool drink?' his grandmother suggested. 'I'm sure we could all do with something refreshing on an enervating day like this.' She gave another of her fleeting smiles, but this one did not extend to her eyes.

She knows, Kate realised, feeling guilty and ashamed.

Chapter 6

They were close that magical summer, she and Joshua. They met each morning on neighbouring Collaroy beach, and sometimes the sun had set before she reluctantly left him, taking a bus home, always hoping her father believed her plausible tales of time spent sunbaking and swimming with girlfriends from school. On New Year's Eve they went to a party at an oceanfront house, where Joshua seemed to know almost everyone and appeared to be the centre of attention, while she pretended to enjoy herself. As if aware of this, immediately after the new year had been welcomed he took her hand and they sneaked away unnoticed. There was only a crescent moon and the beach was semi-dark and empty. They found a secluded spot where they undressed and made love on the sand.

It was a hot night and afterwards they went into the sea. The surf was no more than a gentle swell, the water refreshing. Luxuriating in it, letting the waves that were no more than ripples cover her naked body, Kate could see the distant lights along the shore where the party was still continuing. Up on the hillside directly opposite them the houses were quiet and dark. His grandparents in their weekender would be fast asleep, she thought, or was Grandma Rose, as she liked to be called, lying awake and wondering if . . .

Conjecture was interrupted as something slimy brushed against her, and she gave a startled cry before realising it was harmless. 'Oh, God,' she exclaimed. 'Yuck!'

'What was it?'

'Seaweed. I thought it was an eel or something horrible from the murky lower depths.'

He laughed at this, then wrapped his arms around her and began to fondle her breasts. Kate could feel him growing hard and erect, and herself responding to it as she started to become aroused again.

'That's not seaweed or an eel,' she said blissfully. 'It feels like something very friendly.'

'A friendly shark,' he replied, and she smiled and lent against him, thinking they'd never done it in the ocean before, but any moment she'd discover what it was like. 'After all, this is familiar territory for them,' he whispered in her ear.

'Familiar?' She wondered what he meant.

'I was standing here once when a shark slid between my legs.'

'*What?*' She turned in alarm, staring at his face. 'Joshua, you're joking!'

'No, it's true. I felt this shape . . . I knew it was a shark and I nearly crapped myself. Almost at this very spot.'

'Oh, Christ.' Kate backed away, gazing at the dark sea in alarm. 'I wish . . . I truly wish you hadn't said that!' She started to splash as a reflective protective gesture while heading towards the safety of the sand.

'Kate,' he pursued her, laughing, 'it was long ago, I was only ten years old. And let me tell you the punch line . . . the shark was dead.'

'That's your story,' she replied, shivering as he reached her.

'Truly. I practically broke a speed record getting out of the water, but a few minutes later I saw it washed ashore. Just a baby shark, and honestly . . . it was dead.'

'Even so, I bet you didn't go in swimming again. Not here.'

'Well, no,' he admitted, 'it did occur to me baby sharks have mummies and daddies. I shouldn't have told you.'

'You definitely shouldn't have.'

'I'm a dill. It put you right off.'

'How did you guess?'

'Don't fancy another swim then? Or anything else? Of course you don't. How could you?'

Kate laughed and hugged him. 'How about a run?' she said. 'Let's get dry – and warm. I'm freezing.'

They ran along the empty beach, then jogged back hand in hand to retrieve their clothes. But exhilaration from the naked run led from one thing to another, and it was long after three in the morning when he walked her all the way home to the neighbouring suburb of Dee Why. There was a steady stream of traffic along Pittwater Road returning from late parties, horns tooting and drunken cries of bawdy encouragement as car headlights picked out their enfolded figures whenever they stopped to embrace each other. The walk took over an hour, because the stops became more and more frequent and their exchanges increasingly passionate.

The windows of the flat above the café were dark. They stopped on the corner, and Joshua wrapped her in a final embrace. Her lips were bruised from his kisses, and her blood was racing. She had never been so deliriously happy.

'I hope he's not waiting up for you.'

'I don't care if he is,' Kate said. She imagined her father fretful and listening for her arrival, while he counted the hours since midnight. 'He has to know sometime. After all, it's 1968, and I'm going to be eighteen before this year ends.'

'Here's to us and good things happening in 1968. Make a new year wish.'

'I have.'

'Tell me.'

'I can't, or it mightn't come true. You make one.' She watched him while thinking of her own wish. A simple one, really. A longing that soon he would say he loved her.

'I've got a whole heap of them,' Joshua said, 'and you know this one anyway. I want the lousy Vietnam War to end before I turn twenty and our government forces me to take part in the bloody ballot.'

'It has to end. We all want that.' She felt certain the war was too unpopular to last much longer. The hated lottery to select twenty-year-olds for conscription had already caused a national furore. Soon the politicians would have to listen.

Besides, she thought, on this, the best night of her life, good things must happen and wishes would surely come true.

At the end of January the holidays were officially over and friends started to return. Toby Robinson and his sister, the astonishingly sophisticated Noelene, flew back to regale them with the glitter of Surfers Paradise. Noelene was to sign a lucrative contract modelling swimwear; Toby to resume his second year of medicine at Sydney University. In the first weeks of February, Kate met many of Joshua's circle, and a new routine of parties and barbecues occupied the weekends.

That was when things began to change.

She soon discovered theirs was a close-knit group, an upper North Shore clan who had been mates since attending the same prep school and, until this year, had always spent their holidays together on the Northern Beaches. It seemed a matter of quiet astonishment to them that in their absence Joshua had found himself a new girlfriend – and of all things, she was Greek.

In their well-ordered and laid-back world there were few strangers, and almost no foreigners. She knew that while Greeks were now a large migratory group, they were still stereotyped in Australian society as ethnic and clannish, choosing segregation in inner-city ghettos, generally intermarrying, and often to be found working in family-owned fruit shops or milk bars. It was a biased perception, but one firmly believed in the elite streets of Double Bay and Killara.

Kate was aware of their feelings. She sensed the conjecture: while they were outwardly polite, it was their careful courtesy, an almost overdone politeness, that first made her conscious she was an oddity in their midst. She could imagine the type of surmise when they were alone and able to comment freely. Was good old Josh serious? How on earth did they meet? Would it last? Were they fucking? She was certain there'd be consensus on this – or else why would Joshua, the charismatic good-looking guy so many girls clearly fancied, be hanging around her all summer?

She expected disparagement. After all, her father was the chef of a small Greek café in Dee Why and they lived in cramped premises over it. A stark contrast to Joshua's coterie from affluent homes. And there was the age gap. A mere two years, but his friends were virtual adults now who attended university or were being inducted into family firms, while she was still a form five schoolgirl. They were also graduates of private education; she had always attended the local public schools. The much-fostered illusion that Australia was an egalitarian society, Kate thought, was a total myth. She lived in one Australia; they occupied a quite different country of old-boy allegiance and acquired privilege.

Except for Joshua, she thought. He was not quite the same as the others. His home, for instance. His father the dentist had a practice in remote and unfashionable Lakemba, where he lived with his second wife. It was a matter of embarrassment to his son that for years this had been a playground topic and many of his friends had regarded it with schoolboy hilarity. Some claimed not to have heard of the place.

'You mean Port Kembla,' they insisted, for this was a well-known industrial town and freight harbour.

Joshua did his best to ignore the belittlement. Not that he liked living there, but it was hard to be mocked by his friends about it. 'Beyond the Black Stump' was how one dismissed it, a tag more insensitive when applied to a suburb rather than an outback town, for at least the outback had the status of tradition and romance. Whereas poor old Josh, according to his faction, had to live in a dreary district so his dad could make a quid out of the hoi polloi's teeth. To them it was working class, too far from the coast, too hot in summer, too cold in winter, and had absolutely nothing to recommend it. Which was uncomfortably true. Worse in their eyes, housing was so cheap it had become popular with immigrants, and Muslims had begun to encroach there; it was even rumoured they'd applied for consent to build a mosque. In which case, the friends assured Joshua, we'll buy you a prayer mat.

It was a joke, all good clean fun, they hastened to assure him. But Kate knew it was not always fun to him, no matter how nonchalantly he appeared to accept their teasing. She sometimes wondered if that was why he never invited any of them home, including her, until nearly four months after they had first met, he told her his family was curious about her; would Kate do him a favour – it was bound to be mind-numbing – but one day in the school holidays would she come to lunch?

Of course, she answered, pleased at this acceptance of her existence. She went with high hopes and expectation, but soon realised why Joshua never asked his friends there.

It was a Saturday morning, and he was waiting on the station platform when her train arrived. She had brought a small bunch of flowers, and came armed with good intentions, having spent the previous night making a number of sensible resolutions. If his dad the dentist proved even a bit racist, she would be calm and diplomatic, and it would be best if she avoided all mention of the grandparents' beach house, let alone her intimate knowledge of it.

The main street was busy with women shopping before the stores shut at midday for the weekend. It seemed like any other suburb, although Kate noticed a few Arabic faces, and the occasional woman wearing a hijab. The house was situated on a corner, larger than others in the vicinity. The front part of it, Joshua explained, was the dental surgery and waiting room, so they went in the back way where his stepmother instantly appeared, as if she had been poised waiting for the sound of the door.

She was a thin, nervous woman with tightly permed brown hair. Kate greeted her with the flowers, and was met by a fluster of worried questions from her. She insisted on being called Brenda, and asked if the trip from Dee Why had been tedious. Such a long way. Was Katerina tired from the travel? Was she hot, or had she managed to get accustomed to the awful Australian weather?

'She's lived here since she was six years old,' Joshua said, but Brenda seemed not to hear him.

Lunch was an ordeal, not from his father's expected attitude; he was studiously polite and she could see traces of the charm that must have wooed women in his heyday. No, it was Brenda's constant concern and agitation that was the problem. It seemed to Kate the woman must rarely entertain, for the visit appeared to create an astonishing amount of stress. She'd hired a cook and an assistant for the occasion. As there were just the four of them at the table, and two unnecessary people hovering to serve them, it felt odd and uncomfortable. Even more incongruous, Brenda had made several forays to the kitchen where she tasted the meal and judged it unsatisfactory, so what was served instead was a hasty substitution of salad sandwiches followed by tinned fruit and ice-cream.

A sense of strain inhibited any chance of relaxed conversation. The dentist was clearly annoyed at the ineffectual social behaviour of his wife, Joshua was embarrassed, and Kate had to feign cheerfulness and declare her enjoyment of the surrogate lunch. She was also aware there was an undercurrent of conflict between Joshua and his father regarding his decision to delay university. Dr Maitland declared the idea of a gap year to be foolish. What on earth was the point of taking part-time and dead-end jobs? How did his son imagine working as an assistant stage manager in a second-rate theatre company, or doing occasional days as a cadet reporter could be of benefit when he graduated as a doctor?

It was a relief when the fiasco was over, Joshua supporting Kate's excuse of the long trip home as the reason for an early departure.

Brenda seemed greatly relieved, agreeing it was a considerable way back to Dee Why, and while they were sorry she couldn't stay longer, it was probably sensible to make an early start on such an arduous journey.

'Arduous journey, for Christ's sake,' Joshua exclaimed angrily as they left the house. 'The stupid cow. Where does she think you live? Bloody Alice Springs? Darwin?'

He was humiliated, and she felt upset for him. While they walked to the railway station he revealed his feelings in a way he'd never done before, recounting the death of his mother when he was nine.

'She was killed in a car accident. Dad always said Mum drove too fast. They used to have rows about it. Actually,' he said after a pause, 'they used to have rows about everything. I think they'd had one that morning. She was on her way to see Grandma Rose and Grandad who were spending the weekend down at the beach house. I got the feeling, although no one has ever said anything, that she wanted to talk to them about her marriage . . . about whether she was going to stay with my father or not. When you're nine, you're old enough to know what goes on in the house, and I knew things weren't good. No, that's not true . . . things were really lousy. They were bloody awful.'

Kate took his hand and held it tightly. They waited for traffic to pass, then crossed the road towards the station. A train was visible in the distance, easily catchable, but they made no attempt to hurry for it. She knew he wanted to talk.

'They had awful fights . . . sometimes late at night I'd be woken by their shouting. Mum was Jewish. You know that, you've met my grandparents. She was very beautiful and popular – Grandma told me all the blokes were after her. But she and my dad took one look at each other and that was it. Neither of their parents were keen on the idea. His didn't want him to marry a Jew – hers were worried about their daughter getting wed to a gentile.' He shrugged and gave her a faint smile. 'Religion and racism, it sure buggers up the world, Kate. But you know that.'

'What happened to spoil the marriage?' she asked.

'I suppose it was lots of things, but anti-Semitism certainly played its part. If people fight they say cruel things . . . sometimes things they might regret . . . and then they're out there and can't be taken back. One night I heard Dad shout that the worst thing he'd done in his entire life was to get hitched to a fucking Jew.'

'Oh, God,' Kate said. She felt desperate and wanted to put her arms around him, but they were in a crowded street. So she just clutched his hand even tighter.

'That was only a few days before she went to talk to Grandma. I'm sure it was to ask for help. I can't help feeling she couldn't stand it any longer, but divorce back then was a big step. I bet she'd have just walked out, but there was me. I was the problem.'

'Why?'

'Because . . . I think she wanted to know how she could leave my father and still keep me.'

'What happened?' Kate asked, while dreading his answer.

'The car went off the road in French's Forest; it hit a tree and exploded. She died on the way to hospital. They said . . . a doctor said to my father . . . I wasn't meant to hear, but I did . . . he said if she'd lived she would have been brain damaged.'

At Wynyard, Kate decided to walk to Circular Quay and take a ferry. It was a longer way home, first the boat trip to Manly, then the bus, but the ferry was more agreeable and gave her time to think. She sat outside in the late afternoon sun, watching the busy harbour and the yachts heading back to their moorings after the weekend races, recalling all she'd been told. Once he began Joshua had seemed unable to stop, as though he'd never had so compliant a listener, or perhaps had been unable to confide so much pain to anyone else before, and they'd remained on the railway platform while several trains arrived and left without her.

Less than six months after his wife's death, Dr Maitland had married his dental nurse. Joshua, who then attended a local school, had come home to find they'd been married in a registry office that afternoon. Even at the age of nine he wondered why he hadn't been invited.

A new school term began the following month, and they decided to send him to a North Shore college as a boarder. Sometimes in the shorter holidays, like the Easter break, he was told to remain at school. When he asked the reason, his father explained the dental practice had expanded and they were too busy to cope with him at home. He actually found in the following years he didn't mind this: he was often invited to the homes of school mates, which was how he formed such abiding friendships. But the holiday he most enjoyed was the long Christmas vacation he spent at the beach house with his grandparents. They became his real family, and as so many of his circle had holiday homes in the district the summer months were his real life.

Joshua confessed he found it impossible to like his stepmother. He'd known her from infancy, for she had always been his father's dental nurse. Brenda's domain was the surgery in the front of the residence, until she moved into his father's bedroom and took over the rest of the house. Joshua admitted his antipathy, but said it was not only caused by her taking his mother's place. Even as a child he'd found her disagreeable, rarely showing affection and forever fussing and indecisive, like she had been at lunch.

'She was rather awful,' Kate admitted, but tried to defend her, for there was no point in creating fiction. 'It can't have been easy for her, trying to move into your mother's place and be a mum to her child.'

'You've got it wrong,' Joshua told her. 'She always wanted to take my mother's place. She hated my mum. She'd hated her for years. Even now, she hates her memory.'

'Josh darling, surely not,' Kate demurred.

'So why did she cut off the faces?' he asked.

'What faces?' She had a moment of confusion, not understanding the remark.

'Mum's photographs,' Joshua said. 'There were photos of her all over the house that gradually began to disappear. All except mine. I had a box of them. Then one time when I came back from school they were gone. I asked had she seen them and she said no. So I tried asking our cleaning lady, who wouldn't tell me at first. Eventually she said she'd found them in the rubbish bin and had taken them home to keep, and one day when I was older she felt I should see them. I said I was old enough already, and the next day I went to her house where she showed me.'

He paused, as if having difficulty in continuing, and she gently prompted him. 'What happened?'

'All my mother's heads and faces were gone. They'd been cut out. She'd just left the body . . .' To her distress, tears began to fill his eyes. 'All of them. Just this figure in a dress . . . or sometimes in a bathing costume, once in tennis clothes . . . without a face.'

Kate was stunned. It seemed appalling, unbelievable. She tried to find him a handkerchief but by then, as if ashamed of his emotion, he had angrily turned away to wipe his eyes on his sleeve.

'Does she know you saw the photos?'

'Oh, yes. I made sure of that. But Brenda denied knowing anything about it. She told my father she thought I'd done it to make trouble. In the end they both blamed the poor cleaning lady, and sacked her.' He shook his head. 'That was six years ago, and we all go on living in that house as if nothing happened.'

One day soon, he told Kate, he was going to move away. It was why he'd taken part-time jobs instead of going to university. His father didn't know yet, but he'd already written to the registrar to say he wouldn't be coming next year. University meant being stuck at home, because he'd missed out on a scholarship and would be dependent on his father for the fees and cost of living. That was out of the question. When he'd saved enough he'd quit home without regret. Certainly by the end of this year. Did she understand why he couldn't remain in that house any longer, no matter how it affected his future?

'Yes,' Kate told him, 'I understand.' She also knew this was not something he'd ever shared with his circle of friends, not even Toby. It made her feel special, and quietly happy. Although it did occur to her that others struggled through university by taking part-time jobs. But loyalty kept her silent. 'I'm on your side,' she said.

He hugged her so tight she almost stopped breathing, and when the next train arrived he remained on the platform, waving while she boarded. As it pulled out she tried to catch a last glimpse of him, then put her hand out the window and waved back, until a guard came past and told her a west-bound train would be passing any moment, and it might amputate her arm as it went by – unless she shut the window and behaved. Apart from the loss of an arm, repeating the offence would cost a two-pound fine. Four dollars, he corrected himself, remembering the country had converted to decimal currency.

She had obediently sat down, and spent the time thinking about Joshua. Her first lover. Her first and only lover. The fresh guy on the beach who had such a heartbreak of a life and had never told anyone else about it. Until at last, after all these months, he'd told her. It felt like an unbreakable bond between them.

But the end of this year he'd leave home. So soon. She wondered where he might decide to go, what he would do and how it might affect both their lives.

Chapter 7

It was dark when Kate reached home. Her father was upstairs in the flat drinking *retsina* and watching television. She tried to tiptoe quietly to her bedroom, but he heard her and called out.

'It's just me, Papa,' she said.

'Who else would it be?' he replied. 'Where were you till so late?'

'Travelling,' she answered, as she came into the small living room and dutifully kissed him. 'I took a ferry and the bus.'

'Why?' he asked. 'It's the slowest way.' He didn't wait for an answer, more intent on his next question. 'So what were they like, the family of this friend Joshua?'

She knew the subject would be raised, and had already decided not to tell the truth. The issue of her meeting an Australian boy had already caused friction between them, when Andreas had insisted she stop seeing him. Until then Kate had been compliant to most of his directives for the sake of harmony, but on this she was inflexible. Joshua, she'd told him, was none of his business. They lived in Australia, not Cyprus or Athens, and at her age she would choose her own friends. The rebuff was a matter of great astonishment to Andreas, and rather an agreeable surprise to Kate that she had been so resolute. Since then, whenever Andreas mentioned Joshua's name it had a barbed edge to it. She would not give him the satisfaction of any more acerbic remarks.

'They were nice,' she said. 'Charming people,' she added, in case it didn't convince him.

'And the lunch – good food, or Australian food?'

'Interesting food, father,' she replied, and to her relief he did not pursue this, but turned his attention to the screen where plain-clothes detectives wearing trademark hats were questioning a swarthy suspect.

'Is it *Homicide?*' she asked, sitting beside him.

He nodded, pointed at the scene and shook his head. 'You see?'

'See what, Papa?'

'The crook; this time I think he's meant to be Greek. So why don't they have a Greek homicide policeman, eh? Just for a change.' It was a familiar refrain, particularly after half a bottle of *retsina*.

'I don't know, Papa.'

'Always the bad guys are someone else, not Australian. If you don't know why, I certainly don't know why, so we should ask your smart friend Joshua. Ask him to tell us why the crooks are always foreigners or dagoes.'

'But they aren't,' Kate said, on the verge of annoyance, then decided it was an argument she'd never win. Her father, in his way, was as myopic as Dr Maitland. A plague on both of them, she thought, and went to her bedroom. She knew he would sit watching until he was half asleep around midnight. And in the morning he'd complain the telly was all bloody rubbish and why couldn't they put on decent programs like they had in Nicosia?

His recall of the past was steeped in nostalgia, and unassailable.

It was pointless telling him there'd been no television in Cyprus when he left – just trial transmissions beamed to sets only rich people could afford. Kate had not seen TV until she came to Australia. Though not even the marvel of moving pictures coming from a small box in the corner of the room could console her in those first anguished months.

She closed the curtains and began to undress. There was a note on the bedside table in her father's scribbled handwriting. She assumed he must have put it there and forgotten. She read it and could not help a smile even while she shook her head at the message. It was so truculent, so typically her dogmatic dad. *Another man friend rang. You have too many of these friends. This one's name is Damien. He said to come to a barbecue next Sunday.*

Damien? she thought. Who on earth is Damien?

'Damien Raphael,' Joshua explained as they got off the bus by the golf links, and crossed Pittwater Road. 'He's been away all year in the bush working as a jackeroo, and this is his welcome home barbie.'

'I still don't remember meeting him,' Kate said.

Joshua gave her a sly grin. 'No wonder. Do you remember the New Year's Eve party, and afterwards on the beach?'

'Of course,' Kate smiled, 'the night of the sexy shark. I could hardly forget that.'

'Me neither,' he said. 'Well, Damien was at that same party. Somewhere in the crowd. But I suspect you were too busy thinking of getting me out on the sand and having your wicked way with me.'

She tried to elbow him in the ribs. He laughed, and put his arm around her waist. Kate adjusted her stride companionably to be in step with him. It was a cloudless day, the golf course packed, hang-gliders floating above the Long Reef headland. Ahead of them, at the end of the street, was the sandy beach, the sun reflecting on bright-blue water and animated children flying kites that fluttered and swooped amid their shrill cries of delight.

'A great day for a barbie,' she said. 'Who's giving it?'

'One of his Italian relatives.'

'Is Damien Italian?'

'Sort of. The mother's not. His dad came from Italy when he was a baby. His dad and a twin brother. The twin is Damien's Uncle Angelo. Mad as a cut snake. Plays the violin. Considered seriously weird.'

'Why? Because he plays the violin?'

'No, because he's a fruitcake. Took a mob of us out once when we were schoolkids. We thought he had kangaroos in the top paddock. Mind you, Damien himself is a bit on the weird side.'

'Is he?'

'Got a few peculiar ideas, or at least I think so. Most of our group agree. But you judge for yourself.'

'So is the strange uncle giving the barbie?'

'No, another relative. A cousin, I think. You know how it is with the Eyeties . . . rellies galore. No birth control, by order of the Pope.'

She was about to say that if his father had grown up in Australia and Damien was born here, that surely made him second generation . . . When did one stop being an Eyetie alien and become an Aussie? Instead, she asked, 'How long have you known him?'

'Since prep school. We were in the same year, right through to the leaving certificate. I wouldn't say he was a close friend, but

97

he hung around our mob for a bit. He fancies Toby's sister like mad.'

'Will she be at the barbecue? Noelene?'

'Oh, yes.'

'And Toby?'

'Wouldn't miss it for quids. Italians are famous for putting on a big spread. They always have lots of seafood and plenty of grog. Good old Tobias will be there.'

Bugger, Kate thought. It would've been a break, just once without the ubiquitous Toby Robinson. She could stand his sister, a beautiful airhead, as someone once called her, but Kate never felt the least bit comfortable with Toby.

'What's the matter?' Joshua asked her.

'Nothing,' she said, smiling. After all, she could love him without having to like all his friends.

The house was one of a small cluster in a privileged position that abutted the beach, a gracious old federation bungalow amid palm trees and Norfolk pines. She saw a large crowd gathered on the front lawn around a barbecue. All the usual suspects, she could tell. As well as a slight figure with bright-red hair waving a welcome, who Joshua informed her was Damien.

It was a long and noisy afternoon, fuelled by cans of cold beer and casks of white wine. Amid much hilarity the prize exhibit was brought out in a baby's bathtub filled with ice; a metre-long fish that had been caught within sight of the house, among the rocks fringing Fisherman's Beach.

'A genuine Eastern blue groper,' Toby proudly announced, after vaulting nimbly onto a table to get their full attention, 'better known to we spear fishers as *Achoerodus viridis*,' he added to loud applause, brandishing a hacksaw. Everyone laughed as he pretended to sharpen the saw and scrub up like a surgeon, then they crowded around to watch the giant catch being dismembered into large steaks.

Kate was standing with Damien while this went on, thinking how predictable it was, Joshua's best friend putting on a performance and behaving like the clown prince. 'Did Toby catch the groper?' she asked.

'No.' Damien shook his head. He was rather quiet, Kate thought, for the guest of honour. Quiet and rather shy.

'Who did?'

'I did,' he said after a moment, almost apologetically.

'So why is our Tobe carrying on like a pork chop?' she whispered, and was pleased to see Damien smother a laugh.

'Typical Toby,' he whispered back, 'but he has a very nice sister.'

'Joshua said you're an admirer.'

'Put it this way,' he said. 'I'm in Noelene's queue.'

'What part of the queue?' Kate asked, smiling.

'Hard to tell. We used to go to the movies together every week, but I've been away all this year and may have lost my place.'

By mutual accord they shifted slightly away from the throng in order to talk freely. Apart from the abundant red hair he had clear hazel eyes and freckles on both his face and arms. Not entirely Italian, she thought, and assumed there'd been an Anglo-Saxon branch somewhere in the family tree.

'Whereabouts were you for the past year?'

'On a cattle station in far west Queensland.'

'That,' Kate said, 'is a long way from Noelene and the queue.'

'A long way from everyone,' he replied.

'So you're going to be a jackeroo?'

'No,' he replied. 'If there's one thing I know about the rest of my life it's that I'm *not* going to be a jackeroo. It was a passing phase, and no longer on the agenda. I broke the news to my folks last night . . . which is why my dad's not here today.'

'Is he upset?'

'My old man doesn't actually pass through the stage of being "upset" – he just goes bananas. Gets absolutely livid. He's one of those fathers who thought he had my future all worked out. A few years hard slog to get experience, then manage a property, eventually buy a small place of my own. Run some cattle and sheep, become a modest sort of country squire.'

'But you don't aspire to squiredom?'

'You can say that again,' he concurred with a grin. 'I told him I rejected the whole concept and want to be a writer instead. That was when he lost his cool and shouted that among other things I'm a bloody idiot, a raving ratbag, headed for disaster, disillusion and the dole.'

'Not a man to mince his words,' she said, and Damien laughed in agreement. 'So how did your mother feel about it?'

'She's Irish. Thinks it's romantic. Shades of Yeats and the Celtic poets. She's not one to argue at home, but this time she was bold enough to suggest I should be allowed follow my instincts. Dad didn't like that a bit. Made him even angrier. He said I'm as erratic as my Uncle Angelo, who most people consider a bit around the bend. Not me, though. I think he plays the violin like . . . well . . . as far as I'm concerned, like Yehudi Menuhin.'

'That's some accolade.'

'Angelo is some violinist. He and my Aunt Fanny, that's his wife, are marvellously eccentric. They're nice people. So if I'm as nutty as Uncle Angelo, that's fine by me.'

Kate liked his youthful enthusiasm; it was contagious. And she disagreed with Joshua; she did not think Damien the slightest bit weird.

'So what are you going to do?'

'Get a part-time job, write stories and poems. See what happens. I'm still not quite twenty. I've got lots of time.' He changed the subject. 'That's enough on me. How about you? What's next in your life?'

'I finish school this year. I'll be eighteen. After that . . . I don't know. A lot depends on whether I can get a scholarship to university.'

'And you and Joshua?'

'What about us?'

'I hope all is well.'

'Yes,' she said. 'Everything is fine.' She frowned and glanced at him; something about the question puzzled her. 'Why, what made you ask that?'

'Idle curiosity,' he shrugged.

It was hardly the answer she expected. It felt at odds with the rest of their relaxed conversation, almost evasive, she thought, but before she had time to say any more they were interrupted. Noelene's expensive perfume preceded her, as she joined them and linked arms possessively with Damien.

'I was told to break up the twosome. The barbecue awaits our host and guest of honour. That's if you two have finished your tête-à-tête?'

Without waiting for an answer, she steered him away. The intrusion was like a rebuff. Damien gave Kate an apologetic glance, but allowed himself to be led back to where the main group were now collecting plates and cheerfully lining up for their fish steaks. Kate had a curious moment of detachment, as if she was not really a part of this gathering; the group was chattering among themselves and she realised how deeply their lives had always been linked, whether from attending their exclusive schools or growing up in the same comfortable neighbourhood; whatever the answer might be, they all belonged to an intricate network, and had ever since childhood.

It was like a snapshot, frozen in time for an instant. A beachfront barbecue, and she was an isolated observer. Joshua was deeply engaged in lively conversation with a crowd of his mates around the beer keg on the verandah. Dirty jokes were being told by the sound of their gusts of laughter. There was hilarity and gossip around the trestle tables of food. No one seemed aware of her standing apart, no one called or beckoned her to join them. She was tempted to sneak away, and had an impression that for a time at least, her absence would not be noticed. If she was to leave . . . just walk off quietly . . . would anyone be aware of it, or care?

But she hesitated. That was when Joshua looked up, saw her poised there and beckoned, pointing in the direction of the line-up at the barbecue and making urgent gestures towards his mouth and his stomach. So she smiled, dismissed her ridiculous negative thoughts and went to join him.

It was a long afternoon and they were almost the last couple to leave. The day was fading as they decided to walk back across the golf course; the kites and hang-gliders were gone, there was a new moon and lights were on in the clubhouse. They took the steep pathway down the cliffs to a stretch of beach that led towards the distant lights of Dee Why, removed their shoes and trudged barefoot through the soft sand. Joshua put his arm around her. It made her feel warm and wanted, although the night itself was growing chilly.

'I had a peculiar sensation that something was wrong today,' he said.

'When?'

'At lunch time. That you were feeling out of it. And I know this is silly, but I felt for a moment you were about to do a runner.'

'Me?'

'You. About to shoot through like a Bondi tram.'

'That is silly,' she said, startled by his prescience.

'I told you it was.'

'Why ever would I do a thing like that, Josh?'

'Just a funny gut feeling. I'm glad I was wrong.'

They paused and kissed. The waves were curling in and washing gently on the shore. They seemed almost luminescent. She wished it was summer so they could make love on the beach.

'No sexy sharks tonight,' Joshua said, and she nudged him.

'Too cold for that,' she agreed.

They walked on slowly.

'What did you think of Damien?'

'Quite nice. Rather shy. He wants to be a writer.'

'So I heard. Not a particularly good way to make a quid.'

'Why not? Some writers are rich.'

'Yeah, like Somerset Maugham and a few in America and Europe. Not many like that in Australia. His family's really pissed off, I hear.'

'Except his aunt and uncle.'

'The old weirdos, they don't count.' Joshua laughed. 'Bats in the belfry, both of them. I'll bet he ends up an accountant like his father.'

Oh, I hope not, Kate thought. An accountant, married to Noelene? That would be a pity.

Chapter 8

Whenever Damien Raphael had moments in his life that he wished to share, it was always his Uncle Angelo and Aunt Fanny in whom he confided. It had been that way as long as he could remember. They were far closer than his parents. This, he realised, was clearly obvious to his father, and the reason why they had such frequent disagreements. As he'd told Kate, Fanny and Angelo were largely disparaged by the rest of the family for their eccentricity, but it was their informality and idiosyncratic behaviour that endeared them to him.

The day after the barbecue he took a train, then walked from the station to their astonishing house. Number one Buckingham Avenue was angular and rather Gothic, like something out of a Brontë novel, standing in singular isolation on a rural road in suburban Turramurra, of all places. In the flat landscape of modest bungalows it could be seen for miles, a grey-brick mansion with iron-lace verandahs and a slate roof from which an attic extension projected like some bizarre folly beside the chimneypots. This upstairs garret was Uncle Angelo's domain, where he unceasingly played his favourite concerto, the Brahms in D major, almost every night until the neighbours had complained.

In fact, Damien learnt, they'd made a most unneighbourly move by sending a petition to the local council, saying Angelo's violin sounded like a bunch of copulating alley cats. As a result, Aunt Fanny had invited them all to morning tea, thanked them for their discretion in using the polite word 'copulating', and added that, by the way, it derived from the Latin *copulare*, which meant 'fastening together'. She then won them over by announcing that a local handyman was arriving that afternoon to attend to the windows of the attic, to *copulare*, or fasten them together – known as double-glazing – an act of kindness to those who did not like Brahms or violins.

As befitting a grand house, the living room was immense. It had a polished mahogany floor, classical cornices, stained-glass windows and was bejewelled with a huge chandelier. It was in this vast room at the age of five that Damien had first heard Angelo play his violin, when his aunt had danced like a spirited Pierrette down the sweeping staircase, taken his small hands in hers and waltzed him around the room. He smiled at the recollection; how could a father and mother possibly compare with that?

His parents, in their sensible double-brick home in unadventurous Artarmon, declared the house ugly, a monstrosity of a place, but to Damien it was like an enchanted castle. It had a large garden where fruit trees and vegetables grew, and for some reason that was never explained they kept chickens in the garage. Their car, a stately vintage 1927 Packard phaeton, was parked in a shed that would have been better suited to the chooks, while Abercrombie, their chauffeur – who also served as a gardener and on special occasions put on different clothes and doubled as the butler – lived in a primitive room attached to this shed. Appearances, particularly the size of the house, led most people to believe they were wealthy, but the reverse was true.

'Poor as church mice,' Damien's father regularly stated, resenting the fact that Angelo did not work and received financial assistance from their father, Damien's grandfather, who would drive when necessary to Turramurra with his cheque book.

The brothers had been two years old when their parents decided to leave Italy and emigrate to Australia. As twins they bore a passing resemblance to each other, but were totally unlike in every other way. Damien's father Luigi had been an industrious student, and from high school proceeded to university where he graduated in economics and became an accountant. Angelo, on the other hand, had spent much of his time at school daydreaming of being a renowned violinist who would one day play in New York and London at great concert halls, but being denied this and failing his school leaving certificate, decided he was unsuited to the kind of menial jobs that were available. It led somehow, no one quite knew how, to him becoming a gentleman of leisure. How they came to own a grand old house like Buckingham Avenue had puzzled Damien, until one day Angelo confided that after his very first meeting with Fanny, he had used his entire legacy from an Italian great-uncle to buy the sort of house that might impress her, handed her the keys and asked her to marry him without any delay.

'Mad,' Damien's father declared of this impulsive act every time he saw the house, and always predicted loudly to the rest of the family that his brother had absolutely no regard for money, and hence they would always be poor.

Which they were until the day Aunt Fanny, who unfailingly bought two lottery tickets a week (a habit considered sheer waste by Damien's father), won first prize in the new Opera House Lottery. And six months later, continuing to buy tickets each week, she won it again. He could clearly remember the cry of anguish in Artarmon, and the stunned expression on his father's face seeing this unique repeat triumph rate a headline and a story in the *Sydney Morning Herald*.

'The fucking woman is a fucking witch!' he'd shouted, and Damien remembered his mother rushing in to ask him to please not use that word in front of you-know-who. But by the age of eleven Damien of course knew all such words, because his father often used them when talking about his twin – or about Aunt Fanny whom he always insisted on calling 'the brother's bloody bride'.

It was after her second win that 'the bloody bride' became rather grand. She dressed the chauffeur in livery and occupied the back seat of the antique Packard where she waved to passers-by like minor royalty. On Damien's twelfth birthday she'd swept him off in the Packard to the cinema, the two of them resplendent in the car with the hood down, while she waved to the proletariat (some of whom were astonished enough to wave back), and they went to see Elizabeth Taylor in *Suddenly Last Summer*. When the usherette tried to stop them, declaring he was far too young to see this X-rated adult movie, Aunt Fanny told her not to be ridiculous, insisting Damien was much older than he looked.

'Just small,' she proclaimed with a voice that resonated around the half-filled matinee seats like a trumpet, 'even though this is his sixteenth birthday.'

He was thrust ahead of her into the cinema while his aunt fended off the usherette. He didn't understand anything about the story, which had lots of heavy breathing, searing looks and scenes that made the rest of the audience gasp, but he remembered afterwards confiding in Aunt Fanny that Elizabeth was the most beautiful girl in the world, and how he wished he could grow up quickly and marry her.

'Well, for goodness sake why not?' was the reply. 'She's married four happy chaps already, my duckling. You may as well join the throng and have a turn.'

Fanny loved the movies, everything from Westerns to foreign classic films. Sometimes they went to the local drive-in at French's Forest, where there always seemed to be lots of empty cars. Damien thought this strange, until one night when they were beside a panel van. There was no one visible, but it appeared to be moving up and down as if something vigorous was going on inside. When he asked why, Aunt Fanny told him it was probably people doing their exercise in the back of the van, and to keep his eyes on the screen in case he missed something. Damien, who was fourteen by then, got the giggles and could hardly concentrate on the film; his thoughts firmly focused on the activity that was making the van squeak and quake.

He smiled at the memory, and quickened his pace as he neared the house. His aunt and uncle were sitting in deck chairs on the upstairs verandah, and called cheerful greetings as he entered the ornamental gates. A gin bottle and an ice bucket were on the table, with an empty glass there waiting for him.

'Just in time, my boy.' Angelo welcomed him with an affectionate hug, something Damien's own father had never been able to manage. 'The sun is over the yardarm somewhere in the world, so we thought we'd have a G and T.'

He was a tall, patrician looking man in his sixties, with a leonine head of silver hair and a fine speaking voice, who at times had been taken for a veteran actor or a retired diplomat.

'Good thinking,' Damien said, and kissed his aunt. Ten years younger than Angelo, she was English, and had silky grey hair, soft blue eyes and a ready smile. Long ago she had gotten over her disappointment at not having children, and treated Damien like one of her own instead.

'How was yesterday's barbecue?' she asked, as Angelo poured him a drink and Damien sat between them. 'All the usual crowd?'

'More or less,' he replied carefully, and smiled at her instantly enquiring gaze.

'So . . .' she prompted, 'what does that mean, darling? Tell us who was there and what happened.'

'The regulars. Noelene, of course. Joshua, Toby and all the others. Plus a girl named Katerina.'

'Ah.' Aunt Fanny seized on this as Damian knew she would. 'And who, enlighten us, is Katerina?'

'That's her original name, but she's shortened it to Kate. She's Greek, and her father manages a café in Dee Why.'

'Nice?' Angelo asked. 'The daughter, I mean, not the café.'

'Very.'

'Pretty?'

'Extremely.'

'And . . . ?' It was Fanny this time who persisted. 'Are you seeing her again?'

'It wouldn't be much use.'

'Why not?'

'Because she's well and truly spoken for.'

'Bad luck, old lad. Well, drown your sorrows with this,' Angelo said, adding an extra slug of gin before handing Damien his drink.

Jacarandas were in full bloom, enlivening the streets and making a very early display of Christmas decorations look shabby. It was the second week in November and Kate walked from school to the bus stop near Manly High School with two of her closest friends. She and Melanie Barnes had been in the same class since primary school, and Cheryl Latimer had joined them in form two when her family had moved from Cooma.

They were all in a state of tension with only a week until they sat for the Leaving Certificate, but Cheryl was under the most strain. Her parents were putting too much pressure on her, forever talking about the importance of the exam, telling her that success with a top-of-the-State mark of 100 per cent would enhance the rest of her life, but she must realise that poor marks would very likely ruin it.

'Not asking for much,' Kate said with sympathy. She knew the pushy aspirational Latimer family. The father had been a stock and station agent in the alpine town, and apparently made a quick fortune in land as the Snowy Mountains Hydro scheme evolved. His wife owned two coffee shops and the father was now buying acres in western Sydney and converting them into housing estates. They'd brag about it for weeks if their daughter got honours, and berate her if it was anything less.

'They're so competitive,' Cheryl complained. 'It's always been like this. They go to football games and shout at my brothers if they don't play well. Or yell abuse at the referee if the team loses.'

'Tell them they're giving you the shits,' Melanie said. Mel had grown tall and blonde, and was renowned for speaking her mind to all and sundry.

'Mum would throw a wobbly. Probably insist I wash my mouth out with soap,' Cheryl answered, and they all laughed.

At the Dee Why shopping centre they left the bus and stopped for a milkshake, after which Mel was headed for a swim and Cheryl hurried obediently home. Kate went to the post office. There was a letter waiting for her in the box, her mother's familiar handwriting, and she walked down to the beach and sat in the shade of the pines to read it. There was a new address at the top, underlined for her attention, and a cheque was enclosed for her forthcoming birthday.

Darling Kate,

We've moved to a new address, a nicer and larger apartment because Michel has been promoted again. I will send a birthday card nearer the day, but I'm sure the cheque will be useful.

I suddenly felt a need to write, because your news has been sparse lately. I know this is a vital year for you at school, and I keep telling myself you are occupied in study, but I cannot help wondering what has happened to that young man in your life.

When you met him you weren't at all sure if you'd see him again, but the next letter made it clear you even went to a New Year's Eve party together. Then hardly a word, except a brief mention of how you were invited for lunch and the stepmother was horrible. An occasional mention since, but no hard news. Forgive me for being inquisitive, but you used to tell me everything. Have we reached the time when we stop confiding in each other? I feel I know so little about him – except that his name is Joshua.

Can you tell me more? Or am I intruding into your life, a prying thirty-four-year-old mum, asking about matters that are strictly private? How about taking a photo of him? Then I can see what he looks like.

Does he love you? Do you love him? Tell me something, my pet, even if you write back and tell me to shut up. At least if you say that I'll know that something serious is afoot. Impatiently, and with lots of love as always,

Sofia

Dearest impatient Mum,

First of all, you're thirty-five by my count, not thirty-four. Or have you reached a time when birthdays cease and counting stops? Do you intend to stay thirty-four for very long? It makes me laugh, because I'm still seventeen – almost eighteen and wishing I was already – and all because Joshua will be twenty on his next birthday which is very soon. So there, I've told you I'm seeing an older man!

I am sorry not to have written much in the past few months. Study for the Leaving Certificate is intense, so that's one excuse. Joshua is another because we do spend time together, but the other excuse is Papa. I'm writing this at the beach two streets away from our café, so he can't wonder what I'm doing and pry. It's becoming difficult, and I don't know what to do about him. Ever since Isabella took off with her jazz guitarist he's made no attempt to find anyone else. He really has no friends, male or female, despite all the years he's lived here, and at nights after we shut the café (it's always empty by eight o'clock, so there's no point staying open any longer) he goes upstairs with a bottle of retsina, or sometimes a bottle of ouzo, and just sits and drinks and watches TV. And next day complains about it. I suppose the real problem between Papa and me is simply that I love this country – even if there are times when I feel half Greek and the other half Aussie – but he's never come to terms with it. And he never will.

He's an unhappy man, Mama. There is nothing you or I can do about it, but I have to share the burden because there's no one else here who knows him like we do. It just helps me to say all this to you because I need someone to confide in.

Now, coming to the core of your inquiry about my life. I'm sure when you were seventeen some things were highly secret and classified. So it is with me. I certainly wouldn't dream of saying shut up, but you can assume that it's quite serious.

In fact, dear curious Mama, it's seriously serious. So much so that in my bedroom I've taken down all the pictures of my favourite film stars, and even *The Beatles* have been given the push. I've replaced them all with a single photo of Joshua. He (the photo) watches over me at night while I study, for I'm determined to do well.

I'll ask my friend Cheryl to take a snapshot of Joshua and me, and I'll send it to you before Christmas. In return, you send me photos of you and Michel in your new apartment, and give my congratulations to him on the recent promotion.

Love,

Kate

P.S. I haven't been taking part in 'demos' lately because of studying, but there's a big one when the exams are over. Don't worry, it's strictly peaceful. We hope a quarter of a million people can walk in passive protest against this war and really make our politicians take notice.

By ten o'clock on the morning of the demonstration the city was teeming with people. There were TV helicopters already in the sky getting pictures for the evening news and reporting that all streets were jam-packed with protesters. Traffic was gridlocked; pedestrians who had been arriving by trains, buses and ferries since early in the day were making their high-spirited way along every avenue that converged on Hyde Park. What looked like a cheerful army walked from the eastern suburbs occupying the full width of William Street; likewise Oxford Square was devoid of traffic, and a stream of people, young and old, estimated at over fifty thousand, were approaching from Randwick, Bondi Junction and the beaches. From the harbour to the town hall the streets were all filled with lively crowds.

Kate, Cheryl and Melanie, freed from the stress of exams, if not yet from the suspense of results, were among those in Martin Place.

Coming past the cenotaph they started to sing Pete Seeger's 'Where Have All the Flowers Gone', and people around them joined in until it spread across the crowd. It became a huge emotional refrain, the sound of it rising to the high office buildings on either side of the square. A kilometre away in Liverpool Street, another crowd was lustily singing Glenn Campbell's new hit 'Galveston'.

'God, I wouldn't have missed this for quids,' Mel shouted at the end of the song, and it was met by a chorus of agreement.

'Where are all you flowers from?' a voice asked them.

'Dee Why,' Cheryl replied, cupping her hands to amplify the reply.

'The dee-lightful Dee-Why-on-Sea,' Kate yelled, to be greeted by loud cheers almost drowned by boos. This was followed by a rapid succession of shouts, extolling their territories.

'Canterbury! Glebe! St Leonard's! Ryde! Parramatta! Newport!' came a variety of voices. 'Bullamakanka!' a male voice bellowed.

'Wow! I've always wanted to go there,' Mel called to him.

'Play your cards right, darling, and I'll take you home,' was the reply.

A vast good-humoured and peaceful gathering, filling the city with the sound of protest songs – that was how one journalist had already filed the opening of his story for the afternoon edition – when two merging groups became wedged at the junction of Macquarie Street, directly opposite the State Parliament. The row of heritage buildings were protected by a line of mounted police. People were pushing, trying to keep moving. Within moments the area had filled so completely that it was virtually impossible to proceed in any direction, and the police were clearly concerned. Their horses were on edge. The good-natured singing and verbal exchanges had stopped, and suddenly there was a change of mood in the crowd, a feeling of hostility that they were being prevented from reaching the speakers and the main event in Hyde Park. That was when the mounted police made a decision to clear a space and force people back.

Some tried to give way before their advance, but with such a crowd an orderly retreat was impossible. Bodies cannoned against each other, feet were trampled on, outbursts of crowd anger began to blame the mounted cops and their horses. A few of the wily protesters who had encountered this kind of trouble before had come equipped with marbles, and bowled these under the horses' hooves. The leading horses started to lose traction, slithering and thrown into disarray. One's front legs shot from beneath him, the rider toppling from his saddle and falling with a crash. A shout of triumph erupted from some among the crowd, as the entire line of horses started to back and rear in fright. More of them slid and fell, their riders unseated, the horses flailing and wild-eyed with panic.

Calls for calm and voices of concern for the animals on the ground were drowned in a tumult, as angry police reinforcements arrived on foot. They advanced in a solid and aggressive phalanx and started to use their batons indiscriminately on the crowd, lashing out at any of the protesters within reach. Shouts of alarm, screams and the discordant sound of a loud hailer barking commands blurred into a deafening cacophony, as Macquarie Street became a scene of turbulence and sickening violence.

Kate saw the raised truncheons moving in her direction through the crowd. She glimpsed Mel, then lost sight of her. The police, infuriated by what had happened to their mounted comrades, were using maximum vigour. She saw a woman, arms twisted behind her back, flung into one of the vans being used to hold people in custody. The vans were steadily backing into the crowd, forcing people to give way. In the crush Kate was isolated from her friends. She thought she heard Cheryl's voice calling, but there was no sign of her. A man pushed past, blood spurting from his forehead and flowing down his face. People were on the ground being trampled on. Everything was turning ferocious and wildly out of control.

That was when she heard a shout and looked around. There were no familiar faces. Neither of her former classmates were anywhere to be seen. Then she heard the shout again, a male voice calling her name. 'Kate! Katerina?'

Who was it? She didn't recognise the voice, but there was such a tumult of sound it was hard to even tell which direction it was coming from. Then she heard it again.

'Over here. *Katie!*'

'Yes!' she shouted back, looking around until she glimpsed red hair. A hand was waving. She couldn't see any freckles from this distance, but somehow knew the hair belonged to him. They fought their way through the stampeding mass towards each other. Damien grabbed her arm.

'For Christ's sake, let's get out of here,' he told her urgently, and started to shoulder his way out of the crowd, tightly clutching her so they were not separated in the turmoil. For someone of barely medium height and so slightly built, he was like a bulldozer, Kate thought, as he barged and bellowed curses while towing her protectively behind him.

'Out of the fucking way!' he yelled in the faces of those impeding them. They emerged from the crush and came to a breathless halt as they were stopped by the rushed arrival of an aggressive new group of police reinforcements.

'Thank God,' Damien said hurriedly to a sergeant who was on the brink of ordering his men to arrest them. 'My friend got stuck in that mob. She's trying to get a ferry home, and we honestly thought we'd never make it through.'

'Bullshit,' said the sergeant.

'Is there a new law against ferries?' Damien demanded.

'I live in Dee Why,' Kate intervened hurriedly, thinking he was on the brink of overdoing it and landing them in more trouble, 'with all the streets so crowded I can't get through to catch a bus. A ferry to Manly is the only way to get out of the city today.'

The sergeant eyed them both, studied Kate carefully as if trying to categorise her, then jerked a thumb towards the harbour behind him.

'Hop it,' he said. 'Next time think up a better story. Better still, next time be smarter and stay at home.'

At Circular Quay they bought beakers of coffee while waiting for a ferry. Damien said he would wait until the streets cleared so he could go home by train as he lived on the north shore. Both were relieved to have escaped unhurt and to have avoided arrest, but upset at what had happened.

'Those stupid bastards bringing marbles and targeting the horses.' Damien shook his head with an angry sigh. 'What the hell possessed them to do that?'

'Sheer madness,' Kate said. 'They completely wrecked what was meant to be a peaceful protest. It's been publicised as that all week, but it certainly isn't going to look like one on the evening news.'

'Not with those cameras zooming in on the horses falling. We'll have a million animal lovers changing sides tonight,' he said.

'And the government gets a free kick,' Kate added. 'Can't you hear those right-wing pollies in Canberra giving us heaps?'

'I can hear it loud and clear. I'll even cop it when I go home.'

'So will I,' she admitted, and the thought of the day's crusade ending in such combined parental disapproval all at once seemed blackly comic and made them both smile.

'So we're not going to change the world today, Katie.'

'Maybe next time,' she said. She liked the way he called her Katie; it sounded cosy, she thought, friendly.

They saw the ferry approaching around Bennelong Point, and she finished her coffee. He took their plastic cups and found a litter bin.

'How are things with you and the family?' she asked while they stood waiting for it to arrive.

'Could be worse,' Damien said. 'The old man has at last accepted the idea that I've given up on being a cattle king. Or an accountant, like him. That's a slight step forward.'

'It sounds like a mighty leap forward.'

'He still thinks I'm crazy, but I can cope with that. And if it gets too difficult, I can move in with the other family crazies, Uncle Angelo and Aunt Fanny.' But the way he said it betrayed an affection for these apparently odd relatives.

'You're obviously fond of them.'

'I really love them,' he said quietly, 'and it's mutual. They're the closest people in my life.'

She felt a moment of envy. What did she have in comparison? Her wayward mother, whom she loved at a distance. And her father? Well, of course she loved him, but to have such a bond and be so sure of it . . . Damien made it sound so wonderfully special. How did one's family relationships develop like that? But at least she had Joshua, she reasoned, and he was special in her life.

He was gazing at her, so she asked, 'Anything published yet?'

There was a slight pause. 'Well . . . nearly,' he replied.

'How do you get *nearly* published, Damien?'

'It's quite difficult actually,' he said with a grin. 'Put it this way. I had a couple of stories rejected – I was in despair, then another came back with a note saying it showed promise. So that's hopeful. It's a very promising word, promise. Encouraging. Calculated to keep you trying.'

'And you will keep trying,' she said smiling.

'Of course.'

They stood watching the ferry tie up and the gangways being slid into position as passengers from Manly disembarked.

'Thanks again for the help,' she said. 'I think you saved me from being arrested.'

'I'm glad I was there. I hope your two friends are okay.'

'Me too. We're all waiting for news of our exams.'

'Fingers crossed for that scholarship to get you to uni,' he said, as she followed others and boarded the ferry. She stood by the rail as he waited on the wharf.

'Regards to Joshua,' he called to her, then added, 'if it still is Joshua. I guess it is?'

'Still Joshua,' Kate called in reply, and took a seat towards the bow in the sunshine. Damien seemed to shrug at this reply, then waved and walked away before the ferry moved out. By the time they went past the unfinished shell of the opera house, she had lost sight of him.

Of course it was still Joshua. Why would he wonder about that? Josh had started a job with a touring theatre company, or he would have been there with her.

The ferry was out beyond Fort Denison, an island in the harbour known as Pinchgut in convict days because prisoners were starved there, before she realised she had forgotten to ask Damien if he was still in Noelene's queue.

The following week, just before Christmas, came another letter from her mother, together with a photo of her and Michel in their new apartment. Kate remembered him as a polite young purser. Now, twelve years later, he seemed comfortable and assured, his arm around Sofia. They looked, she thought, very happy.

My dear sweet girl,

Thank you for the snap. You and Joshua make a fine couple, and he's a handsome boy. It's wonderful to be eighteen and in love. But do be careful, and don't be too much in love. As an old lady of thirty-five – if you insist – that's all the sage advice I can give you. This time I'm speaking as your . . . Mama.

P.S I saw a protest against the Vietnam War on our TV that turned into a riot. I thought it must be in New York, but it startled me to find out this one was in Sydney. It's the only news we've seen about Australia all year and it was very violent and thoroughly disconcerting. I certainly hope you weren't there.

Chapter 9

They ran down the beach hand in hand and dived into the surf. An unexpected wave caught them, its strength a surprise as it dumped them back onto the sand. They picked themselves up, laughing with youthful exhilaration. It was mid-summer, and the first time they had seen each other since his grandfather's sudden death and the funeral. After that day Joshua had been away on a country tour as assistant stage manager with the theatre company, and Kate had been helping in the café during the busy January holiday period.

They held hands and braced themselves as another breaker rolled over them, then they started to swim for the calmer water further out. When they reached the next wave they dived under it, this time before it crested, and emerged with their arms wrapped tightly around each other. Kate could feel the rush of heat this generated. Joshua's eyes sparkled as his hands roamed and he began trying to peel off her new bikini pants.

'It's impossible,' she told him, but without much conviction.

He held her against him, while their legs moved gently to keep them buoyant in the water. It felt sexily titillating. The warmth of the sun and freshness of the sea invigorated them. When the next wave rolled past, they trod water and kissed.

'Your grandmother will see us,' Kate protested.

'Even she can't see under water,' Joshua replied.

'You're awful sometimes,' she said fondly, as a new breaker swamped them. She emerged with eyes streaming and a mouthful of salt water. She grabbed hold of him – purely for safety this time – because she had never dared venture this far out alone.

His grandmother was sitting on the beach, a distant figure beneath a striped umbrella, reading the newspaper while listening to a transistor radio. Or making a show of reading and listening, Kate thought. It was hard to tell. Rosetta Morris was of the old school; she kept her emotions under tight control. It had been only two months since her husband's death, and Joshua was staying with her at the beach house.

The funeral had been strange; Kate could think of no other word for it. Grandma Rose had not attended. Nor had any woman, except Kate herself. Strange indeed; just her and Joshua, and six men in dark suits whom she had never seen before, but assumed they were either relatives or business associates. There had been no minister or even a celebrant, no one presiding like at most funerals. No music or prayers offering expressions of comfort, just total silence and not a word spoken; the tiny group simply bowed their heads for a few bleak minutes while the coffin slid forward into the flames, then the men turned and abruptly left the chapel. And Kate, bemused and feeling she should not really have been there, wondered who on earth they were, and why any of them had bothered to attend.

'They weren't friends,' Joshua tried to explain when the group had gone and the pair of them were alone outside the chapel.

'Then who?'

'They were employees.'

'You mean in his stockbroking office?'

'Not exactly. Sort of employees, I suppose you could call them. He ran an illegal betting shop, and they worked for him.'

'Truly?' She was astounded. Standing there confused, a throng of people from another funeral fled past them. 'But I always thought he was a stockbroker.'

'He was, from Monday to Friday. On Saturdays he ran his betting shop.' Joshua grinned at her stunned expression. 'He made more on those illicit Saturday afternoons than he did all week being respectable.'

'I'd never have guessed,' Kate said, trying to visualise it. 'But why did they come?' she'd asked. 'They didn't seem to like him much.'

'They didn't like him at all. Grandma paid them to come.'

'What?'

'They all owed him money,' Joshua explained. 'Usually on Saturday nights after the races they played poker, and grandfather always won. Everyone knew he cheated, but nobody dared say so. At least not while he was alive.'

'Golly,' she said, unsure if he could be serious or not.

'It's true,' he assured her. 'Gran promised to repay their losses if they turned up, because he'd refused to let anyone else attend. She thought for appearances sake someone should be here.'

'That's bizarre,' Kate exclaimed.

'Well, he was an odd-bod in his way,' Joshua agreed. 'A strange old codger, and not everyone's idea of fun. Ferociously anti-religious, claimed it had caused most of the wars throughout history – well, he had a point there, didn't he? Anyway, he had a real aversion to it: rabbis, synagogues, Bar Mitzvahs, funerals. He and Grandma Rose had a pact – that whoever went first, the other wouldn't be at the ceremony. Our few relatives were told it was his wish they didn't come today. As for friends . . .' he shrugged and said, 'I don't think that was much of a problem. He didn't have any.'

'But you came. Despite his wishes. And brought me.'

'I sort of wanted to be here, if only to find out if the silent six turned up. And I needed a bit of moral support.'

'So that's why I'm here? As a bit of support for you?'

'I knew you wouldn't mind,' he said, his grin taking this for granted. 'Besides, if Grandpa's right and there is no hereafter, he'll never know I'd disobeyed his last request.'

'Bizarre,' she repeated, thinking of his stolid grandfather in his conservative collar, tight-fitting suit and lace-up boots. An illegal off-course bookmaker, a cheat at cards, and his wife paying to have people attend his funeral! Joshua's family, she decided, was as wacky as hers. Which was a relief in a way, for she'd always been in awe of them. Always felt her own family was inferior. After all, a couple of rooms over a Greek café could hardly compete with a handsome apartment in the eastern suburbs, and a holiday beach house with an ocean view.

Not that she had ever seen the apartment where they lived, but she knew it would be handsome. His stylish grandmother would settle for nothing less. Kate was unsure where it was, but knew she was unlikely to be invited there. She had never measured up to the appraisal of those perceptive eyes since the first day they met.

Rosetta Morris sat in the shade of the beach umbrella listening to news on the transistor and felt afraid. It was something that would surprise those people who found her rather daunting. The morning paper was discarded on the sand beside her; she was no longer even conscious of the two figures frolicking so far out beyond the surf – much too far out, she'd been thinking – until she heard the announcement on the radio with a sudden sense of dread.

She had lived through difficult times. As a girl in South Africa her fiancé had joined the volunteer Cape Corps to fight with the British forces, and been killed on the Somme a month before the armistice in 1918. The following year her father's lucrative export business had failed through a worldwide shortage of shipping. A fire that consumed his warehouse had seemed providential – far too providential, in the view of his insurers – and after a police inquiry he was charged with arson, pleaded guilty and was sent to prison. It meant bankruptcy and the loss of their comfortable family home, forcing Rosetta and her mother to move into cheap lodgings in Durban. Her mother, who had never worked, lived on the charity of relatives; Rosetta found a job in an accountant's office. It was there, aged twenty-two, she first met Aaron Morris, who was then a stationery salesman.

A week later he asked her to marry him. She refused, and had little difficulty in doing so. He was fourteen years older than her, and hardly a romantic figure: he was short and stout with receding hair, rather socially reticent, and quite unable to compete with the heroic memory of her dead fiancé.

When she refused his second proposal the next month, her mother begged her to reconsider, and not to be stupid. He was a steady sort of man, she pointed out; he clearly adored her, and what was the alternative? Would she prefer to accompany them to Northern Rhodesia when her father was released from prison, to a country town outside Lusaka where a relative had offered him work as a tally clerk in his wool store? Would she enjoy that? Life there would undoubtedly be awful, but they had no choice except to move far away from the finger-pointing and the scandal.

Our own lives are ruined, her mother told Rosetta, but she at least had an alternative. Aaron Morris should be accepted with gratitude.

When Rosetta explained she didn't love him, her mother said she was being immature. Love was not essential for a sensible and prudent marriage. She should realise it was a simple choice: Northern Rhodesia or Mr Morris.

They were married in a civil service, and a year later she gave birth to their only child, a daughter. When the girl was ten years old, troubled by the rise of Afrikaner nationalism, they emigrated to Australia. It was not the best time to arrive, in 1936. The worldwide Depression still gripped the country; thousands were unemployed, and resentment was high against refugees and newcomers.

But we coped with that, she thought, remembering the lack of welcome. We even prospered. Her husband found work as a clerk in a firm of stockbrokers, and during the war with staff away on military service, had been promoted to a dealer in share trades. After the war he'd opened his own investment business. He had built up a modest clientele and achieved some success, although it was his covert Saturday activities that brought them real prosperity. Those illegal and alarming Saturday afternoons . . . she still recalled her angry disbelief when she'd found out.

But I even coped with that, she recalled, if never comfortable about it. No, it was what came afterwards that had been so devastating. Her daughter, whose accomplishments had enriched their lacklustre marriage; her amazing child who had won scholarships, become dux of her final year and school captain; the popular girl pursued by all the most eligible males had fallen in love with Edward Maitland, a student in his final year of dentistry. He was a fine athlete, the champion swimmer of the surf club, a handsome young man sought after by all the girls, but it had been a disaster.

She could never forget how her daughter's disenchantment and her growing unhappiness had culminated in her decision to end the marriage. And that awful day, her phone call pleading for help, the wild drive and the agonising hours after the crash, hearing nothing until the bleak hospital message informed them of her death. Rosetta had been broken-hearted, her own life seeming a wasteland, the only salvage from it the grandchild who every year since then had spent the summers with them.

She had occasional misgivings about Joshua and his continuous pursuit of a hedonistic lifestyle. She sometimes feared there was too much of his father there; clearly they had the same magnetism for the opposite sex, and she knew there had been several before this one. They had all, like Joshua and Kate, used the beach house for their sexual couplings at every opportunity, and while she restrained herself from making it an issue, it had been an impropriety that upset her. She blamed the girls, although she knew in her heart who was really at fault.

But he was the one person left in her lonely life that she cared for. And now the radio had reported another national lottery to select a new batch of army recruits. A lottery! she thought indignantly – what a travesty! How could a civilised country tolerate a system where twenty-year-olds whose birth date matched a number drawn from a barrel would be forced into the army as conscripts? It had seemed like a bad joke when first passed through parliament three years ago. A sweepstake to choose who would serve in this unpopular war.

Her grandson would soon be twenty. Not yet old enough to vote, but if the forthcoming ballot picked his number, then old enough to be trained and sent to fight in Vietnam.

Chapter 10

The summer had gone too soon, and Easter was capriciously cold. Sharp winds scattered the sand, flattened the surf and emptied beaches. On prime sites in the rapidly changing township of Dee Why, wrecking balls swung over weekenders, acrid dust rose in a miasma that choked the air, and demolition gathered pace for apartment blocks and new motels. All year Kate had seen the growth of scaffolding and cranes from her bedroom window. And now, like the landscape outside, so much in her own life was changing.

It was hard to believe how everything had altered since summer and the thrilling news of her high marks in the Leaving Certificate. She had been in the top 5 per cent of the State, and *The Manly Daily* had claimed her achievement with a photograph on its front page. LOCAL GIRL'S SUCCESS was the caption, and she had cut the page out and sent it to her mother. A rapturous letter had resulted: Sofia was euphoric about her clever daughter and wondered if she might go to university.

Kate wrote back to explain they could not afford the fees, but there was talk, still to be confirmed, of being listed for a scholarship next year. She was going to wait, work the rest of the year in the café, and study in her spare time for the entry exam. But only days after the letter was posted, no doubt before its arrival, this anticipation had been eclipsed by other events. A childhood of upheavals should have accustomed her to change and disappointments, but these came with a numbing rapidity.

First was the arrival of Montague Packard, a man she had often heard about but never met. A voice on the telephone until now. Mr Monty Packard, cherubic and grossly overweight, a one-time popular comedian on television and now a wealthy man who owned their café and the string of shops adjoining it, had come to inform Andreas the café was to close.

'Close?' Her father seemed perplexed by the word. 'You mean for the repairs? For renovations?'

'For good,' Monty Packard replied. 'The place shuts next Saturday. On Sunday we knock the building down.'

'Knock it down . . .' her father echoed with an astonished look of disbelief, then summoning a nervous smile. 'Is a joke, yes?'

'No joke, Andreas. Sunday morning – I've got the demolition team lined up.'

'Lined up?' He seemed unable to grasp what was being said.

'For Christ sake, quit repeating everything I say.' Packard sounded tense, eager to settle this and leave. 'They're coming with bulldozers and trucks. It's going to be flattened. You've got a week to find somewhere else to live.'

'But you can't do this!'

'Of course I can bloody do it, mate. I own this place, as well as the shops next door with their freeholds. The flaming lot, they're all for the hammer on Sunday.'

'No! It's vandalism, against the law. We'll go to court.'

'Don't be stupid. It's completely legit, passed by the council.' He took a document from his pocket. 'Here's a copy for you.' When

Andreas shook his head, refusing to accept it, Packard placed it on one of the formica tables and secured it with a salt cellar. 'When you calm down, just read it and you'll see. It's all cut and dried, and nobody's going to court.'

'But why? Why do you do this?'

'Use your brains, Andreas. Think of what's been going on around here for years. I've let it ride till now, and it's gone gang-busters. Now it's bonanza time.'

Kate, seeing the look of bewilderment on her father's face, intervened. 'He's talking about land prices, Papa. Profits.'

'And why not, eh?' The huge man looked at her. 'A bloke has a right to make a buck, doesn't he?'

'Of course, Mr Packard,' she answered.

'This whole side of the street, it's going to be a motel. I always warned him one day it'd happen. He can't say I didn't tell him.'

'But you never told him you'd kick him out at a week's notice. One week to find somewhere else to live. Do you think that's fair?'

'I gotta grab the wreckers while I can get 'em.'

'And you couldn't care less how you treat a man who's worked for you for . . . how long is it? Thirteen years? Nearly fourteen?'

'He got his wages paid regular each week. And free board all this time. You're out of order, Miss Vassos.'

'And you're a nasty ungrateful prick, Mr Packard.'

He stared at her, his eyes suddenly hard and malevolent. 'You watch your language, you little dago bitch.'

The words were like a slap in the face. Nobody had called her that for so long, she'd almost forgotten what it felt like. A teacher at her primary school long ago had told her something she still remembered. You laugh at them, she said. It's no use getting upset, because that's what they want. Laugh, and you perplex them. So Kate laughed.

'You think that's funny?' Packard asked, staring at her.

'No, I think it's absolutely pathetic,' Kate retorted, 'if the best you can do is a cheap racist remark. I was six when I came to this country, Mr Packard. How long do I have to live here not to be a dago or a wog?'

There was a delay while he studied her more carefully. 'I apologise,' he said finally, 'but you want to watch your own mouth and guard your language, young woman.' He went to the door, turned for a last word directed at her, ignoring Andreas. 'The crew will be here early on Sunday, so make sure you find somewhere else by then.'

Kate watched him leave, crossing the road to a large European car. As he drove away she heard a harrowing sound, and realised it was her father. It was the first time she'd ever seen him show such distress. Tears were streaming down his face. Not knowing what to say, she put her arms around him and let him sob on her shoulder.

Kate knew it was futile, but they went the next day to lodge a protest at the Warringah Municipal Council. After a wait of almost an hour they were granted a brief interview with an assistant from the town clerk's office, who assured them the development application was in order. Mr Montague Packard was within his legal rights. Of course they could seek their own advice, but it would be a costly gesture and bound to fail. The assistant sympathised with their situation, he said, and would hate to see them lose money in pointless litigation. It was apparently meant to sound conciliatory, but felt more like a threat.

Later that week Kate found them temporary accommodation

in an old boarding house on Pittwater Road. Andreas complained the room was shabby, the bed uncomfortable and the continuous traffic kept him awake at night. He made no attempt to be sociable with the other residents, and railed endlessly about the injustice of his treatment. All the years he'd spent serving tedious mixed grills and other local food, and now, when at last there was a clientele with civilised tastes, now when he had regular customers who enjoyed a proper Greek menu, when they were finally making a profit and the future seemed bright, now it was all snatched away.

It was morally wrong and terribly unfair, no matter what the law said, he kept telling Kate. The second time in his life he'd worked hard to build up a good business for someone else, and each time he'd been cheated and betrayed. She did her best to be patient with his incessant complaints; she knew how deeply the abrupt dismissal and the loss of the café had humiliated and wounded him.

She thought it unwise, but he insisted on seeing the demolition take place, so on the Sunday they had joined a curious crowd to watch as bulldozers ripped apart the building that had been his livelihood and their home. Not content with that, Andreas remained while all the adjacent buildings were destroyed, and the entire area was reduced to rubble. Chain fencing was being erected around the site when they finally left. A sign attached to it declared the construction of a new first-class holiday motel would soon begin.

'We'll look in the newspapers for a job,' Kate tried to encourage him, 'you'll easily find work.'

Andrea's attitude expressed his scepticism about this. He made no attempt to help her search the Positions Vacant columns. For weeks he sat brooding in the garden of the boarding house, hunched in a thick coat as the weather grew colder, absorbed in his own misfortune and debating alternatives for his future, while oblivious to other events that had begun to disturb his daughter. She needed someone with whom she could share her anxiety, but in his present state her father was the last person she could confide in.

Kate attempted to be sanguine about it. She tried to dismiss the fear that she'd missed her period, and to think of it as merely being late. Overdue sounded better; it surely couldn't be anything else. She'd been so meticulous each day, ever since she had first seen a doctor in Manly and been given a prescription.

Could she have forgotten? She tried to think about it rationally. The weekend she and Joshua had borrowed a boat and gone sailing? Or could it have been one of those rushed mornings, trying to juggle work in the café with the hope of meeting him to make love beneath the beach house? Surely not, and besides, this was not quite as frequent of late. He was often doing a shift at the newspaper office, or busy with the theatre company; these were just two of several jobs he was willing to tackle now he'd broken away from home.

She was glad he'd made the break, but concerned he had no constant address or regular phone number any longer. He often stayed with friends and would call her whenever he had free time, but because of what had happened to the café and the weeks spent still trying to solve the problem of her father, she realised she was seeing a great deal less of him.

Two weeks overdue became three. At the end of the month optimism was giving way to anxiety. She tried to envisage how Joshua would take the news of fatherhood, while hoping it might yet prove to be a totally false alarm.

Another new conscription ballot had been held, but like previous lotteries the results were not made public. Don Chipp, the Minister for the Army, was on record as stating the names were a classified matter – it was a private contract between those selected by the draw and the military. A strange comment, declared newspaper editorials, while letters from their readers condemned the clandestine strategy, asking what reason the government had for continuing this furtive and undemocratic secrecy.

Rumours began to circulate, but Kate heard none of them. This was until walking past the cinema in Collaroy, when she heard someone call her name. It was Andy Scott, who had been at school with Joshua.

'I've been trying to reach you for a few days,' he greeted her, 'but the phone line was disconnected.'

'Not only the line,' she said, and told him about the demolition.

'What a bugger,' he said sympathetically. 'Sounds unfair. I'm really sorry to hear it, Kate.'

Andy was two metres tall with a mass of blond hair and an easy smile. She had always liked him more than many of Joshua's friends. He was in his second year of medicine, a front-row forward for the university; a gentle giant, people said, except on the rugby field.

'I wanted to find out if it was true,' he said to Kate, unaware of admiring feminine glances as a group of women passed them.

'If what was true?' she asked.

'About Josh . . . You must've heard by now.'

'Heard what, Andy?'

'The ballot . . . you mean you don't know? Oh, strewth.' His good-natured face was flushed with embarrassment. 'Am I breaking the bad news? They drew his birthday in that bloody lottery.'

Over an iced coffee in the milk bar next door to the cinema Andy told her that Joshua had undoubtedly been sent his call-up papers already, and that was probably why he hadn't been in touch. It was well known that recruiting was hotting up, the government was concerned about the urgent need for troops, and things were being rushed. Andy had heard of other cases like this. Joshua could even be in the army by now.

'Still, he probably didn't want you fretting, Kate.'

She knew it was meant to be a kindness, but was troubled by the lack of word from Joshua and found it difficult to understand.

She rang from a public phone box on her way back to the boarding house and his stepmother answered. Brenda sounded flustered, declaring it was a busy afternoon and inconvenient; there were patients waiting. Despite that she found time to say it was extremely worrying and nobody liked the ballot but, after all, the government needed troops, and Joshua had clearly burnt his bridges. Since he had rashly chosen not to go to university, he'd jettisoned the only legal means of army deferment. As a medical student he would obviously have been exempt until qualifying, and by then the war would be over. It proved how impetuous and foolish he'd been to have rejected his father's offer to support him.

And no, she had no idea where he might be, but that was hardly surprising, was it, because he was never at home nowadays – he'd been drifting between his pointless part-time jobs and staying with friends, but if he did happen to get in touch she would pass on the message that Katerina Vassos would like him to telephone.

'I'm not at the same address or phone number,' Kate started to say, but Brenda had already hung up.

The following day Kate went to the beach house, but it was locked and empty. It was no surprise Joshua's grandmother was not there at this time of year. It had been a vain hope, for she knew Mrs Morris's home was an eastern suburbs apartment, but had no idea of the address. Nor could she find out; the phone there was clearly a silent number, for her name was unlisted in the directory.

In the end Kate reluctantly decided the most likely person to be able to help would be Toby Robinson, or his sister Noelene. She had never been to their home, but knew it was in Killara, on the upper North Shore. She looked up the address, debated for a time about phoning, then decided against it. Armed with a street map she took a bus to North Sydney and from there boarded a train to Killara. Although in the directory it appeared relatively close to the station, it turned out to be a long walk with street after street of substantial houses, grass tennis courts and expensive cars. Everywhere she looked were signs of undoubted affluence. Too late she began to wonder whether it would have been wiser to phone.

The Robinson house was equally as large, but had the advantage of privacy from a long driveway abundant with a canopy of wattle and wisteria. It was a picture-book home, a kind Kate had rarely seen anywhere. She crossed an immaculate lawn and went past a swimming pool with an Olympic-style diving board. Around the house colourful flowers trailed in hanging baskets, and masses of azaleas and rhododendrons grew in tidy flowerbeds awaiting the spring.

At least someone is home, she thought with relief after her long walk; the front door was wide open and there was a distant sound of a radio. Upstairs there were gable windows, their curtains fluttering in the breeze. On a patio in front of the house a labrador lay dozing in the sun. He lifted his head and his tail thumped the tiles in welcome. Kate leaned down to pat him as Toby appeared.

'Hello, Toby.'

'Kate!' He seemed surprised, and not altogether pleased to see her.

'Just admiring your dog.'

'Everyone does.'

'What's his name?'

'Oscar,' he replied, adding, 'this is a bit unexpected.'

'Sorry to intrude, Toby. He's lovely. You are,' she told the dog, 'you're lovely, Oscar.' The labrador licked her hand, then with a final twitch of his tail went back to sleep.

'For Oscar Wilde?' she asked.

'No. Oscar Hammerstein.'

'The composer?'

'Actually, he's a lyricist. Writes the words. My mother's mad on his shows, *South Pacific*, *Oklahoma*, all that stuff.' He was clearly impatient with this trivia, Kate realised. She also had an odd feeling he was on edge; uneasy about her being there.

'I should've phoned,' she said.

'It is a bit out of the blue.' The reply, ungracious, clearly confirmed a phone call might've been best. 'I mean, we haven't seen much of you lately. I expect you've been busy, waitressing in the café?'

'Not any more.' She told him what had happened.

'A shame,' he remarked. 'We'll miss those famous mixed grills.'

Not really, Kate knew. He'd only been there once, with a batch of friends who did not include Joshua. They'd come from a local hotel after a few beers too many, a bit too loud, embarrassing her when they'd drunkenly patronised her as one of their local followers. Making her sound, she'd always thought, like some kind of groupie.

'So what brings you here?' Toby asked.

'I wondered if you'd seen Joshua.' She watched the expression on his face become guarded.

'Josh? Well, no. At least not lately. Haven't you?'

She felt sure he knew the answer and did not reply. Instead she tried to be casual and friendly. 'His birthday number came up in the ballot. You must've heard.'

'Well, yes, of course I did,' Toby replied. 'Lousy luck.'

'So what's happened since then?' she asked. 'Where is he?'

'Why come here and question me?' He shrugged expansively. 'I mean, if you don't know, what makes you think I would?'

It sounded disparaging, and was meant to be. It prompted a sharp rejoinder from her. 'You might know before anyone, including me. After all, you've been bosom buddies ever since prep school.'

'What the hell is that supposed to mean?' Toby demanded. He stared at her, his face growing red and angry. 'Maybe you don't realise it, Kate, but that either got lost in translation or you meant it to sound homophobic.'

'Oh, c'mon,' she chided him. 'That's not what I meant.' Seeking to diffuse his reaction, she tried another tack. 'Perhaps your sister can help. May I talk to Noelene?'

'No,' he answered.

'No?' She stared at him, and saw from his expression he was goading her. 'Just like that? I'm sorry, I don't understand this, Toby.'

'You can't speak to her because she's not here.'

'Couldn't you have told me that?' After a pause, when it seemed no answer was forthcoming, she tried again. 'Am I allowed to ask when she'll be back?'

'You can ask, but I haven't the remotest idea. So I'm not able to tell you.'

'Am I allowed to ask where she's gone?'

'You're giving me a real pain in the arse, Katerina.'

'That's no surprise, Toby. You've never liked me.'

'I never have,' he agreed readily.

'Well, now we have consensus on *that*, would it be too much to ask how do I get in touch with her?'

'She's left home. No forwarding address as yet.'

'Left home?'

'Moved out.'

'Thank you for explaining what it means,' Kate retorted, aware the exchange had become wildly and unnecessarily acrimonious. 'And of course you wouldn't know the address of Joshua's grandma?'

'You could try the phone book.'

'I have. She's ex-directory.'

'Sounds like you've been busy,' he gazed at her curiously. 'Been making quite a search for him. What's all the panic?'

'No panic.'

'Bullshit.'

'I just haven't heard from him,' she answered quietly, resolved not to let him start guessing games. Toby was the very last person she'd choose to confide in. 'Naturally, the news was a shock, and down at the beach they're saying he might be sent to Vietnam.'

'Down at the beach they know bugger-all.'

'I just need to find out for sure. I'm worried.'

'Yes, you would be. It'd spoil your games.' He gave a derisive smile. 'Imagine it. Joshua in jungle greens, killing the Vietcong.

And you, waving your protest banners, calling him and his mates fucking murderers. He'd love to hear that when he came home, wouldn't he? Really love to hear it.'

'And of course, you'd be the one to tell him.'

'It'd be a pleasure, Katerina.'

'You keep calling me that. My name is Kate.'

'Not to me. You're Katerina, the wog girl who opened her legs for my good friend. Because that's the only way you'd have kept him hanging around you for the past eighteen months. Most of us thought it was a bit of a joke at first. Joshua getting his end in. Now we find you plain pathetic and boring.'

I mustn't lose my temper, she thought. Try to laugh, like she'd been advised. But she couldn't laugh, not this time. In Toby Robinson's scornful face was all the dormant prejudice she'd sensed when he and the others had returned from holidays to learn she and Joshua were an item. Their mate Josh and the daughter of a chef in a Greek café. If she hadn't fully realised before, this was confirmation of how most of the circle had instantaneously disliked her.

'You're clearly in favour of the war,' she said, trying to remain calm, 'whereas I hate them dropping napalm bombs on villages. We'll never agree on Vietnam. But surely you'd worry if Joshua was there. At least we're both concerned about what happens to him.'

Toby started to laugh, as if she'd said something hilarious. It was loud enough to make the labrador lift his head inquiringly.

'You stupid bitch,' he said coldly, when he stopped laughing. 'I swore I wouldn't tell, but I can't resist it. Joshua isn't going to Vietnam. He's too fucking smart for that. He's on his way somewhere that's safe from the government and their lottery call-ups.'

Thank God, was her instinctive thought. But where did he mean? Where was safe?

'Where is he?' she asked, but Toby shook his head. 'Please?' She knew she was begging, but couldn't help it.

'Forget it,' he said. 'Nobody is to know, and that most certainly includes you. In fact it includes you more than anyone.'

'But why, Toby? I'm his girlfriend.'

'I can tell you one thing, but you may not like hearing it.'

'Tell me,' she pleaded.

'Okay.' He smiled. 'Joshua may have liked shagging you, but when it mattered, when he needed someone to trust, he chose my sister. Noelene helped him get away. I won't tell you where they are, but they'll stay there till the war's over. He's safe, she's with him, and the next time you see them I think you can count on them being happily married.'

As if there was nothing else to say, he went inside the house. The door shut firmly behind him. The labrador, seeing Kate was alone and whatever had been happening was now over, dropped back to sleep. She stood there helplessly for a few moments, but knew it was futile. She felt sure Toby was at one of the windows watching her walk away, but had no intention of looking back to find out.

In the street as she braced herself for the return to the station, she was hardly aware of anything, the luxurious homes, the way back to the railway, anything at all. She felt as if she was in a daze, quite unaware of not being alone until she heard a voice call her. She turned and saw a familiar face.

'Kate . . . ?'

'Oh, hello,' she said. And then her mind went totally blank. Who was he? One of their friends, she realised. The one who'd gone to be a jackeroo in Queensland and no longer liked the idea, who'd told her he was going to be a writer at the barbecue . . . The friendly

one who'd caught the fish; the one with freckles and red hair . . .
She tried to think of his name, but her mind was so shattered by
what Toby had said that everything seemed a void.

'Do you live around here?' she asked, still searching for what to
call him and feeling awkward because she had no idea.

'Not me,' he answered with a friendly smile. 'I live in what Toby
likes to call outer Siberia. Down in Artarmon. I'm spending a week
or two with my Uncle Angelo and Aunt Fanny. They're a few stations
up the line, in what they like to call rural Turramurra.'

'Your eccentric and favourite relations.' She could remember
that, but not his name. She tried visualising the rally, the police
horses, but his name was a total blank . . . what on earth was his
name?

'You have a good memory,' he said.

Not really, Kate thought. If only he knew.

'I dropped by to find out if Noelene is free,' he said. 'There's a
good movie at the State Theatre . . . in case she'd like to see it.'

'She's not at home,' Kate answered him carefully, 'or so Toby
just told me.'

'Oh well.' He gave a wry smile, as if becoming familiar with this
disappointment. 'Are you on the way to meet Joshua?'

'No. Well . . . I was . . . but I'm not sure where he is, either.'

'Bit of a frustrating day for both of us,' he said, seeming to
accept this confused reply.

'It is,' Kate agreed, and the more she tried to recall his name the
further away it seemed. She wished he would go before she made a
fool of herself. Or else she'd just have to walk off with nothing more
than a wave or a nod, but that would be abrupt and unkind.

She didn't want to be unkind to anyone, except perhaps Toby
and Noelene – and even maybe Joshua – but certainly not to this

boy. He was called Raphael . . . but that was his surname. She could hardly call him that. What, for God's sake, was his Christian name?

She realised he'd been talking and she'd missed it. 'Sorry, what did you say?'

'Just that . . . I don't suppose you want to come to the flicks, Kate? A new film with Steve McQueen. It's supposed to be a great movie.'

'I can't. I'd really like to, but I can't. Not today.'

'Oh well,' he repeated with a smile. 'Give my best to Joshua. I suppose you and he are still . . . still getting along?' When she couldn't find the way to answer that, but nodded instead, he seemed to nod in acceptance. 'Must have been a shock for him when he cracked the army ballot. For you, too.'

'Yes,' she replied, but her mind still struggled. If only she could think what to call him. How could she lose her memory like this?

'So long, Kate,' he said.

'Goodbye.' She flicked a casual wave and started to leave. His name, she pleaded. His name was . . .

'Damien!' she turned and called to him.

'Yes?' He swung around, as if hopeful she had changed her mind about the film.

'I just remembered something,' she improvised hastily. 'Have you written any more short stories?'

'About ten,' he replied.

'Sold many?'

There was a slight pause.

'None, so far.'

'Well . . . I'm sure you will.'

'To be honest, Kate, I'm beginning to doubt it.'

'You will. Don't give up.' She saw his uncertainty. 'I mean it. Please don't give up.'

'The old man says I ought to be sensible and take a job in a bank.'

'And if you do that, he wins, doesn't he?'

'I suppose so.'

'He'll be pleased he got his own way, and you'll be miserable. It's your life, Damien. For Christ's sake, don't let him live it for you. Don't let anyone do that,' she said vehemently.

He stood staring at her with conflicting sensations of surprise and gratitude on his face.

'You're right, of course.'

'He's really trying to make you into an accountant, like him.'

'You're right again.' He smiled warmly. 'I mean, you definitely are.'

'You'd hate the bank.'

'I would.'

'So tell him.'

'I will.'

'Promise me.'

'I promise.'

'And don't ever give up.'

'I'll try not to. And Katie . . .'

Of course I should've remembered, she thought. He's the one who calls me Katie.

'What, Damien?'

'. . . thanks for the vote of confidence.'

'I just have this feeling you're going to make it. Truly.'

'I'll remember that.'

'Take care, Damien.'

'You too,' he said.

She began the long walk back to the station, where she caught a train to Chatswood then a bus to the northern beaches. It felt like an endless journey. She hoped she had helped Damien. It would be nice to think so. If only she could help herself as easily, but she had no idea of how to do that.

Chapter 11

She woke in the middle of the night and could hear the surf pounding on the beach, and the swish of tyres from traffic passing in the rain along Pittwater Road. She lay awake for a long time, her thoughts in a jumbled disarray as she again relived the shock of Joshua's betrayal. So many questions beset her since that dreadful day, questions Toby had taken pleasure in refusing to answer. Where could he be? Where was *safe*? And why hadn't he told her? When she came to this particular query she knew that sleep was once again impossible. She reached for her dressing-gown, sat on a stool by the window and watched the steadily falling rain lit by the gleam of car headlights. She refused to cry.

When the traffic began to cease she could hear the man in the next room snoring, the sound of it through the thin fibro wall disturbing, for it reminded her of her father. Perhaps she could cry for him, but not for Joshua. Andreas had looked so helpless at the airport, as if aware that this could be the last time they'd see each other. Nervous, too, because at the age of forty he had never flown before, and now was committed to long hours on a Boeing 707, via Darwin, Hong Kong, New Delhi and finally Nicosia, taking him back to a corner of the world he should never have left in the first place.

It had happened suddenly. Of all things, a letter from her mother – in response to the concerns Kate had expressed about him the previous year, as well as the news of the café being sold – had brought with it the surprise of a plane ticket from her.

It's a ticket direct to Cyprus, she had written,

so he can't stop off in Athens even if he wants to thank me, but you needn't tell him that. Ever since you wrote last year I felt troubled that he does not fit in there, and now the business has been sold and he has no plans, it seemed a possible solution. Michel was able to get a special deal on a one-way flight, but don't tell him that either. If your father is upset or too proud to accept this chance to leave, then send me back the ticket and we can return it without cost to us. But it does feel to me he would be much happier back in Cyprus – at least he has friends there and likes the climate, so this is my small attempt to help him after the grief I caused him. But don't tell him any of this, please. I hope you're well, my darling, and working for your place at university. I trust the beautiful young man is in devoted attendance, but not taking up all your time.

Much love,
Sofia

From the panoramic viewing windows of the departure lounge Kate had seen the Boeing in front of the terminal, and watched Andreas as he climbed the flight of steps to board. While proposals for enlarging Kingsford Smith into an international gateway were in the planning stage, the airport was still small and friendly; it was possible to mingle with passengers in the departure lounge, kiss them goodbye at the gate, then see them walk to the plane and, once inside, those with seats that had a view of the terminal could wave farewell as the engines revved.

Her father, after some argument and prevarication, had agreed to give up and return to Cyprus. The decision made, it seemed to Kate he was glad to be going, to leave the depressing accommodation in the boarding house where he felt out of place, and the lack of any real future. Nearly sixteen years in a country he had not liked and that never accepted him had broken his spirit.

He would go back – to what, she didn't know; her memories of Cyprus were those of a young child, and fast fading, but she hoped it would be better for him than here. She was uncomfortably aware that he would not have gone had she confessed her pregnancy, so she'd said nothing. What could he possibly achieve by remaining, other than to reproach her?

Kate had already resolved this would be her child. She would not yet inform Sofia, whose remark about the beautiful young man went unanswered, nor attempt to seek out Joshua's grandmother. Nor would she ask anyone for help. Her one interview with a local doctor had made up her mind on this. His attitude had been abrupt; it seemed to convey she was to blame for carelessness, and had been unwise in her choice of a partner since he'd apparently abandoned her. It had felt like an indication of what lay ahead. When the doctor obliquely reminded her abortion was a crime, and suggested she should have the child at a private clinic like a Sister of Mercy hospital where he could arrange for its immediate adoption to a good family, she tersely told him it was her baby and she would make her own arrangements.

What these arrangements would be she still had no idea. But she did know there would be no abortion, and decided there would certainly be no adoption to a family of anyone else's choice, however good and well connected they might be.

She had stood watching and waving as the plane engines surged,

149

and her father peered from the window and waved a last agitated goodbye. That was when she had wanted to cry, but instead a phrase ran repeatedly through her mind. 'If you have tears . . . prepare to shed them now.' Words from Shakespeare's *Julius Caesar*, in which she had been Calpurnia in the school play. *If you have tears . . .* but she knew she had none. None for her defeated father, none for her deceitful lover. And certainly none for herself.

It was a pivotal moment and a decision had been made. She was now entirely alone, and she had to get on with the rest of her life.

It was important to disconnect from the locality where she'd grown up and from all the people who knew her. Much as it hurt to give up Mel and her other close friends from school, it had to be done. At the end of the week Kate left her room in Collaroy, and moved to a cheap boarding house on Broadway almost opposite the Central railway. The following day she found a job in Park Street near Museum Station as a waitress in a coffee shop. She was paid $25 a week, and could earn a little extra with overtime. Almost half of this went for rent. By eating only breakfast and dinner each day, and walking to work to save on fares, she could afford a cinema seat once a fortnight in the cheap front stalls. Every month she made sure she had two dollars saved for a visit to Dr Marion Scott, a general practitioner in Glebe who charged her only the newly instigated common fee. Marion Scott was a large capable woman in her forties, who never once mentioned the word adoption.

This routine came to an abrupt end when she was over seven months pregnant, for the coffee-shop proprietor said that because of her advanced condition he could no longer employ her. A week's notice was the best he could do. It was a pity; she was a good worker, but his customers were starting to make comments. Unfair, perhaps, but it was disconcerting to hear them speculate on whether the baby or the coffee would arrive first. Also, his insurance did not cover unexpected events like a possible miscarriage or sudden birth during the lunch-time rush hour.

A mean old bugger, declared Mandy Pollard, one of the girls Kate worked with, and advised her to try applying for a maternity benefit from the government. Kate took a morning off work without pay to do this, but was told there was no fund available for single mothers. However, if she wished to fill in the father's name they would attempt to obtain a disbursement from him. She declined to give a name, and when pressed on this gave the only possible answer.

'I've no idea where he is,' she admitted, and the raised eyebrows of the middle-aged interviewer indicated disbelief. Or was it contempt? In his world it was no doubt regarded as an impetuous one-night stand, not eighteen months of what she had believed was love, but she knew it was pointless trying to explain this.

'Without the father's name, we can do nothing,' she was told. She would receive benefit payments just before and after the birth of the child, but no other assistance was available. That was when Kate realised she was in deep trouble. Coping with her final week at the coffee shop she knew there'd be no hope of any other job. She was lucky she'd been able to work this long. She was large, the size of a house, she told herself when seeing her reflection. Truly, as her friends at school would have said, 'Up the duff and in the pudding club'. She was feeling tired most of the day, and her feet hurt constantly. A month ago she had to give up walking to work and saving fares. Her rent was only paid for two more weeks, and by using what little remained in her bank account she calculated she could manage until the end of the month.

And after that? Have it adopted, she was told bluntly by Mandy, who had run out of other suggestions. When you've got no other choice, that's a way out. People who want to adopt will make sure you're okay for food and rent till the baby's born, and even pay you to sign over the papers. Get the right parents and you end up with a nice little nest egg. Later on you can afford to have a kid to keep for yourself.

It was her second-last day. It had been a hectic rush at lunch hour, and her feet were painful. Her legs felt like lead weights. Thankfully there were only a few people left. Just a couple holding hands at a table in the annexe, and a young man in a three-piece suit sitting alone and intently studying a document.

Kate knew him as a regular, 'the long black from the Magistrate's Court', her forthright friend Mandy had named him, which was not a racially prejudiced description of the man, but was prompted by his choice of coffee and place of work. In fact he was comparatively short, white skinned, with light brown hair, and his order never varied.

'A long black,' she said, bringing it to him, as he glanced up from the document and nodded.

'Thank you.'

She watched him take the spoon and stir the cup without any sugar, as he looked up to witness her observing this. 'A peculiar habit,' he said with an amiable smile, 'because I've never used sugar in my life. I often wonder why I do that.'

'To see there are no coffee grains lurking at the bottom of the cup,' Kate suggested. 'Besides, we all have our funny habits.'

'Do you have any?' he asked her.

'These days I'm inclined to check my silhouette in shop windows. Watching my tummy go by, followed by the rest of me.'

He laughed. Kate gave him his docket and was about to return to the kitchen when he asked if she'd like to sit down.

'I'd get the sack,' she said.

'I thought that had already happened.'

'It has,' she agreed. 'Although it's not strictly the sack. More a termination of employment for being in the family way.'

'That's technically unfair, and might even be unlawful,' he told her, pulling out a chair as she hesitated uncertainly. 'Please . . . do me a favour.' She sat down with relief. 'Feel better?'

'Much better off my feet.'

'I gather you're leaving tomorrow?'

'That's true,' she confirmed.

'It could be construed as discrimination,' he said, while giving his unsugared coffee another brisk stir.

'You've been talking to someone,' she replied.

'One of your workmates.'

'Mandy,' she guessed. 'The one with blonde hair and glasses?'

'She said you have a problem.'

'Why did she tell you?'

'Because I'm a lawyer.'

'Oh,' Kate said, careful not to say that she had supposed he was probably an usher or a clerk at the Magistrate's Court. Not what he'd like to hear, she thought. 'A solicitor?'

'At present, appearing mostly in the lower courts, but I'm hoping some day to become a barrister.' He took a sip of his long black.

'Coffee okay?' Kate asked.

'Perfect. Mandy said your name's Kate Vassos. Unmarried.'

'Yes.'

'No parents?'

'I've got them, but they're separated and both live overseas.'

'No supporting family here?'

'None.'

'Where's the baby's father?'

'I don't know,' Kate replied, becoming disconcerted by the rapid series of questions.

'Is there any way of finding him?'

'I hardly think I'd want to.'

'I don't mean to upset you,' he said quietly, 'and if I'm intruding you only have to say so. Can you tell me what happened to the father?' As she paused and frowned at this request he continued, 'If you'd rather not, then tell me to shut up and mind my own business.'

'We had a love affair,' Kate said, after a few moments of trying to decide where this was heading. 'My first and only love affair. His number came up for Vietnam, and he ran away to avoid being conscripted. I don't know where he went – and I don't blame him for running away because I'm completely against the war, but he ran away with another girl.'

'Did he know you were pregnant?'

'No.' After a moment she added, 'I hadn't told him. I was unsure at the time.'

'Do you think it would've made a difference?'

'That's a rather unfair question . . . I don't even know your name.'

'Hugh Forrester.'

'It's an unfair question, Mr Forrester. But I suppose in view of everything . . . I mean the way he went, the lack of honesty or disclosure, if you prefer that kind of word . . . I have to say I don't think it would've made any difference at all.' She looked directly at him and said, quietly, 'I was yesterday's girlfriend.'

'Would you be prepared to talk about this in front of other people?'

'I think I'd absolutely hate it. What would be the purpose?'

'The firm I'm indentured to works for a group. They're very concerned with what's going on at a lot of hospitals. Young girls being talked into adoptions, and later coming to regret it.'

'I've encountered a bit of that kind of thing already.'

'So Mandy told me. She also told me you're short of money.'

'Mandy knows too much about me.'

'It was done with good intentions.'

'I know,' Kate said quietly, 'she's been a good friend.'

'This group might well be prepared to fund you, to recompense you for the loss of your job, and pay all medical and hospital expenses so you can have the baby and keep it.'

'You mean, if I tell them what they want to hear?'

'If you tell them the truth. That's what they want to hear.'

Kate put her arms on the table and propped her chin in her hands as she studied him carefully. 'Mr Forrester, it sounds too good to be true. This is where you tell me I'll be on the front page of a newspaper.'

'I can promise you won't be. Your name will remain private. The father's name will not be recorded, unless you choose to give it to us.'

'I'll never do that. He may have done the dirty on me, but even a shit has a right to privacy.'

Hugh Forrester looked at her and nodded approvingly. 'So when they sack you tomorrow, Miss Vassos, will you let me take you to lunch and introduce you to this group of people?'

There was a quiet sincerity that belied his lawyer's manner and felt surprisingly kind. So she nodded. 'I'd be grateful, Mr Forrester.'

Kate had just turned nineteen when her daughter was born in St Luke's Hospital. She broke the news to her parents by arranging to send each of them a photograph of the newborn infant with a handwritten note. *This sweet wrinkle-faced little person is Juliet Vassos, your granddaughter, born January 20th, 1970.*

Her mother arrived in Australia two weeks later.

PART 3

1970–1991

Chapter 12

It was a warm, peaceful morning. Kate was resting in the garden of a nursing home where Hugh Forrester's charitable group had arranged for her to stay, the baby in a bassinet beside her sleeping peacefully, when a nurse came out of the main building looking agitated. She had a visitor, she told Kate; it was not the permitted visiting hours – this part of the day was strictly for the mothers to breastfeed and then rest – but this visitor who refused to give her name was being insistent.

'I'm not a visitor,' came a familiar voice behind her that made Kate sit up in shock, 'I'm her mother. And I didn't give my name because I wanted to surprise her.'

'Well, you've certainly done that, Mama,' was all Kate could say, dumbfounded at this sudden appearance. It felt unreal, like a dream or a nightmare; she was not sure which as yet, but it looked as if her mother – who had so abruptly walked out of her life all those years ago – was about to re-enter it. It was hard to believe it was actually Sofia, well dressed and looking glamorous, swooping to hug her and then picking up Juliet from her bassinette to admire her, waking her and causing the nurse to shake her head in admonishment when the baby began to cry.

'That's why we have strict visiting hours,' she said witheringly.

'Babies don't need too much sleep. It makes them fat,' Sofia retorted, a statement so patently absurd and exactly like the mother she remembered that Kate had to laugh. The nurse shook her head in mute disbelief. They both watched as Sofia jiggled the tiny bundle and made clucking noises. The crying stopped.

'There. Look at the darling girl, she's smiling at me.'

'It's wind,' was the nurse's caustic reply.

'You think I don't know the difference between a baby wanting to fart and a big happy smile?' Sofia demanded. 'She knows a friendly face when she sees one, don't you my angel?'

Kate, thinking it was time to intervene, explained that her mother had apparently just arrived from overseas. Utterly unexpected. It had been a very long time since they'd seen each other. The nurse, after due consideration, grudgingly agreed that in view of this she could remain, despite the rules, but only for a short stay. She could then return if she wished at four in the afternoon, as these were the proper visiting hours. 'And please, try not to excite either mother or child,' she warned, before leaving them alone.

'Like a rottweiler, that one,' Sofia said.

'Settle down, Mum. Give me the baby, find a chair and then tell me how you knew I was here.'

'From the lawyer,' Sofia replied, as she shifted a garden chair alongside Kate and made lip-smacking kissing sounds to Juliet.

'You mean Hugh Forrester?' When Sofia nodded, Kate asked her how that had happened.

'You asked him to post the photo and your little note. He sent it with his compliments slip. So I rang him from Athens. I woke him up in the middle of the night, but I couldn't help that. After all, it was only early evening in Greece.'

'We do have different time zones,' Kate reminded her, gently placing the baby back in the bassinet, and gesturing to her mother to calm down and stop making funny faces. 'Let her go back to sleep.'

'She's beautiful, Katerina.'

'Of course. She's your granddaughter.'

'Yes.' Sofia frowned for a moment, reflecting on this. 'When she starts to speak, darling, I don't think I want to be called Granny.'

'We've got time on our side to deal with that, Mama. Now, c'mon, tell me everything. For a start, where's Michel?'

'In Athens.'

'You haven't broken up?'

'Of course not. Still the lovebirds,' she said with a smile. 'And he's a big cheese now in the shipping company. But we talk about you first. I want to know everything. Why didn't you write to say you were pregnant? And what about this lawyer, who is so polite to me in the middle of the night – so helpful and concerned about you. Who is he? He can't be the father, even if he acts like one. I'd say the father must be Joshua, so what's happened to him?'

'Not now, Mama,' Kate said quickly. 'When did you arrive?'

'Today. This morning. What a long flight!' She shook her head at the immensity of it. 'One hour, two hours, that's okay, I don't mind two hours. But nearly two days, listening to those engines, eating that food, oh-mi-god, it's like the moon, only further!'

'Where are you staying?'

'A hotel Michel arranged. I go there, drop my luggage, take a quick shower, after that a taxi here to see you. Then the Gauleiter nurse nearly won't let me in. Now come on, darling, where's the handsome Joshua? When do I meet him?'

'It's a long story,' Kate said, 'and it'll keep until another time.'

She looked at Sofia, still young and good looking; her *thirty-six*-year old mother who'd typically arrived without warning after so long. 'Are you thirty-six or thirty-seven?' she asked impulsively.

'What sort of a funny peculiar question is that? I've decided to stop counting,' Sofia replied. 'I'm as young as I feel, and as young as I look. How do I look?'

'You look wonderful.' Kate felt sudden tears forming. She tried to wipe them away.

'Katerina, you're crying.'

'No, I'm not.' She shook her head, smiled and gave up trying to stop the tears rolling down her cheeks. 'It's just such a truly lovely surprise, Mama. It really is. I've spent all these years thinking I'd never see you again.'

The nursing home was in Greenwich, looking across the river towards Cockatoo Island. A full moon hung above the summer night, and Kate could see distant lights from the waterfronts on Birchgrove's Louisa Road. It was like a sanctuary, this place that Hugh had found, after insisting she could not go back to her room in Broadway, certainly not with a newborn baby. Some time spent here would give him an opportunity to find her accommodation that was suitable and affordable. She felt deeply indebted to him, but he insisted it was his group of worthy citizens paying for this convalescence. At least a fortnight of recovery was needed, he said; she might not think so, but her doctor felt she was badly run-down. Too many months of working long hours in the coffee shop, on her feet all day when she should've been resting, and in addition the many sleepless nights fretting about the future.

She had not known until she came here the relief and pleasure of being able to sleep whatever time of the day she wished, to walk and read if the mood took her, requiring only to feed, nurse and grow fond of her daughter. Juliet gave no trouble; the staff, including the protective duty nurse who had tried to bar Sofia, were friendly, and almost two languorous weeks had passed contentedly.

It gave Kate leisure to realise she had never known this kind of peaceful relaxation. Her teenage years had been fully occupied both with school and helping her father in the café. Then she had met Joshua; there were the snatched hours with him, at the beach house or anywhere they could find a place to make love, trying to balance her romantic life with the stress of studying for exams, and the unromantic daily chores of washing up or peeling spuds. It had been wonderfully exhilarating with Joshua, but there were also dark days, concerns and tensions. She remembered his grandmother's attitude, her father's barbed comments, her own growing disquiet that she didn't really belong . . . and how true in the end that had proved to be.

She tried to stop thinking about him, to obliterate him from her mind. It was proving far more difficult than she'd imagined, though. Even today, having to tell Sofia what had happened when her mother returned in normal visiting hours had been almost unbearable, bringing the betrayal and torment so sharply back again.

'A bastard!' Sofia had exclaimed after hearing the whole story, except for the humiliating encounter with Toby Robinson – Kate had no intention of ever sharing that with anyone. 'Such a beautiful young man, but a bastard. The beautiful ones often are. And you don't even know where he's gone?'

'I don't want to know, Mama.'

'One day you'll have to know.'

'Why?'

'Because Juliet will ask. When she's older she'll want to know who is her papa. You must face that one day.'

'I'll face it one day, but certainly not today, Mama, if you don't mind,' Kate replied so firmly that to her relief her mother nodded and changed the subject. That day was part of a distant landscape, and not something she wished to even think about at present. Her thoughts instead strayed to the two people who had been her friends and main support recently. Mandy had come to visit regularly, both in hospital after the birth and here in the nursing home, bringing magazines to read and recounting items of gossip to make Kate laugh. She said the regulars at the coffee shop all agreed the place had gone downhill since her departure. They missed her bright smile and the daily ritual of taking bets on how long to go before she dropped the baby. Mandy said 'the long black' still came from the court each day for his coffee, still regularly stirring it even though it contained no sugar. It was her considered opinion that Hugh Forrester was keen on her.

Kate derided the notion.

Mandy insisted. Talks about you a lot. Sits there looking forlorn.

Get off, Kate said.

I tell you, kitten, he fancies you like mad.

Kate scoffed, although she suspected there was a grain of truth in it. He had been a regular visitor, but she didn't want to imagine the future with anyone except Juliet. And, for a brief time, after her sudden and unexpected appearance, with her mother.

In the morning she would have to phone both Hugh and Mandy, to tell them she would be moving from here. Sofia had speedily taken over, saying she was staying in Australia for two months and wanted them to spend it together. Kate had not resisted. Her mother's arrival had both stunned her and created a huge emotional upheaval.

'If you have tears . . .' she remembered. She certainly had tears that afternoon in the garden. She had gladly agreed to spend the time with Sofia, but she could hardly believe the announcement they would be living at the up-market and prestigious Pacific Star Hotel near Circular Quay and The Rocks. Could they possibly afford it? she asked.

Apparently so. Michel, who Sofia repeatedly said was now a big cheese in the shipping firm, had organised it.

Sofia had a hire car waiting. Not a taxi, but a luxurious looking limousine. Kate said a fond goodbye to all the staff, gave a particular hug to the duty nurse while Sofia managed a sardonic lift of her left eyebrow at her adversary, and escorted her daughter and tiny Juliet to the limo.

'It's unreal,' Kate said when they sat back in the car, after the uniformed chauffeur had closed the car doors for them. 'Are we showing off,' she asked quietly, 'or can we actually afford all this?'

'We're not paying for it,' Sofia told her.

'Then who is?'

'The shipping firm. I told you, Michel is now a big cheese.'

'How big?'

'Big enough. He's assistant manager of the department that runs luxury tours to Asia and Australia. His firm have just bought the Pacific Star Hotel in Sydney, so Michel persuaded them he should send someone trustworthy to inspect it, with a view to seeing if there were any changes that needed to be made.'

Kate turned and looked at her mother incredulously. 'You mean . . . my God, you do. You're the inspector!' she said, and began to laugh.

'Why not?' Sofia replied. She gestured a warning in the direction of the driver, then leaned towards Kate and whispered in her ear. 'The chairman sends his wife to Bermuda each year, to "check" on the company hotel, and his mistress goes regularly to Hong Kong. The firm have lots of hotels overseas. The management all get free family holidays doing so-called inspections, and they're written off as a tax expense. It's called executive enterprise.'

'Or corruption,' Kate whispered.

'Or corruption indeed,' Sofia murmured. 'In the past Michel had to stand by and watch them all put their fat hands in the cookie jar. Now that he's promoted he can join in. The day we got your news he decided it was imperative an urgent inspection be made. So don't knock it.'

'I wouldn't dream of knocking it! Not if it means your tour of inspection can last two months.'

'It has to last two months.' Sofia tried unsuccessfully to stifle a giggle. 'Because that's when the assistant tour manager arrives here to receive my report in person.'

'Do you mean . . . Michel?'

'Who else?'

'He's coming for a visit?'

'In two months' time.'

Neither of them could control their mirth. Sofia's body began to shake as she laughed, and the movement woke Juliet. She looked up at the two faces, and raised a small pudgy arm as if calling for attention or perhaps silence. The idea of this set them both laughing again.

The chauffeur glanced at them in his mirror. Wonder what's so funny? he thought. Hope the baby hasn't crapped on the lambswool seat cover. Nice looking pair of wimmen. Look like sisters. One a bit older than the other, but either of 'em could put their slippers under my bed any time they liked, he decided.

The Pacific Star Hotel in the old part of Sydney known as The Rocks had a long history of failure. Built in the last colonial days before Australia became a nation in 1901, it had survived precariously as a 'grog shop' for sailors and a place of assignation for anyone. Because of this, extra floors were built to accommodate a rash of squalid rooms that were available by the hour or night.

It flourished in the 1914–18 war, a last embrace for soldiers on final leave before their troopships sailed, but later fell on hard times due to the influenza pandemic and the Depression. With more luck than good management it survived the fate of other whorehouses in the district, and passed from one owner to another, until heritage became a popular word. Then the sandstone streets were preserved and cherished, the historic premises were taken over, rebuilt, refurbished, and it acquired the status of an elegant and exclusive hotel with spectacular views and prices to match.

Kate could hardly contain her astonishment as they were warmly welcomed at the reception desk and shown up to a suite on the top floor. It contained two bedrooms as well as a sitting room and a small balcony with an immense view down the harbour towards South Head. She saw king-sized beds with soft continental quilts, massive towels in each of the ensuite bathrooms, twin settees facing across a bentwood coffee table, a large colour television set, ornamental mirrors and a chandelier. She had never encountered luxury like this in her life before now.

Sofia came to stand beside her at the window, admiring the view. The Opera House dominated the foreground, its interior still unfinished but the outer shells pristine and gleaming as they reflected the sunlight. Even Kate, who had often seen its progress from the deck of passing ferries, felt the full impact of the inimitable design from this height. She heard Sofia's intake of breath, like a gasp of disbelief as they stepped out onto the balcony to admire it. Without the window glass between them and the view, it felt even closer.

'Magical, isn't it? I don't suppose you remember, but I once wrote in a letter that perhaps some day I could visit here and we'd see Utzon's building.'

'I remember,' Kate said.

'So there it is . . . and here we are, after all this time. Hard to imagine how happy this makes me.' For a moment Kate thought that Sofia was on the verge of tears. 'It feels like a dream, Katerina. I thought that's all it would ever be.'

Kate smiled. 'I remember that too. Somewhere I still have the letter. You said, "if it seems unlikely we can but dream".'

'So, no need for dreams any more. Tomorrow we go for a walk down there. I'll take a picture of you holding Juliet in front of the Opera House to prove it's real. Then you can take some of me to send to Michel and my friends in Athens.' As mercurial as ever, she threw her arms wide in an excess of sudden joy. 'My God, I never imagined something like this could happen. Not to us!'

Nor did I, thought Kate, sharing her enjoyment. But she kept trying to remind herself that this wasn't permanent – just two months out of the rest of her life. So it was best, she decided, not to wonder what would happen when this time was over.

Being realistic, she knew one thing; after luxury like this, the only direction to go from here would be down.

Whenever Mandy had any spare time from work she insisted on minding Juliet for them, leaving Kate free to show her mother the rest of the city. They went on occasional guided tours, and while Kate herself relished this rare chance to discover parts of the town she'd never known and learn more about Sydney's early history, Sofia had little interest in excursions to architectural gems of the past.

'I'd rather see the places where you grew up,' she said, 'than listen to a tourist guide telling me about convicts.'

'But the place where I grew up isn't there any longer,' Kate tried to explain.

Despite this, the next time Mandy was free to babysit they went on a ferry to Manly and from there took a bus to Dee Why, where at Sofia's urging they went to see the street where the café once stood. The motel building was making significant progress; it had now reached the second level, and high above them on scaffolding a team of bricklayers was hard at work.

Seeing it, Kate wished she hadn't been persuaded to come back here. What had once been a friendly neighbourhood of small shops was now just a bleak memory of the bitter Sunday when she'd seen them all bulldozed . . . holding her father's hand as the bricks and mortar crumbled. The visit also proved a disappointment to Sofia, who found it difficult to imagine a Greek café had stood there, let alone that her husband and daughter had lived above it all those years. She was unusually subdued when they walked to the beach and sat on a bench beneath the pines.

'Poor Andreas,' she said at length, rather diffidently, 'he divorced me last year. I never told you.' Kate turned to register her surprise, but Sofia's gaze was fixed on the crowded beach and the surfers in the water. Eventually, she said, 'Michel and I didn't ask for it; we never cared one way or the other. We didn't feel a need to marry. But perhaps this means your papa has at last found someone. I hope so.'

Kate remained silent. Despite all the years her parents had been separated, a divorce seemed unexpectedly final. She felt desperately sorry for her father, and wished she could have been closer to him. He'd had no luck one way or another – no luck with his work or with the few women in his life. He had written just once after his return to Cyprus, a short scribbled letter to say he had arrived safely, and she had replied, asking him to write with more news when he was settled. There'd been nothing since then. She hoped she was wrong, but remembering his lack of success with Isabella she rather doubted if he would even make an attempt to find someone.

'It was a mistake coming here, Mama,' she said, suddenly anxious to get away from the memories this place evoked.

It was strange about Hugh Forrester. In the three weeks since Kate had left the nursing home, there had been no word from him. It puzzled her; he'd been so anxious to help her find a place to live. Kate rang Mandy at the coffee shop to ask if she'd seen him.

'Not this week,' Mandy answered. 'The last time he was in he didn't crack a smile; looked like a wet weekend. Maybe he's gone on holiday, or else he's ill.' She promised to check at the Magistrate's Court across the road to find out.

'But don't say I was asking,' Kate requested.

'Why not, kitten?'

'Just because,' she replied. 'I don't want him to feel obligated, if he can't help me any more. Decent rooms are bound to be hard to find. Especially with a baby. Just say . . . look, I don't know . . . try to be discreet.'

'But you know me, mate. I'm always discreet.'

'That'll be news to most of us,' Kate said, smiling at she hung up.

'Worried about something?' Sofia asked. She was sitting on the balcony wearing white shorts and a sun top, reading mail that Michel had sent from Athens.

'No, just curious about Hugh. He was so eager to help me find a decent place to stay after I leave here. If that's changed, I need to know.'

'But there's no hurry, surely?'

'Only five more weeks, Mum.'

Sofia gave a mock sigh. 'Do you have to call me *Mum*? Mama is quite bad enough. Sofia is preferable.' She pointed to the other chair. 'Why don't you sit down, darling?'

'I've got to feed Juliet in a minute.'

'She's fast asleep.'

'In a minute she'll be wide awake. Like a clock, that one.'

'Then give me that minute of your valuable time, please.'

Kate looked at her. Sofia smiled and patted the chair beside her as she checked through her mail and found a brochure.

'Michel sent this. He asked me to show it to you.'

Kate took it. It was an advertisement of what appeared to be a studio apartment, surrounded by luxuriant foliage with photos of young adults playing tennis and small children in a swimming pool.

'Why?' she asked, mystified.

'Because the shipping company owns the block, and we could get you a small apartment, enough for you and Juliet.'

'But this is all written in Greek.'

'Of course. The apartment's in Athens.'

Kate stared at her.

'Or rather just outside Athens. Near the sea, and far nicer than the city. Half an hour from where we live . . .'

'No, Mama —'

'Think about it, Katerina. There's no rush. Michel's put a reserve notice on one, so it's yours if you choose. The company will pay the rent for six months, until you get settled.'

'No, Mama —'

'We'd get a maid to look after Juliet. You'd be able to work.'

'Are you hearing me, *Mum*?'

'My pet, all I ask is that you think about it. After all, that's where you were born. It's not such a big step to return to your own country.'

'*This* is my own country,' Kate said, trying to remain calm but on the verge of losing her temper. 'Here, the country where you left me at the age of six.'

'You know how much I regret that. I want to make up for it.'

'Not this way, Mama.' Kate crumpled the brochure and dropped it on the table between them.

'But how can you manage here . . . with the baby?'

'I'll work it out.'

'It's going to be hard for you without support, no matter what your lawyer friend says . . .'

Inside the apartment Juliet started to cry. Kate heard this with a feeling of relief. 'Sorry, that's my little alarm clock going off,' she said, starting to remove her shirt, then turned with a slightly puzzled look. 'What do you mean – about my lawyer friend? You haven't met him.'

'I've spoken to him on the telephone.'

'Of course,' Kate remembered. 'From Greece. You woke him up in the middle of the night.'

The baby's cries were becoming louder. Sofia seemed to be waiting for her to go and feed her, but there was something about what her mother had said that bothered Kate.

'She sounds as if she's starving, Katerina,' Sofia said, as if surprised at the delay, and Kate went inside to her bedroom where Juliet was red-faced, her hands waving, feet kicking, her furious cries ceasing the moment she was lifted from the bassinet.

'Little bugger,' Kate said fondly. 'Mummy's here, and the milk bar's open.'

It was while Juliet was contently sucking on her breast that Kate thought about that middle-of-the-night phone call. *It's going to be hard, no matter what your lawyer friend says.*

Her mother's remark suggested they'd had a discussion about the problem of her future. With Hugh, woken by a stranger's call? And the seven-hour time difference, meaning it was about two or three in the morning?

It hardly seemed likely.

She rose carefully, holding Juliet. One breast was starting to feel tender, so she moved her to the other. After a murmur of protest at this interruption Juliet greedily accepted the change. They went out to the balcony where Sofia was now engrossed in a Greek magazine. She looked up as Kate sat down again with Juliet feeding.

'A hungry little alarm clock. You were right, darling.'

'Sofia . . .'

'Yes, my love?'

'When did you talk to Hugh on the phone?'

'I told you . . .'

'Not that time. When did you last speak to him?'

There was an imperceptible pause. Sofia looked thoughtful, giving the impression she was trying to remember. 'A few days ago; I think it was Tuesday. Yes, Tuesday,' she confirmed, 'I meant to tell you.'

'But you forgot.'

'I'm afraid I did. He only phoned to ask if you were well. I told him how much we were both enjoying it here. He said there was no message.' She smiled as if that matter was disposed of, then picked up the crumpled brochure Kate had left on the table, and carefully smoothed it. 'I do wish you'd give this idea of Athens some more thought, darling. It really is the answer to everything.'

The coffee shop was half empty when she arrived with Juliet in a carry cot, but Hugh was already waiting for her at a corner table. There was a new waitress who had a special smile for the baby, delaying Kate by admiring her and marvelling how anyone could be that cute and tiny. By the time Kate reached the table and Hugh greeted her, Mandy had emerged from the kitchen. She stood gaping at them in disbelief for a moment. Then she was quickly alongside them, pad and pencil poised for their order as if she'd never seen either of them before.

'A long black?' she asked Hugh formally.

'Thank you,' he replied.

'And for the lady?'

'A glass of your very best milk,' Kate said, poker-faced. 'And a big dollop of ice-cream.'

'Sounds delicious.' Mandy could no longer contain herself. 'I thought I was to be your emissary,' she said to Kate. 'Your *discreet* emissary?'

'There was no longer a need for discretion,' Kate said, promising to explain later. 'Don't forget the dollop of ice-cream, will you?'

Watching her return to the kitchen with a last baffled look back at them, they shared smiles.

'I asked her to find out what was wrong because I hadn't heard from you. Then my mother tripped over her own devious tactics. How many times did you try to phone me?'

'Three times. She either told me you were having a rest, or else feeding Juliet. I got a bit fed up that you never called back, but the third time when she said that you'd decided to go and live in Athens, it sounded so convincing, that I thought . . . well . . .'

'What did you think, Hugh?'

'I suppose I thought, that's it.'

'The ungrateful bitch is going home to Mummy.'

'I certainly didn't think that,' he said. 'It was a disappointment, but there was a certain logic to it. After all, you were born there.'

'Now don't you start,' Kate said softly, and smiled.

'Anyhow,' Hugh continued, looking into her dark-blue eyes, 'I'm bloody glad you're not going. In fact I'm seriously delighted. It would have been far more than a disappointment, never seeing you again.'

Neither said anything for a moment. Mandy came back and had to give a warning cough before they realised she was there.

'Excuse me! A long black and milk with a dollop.' She placed the orders in front of them. 'Any slight chance of telling me the score?'

Kate looked up at her. 'My mother was intercepting Hugh's calls. She had plans for me that I didn't know about.' She quickly explained about the seductive brochure and the flat near Athens.

'Crafty old thing,' Mandy said. 'How's she taking it?'

'Mama is not gracious in defeat. She's too accustomed to getting her own way.' She laughed and added, 'She'd hate you for the word "old".'

'So when is she going back to Greece?'

'When Michel gets here, in five weeks' time. By then she'll have tried every trick in the book to change my mind.'

'It sounds,' Mandy said, 'as if it's going to be a long five weeks.'

Chapter 13

They stood outside the terminal, watching the aircraft take off and turn northward for the flight across Australia. Kate raised a hand in a farewell that she knew neither Sofia or Michel would be able to see, but remained standing there like that until the plane was out of their sight.

It hadn't been so bad, she thought – the last few days with Michel there had helped, and as if reading her mind, Hugh said despite the dire predictions it could have been a whole lot worse.

'It could've,' Kate agreed. 'In fact, we ended up almost friends. That's not bad for my mother and me.'

They linked hands and began to walk towards the car park. His MG sports was some distance away, its shiny red colour making it easily discernable.

'We'll be close friends again in our letters,' she said jokingly. 'It's where we're best with each other, on paper and at a distance.'

'You were thrilled when she arrived.'

'I was. It was really lovely for a few weeks.'

'Only that long?'

'Until the bloody brochure,' Kate said. 'That spoilt it.'

'I suppose in her own way she meant well,' he said.

'You're too tolerant,' she chided. 'She meant to make amends to herself for dumping me. Take us over, me and Juliet, acquire an instant family, become a matriarch . . .'

'You can be pretty tough sometimes,' he said affectionately and put his arm around her. She leaned against him as they walked through the rows of cars, thinking about this.

'If I am, I learnt it from her. The day she brought me here, then caught the same boat back to Athens . . .'

'You don't forget.'

'Would anyone?' she asked. 'Michel's a nice man and I'm glad they're happy, but I can't forget.'

They stopped at the MG. The hood was down. He put both arms around Kate, kissed her, lifted her gently and placed her into the front seat. Then he went around and nimbly stepped over the driver's door to sit beside her.

'You'll miss doing that,' Kate said fondly.

'It's a young man's car,' Hugh said. 'At the age of thirty it's time I grew up.'

'But are you sure?' she asked, concerned at how much he loved the speedy little MG, and thinking of the sedate Vauxhall Victor he'd arranged to take as a trade-in.

'I'm certain. It's been fun to drive, but it's like a wind tunnel with the hood down, and we don't want our Juliet to blow away.' He leaned across to kiss her again. 'Do we?'

Kate shook her head in reply, feeling happy and safe. *Our* Juliet, she thought; it sounds just the way I hope it will be. She fastened her seatbelt as Hugh revved the sports car, and they drove off to exchange it for a family sedan.

~

My dearest girl, the letter began, confirming Kate's prediction of their amity on paper,

I do miss you. I miss the view of the marvellous Opera House and the harbour, and what a joy it was, living in that smart hotel together and sharing our brief spell of luxury. Nice to remember the fun we had, and forget the silly disagreements that were not important. I'm glad we finally met Hugh, who I think is a pleasant and considerate man, and Michel agrees that he is very fond of you. We hope things work out for you both, and this relationship is lasting.

My love to darling Juliet. Send me news and photographs of her as she grows up. Do you have a harbour view from the apartment you share in Paddington? Although we have only been home a few months I am already forgetting my geography, and can't remember where this suburb is.

Much love,

Sofia

P.S. A little unexpected drama here. The shipping company has been taken over by a multinational, and we are not sure what happens next.

Juliet was three years old when Katerina Vassos became Kate Forrester in a ceremony held near Mrs Macquarie's Chair under a Moreton Bay fig tree. It was a blissful spring day, sunlight danced on the harbour, and the weather could not have been kinder as they took their vows.

Hugh had brought up the subject of marriage several times since they had begun to live together. At first unsure if she wanted to commit herself so completely, Kate gradually found no reason not to do so. Hugh was a warm, loving man, and if the sexual chemistry was not quite the same as with Joshua, his affection for her and

Juliet was genuine. The ceremony was a private affair, attended only by Kate's daughter, Mandy and the groom's choice of best man – a young lawyer named Roger Montgomery.

'Roger the Dodger,' Hugh introduced him, when they met under the tree. 'We went through law school together.'

They were both in their early thirties; Roger now a junior partner in his family's firm. Friends attracted opposites, Kate thought, for while Hugh was seriously inclined and dressed conservatively, Roger was extrovert and modish, his sandy hair a trendy shoulder-length and his preferred attire, when the occasion allowed, a T-shirt and jeans.

'My father hates the hair,' he confided with a grin, 'he says it makes me look like an extra in *Jesus Christ Superstar*.'

Mandy arrived with flowers, hugged Juliet to whom she was unofficial godmother, and managed to withhold her surprise at the lack of other friends. She did not raise the subject until months later, when she came for lunch. Hugh was at work, and Juliet had only recently started to attend play school.

'How does she feel about it?' Mandy asked, with the proprietary interest of one who'd assisted in the outcome.

'She was so excited the first day – until we met a small boy, also new and sobbing his eyes out. So she burst into tears and cried in sympathy with him,' Kate said.

'Poor little thing.'

'It had a happy ending,' Kate assured her. 'Now she loves it, can't wait to go, and the small boy is her best friend. They're thinking of becoming engaged.'

'Good.' Mandy smiled, then in her typical direct fashion asked, 'And what about *your* best friends? I thought they'd have been at the fig-tree nuptials.'

'We decided to keep it private.'

'You certainly managed that. Do you intend to cut yourself off entirely from the past? It's three years since Joshua.'

'Four,' Kate corrected her. 'The longer the better. Time becomes elastic. Hugh and I can say we've been together since then and they'll assume he's Juliet's father.'

'So Joshua's history?'

'He is now.'

'You're never going to tell her?'

'Not if I can help it.' A frown betrayed some insecurity. 'It would mean being civilised. I don't feel up to being civilised.'

'Fair enough, kitten. Your choice,' Mandy said. 'A brand-new name and marital bliss with dear old "long black" – and I must stop calling him that!'

'You must.' Kate smiled. 'In a few years with any luck he'll be Hugh Forrester, Barrister. And maybe one day Forrester Q.C.'

'My word!' Mandy said with a giggle and a genuflection. 'If he becomes a judge he could be knighted. Would that make you a dame?'

'Come off it!' Kate laughed. 'Just a working wife.'

'Have you found a job?'

'Part-time, with a promise of full-time when Juliet starts primary school. Roger's father has offered me a job clerking with his law firm, Montgomery & Associates. Meanwhile I'm going to do a correspondence course in legal studies.'

'Almost a legal eagle.' Mandy rolled her eyes and set them both laughing again. 'It sure beats that sweatshop coffee lounge.'

'It had its moments,' Kate replied, thinking of the friendship they'd forged there.

Over lunch Mandy asked for news of Sofia. Since the takeover of the shipping company there'd been casualties among the senior staff, and for a time it seemed Michel's position might be in jeopardy.

'But he's still there,' Kate said. 'He's one of the survivors, to their relief. But Mama says he's no longer such a big cheese. I think it means he was moved sideways.'

'I still think fondly of her,' Mandy observed. 'With all her scheming, it was hard not to like her.'

'My problem exactly,' Kate answered.

After a leisurely lunch they walked to the bus stop, making plans to see a film on Mandy's next free day. She had a new job, assistant manager at The Mock Turtle, a recently opened restaurant in the city. As the bus arrived she gave Kate a quick hug, then stepped on board.

'Love to the world's best-looking goddaughter and to Hugh,' she said, while the driver waited impatiently for her to move so he could close the remote-controlled door. But before he could she called out, 'and I'm so glad the other miserable bugger is history!' Kate and half of those on board heard it, and she could see Mandy still laughing as the bus drove away.

Not quite history, she thought, while walking home. After her childhood where love had so often been lacking, Joshua had completely changed her life. She had been naïve, she now knew, to think it would last, but to leave without a word . . . and to allow Toby and his sister, who had never been her friends, to share in her humiliation. That would always hurt.

She was quietly determined he'd never know about Juliet, for the child's sake as well as her own. Joshua would be flattered with this small and cute progeny; he'd shower her with gifts and try to take her over. It'd be a battle for the heart and mind of one little girl, and they'd all be affected, Hugh as well. Perhaps Hugh most of all. She did not want him to be hurt. She was aware she didn't love him in quite the same way, but she felt happy with him. Happy and completely safe.

But a feeling persisted that to be entirely free of Joshua she had to know *why* he had gone without even a moment's thought for her, no matter how desperately he wanted to avoid Vietnam. And why he had ruthlessly ditched her as if she was nothing better than a one-night stand.

One evening there was a paragraph in the newspaper. About to use it to wrap dinner scraps, Kate saw a name she instantly knew. Alongside the name was a small photograph that barely escaped being obliterated by the leftovers of their spaghetti bolognaise. *Damien Raphael, the winner of the recent short-story competition in this newspaper, leaves for London tomorrow by sea.*

'You beaut,' she said aloud. 'How bloody wonderful!' Her voice was so triumphant it brought Hugh in to ask what was so wonderful.

'A friend of mine won a story competition,' Kate told him. 'Do you remember me mentioning Damien?' She showed him the paper.

'He has an uncle who plays the violin,' Hugh recalled. 'Uncle and aunt are both considered slightly unusual.'

She laughed. 'Bloody weird, certain people used to call them. Anyway, that's him. On his way to England tomorrow.'

He could tell from her delighted face how much this pleased her. 'He was one of the good guys?'

'He was. I'd love to tell him how glad I am.'

'Why don't you?' he suggested. 'Why not go and see him off.'

She thought about it while she cleaned the kitchen, then poured two glasses of wine from a cask and took them into their bedroom where Hugh had set up a small desk in the corner. He was already starting to study for a bar exam. 'Aspects of Evidence' was one of three subjects that aspiring barristers had to pass to be considered for advocacy before the courts.

'Are you winning?' she asked, kissing his cheek as she put the wine glass beside him.

'This might help.' He picked up the glass and touched it against hers. 'You realise I'll be grilled by a mob of legal luminaries, who try to fail us, thus keeping their hallowed ranks lean and prestigious.'

'You want me to test you with some hard questions?'

'In a minute,' he said, tasting the wine, then asking, 'why don't you go and say *bon voyage* to your friend Damien?'

'Because I don't know what ship he's travelling on.'

'Shouldn't be difficult to find out.'

'I wouldn't know where to begin.'

'Of course you would. You don't want to go.'

'I'd love to, but . . .'

'But some of Joshua's friends might be there,' Hugh said.

'They might.'

'The odious Toby Robinson, for instance.'

'That would certainly help ruin the day.'

'Kate, darling, please go.'

'Let me think about it.'

'Please. Don't entirely shut out the past like this. And if Toby or anyone else gives you trouble, kick him in the balls. Or give me his address and I'll gladly do it for you. That's if Toby's got any balls.'

But she had not made up her mind by the time they went to bed. That was when Hugh switched out his bedside light as if preparing to go to sleep and said, 'By the way, his ship is called *The Montana*. It leaves tomorrow afternoon from Woolloomooloo.'

Kate put aside the book she was reading to gaze at him.

'I looked up various Raphaels in the phone book. Got his home second try, spoke to his mother and then to Damien.'

'When did you do this?' she asked.

'While you were reading a story to Juliet.'

'And what did you say?'

'I said I was ringing on your behalf, because you were busy with our daughter.'

'What did *he* say?'

'He said good heavens! He had no idea you were a parent.'

'And then?'

'I said you'd been one for several years.'

'What did he say to that?'

'That he'd been wondering where on earth you'd got to all this time. You'd dropped out of sight and nobody seemed to know where to. So I said that you'd dropped out of sight with me.'

'Mmm,' she murmured. 'Clever clogs.'

'And we couldn't invite anyone to the wedding because we eloped nearly four years ago, before the baby was born.' Kate's head, already close to Hugh's on the same pillow moved closer, and her expressive eyes, if possible, opened wider as he continued. 'Then I explained you'd always wished we'd invited him, and you'd love to see him tomorrow if you wouldn't be likely to run into any of Joshua's old mob, or especially Joshua himself.'

'When you're a barrister,' Kate said, edging her body closer to his warmth, 'you'll be very adept at embroidering stories in court.'

'One hopes so,' Hugh answered.

'So . . . who'll be at Woolloomooloo tomorrow?'

'Just his family. Parents, maybe a few cousins, plus the eccentric aunt and uncle. Not necessarily with violin, although I did suggest he ought to bring it to play 'The Maoris' Farewell'. Damien thought that a hoot.'

Kate laughed softly and let her head rest on his shoulder. 'And . . . ?' she prompted.

'. . . and he'd love to see you. I said I'd stay home to collect Juliet from kindergarten, but you'd definitely be there. So you won't make a liar out of me, will you?'

'My darling, I wouldn't dream of making a liar out of you,' she said, turning out her light and snuggling happily against him.

The Montana, she thought, was the kind of ship she would love to travel on. Nothing remotely like the *Ottoman Star* with its crowded migrants. A freighter, just a few passenger cabins, taking a leisurely route via Cairns, Borneo, Singapore, across the Bay of Bengal to Madras, then the Gulf of Aden, the Suez Canal, Athens, and finally to the Atlantic Ocean and Southampton. A three-month voyage, but far cheaper than any of the passenger vessels, Damien enthused to Kate. And he had a tiny single cabin which he proudly showed her; it was the size of a large cupboard where he hoped to spend much of the time at sea writing plays that he'd try to sell to British television.

'What about your poems and short stories?' she wanted to know. 'Have you given up on those?'

'I knew you'd ask,' Damien said. 'I sold a poem and they sent a cheque for five dollars, but the magazine went bust and the cheque bounced. So I decided poetry might be a hobby . . . for when I'm older.'

'What about the short stories?'

'Well . . . I've sold six.'

'That sounds pretty good,' Kate said.

'Not when I admit I've written over forty,' Damien replied. 'But . . . I have sold some radio scripts and one television play. Fanny and Angelo think I'm about to be famous, but Dad so kindly worked out the ratio of time spent against money earnt, and told me I'd actually averaged nine dollars a week. Not even half the basic wage! Trust an accountant to figure out a thing like that!'

She met his parents together with Uncle Angelo and Aunt Fanny in the passengers' saloon. The father, she could see at once, was rather formal and traditionalist; she could well imagine his disapproval of a literary career, and he appeared to feel this overseas trip was a wild adventure from which no real benefit could emerge. The mother had the same bright-red hair as Damien but none of his spirit; she seemed passive and totally compliant to her husband's loudly voiced opinions.

Kate took an instant liking to Aunt Fanny, and quietly asked her if Angelo had brought his violin.

'I made him leave it at home,' Fanny murmured. 'But now I'm sorry. He would've enjoyed serenading a pretty girl like you.' She leaned close to whisper: 'And my stick-in-the-mud brother-in-law would've gotten so upset. It is great fun to see him . . . what is the Aussie expression? . . . Ah, yes, great fun to see him go bananas and lose his block.'

Kate tried not to laugh, and ended up with a coughing fit. Damien took her off on the pretext of showing her around the ship.

'My aunt is a wonderful woman,' he said, 'and rather wicked. She likes nothing better than goading and annoying my dad.'

'She's gorgeous,' Kate answered. 'I wish I'd had a chance to know her before this.'

'I wish you hadn't disappeared the way you did. It didn't take me long to work out it was entirely because of that bastard Joshua.'

'Don't let's waste time on the past, Damien. Or on him. How long are you going to stay in England?'

'Depends how things go.'

'How did you save the fare – on your average nine bucks a week?'

'Part-time jobs. Mowing lawns, washing cars, minding kids. My folks don't know this, but I only saved enough for a one-way trip.'

'How will you get back?'

'Haven't the faintest,' Damien said, happily unconcerned. 'Mow English lawns, I guess, wash their cars, mind their kids . . . On the other hand, if I get lucky I might not want to come back.'

'Will you write to me and let me know how things are?' Kate had a sudden premonition they might not meet again.

'Give me your address and I will. And if you don't want to talk about it now, I can write and give you the low-down on what became of Joshua. Unless you know the details already.'

She turned and stared at him. *'What became of him?* You mean you know?'

'I found out. You don't know?' When she shook her head, he asked, 'Do you *want* to hear?'

'I suppose I do,' Kate said, then after a moment added, 'but I'm not sure. I mean, he really is a figure from the past to me now; I've got a husband and a daughter . . .' She was uncertain how convincing it sounded.

'Is he the father?' Damien asked. 'Hugh, the guy I spoke to?'

'Of course,' Kate said, but had a feeling she'd paused a moment too long, and lying to Damien was not as easy as telling lies to others.

'I apologise for even asking that,' he said promptly.

By then they had made a brief circle of the ship and returned to where his parents and relatives were waiting patiently. She realised departure was near and she was intruding on his family's farewell.

'It's been lovely to see you, Damien. I really must go.'

'Regarding Joshua,' he said, '*do* you want to know about it?' As she hesitated he suggested, 'How he ended up, and all the rest. If you wish, when I write to you I could include what I found out.'

Kate nodded. She scribbled her new name and address on a piece of paper she discovered in her handbag and gave it to him.

'Kate Forrester.' He read it aloud and she could tell the name felt strange to him. 'On the phone Mr Forrester sounded like a nice bloke.'

'He is.'

'I'm glad you're happy,' Damien told her.

They joined his family, where Kate said goodbye. She knew the parents were pleased to see her leave. Aunt Fanny gave her a warm hug, and said to come and see them one day, and bring her husband and little daughter. She started to shake hands with Uncle Angelo, who instead enveloped her in a bear hug that left her almost breathless.

'Take good care of yourself,' he said. 'Damien was a bit slow. He should've brought you to us long ago.'

She went down the steep gangway to the dock, where preparations for the ship's departure were in progress. She realised it was the same wharf she arrived at when six years old – the first time she had been on it since meeting her father on arrival in Australia, the day her parents had gone their separate ways for the rest of their lives. It reminded her that Damien's ship was calling at Athens; she had meant to suggest he might like to phone her mother, perhaps meet for a meal or a conducted tour – but with all they'd had to talk about, had forgotten it.

Just as well, perhaps, she thought. Sofia's knowledge of the truth could embarrass her contrived story. Even with the best of friends, it was necessary to be guarded. In the past she'd been upfront and gregarious; it was awful being entrenched in secrecy. Especially to someone she could surely trust, like Damien.

At the dockyard gate she turned for a last look back at the freighter. He was alone at the rail, red hair ruffled by the breeze, watching her leave. He stood there waving until she was out of sight.

Chapter 14

The letter from London came nearly five months later. Damien apologised for the delay, but the journey had taken a few extra weeks because the ship had detoured to pick up cargo in Ceylon and then changed course in the Mediterranean to deliver it to Marseilles. Not only that, but since arriving in England he'd been flat out like a lizard – trying to make appointments to meet television producers and battling to find a decent room to live in.

Meeting TV executives was not easy, he'd rapidly learnt. He had begun by ringing one producer's office at 8.30 in the morning, to be answered by a female voice. He went through a prepared spiel and asked if he could make an appointment with her boss – assuming that he was speaking to the secretary – but was told in fact he was speaking to the office cleaner. The secretary would be in at 9.30, and the producer perhaps an hour later. The cleaner had detected he was Australian, not only by the accent. Australians, she said, always rang too early, especially when they were brand-new off the boat. It was probably something to do with the strange time zones down there at the bottom of the world, she told Damien.

Accommodation had also been full of potholes. It was hard to find anything pleasant and cheap enough to suit his modest budget in central London. But it was where he had to be. It was pointless coming all the way and not living right in London itself, for that was where the action happened. He had finally found an ideal room in Earl's Court Square.

I cracked the jackpot because it overlooks the square's private garden which is actually a couple of acres, and all these big nineteenth-century houses full of flats or rooms to rent are built around it. Spring is being sprung here, and each day the trees in the square show new buds and fresh leaves. It's the first time I've ever seen this complete transformation. Apart from the advent of spring and trees all springing to life (sorry about that), it's comforting to hear so many Aussie accents around here in the shops and tube station. It's a friendly neighbourhood, close to everything, and I already feel quite at home.

I wrote two plays on board the ship, one for radio and one TV opus. Sent them both off, and had two fairly prompt letters of rejection. The radio epic seems doomed, for the BBC is the only market that I know of. But there are lots more TV outlets, so I shall send that one on a journey around the various companies and see what happens. In the meantime I've put an advert in The Kensington Post offering gardening, babysitting and car-washing services.

Now, the story of Joshua Maitland. I wrote this on the boat, and put it in a sealed envelope that I almost mailed you from Port Said, but decided to wait and enclose it with news after I arrived here. If you don't want to revisit the past then just burn the unopened envelope and that's the end of it. But I suspect you must wonder where he went and why he behaved the way he did, in which case read first, then burn. I hope Juliet is growing up to look like you, and my regards to Hugh.

All best wishes,

Damien

Kate hesitated, then opened the other envelope and took out a cluster of typed pages. Set out like a story, she thought, and settled down apprehensively to read it.

I should preface this by saying that I never really liked Joshua. So if my words seem critical at times please forgive an innate aversion, or perhaps it was envy on my part, because he had some kind of charisma that eluded me and always made him hugely popular.

We met when we were both aged nine, on our first day at the same school when he began as a boarder and I started as a day boy. It was a rather snobbish sort of school, and we both had a mutual disability at first. This – extraordinary as it might seem – was a geographical handicap from the address of our homes. Neither of us dwelt in the blue-ribbon strip of the North Shore where most day boys lived. Mine was in Artarmon, which was considered a working-class district to the deep south of Chatswood back then, and Chatswood itself was rarely spoken of without a shudder. Joshua came from the absolute 'no go' area of Lakemba, scorned by one and all, as most boarders came from the country and their families owned sheep stations or local businesses and were members of the Country Party. At our exclusive school the west of Sydney was usually ridiculed as a place where no one would wish to live. 'Dunny country' or 'Shitsville' were two of its milder epithets.

So we had this strange affinity of being 'outsiders' for a while, which established a defensive relationship. But within a year or two Joshua grew taller than me, more assertive, and quite soon far more popular than me. He really worked at it, determined to make them forget where he lived and accept him as one of 'their crowd'. Soon he was not merely one of them, he was the virtual leader who promptly detached himself from close association with me and became best buddies with Toby Robinson.

Because he was often left at the school boarding house during the short holidays, he was soon invited to stay at Toby's place and other homes of his friends. They formed a sort of cabal, a tight circle of mates, and by chance Joshua's grandparents had a holiday beach house at Collaroy, which happened to be where lots of the others spent summers during the 1950s and early '60s. Even I came into contact with them at times, because my cousin lived at Fisherman's Beach in the house where you came to a barbecue. But I was never really one of the clique. Just a figure on the fringes.

One memory probably best sums up my relationship with them. On my twelfth birthday, Uncle Angelo took a group of us from my class to the AWA tower. Remember the big radio mast on top of the AWA building in Clarence Street that used to be famous as Australia's highest structure? He took us up to the viewing platform about a hundred yards above street level, where we could see the beaches of Bondi and Tamarama, as well as west to the Blue Mountains and south beyond Cronulla. It was scary at such a height; cars in the street below looked like toys, and Angelo said the crowds of tiny people reminded him of ants heading home to their nests. It's actually a diminutive replica of the Eiffel Tower, and he said one day when we grew up we must all travel to France, especially Paris, where we could see the real thing. None of them seemed to like the idea. I heard a loud whisper from Toby: 'Yuck! France is full of frogs who eat snails.'

The other boys all giggled. Angelo tried to ignore this and enthuse, although I knew he'd heard the remark. He told us that in our lifetime the ease of air travel would mean trips to France would be on the agenda for all Australians. So learning French could be a useful asset for us lads.

That was when Joshua chimed in, acting the class clown.

'Not me,' he said deliberately loudly, and proceeded to chant the old schoolboy refrain, 'Bugger Latin, bugger French, and bugger sitting on a hard-board bench!'

You can imagine how all his coterie thought it clever and laughed as if Angelo wasn't there.

I felt angry with them, but timidity kept me silent. Joshua and Toby were the hub of popularity, and to quarrel with them was to end up an outsider. So for years I ignored or pretended not to hear snide remarks about my relatives, feeling secretly ashamed but willing to compromise to remain one of their group. Never a core member, not one of the close circle, but tolerated. Even thinking of it now, writing this far away in the Bay of Bengal, I wish I'd been braver. Their offhand and cavalier friendship was never worth it.

Forgive the preamble, but that's my mea culpa. I'm not proud of it, but school is an odd place, and you can either be tolerated or ostracised. I was tolerated.

I'm glad I can confess all this to someone I trust like you, and now I know you want to read the rest. Where did he go and why? I got this from the horse's mouth the last time I spoke to her, and since I was leaving and neither of us cared for each other any longer I believe that Noelene told me the truth.

Being selected for conscription in the ballot came as a real shock to Joshua. He'd rejected university so that wasn't a way out. He went to a doctor friend of his father's and tried to get help, explaining he'd heard of doctors who prescribed certain pills that could help to fail the army medical. Apparently he got an earful instead. He picked the wrong doctor; this one had been in World War Two and told Joshua he was shocked and inclined to report the matter to the authorities. He rang Joshua's dad and told him about it, saying if his son did happen to get a medical exemption he would ask the army to investigate.

I gather he got another bollocking from his father, who said it was his duty to go off and fight the little slant-eyed Commie bastards – which seems to tie in with me being told by someone (maybe Joshua himself) that his old man was a red-hot anti-Com and a redneck racist.

Anyway, after this, all outlets seemed blocked so he went to confide his troubles to Toby, and it was Toby and Noelene who came up with the idea.

Mainly her, or so she says. It sounds more like Machiavellian Toby, but maybe there's a touch of Lucrezia Borgia in her as well.

They said the only option was to get out of the country. Joshua felt it was impossible. If he tried to use his passport he'd never get on board a ship or a plane. The government had placed travel restrictions on anyone who might be subject to the draft. No airline or shipping firm could issue tickets to twenty-year-olds without a departmental certificate.

He complained there was no way he could get an exemption. Aborigines and Quakers were exempt, but not him. On the other hand, if he tried to hide somewhere, it'd be tantamount to desertion and land him in real shit. So what else was left? In his opinion, nothing.

According to Noelene, she was the one who told him to shut up and listen. Young men his age were going to New Zealand. They didn't need passports between the two countries and nobody could stop them from going there. Apparently Joshua argued with her. He'd heard the special branch were taking the names of everyone boarding a plane to the land of the long white cloud. And they were compiling a nasty long blacklist, which would cause a pack of trouble some day when those guys wanted to come home again and get a job.

Noelene said he wasn't going by plane. She reminded him the family had a sea-going motor cruiser moored at Rushcutters Bay. And her father was an exporter whose business involved the dispatch of goods overseas. He was sending a consignment of wine to Lord Howe Island and another cargo to New Zealand by freighter at the end of next week. She and Joshua, together with a skipper and crew of one, would leave long before this. They'd take the cruiser to Lord Howe, meet the freighter and be transferred on board. Two days later they'd both walk off as crew in Auckland.

Noelene was quite candid; it suited her. She was bored with Sydney, she'd just given a boyfriend the push, and staying in NZ and living with Joshua appealed to her. She'd also been in touch with agents there who assured her there would be modelling jobs available. He could easily find casual work, and as far as the call-up was concerned, there would be no way anyone could trace him. He would just disappear.

Joshua liked the idea, and thought his grandmother would be in favour when she heard about it. That, they told him, could not happen. Nobody must hear about it; not yet. Maybe later on he could write to his grandma, but secrecy at this stage was essential.

That was when he asked about you. He ought to tell you. Toby told him to forget it. This was about getting him out of nasty dangerous Vietnam to somewhere safe, and what was safer than across the Tasman, in an apartment the family had arranged, tucked up cosily in bed with his sister? Apparently – and I can only quote Noelene on this – Toby declared it was a situation that neither of them had minded since they were sixteen, when they used to fuck every afternoon after school.

So Joshua agreed to leave without seeing you. And, though I don't like mentioning it, when she told me this Noelene seemed to relish how easily he was persuaded to do exactly what they wanted.

I'm afraid that is the not-very-pleasant story of why he disappeared from your life. Despite my feelings I've tried to be fair to him, to show he wasn't a complete shit. But not a very nice guy either. A bit of a coward, and weak under the show-pony bravado.

Anyway, they took the yacht, boarded the freighter as planned, and stayed in New Zealand until our troops were withdrawn from Vietnam. She and Joshua came home after Gough's government ordered the release of those imprisoned under the National Service Act, and stopped the further prosecution of draft evaders. That was when all the call-ups in the pipeline were cancelled. And Joshua was able to creep back into the country without anyone concerned or caring where he'd been.

While they lived together for those years in New Zealand they never married, and from what Noelene said it was not a very harmonious time. I get the feeling the relationship never recovered from the death of Joshua's grandmother, which apparently happened before he had been able to get in touch to tell her of his whereabouts. Noelene said he was very upset about that, and angry he had been forbidden to contact her. Joshua felt she died feeling abandoned by him, and he was always unhappy and difficult afterwards. They parted when they returned to Sydney and she hasn't seen him since. What Toby thinks of it all I have no idea, because I had no wish ever to talk to him. He's the real Iago in this web of deceit.

I did think of softening this letter and avoiding some of the direct quotes from Noelene. But I thought you should know the full truth. The way they didn't care about you, not one of them. At times I was concerned he would let you down, but could never bring myself to say so. Maybe I should have . . . but I doubted in those days if you would have believed me. So now burn this. Forget the past. Get on with the rest of your life.

P.S. I suppose, thinking about it, I was one of the lucky ones whose birthday number was not drawn out of a barrel. In hindsight it seems a pretty stupid way to raise an army.

Kate closed the letter, wondering exactly when Rosetta Morris had died, and whether it was after Juliet was born. She had a moment of guilt, feeling she might have deprived her of the chance to welcome a great-granddaughter, but on reflection doubted if the news would have been happily received. She was aware, and always regretted, that because of Joshua's facile remark the first day they had met at the beach house, his grandmother had not liked her. That he was so upset about Grandma Rose's death seemed like the only trace of the caring Joshua she had loved so deeply.

While burning the pages as suggested, Kate felt grateful Damien had been so candid and not spared her. With it came a sense of release. That night she made love to Hugh, and not once did an image or a memory of the past occupy her mind.

Joshua truly was history at last.

Chapter 15

When Kate replied to Damien, thanking him for his letter and the information he'd given her, it commenced an exchange of letters between them that was to continue for many years. *Your revelations about Joshua help to wipe the slate*, she wrote, leaving him to make what he would of that, and went on to tell him about a clapped-out house in Northbridge she'd found that was for sale – *found because my old banger of a car broke down* – describing the property as crummy but adorable, utterly condemned by their surveyor and disparaged by the bank manager when they went to obtain a mortgage.

The Manager, Mr Marshall, threw up his hands in horror. He told us this place had been on and off the market, sold and resold ever since he could remember, and if we wished to buy a home in the district, he would advise us not to touch this one. Not even with a barge pole!

'Well, that's too bad,' Hugh told him, 'because my wife has fallen in love with it, and we've clearly come to the wrong bank. We'll try your opposition across the road.'

That's when he suddenly changed his tune and lent us the money. So we've moved house, and this is our new address. I'm working full-time now, trying to complete my legal studies at night, and doing my best not to even think about the intimidatingly large mortgage.

She added that because of the repayments, Hugh was in two minds about sitting for the bar exam at present, and was still working as a solicitor.

Damien responded with his own news. He had at last managed to sell his much-rejected TV play to one of the small stations on the ITV network, which was not quite the heights he'd hoped for, but it was a start, and might even have raised a faint look of approval on his father's face, although he would not guarantee this. More likely his parent was busy calculating the amount of time spent versus fee paid, and proving it really meant he was still earning less than the dole.

Once they began corresponding it seemed natural to continue. Kate reported her daughter's progress in primary school, and a few years later the news that Hugh had at last decided to sit for the bar exam, and the following year that he had successfully passed it. She was thrilled for him because he'd always wanted to be a barrister, but the difficult part now lay ahead – finding chambers and then putting up his flag and waiting for hire, like a taxi. Hugh's own words, she told him, not hers.

She wrote of how their neighbourhood was changing: going up in the world according to real estate talk, although she wasn't sure this was a good thing. It meant some of their nicest neighbours saw a handy profit and moved away.

Sadly, house prices are an inescapable topic at dinner parties. People keep talking about cashing in to upsize or downsize. I make no contribution to this dialogue, as our once-crummy house has become a proper home, and the nicest place I've ever lived in. I seem isolated from the mainstream, because so many people want to jump on the property bandwagon. Meanwhile Sydney itself is being transformed, not for the better I feel, by vast reconstruction. Gracious old buildings that should be protected are demolished. Tall anonymous tower blocks rise instead, the sun shines less brightly and the streets feel like wind tunnels.

A friendship grew on paper between them in the same easy way as her friendship with Mandy. Just occasional letters, sometimes only one a year, but always welcome. Kate found it a release; to Damien she was able to confide her most private concerns, in particular how Hugh was still waiting hopefully for hire, but times were tough for barristers and so far briefs were not being offered to him. She was sure this would change, but it was lucky she'd been promoted at work as inflation was causing interest rates to rise alarmingly, and they looked like going higher.

In between news of their changing lives, Kate took pleasure in Damien's growing success as he became a regular writer on television shows, then a few years later wrote a stage play that toured around England. *The purpose of this*, he wrote,

is to try it out on audiences, and see if we can make improvements. Every night after the show I meet over a late dinner with the cast and director and come away with a bundle of notes and suggestions, and while they go off to bed the poor bloody writer has to sit in his hotel room the rest of the night, with only his portable typewriter for company, and do the rewrites by the next morning. Then he fronts up to these well-rested actors to see if the changes work.

But it's exciting, really – much more than television or films, and better rewards at the end of it if we succeed. Not that we'll know that for several weeks yet, while we continue to tour in the hope the show will transfer to London.

In a later letter he told Kate the try-out tour had been worthwhile because the play had made it to a theatre on Shaftsbury Avenue in London's West End, but she already knew this because his success had been trumpeted in the local newspapers.

'Is he a friend of yours, Mum?' The question came from eleven-year-old Juliet at breakfast time when she read the story and saw Damien's photo in the *Sun-Herald*. 'Because according to this, he seems to be quite famous. I didn't know we knew any famous people.'

'Just this one,' Kate said with a smile.

'Do you know him, Dad?' she asked.

'No, my darling,' Hugh replied, 'he's your mum's famous person. But I once spoke to him on the telephone. Only I don't think that counts, because he wasn't famous then.'

Juliet looked at him suspiciously. Hugh hurriedly disappeared behind the business section of the paper, while Kate had difficulty in preserving a straight face.

'You're sending me up rotten,' Juliet said, laughing.

'A smart babe like you? I wouldn't dare,' Hugh said lowering the paper, but unable to prevent a grin.

She went and hugged him, and reminded him that he'd promised to take her ten-pin bowling.

'Five minutes while I finish this coffee?' Hugh asked.

'Okay,' she said, 'but our science teacher Miss Bradshaw said coffee's bad for you.'

'Well, Miss Bradshaw is undoubtedly right, Jules. But we old fogies are stuck on our bad habits.'

'You're not old,' Juliet said. 'You're only . . . thirty-something?'

'Nearly right. A mere forty-one.'

'Gosh, that is old, Dad. Because after all, Mum's only thirty.'

'I know. It's a bit of a worry,' Hugh said to her with great gravity. 'The difference in our ages is well known in this neighbourhood and it keeps me awake at nights.'

Kate loved these leisurely weekend breakfasts when she did not have to get Juliet off to school and then drive to the office. Hugh finished his coffee and extended a hand to Juliet, who blew a kiss to Kate as they went out to the car. She watched them feeling such affection: Juliet busy chattering away, Hugh patient and so wonderfully good with her, as they climbed into the same old Vauxhall Victor. There was a nearly-new Mazda in the garage that she took to work each day, but he insisted on keeping the old bomb until he got regular work as a barrister. If only he could, she thought, but assured herself it must happen soon.

Now that Damien had achieved success he rarely wrote of his increasing status in letters to Kate over the ensuing years. She had to learn from the papers that he'd won a BAFTA award, and was nominated for an Emmy. And the television news revealed that his last stage play had opened with good reviews that predicted success on Broadway. Damien himself wrote to Kate more about his personal life; told her candidly of a break-up with a long-time live-in girlfriend, then a year or so later enthusiastically confided that he'd met someone truly special, an Aussie actress on location in Morocco who had a small role in a film he'd written.

The film, he wrote dismissively, was a bit of a potboiler and the director was a pain in the bum, but the actress was an absolute doll. Her name was Ingrid Barclay, originally from Adelaide, now firmly based in England, and they'd become an item. *Great word, item,* he wrote. *It has such warmth when you're a part of one, and this time I believe there won't be an unhappy ending. Romantic music over closing credits, and the joyful couple walk off into the sunset, I hope. But I'll keep you posted.*

She passed the letter to Hugh, who smiled over it, which pleased Kate, for it was rare lately that he smiled. The cab on the rank was no longer an amusing metaphor; there were a great many barristers feeling the pinch of a minor recession, none of them more than Hugh. Some were returning to work as solicitors: he was trying to resist this defeatist move, but she knew it was constantly on his mind.

It was doubly ironic, because of her own surprising ascent. There was a total transformation in their lives, in which she had become the major earner. After the first few years, her job at Montgomery & Associates had led to a post as secretary to one of the partners, then advancement as private assistant to the head of the firm, Edward Montgomery, and finally the astonishing day when Mr Monty, as he was familiarly known, had offered her the position of office manager. Her letters to Damien about this became cautious – she could write about the thrill of the promotion and her move to the top floor with a brilliant harbour view – but did not want to emphasise Hugh's lack of work and his growing melancholy.

Like most people, Kate had always assumed barristers were the stars of the legal system and the ones who earnt big money, but she now knew that while a small group of famous names made huge incomes at the bar, there were many more who struggled. In times of recession like the present there was a lack of common law work, as well as greatly diminished commercial litigation. As a result there were a growing number of barristers without chambers – barristers who could no longer afford the costs of this permanence and met their clients in coffee shops or clubs. Those who aspired to a wig and gown, it seemed, had to be brilliant or lucky. Most importantly, they needed instructing solicitors to brief them for court appearances. But Kate found that not even Roger Montgomery, Hugh's closest friend, could help in this regard.

'I've tried,' Roger told her one day when they lunched together. 'But you know I'm just a cog in the firm. My father runs the place like a bloody dictator.'

'A benevolent despot,' Kate suggested, for she owed her own rapid promotion to Mr Monty's belief in her.

'Benevolent to some, a bastard to others,' Roger insisted. 'He's decided Hugh doesn't have an energetic-enough style in court. He likes forceful, aggressive counsel, so Hugh's not on our list. I've tried to suggest him to other solicitors, but they all tell me if he's that good, then why isn't your own firm instructing him?'

'It's unfair,' Kate said heatedly.

'I know it's unfair. You know it is. Try telling my pa, who's a man of strong opinions. It's doubly ironic that you're so highly esteemed by the old bugger. Must make things difficult at home.'

It would, Kate thought, with a less charitable man. Hugh professed to be pleased with her success, even though he had finally bowed to pressure and sublet his place in chambers and was now trying to work from home. It was not a good career move, she knew, and had argued against it. If he stayed in chambers he might receive referrals from other barristers. Or, Hugh said with a wry smile, he might spend each day busily employed in doing the crossword. It was the one shadow in her life, that wry smile.

She knew how much the increasing years of failure were hurting him.

It was during this time that Damien's joyful letter arrived with news that he and Ingrid were to be married. He'd suggested they elope to Paris, but Ingrid's parents had flown post-haste from Adelaide with big plans. As a result she and Hugh would shortly receive an invitation to St Benedict's Church in Chelsea (even the Barclays from Adelaide found they couldn't book Westminster Abbey, he put in a handwritten aside), followed by a reception at the Hyde Park Hotel. He knew Kate would not be able to come and, much as he would like to see her, he was spared her reaction on seeing him in morning dress and topper. *Looking like a dill*, he wrote, *but a happy dill with a daft look on his face because of being madly in love with the bride.*

The weekend following receipt of their invitation Kate went looking for a wedding present, and had almost given up when she went into an art gallery run by a friend and there on the wall facing her was the perfect answer. A graphic oil painting of storm clouds over Long Reef and the Basin: it cost more than twice what she'd intended to spend, but was so evocative she felt sure Damien would love it. She brought it home and hung it on the wall, deciding she and Hugh would enjoy it for a few days before she wrapped and sent it.

'It might make him homesick,' Hugh warned, but Kate said he was doing far too well to come home. She knew this from the increasing plaudits in the local press. Australia loves to lay claim to our achievers overseas, she thought, wondering if Damien's father was still alive and surprised at his son's success.

That weekend was warm and sunny, typical spring weather,

and Kate and Hugh spent it working together in the garden. It was something they both enjoyed, especially at this, their favourite time of year. The shrubs they'd planted when they first moved in had now thoroughly matured, and the result was a brilliant display of foliage that not only transformed the look of the property, but created a colourful screen that increased its privacy. In the streets around them things were continuing to change, and seven days a week now there were builders at work. New house frames were being erected as old homes were demolished; the clatter of hammers and the snap of nail guns was a familiar sound.

A car pulled up at the bottom of their driveway. Kate knew the man who got out and walked up the sloping path towards her. He was a local estate agent with links to a developer, and several times had attempted to talk to them about the sale of their property. He wore a lightweight summer suit, the armpits of which were damp with sweat, and sported a panama hat, removing it with a rather overdone gesture as he approached. His name was Howard Miller.

'Mrs Forrester,' he called cheerfully, 'what a simply splendid day God has given us.'

'Yes, hasn't he, Mr Miller,' she said, while trying to think of how to get rid of him. But Howard Miller, who liked to be called Howie, was not easily discouraged.

'I've been researching you,' he announced to her, as if he was the bearer of good tidings. 'All in here,' he opened a file he carried, and from it seemed to know exactly how long ago they'd bought the property and the price paid for it. He was keen to explain the great opportunity it presented, and started to elaborate on this as Hugh finished pruning a bougainvillea and came to join them.

'Just dropped in for a chat,' Miller said, and tucked the file beneath his left arm while vigorously shaking hands with Hugh. 'Explaining to the lady wife how you could make a tidy profit on your investment.'

'And I was about to explain the answer is thanks for telling us, but no thanks,' was Kate's prompt reply, to whom the description 'lady wife' was anathema.

'I don't mean now' – the agent swiftly changed his sales pitch in the face of her resistance – 'but in a few years the area will be even more population intensive. It'll be all villas and townhouses. And you'd make a nice killing . . . after all, they could fit at least six new homes on this block.'

'What sort of money are we talking about – with this killing?' It was Hugh who posed the question.

'At least twice what you paid, easily,' Miler estimated. 'But I'd be happy to do a free valuation and give you some figures to consider.'

'It's still no thanks, Mr Miller.'

'But Mrs Forrester . . .'

'I have to tell you,' Kate interrupted him, this time close to losing patience, 'that I love this house. It's not a commodity we bought to make a profit. And I can't bear the thought of it being bulldozed to make way for new villas, let alone six of them. The idea of our home being crushed into rubble and loaded on trucks to be dumped somewhere and used for landfill makes me shudder.'

'Just as well not everyone is as sentimental,' the agent replied, 'or there'd be no such thing as progress.'

She sent him on his way, suggesting he and his developer friends progress the rest of the district and leave them alone. Miller insisted on them taking his card, in case they changed their minds. When Kate shook her head at this it was Hugh who accepted it.

'Bloody man,' Kate said, 'he's a serial pest. None of his business what we paid. We didn't buy it off him.'

Hugh was more reflective. 'I suppose we could've let him rattle off some figures,' he said as the agent drove away. 'Possibly fanciful, but if we got a really big price we could always buy somewhere else and be mortgage-free.'

'Darling, I don't want to live anywhere else. Do you?'

'Well, no,' he answered after a slight pause. 'But it would make the bank happy.'

'Bugger the bank. The bank is rich enough not to need our help.' Kate tucked her arm in his, and they walked back to where he'd been working on the bougainvillea. 'I want us to be the happy ones. And we are happy here, aren't we?'

'Of course.'

'And Juliet loves it. All her school friends live close by.'

'We all love it,' Hugh agreed. 'It's that wretched mortgage . . . and the great bloody whack we pay each month that hardly seems to reduce the size of the loan.'

'We can cope,' Kate assured him.

But they both knew she was the one who would do the coping, and she realised it was humiliating him. His complete failure as a barrister had become a double-edged defeat; he had totally lost confidence in himself. What's more, she had come to believe that, although he did his best never to show it, her success at Montgomery & Associates was another open wound. But what could she do about it? Even though old Mr Monty paid her well, they were just barely keeping ahead. Perhaps the house actually was an albatross; as much as she loved it, would selling it and freeing themselves of all trace of debt help to energise Hugh?

'Tell you what,' she said that night in bed, 'why don't we give it another year in this house. See how we are then. The interest rates might always go down . . .'

'Or up.' He tried to say it with a smile, to suggest he was not being overly pessimistic.

'Or up,' Kate agreed, 'and if that happens we'll contemplate a move, though perhaps we'll deal with someone a bit nicer than Howie Miller. That can be Plan B. Plan A is that we stay here for two more years till Juliet finishes school, then maybe think about a smaller house or even a unit, and have a fat bank account. And you, my love, could reclaim your chambers and give it another go. Is that fair?'

'You'd hate moving.'

'Not if it makes you happy,' Kate said.

'You make me happy,' he replied, 'no matter where we live.'

Chapter 16

Damien's next letter came from Venice, where he and Ingrid were on their honeymoon.

My dear Kate,

It is a wonderfully thoughtful present – one I will treasure because each time I look at it I remember my summer childhood on that beach, and also the day of our meeting at the barbecue on my cousin's lawn. It will hang in my study and remind me of those remote ambitions and dreams that seem, astonishingly, to have come true.

Venice is a delight. We did the tourist bit and took gondolas where the boatman feels obliged to sing 'O Sole Mio', but now we prefer to go by vaporetto, which are water buses that take you anywhere at half the cost and without the singing!

The wedding went well, despite morning dress and topper. Ingrid's parents in Adelaide have a share of a small vineyard in the Barossa, so we've promised to come and visit them. Be sure to bring the grandkids, they said, but we plan to have a few kid-free years while Ingrid gets on with her career, so the visit may be a while off yet. All my best to you, Hugh and Julie. Imagine her now at high school! The mind boggles how time passes; we've reached George Orwell's dreaded 1984 without the world descending into

*chaos or anarchy, but I'll be thirty-five this year. A relentless reminder I'm
halfway through Shakespeare's seven ages.*

As always,

Damien

Sometimes, in the days when she still occupied an office on the top floor of the building in Macquarie Street with its view of the Opera House and harbour, Kate tried to put an exact date on when these regular letters had come to an end. When, in fact, Christmas cards had replaced their airmail exchange, and become the staple by which they managed to keep in touch.

There were still occasional letters, of course, but as the situation with Hugh's lack of work became increasingly acute, Kate found it more and more difficult. The communication with Damien had always been a friendly exchange of family news; with her life now much less congenial, the brevity of Christmas cards felt easier. But even these began to seem like a rather arid exchange; the brief messages – polite, dutiful and clichéd – became nothing more than a few rushed words in order to catch the December mail. Quite soon even the cards became sporadic, then simply stopped altogether.

She could remember the date. The Christmas of 1987, just before the bicentenary; the year Juliet sat for her HSC. A few weeks after this on Australia Day, from the very same office windows, she and Hugh had watched the entry into Sydney Harbour of the high-masted tall ships, an enactment of the arrival of the First Fleet. Along with a million and a half others, they had celebrated the two-hundredth anniversary spectacular, where the Prince of Wales had addressed the crowd on the forecourt of what had been the scrap of land named for Bennelong, Aboriginal friend of the first governor and trophy native taken to be paraded in London.

She could recall how Prince Charles had told the crowd in front of the Opera House, '*As history goes, two hundred years is really a heartbeat, yet look around you and see what has happened in that time. A whole new free people. The people of a country called Australia.*' While her friends were not all monarchists or enthusiastic about Charlie, they enjoyed the words.

After that she and Hugh had gone to join Roger Montgomery, his wife Anna and a bunch of friends for dinner. Later they'd all trouped back to Kate's office to drink champagne and watch the massive fireworks display, where the Harbour Bridge seemed incandescent and the sky was ablaze with colour. Juliet and two of her friends had arrived to witness this, celebrating the end of school and planning their gap year and a long backpacking trip overseas.

She remembered the night so vividly. January the 26th, 1988.

The last good moments in what became a harrowing year. A few weeks later Hugh had experienced a dizzy spell at breakfast, but seemed better by that afternoon. She had suggested a visit to their doctor, but he dismissed the idea, declaring he felt sure it was nothing. Later in the day he seemed in good spirits, pouring over maps and tourist brochures, helping Juliet plan her trip, even driving she and her friends to the airport when they left at the end of the month.

Six weeks later he had a fall in the shower, and she had helped him stumble out of the bathroom and led him to the bed to lie down and rest. She was determined this time the doctor must be called; Hugh seemed to be having trouble walking, and his speech was slightly confused. She rang the office to warn them she would be late, made him a cup of tea and took it into the bedroom. The shock of what she saw almost made her drop the cup; he was awake and struggling to talk, but only managing to make sounds she could not understand, while vainly trying to move his right arm. She could see at once he had no control over it.

She rang their local doctor. His receptionist said he was busy with a patient but would call back.

'It's an emergency,' Kate said urgently. 'He can't speak, and seems hardly able to move.'

'Just a minute,' she was told, and waited in growing fear and frustration until the receptionist came back to tell her what she'd already begun to realise, that she must call emergency and ask for North Shore Hospital to send an ambulance.

Panic made her fumble through the phone book looking for the right number until she remembered it was triple zero. Her ineptitude both angered and distressed her. The emergency call seemed to take far too long, a calm emotionless voice asking her to explain the symptoms she had witnessed, then to give careful details of her address.

'It's easy to find,' she said anxiously.

'We need the name of the nearest cross street,' came the answer, and for an insane moment, despite all the years she had lived here, she could not remember it. She kept rushing to the bedroom to tell Hugh an ambulance was coming, but was unsure any longer if he could still register what she was saying.

When it did arrive there was more delay as the paramedics debated on how best to transfer him to the ambulance. She wanted to scream, but tried to tell herself they were being conscientious. When she sat in the back with Hugh they drove fast and used the siren all the way to the hospital in St Leonard's. She knew it was essential and commonsense, but the sound of it induced in her a heightened sense of alarm.

Kate was left in the emergency ward while Hugh was placed on a hospital trolley and taken for tests. An ECG, someone told her; there'd be a neurological examination, another said; the whole day felt full of kindly and well-meaning people telling her to relax because he was in good hands. But she couldn't relax, and the longer the wait for news the more stressful it became. In the end it was late afternoon, and she began to realise they'd forgotten she was still there. A young doctor came to apologise, and to confirm Hugh had had a stroke. They'd admitted him and he was sedated and in intensive care. The doctor asked if there were there any other relatives who should be advised.

Our daughter, Kate said, except there was no way to contact her. Juliet and her two friends were on their overseas trip, at present somewhere in Asia, then in a month or two would be heading to Europe. She'd already received postcards from Thailand, and doubtless there would soon be others from India, then Spain, France and ultimately England, but she had no forwarding address until after Easter. By then Juliet was hoping to reach Athens where her grandmother was eagerly waiting to see her. Kate could do nothing except phone Sofia that night with the news, report that Hugh was in hospital, and tell her not to worry.

'Of course I'll worry,' Sofia replied, as if the mere thought of her not worrying might suggest she was uncaring.

'I'd prefer you didn't, Mama. It doesn't help.'

'Why shouldn't I worry? You'll worry, so will Michel when I tell him. And Juliet – at her age I certainly worry about her travelling all alone like this.'

'For goodness sake, Mama, she's with friends. And she's not a child, she's eighteen. You were married at that age.'

'Don't remind me,' Sofia retorted, then added, 'but if you think about it, Katerina, that's a good reason for all of us to worry even more. God knows what sort of men she might meet in some places. And if she's backpacking, she should be ringing you from phone boxes each week, just to keep in touch.'

'Mama, can't you understand these girls have gone off to see the world, not look for phone boxes to call home? Besides, calls to Australia are not only expensive but awkward because of the time difference. We didn't ask her to keep in touch because we didn't expect trouble. She would have no idea anything's happened.' Oh God, she thought, I don't need this, and realised she had missed her mother's reply. 'Sorry, Mama, I didn't hear that.'

'I said it must be possible to trace her.'

'How? I can hardly go alerting Interpol.'

'I don't see why not. What else are they good for?'

'Listen to me, please. Will you listen, Mama?'

'Of course I'll listen.'

'Good. I want you to realise that I've been assured he's in no immediate danger. If she does happen to call me, I'll tell her that. If she happens to phone you by chance, give her the news but say there's nothing she can do. He's being well looked after.'

'That's good,' Sofia said. 'He's not old . . . he shouldn't have a thing like a stroke, not at his age. He can't be much over fifty.'

'He's forty-eight, Mama,' Kate corrected her, thinking what the hell had that got to do with it, and wishing she'd never made the phone call.

'Much too young,' came Sofia's voice. 'So think about this. Maybe it isn't a stroke; after all, doctors act like they're God, but they can be wrong. You keep me informed, my darling, and please for Christ's sake stop calling me Mama.'

Kate hung up, and despite her anxiety could not help wondering

217

what would happen when Juliet reached Athens and called Sofia Grandma. Her mother, she thought, would go ballistic.

It was the little things that were so difficult. Things normally taken for granted; unexceptional things like conversation. When one person could talk and the other had no means of reply, words that were once such an important link became an encumbrance, a liability.

Kate took a week off from Montgomery & Associates, and when Hugh showed no signs of improvement she took several more weeks, spending each day sitting at his bedside. She'd persuaded the hospital to move him into a single room, and when asked if she had private health cover because it would be costly, told them it didn't matter. They could afford it, she asserted. In fact they'd opted out of their health fund after Juliet finished school, deciding Medicare would cover their future needs.

Hugh was conscious most of the time, but unable to respond when she spoke to him, except by a slight nod or a shake of his head. Even this seemed difficult some days. As his left side was unaffected, Kate tried to work out an easier way for him to answer questions. A clenched hand for yes, an open palm for no. As for a response like 'I don't know', she scratched her head and said to him she simply didn't know how to frame a reply for that. When he blinked his eyes several times and she realised he was suggesting this as his answer, she felt close to tears because he was trying so hard to help her.

'That's brilliant,' she said, 'so we've got our semaphore system working. We ought to patent it for other cases.'

He clenched his hand to agree, and tried to smile.

Most days she brought the morning papers and read aloud the current news to him. In the Middle East, Iraq and Iran were again at war. The Queen arrived in Australia to open the new Parliament House. Steffi Graf won Wimbledon, beating Martina Navratilova. And in Queensland the Fitzgerald enquiry called the former premier Joh Bjelke-Petersen to answer questions about corruption.

Sometimes, disinterested in these events, he fell asleep. Whenever this happened Kate continued reading, determined he would wake to hear her voice. One day, in an attempt to rouse his attention in something different, she brought in a book. It was a thriller called *The High Commissioner* by Jon Cleary, a favourite of hers.

She showed him the cover. 'Have you read it?' she asked.

No, he answered, by showing his open palm.

'Do you think you'll like it?'

He blinked his eyes to reply that he didn't know.

'Listen to the opening lines,' she asked him, and read aloud: '"We want you to go to London, the Premier said, and arrest the High Commissioner for murder."' She looked up. 'Like me to go on?'

He nodded and at the same time clenched his left hand. A double yes was the answer, and another attempt to smile.

'It's becoming rather difficult,' George Haines told Kate. The tall, gaunt and almost skeletal senior partner had taken over as chairman when its founder Edward Montgomery died. In the office he was surreptitiously called 'the wraith' or 'the long stream of pelican shit'. 'We realise this is a most distressing period, and it's quite understandable that you wish to spend more time at the hospital, but on the other hand . . .'

He was a man who rarely completed a sentence, leaving it poised as if presuming his meaning was clear. It was a technique that saved him the unpleasant task of being forthright.

On the other hand, Kate knew, was his way of inferring that he and the senior partners were becoming impatient of her bedside vigil, now in its fourth week. Some of them had formerly opposed her rapid promotion under old Mr Monty, and doubtless still did.

'I'm sure he's in very capable care,' Haines said, 'and everything possible is being done. After all, we hear he's now in a stable condition, and that being so . . . well, I'm sure we can rely on you . . .'

Another broken sentence, she thought, as he bestowed what was meant to be a benevolent smile and walked off, his attitude suggesting the message had been delivered and he was sure it would be understood. She wanted to tell the Wraith that a stable condition merely meant Hugh was alive without the help of machines, still unable to speak and clearly frightened of the future. From the nurses she knew he was listless and disconsolate when she was not there. One of them said his pulse rate radically improved the moment she walked in. Whether that was true or not, she knew her daily presence was important to him. But the senior partner had virtually given her Hobson's choice: loyalty to the firm or to her husband.

What to do? she wondered. She could not risk losing her job. They had precious little savings, and nothing of any value that she could sell. At times they had lived precariously, but never with the prospect of a crisis like this. The hospital bill was going to be considerable, and she could not have guessed when they gave up private insurance how badly they would one day need it.

～

Alistair Marshall was a bank manager in his forties, a brisk man who had a neat moustache and was in the habit of steepling his hands at times of pleasure or anticipation. He did this before rising from his desk to welcome Kate. It was said in the bank that he rather fancied her; most of the staff agreed he had an eye for all good-looking women clients, and Kate Forrester certainly came into this category.

'Mrs Forrester,' he said, and shifted a chair in front of his desk as he invited her to sit down.

'Mr Marshall.' She gave him her best smile. 'Thank you for seeing me so promptly.'

'Always a pleasure,' he replied. 'And how is our house?'

It was his customary greeting now, so totally different from her first time in this office when she and Hugh came to apply for a mortgage. Kate could remember him ridiculing the place, declaring it to be old and dilapidated, and clearly not worth the price they were paying. Several years later, when the rooms were all renovated, the entire house repainted by their weekends of shared work, they had invited him for a drink and enjoyed the expression on his face as he saw the transformation.

Since then he'd come to regard it as an astute purchase. Three years ago, he had even approved an increase in their loan to cover some of the extra costs they'd incurred. It added to the length of the mortgage, but had given them money in their bank account. That was when he had begun his jocular referral to it as 'our house'. Recalling that, and looking for an answer to her predicament, was the reason why she had come to see him.

'I was extremely sorry to hear of your husband's illness,' he said. 'I do hope there's been some improvement.'

'There is,' Kate assured him. 'A little bit each day,' she added, trying to conceal her relief as he produced the documents for her to sign. Kate thanked him, saying that she'd told Hugh of the bank's generosity. It had pleased him, and solved their immediate problems.

Alistair Marshall chuckled, and waved an admonishing finger as he pointed out generosity was not strictly the intention. Banks could not afford generosity. He was pleased he could increase the mortgage as the value of her home had risen, but the interest rate was something he could not control. Nor the rather strict conditions.

'Blame the government,' he said.

'I will,' Kate replied as she signed to repay the new mortgage at the current rate of seventeen percent. It was adjacent to a clause stating if the mortgage was not repaid when due, the bank was entitled to take possession of the property and sell it to recoup their losses.

'You've done what?' Mandy looked at her and hoped she was joking.

'I've resigned from Montgomery's,' Kate said. 'They literally gave me no choice. It was the firm or Hugh, so I found it easy to choose. And Alistair Marshall at the bank has made it possible.'

'Jesus Christ,' Mandy said when she heard the details, 'you are such a financial drongo, kitten. Don't you realise the banks are not charitable institutions? The buggers will own the house one of these days, if you keep re-mortgaging.'

'One of these days is a long way off,' Kate replied, 'and in the meantime when Hugh comes out of hospital, I'll be able to take care of him.'

'Did it never occur to you, if you'd kept your job you could've paid a full time nurse to live in?'

'It occurred to me. But he doesn't respond well to strangers looking after him. I've seen that in the hospital. So don't give me an argument, Mandy. It's done.'

But Mandy was not content to leave it at that. She was shocked Kate had given up after such a spectacular rise to her present position in the law firm. 'You've chucked a job most people would kill for.'

'To take care of Hugh.' She seemed suddenly diffident, speaking so quietly Mandy had to strain to listen. 'And that matters more than any job, no matter how good. Because he was the one – with your help, I hasten to add – who saved me from ending up in some shady hospital where they'd have given me a bed if I gave up my daughter in return.' She paused for a moment as if thinking back to that time. 'You and him, remember?'

'Yes,' Mandy said, 'but listen —'

'No, *you* listen,' Kate replied. 'I want you to understand. He looked after me. We had all those good years bringing up Juliet together. Wonderful years. Then things went haywire with his career. Maybe he was wrong wanting to be a barrister, but it's not fair to say that. Besides, I happen to believe given the chance he would've been a good one. I think the stress over the lack of bloody work brought on the trauma, and may have caused the stroke. Whatever the cause, it's now my turn to look after him.'

Mandy was silent for a moment, trying to absorb this. It had been almost twenty years since they had met and worked together in the coffee lounge opposite Museum Station.

'You always managed to surprise me,' she said at last. 'You got over that selfish bastard Joshua and made a new life. Whereas Hugh

223

is neither selfish nor a bastard. Maybe if he was he'd have been a success at the bar. Instead he's a sweet, gentle guy. You may not agree, but I think you love him more than you ever did that beach bum.'

Beach bum? Kate was reflective that night. Maybe that's all Joshua was to Mandy, who had only ever heard the worst side of him. She knew nothing of the affection he'd felt for his grandmother, or the pain he'd experienced growing up in that house after his mother died. There were some tender moments to balance against the cruel betrayal.

The day on the railway platform, the angry tears about the treasured photos with their heads cut off . . . Even the boy ridiculed at boarding school because of the unfashionable place where he lived. But, on the other hand . . .

On the other hand, she would never have had the secure and happy life she'd led with Hugh. So Mandy was right about who she loved the most. And it was a small price to pay, giving up her job, and taking care of him for as long as it took.

Chapter 17

At the end of the following month Hugh was pronounced fit enough to return home. Kate was given the news by the junior attending doctor, who said there was some progress, enough to suggest he might be happier in his own environment, which all sounded rather detached and clinical to her. She felt unsure about it, and asked to speak to the senior consultant. He confirmed there was very little more they could do for him, and physiotherapy and home care seemed the best solution.

When? she asked.

Tomorrow, the senior doctor suggested. No point in keeping him in over the long weekend, when there'd be only minimum staff.

But when she started to make arrangements to collect him by car, it was deemed better for the patient that he be sent home in an ambulance. So she waited at the house for it to arrive.

'You know what I think?' she said to Mandy.

'No – but I suspect you're going to tell me.'

'I think he's not really well enough to leave hospital at all. I get a nasty feeling that they're discharging patients too early, because they need the beds.'

Mandy didn't like to say so, but she was inclined to agree. They were both aware Hugh still had difficulty in speaking clearly and was unable to walk without help. His right side was still virtually paralysed.

Looking at him as he was helped from the ambulance, Kate felt confirmed in her fear. She saw him try to take an awkward step, but by then the attendants had the wheelchair ready, and they carefully but firmly helped him into it. She watched Hugh's attempt to remonstrate, his effort to assert his independence to stand upright, and remembering how lively and active he was when they first met – how he loved to vault into his beloved MG – she thought her heart would break.

In the local village people spoke to her, offering their concern. How was he, her nice quiet husband, who they often used to see doing the weekly shopping? Or sometimes collecting their daughter – who must be nearly grown up by now. They expressed surprise on learning that Juliet's school days were well and truly over, and hoped that Hugh was making good progress.

'It's slow but steady,' she replied to them. It was becoming easier to tell this lie. Despite her care and having a physiotherapist visit the house daily, there was little improvement. Kate did her best to appear composed, but there were times when things seemed to be falling apart. The strain of caring for him rarely varied. From the moment she woke in Juliet's room, having given him their own bedroom, each day was long and exhausting. Hugh had to be washed, he had to be helped to the toilet; he was often fretful, impatient with himself and perhaps with the whole world, she thought, at being so helpless.

Sometimes when the weather was warm that winter she took him in his wheelchair out into the garden. Occasionally a neighbour, Daphne Ennis, came in to have coffee with Kate and brought delicacies she'd baked to tempt Hugh. Daphne was in her early sixties, the widow of a former diplomat, and one of the few remaining residents who had been in The Crescent almost as long as Kate. With the rash of development and abundance of townhouses, there were many new neighbours.

One, calling himself *Captain* Victor Henderson, had already antagonised several of the residents in the few months he'd been there, and had sent Kate a letter complaining about the height of her gum trees.

'An odious man,' Daphne commented, when they met at their respective mail boxes on the roadside and stayed to chat. 'Complains to the council all the time. About your trees, about my fence, about bloody nearly everything. Steps out each morning and evening for a walk, as if he's on a parade ground.'

'I've seen him marching past,' Kate said. 'His poor wife probably has to salute when he arrives home.'

She took the mail to show Hugh. The only item of interest was a yet another postcard from Thailand. A picture of a pagoda in Chang Mai with Juliet's scribbled note, sent so many weeks ago that it had clearly gone astray. Kate was beginning to feel anxious, wishing Juliet would phone, or else give an address so she could make contact. Then, a few days later, in the haphazard way of postcards, came another one with a photo of Piccadilly Circus. It seemed she and her friends had skipped Spain and Portugal, had found jobs in London working in a nightclub, and plans were all being hastily reversed. They might not start their tour of the continent till later. Juliet had sent a card to Sofia telling her that it meant she would probably not reach Athens until July or August, but still in time for the European summer.

This had prompted an urgent phone call to Kate, Sofia choosing her own convenient time just after dinner in Athens, which was 2 a.m. in Australia, declaring it ridiculous an eighteen-year-old was not only allowed to travel alone like this, but was permitted to work in a nightclub.

But she's not alone, Kate had sleepily tried to point out. There are three girls in a group, and at the age of eighteen in this country they are adults. She attempted to point out that she had told her mother this before, but Sofia had seemed unable to recall it.

She also said the postcard from Juliet had called her Gran, which irritated her greatly.

There were times when Kate felt a desperate need to get out of the house. At the Cremorne cinema was a film she dearly wanted to see. *A Fish Called Wanda* was the year's comedy hit, nominated for an Academy Award and featuring some of her favourite actors. Mandy was not free so Kate sat alone amid an afternoon audience, laughing at the antics of John Cleese, then drove home feeling guilty she had left Hugh with a carer, even though it was someone known to him.

It had been difficult to find a suitable person for the rare occasions when she had to leave the house for a few hours. Strangers definitely upset him, so she had been forced to rely on a woman they both knew; Mrs Wheatley had once been a babysitter for Juliet, and a house-sitter in the times when they'd taken holidays. She was not an ideal choice: she talked non-stop – mainly about a growing disaffection for her husband – and like many verbose people rarely listened to anyone else, but she was available at short notice and at least Hugh recognised her.

'He had a nice sleep,' Mrs Wheatley greeted her as she arrived home, 'but I thought if he slept too long he wouldn't get any proper rest tonight, so I woke him up with a cup of tea. Only he didn't want it.'

Oh brilliant, Kate thought, but she smiled and said not to worry.

'Just moved his left hand and shook his head, so I knew that meant to take it away. Sad he can't talk, Mrs Forrester, but then he always was a quiet one. Not fond of a chat, like you and me.'

Speak for yourself, Kate was on the verge of replying, but stopped herself in time.

'What I mean is' – the carer was relentless in full flow – 'he hardly used to say a word when I babysat your Juliet . . . mind you, that takes us back a bit, doesn't it? Is there any more news from her?'

'Not yet,' Kate said, and in haste absently paid her for three hours, although it had been just over two. Mrs Wheatley registered the extra amount with a nod, put the money in her handbag and said it was always a pleasure to spend time here; it reminded her of when little Juliet was a tiny tot. Not so little now, of course, travelling around the world, and what a pity there was no way to contact her.

'There isn't, I'm afraid,' Kate said, and felt an immense relief as Mrs Wheatley opened the kitchen door, the first stage of a move in the direction of her car parked outside the garage.

'Hooroo.' It had always been her inevitable parting word.

'Hooroo, Mrs Wheatley. Don't forget next week.'

'Shan't forget, dear. I'm like an elephant; I never forget a thing. Three afternoons next week, from four till about seven o'clock.'

'That's right. The meetings are at Montgomerys, and I'll leave you a number.'

'At your old firm?' she said, surprised. 'I thought you'd left 'em.'

'I have left. But this was something they asked me to attend. The meetings should be over each night by seven. I hope that won't interfere with any of your arrangements at home.'

'With *him*?' Mrs Wheatley said, with withering scorn. 'Too bad. He can get his own tea . . . *if* he's home. Be at the bowling club though, won't he? On the pokies, emptying his pockets while he gets as full as a boot. That's the story of our married life, Mrs Forrester.'

She departed with a last wave and Kate heard her car start. She went to the living room where Hugh was lying on a portable day-bed with his eyes shut. She kissed him on the forehead and he opened them to look at her.

'I nearly got the story of her life again.'

He managed a nod and a smile.

'Sorry she woke you, darling.'

He shook his head, the nearest he could come to replying that it didn't matter. Their ability to communicate was still limited, but at least his mind was unimpaired. She was grateful for that small mercy.

'She's coming again next week, when I have to attend meetings at the office. Remember I told you about that? The merger meetings?'

Another nod, a tired smile this time. Clearly the proposed merger of Montgomery & Associates with another big law firm was no longer of interest to him.

She took his hand and held it to her lips. At least she'd solved their financial problems for the immediate future with Alistair Marshall, and on top of that the generous fee she would earn for a few hours' attendance at her old firm was an additional help. If only there could be a breakthrough . . . It was perfectly possible, one of the doctors had told her. A stroke was a disturbance in the blood vessels that supply the brain. A cerebrovascular accident, he'd called it. It could improve with supportive care, physio and occupational therapy.

But Hugh was having that every day, and there was no discernable improvement. Not yet . . . but it was too soon to give up hope. Maybe tomorrow there'd be a change. Perhaps if something startling occurred, some unexpected event . . . like Juliet walking in the door to say 'Hello, Dad'. If only they knew where she was. If she would just ring up, instead of the avalanche of postcards. But, of course, they'd told her not to waste her money.

'I had another call from Sofia last night,' she said, and saw Hugh's eyes show a flicker of interest. 'Two o'clock in the morning again; I keep telling her to ring at a decent hour, but she's as bad as Mrs Wheatley – she never listens. I'm afraid there's still no word of our roving daughter, but I'm sure she's having a ball . . . somewhere in England, or Scotland, or maybe Ireland . . .'

He nodded in agreement with this, reached for her hand and held it to his own lips. Kate felt a tremor of excitement. It was still the left hand, the one that was unaffected, but the abrupt movement, the sudden loving gesture – these were new. Perhaps it was a hopeful sign. When the physiotherapist came, she'd ask her if it was a sign.

In the boardroom it was growing late, and they seemed unable to reach a decision. Kate sat there, wishing she'd never been talked into taking part, while becoming concerned about the time. This was the third and decisive meeting of the partners, and the expressed intention was to remain in there until agreement had been reached, but that was proving elusive. Ever since the death of Edward Montgomery the previous year, a merger with other large law firms had been planned. The intention was to create a huge legal multinational. But the ambitious proposal was causing bitter division, that was apparent from the blunt opinions and the body language of those around the table.

Roger and several of the other younger partners were implacably against the merger, but they were clearly a minority. Most of his family and all the senior partners were in favour. Kate was in secret sympathy with Roger's stance, but had no opportunity to influence opinion or to vote. Despite no longer being a member of the staff, she had been asked to attend and keep the minutes.

'Just the three evenings,' George Haines had proposed, 'the first two for discussion and the airing of opinions, and the third one to vote. Of course there will be a fee, within reason, needless to say . . .'

She had declined the offer. The next day there had been a phone call from James Montgomery, Edward's brother, asking her to reconsider. And before she could refuse again, he had suggested ten thousand dollars to cover her time and circumspection.

'We need someone we can trust,' he explained. 'The matter is too sensitive for anyone on the staff and must remain confidential.'

To Kate it seemed that every member of the staff would know; the very secrecy, as well as her sudden reappearance, would alert them. But ten thousand dollars was an inducement she could hardly refuse, and so Mrs Wheatley had been recruited to mind Hugh. She glanced at her watch again, and saw it was after eight o'clock.

They were still fiercely arguing. She tried to concentrate, to keep up with recording the minutes. It had been unexpected and rather awkward when, halfway through the night's proceedings, Haines had declared it a closed meeting; there were to be no interruptions in an attempt to get consensus, and a deciding vote would be taken by 8.30.

She wished she could call Mrs Wheatley to explain the delay, but at least the woman was reliable and trustworthy. It was only in the past years that she'd become so garrulous about her husband and his addiction to poker machines and alcohol. Kate felt sorry for her, unable to afford to leave him and too old to find someone else.

'Well, that's it, I believe. All done and dusted,' George Haines said with satisfaction as the meeting ended. Roger had been completely outvoted, the matter was concluded and the firms would be amalgamated. Kate completed the minutes, recording the vote, waited for the details to be signed, then left the room to make a hurried call to Mrs Wheatley, who by the sound of her voice was not well pleased.

'I phoned the number you gave me twice but you were not allowed to be disturbed, they said. Still in the meeting, I was told. There's been some trouble.'

Kate had a moment of alarm, but the trouble was with Mrs Wheatley's husband. She needed to get home urgently, because he was on the rampage again.

'I'll be there as quickly as I can,' Kate promised, only to be given the full story. Bert Wheatley had come home from his bowling club as drunk as a skunk, and had had a bruising encounter with one of their neighbours.

'Wasn't his fault,' Kate was told. The other neighbours had

ganged up, locked him in one of their garden sheds and threatened to call the police. She had to go there to sort things out . . . that was why she'd been trying to get in touch for the past hour.

'Look,' Kate said, to stop the flow of words, knowing she would continue endlessly, 'if Hugh is settled and comfortable, then please go and take care of it.'

'The hide of them!' the other was saying, clearly not hearing what Kate had suggested. 'Locking him in a garden shed . . . I call that taking the law into their own hands, Mrs Forrester . . . and there's going to be trouble, unless I sort it out.'

'Please, Mrs Wheatley, you go straight there and do that.'

'But I couldn't possibly leave your hubby here alone,' was the shocked reply.

'If we both get off the phone right now, then I can be there in fifteen minutes,' Kate insisted. 'Lock the door. Explain to him I'm on my way and he's not to worry.'

She hung up in order to prevent another cascade of words, and hurried to the car park. But it was a busy Friday night and there'd been a multi-car smash on the Cahill Expressway. As a result traffic was clogged and banked up all the way across the Harbour Bridge. Even after finally crossing the bridge and reaching Falcon Street the stream of cars still crawled slowly towards Cammeray, and it was almost an hour before she reached home. Mrs Wheatley's car was gone, which was a blessing. Lights were on inside the house and all seemed well. Kate unlocked the door, called to Hugh to say she was home, and heard a noise she could not identify.

It came again and sounded like a whimper.

'Hugh?' she called again, feeling a sudden cold fear envelop her.

Another noise like a moan. It terrified her.

'Hugh?'

She ran into the living room, where the television had been left on but without any sound. She realised he must have been trying to reach it. He was sprawled on the floor where he had fallen from his wheelchair. His eyes were open, his mouth trying helplessly to frame words he could not seem to utter. She knelt beside him and gathered him in her arms, holding him gently, murmuring entreaties and nursing him like a baby.

She held him until an ambulance came, but by then he was dead.

Chapter 18

The funeral was well attended, but looking at the rows of well-clad lawyers with their solemn faces, Kate felt their presence almost duplicitous. She wished that only Roger, his wife Anna and Mandy were there with her. And Juliet, of course, but she was somewhere in Europe, her last card written on a cross-channel ferry and about to hitchhike to Paris, still oblivious of what had happened.

It felt like a day of terrible regrets. There was her own remorse at being late home that night. And all these sombre-suited solicitors – if only some of them had bothered to think about Hugh when he was alive. Kate was sure the stress of his failure as a barrister had led to this. The pressure of trying to conceal how much he cared, pretending not to notice when former contemporaries became elevated to Queen's Counsels or made into judges had surely been a constant heartache. He had even tried to appear enthusiastic when finally he was obliged to retreat to corporate work, which was a far cry from everything he had hoped to do.

If someone had only given him a chance, she thought – they may not have acquired an aggressive and forceful advocate, but perhaps might have been surprised to find one who was warm and kind and decent. However, combat in the courts, Kate realised sadly, was rarely won by kindness and decency.

She had other regrets; Juliet's absence, for instance – perhaps Sofia had been right about the backpacking trip being foolish, although no one could have predicted this situation. When they had farewelled Juliet at the airport she could still remember Hugh telling her to send them a card from each country, but not to bother calling home unless she had a crisis and needed their help.

'But what if *you* have a crisis, Dad, and need my help?' she'd replied with a wide grin, and Kate recalled how they'd all laughed at the improbability of this, then hugged each other and stood waving until the sliding doors at immigration finally obscured her. The memory of it made her feel a rush of inconsolable grief.

If you have tears . . . Oh God, she thought, this time I have tears. I just don't have a handkerchief to mop them up, and fumbling for one felt first Mandy on one side, and then Anna Montgomery on the other, each slip one into her hand.

I wish this bloody minister would stop droning on, she thought. It was a mistake to get him. The whole awful day was a mistake. It should have been small and private, like their wedding. Roger could have said a few words, told a few jokes about their university days. Mandy could have made them smile with her memories of 'the long black'. Not this tedious attempt to console, to find some validation for his too-short time on earth. And not the dutiful attendance of his uncaring peers.

It should have been just those who really loved him. Most of all me, she thought, whose life he saved when he asked me to sit down and talk to him in the coffee shop all those years ago. And then took me to see his group of important and high-minded people. Nice people, a strange cross-section of concerned older men and women, a bit remote with their wealth and social status, but genuinely disturbed at the way some doctors were intent on steering pregnant girls into certain private clinics that specialised in adoption.

Where would I have been without Hugh? she wondered.

Where would my beloved daughter have been, instead of somewhere in Europe, unaware that her father – the one person who deserved to be called her father, because from the day of her birth he loved her like his own – is lying here dead?

The handkerchiefs she held to her eyes were both soaked as she realised the minister had stopped, people around her were rising, and mercifully it was over.

It was another month before Juliet returned, without ever meeting her grandmother. She had telephoned Sofia from Vienna to say she would get a train to Belgrade, then hitchhike the rest of the way to spend a week with them in Athens. But on hearing the news she cancelled her plans and three days later arrived home, shocked and bewildered at how it had all happened so suddenly.

It was not an easy time for Kate; she had to relive the pain of it all over again, and there were awkward questions about why Hugh had been left alone that night, and no simple answers. The troublesome Mr Wheatley and a traffic jam did not satisfy her devastated daughter.

'But how could she have left him like that? Just because her husband was drunk! He was nearly always drunk.'

'She left because I told her to, darling. I thought I'd be home in a quarter of an hour. Please, Jules . . . hindsight doesn't help. *If* she'd left the television sound on . . . *if* I'd made her wait for me . . . Thinking of what might have been just hurts and can't make a difference. It was a second stroke . . . the doctors said it could've happened at any time.'

Juliet was not consoled. There was a strained and uncomfortable void in the house without Hugh's presence.

The following day they went to lay fresh flowers at the Northern Suburbs cemetery. The memorial plate and its inscription was shiny new.

HUGH FORRESTER
Aged forty-eight
Beloved husband of Kate and loving father of Juliet
1940–1988

Kate knelt and arranged the flowers in one of the small plastic pots supplied for the purpose, while Juliet stood beside her, looking down at the wording. Eventually she stooped and rubbed her fingers lightly across the letters. Kate watched this, wondering what was going through her mind, unsure whether it was too soon to have brought her here.

It was a silent drive home, with Juliet thoughtful, her monosyllabic replies discouraging Kate's attempts to make any conversation. They had almost reached the house when Juliet abruptly turned to her.

'Was that the truth, Mum? Those words you put on the plaque?'

The question took Kate so completely by surprise, she had no time to answer.

'Was he really my father? Because if so, then who was Joshua?'

~

The phone rang for a long time, then a sleepy voice answered in Greek, her mother's voice complaining it was too early for people to ring up and grumbling that she had been woken.

'My turn to wake you, Mama,' Kate said without apology, for she had already been waiting hours because of the time difference and was prepared to wait no longer. 'I want to ask what you thought you were doing.'

'Katerina . . . ?' Her mother sounded alarmed. 'Is it you?'

'Yes, it's me.'

'Please, not more bad news. Is Juliet . . . did she get home, is something wrong?' Anxiety made her sound older, almost querulous.

'Juliet's fine. She's home, but —'

'You nearly give me a heart attack, Katerina. It's the dawn here. Bad news always comes at times like this.'

'I'm sorry,' Kate said determinedly, 'but I have to ask, when she rang from Vienna why did you feel it necessary to tell her about Joshua?'

'But I thought she already knew.' Sofia sounded astonished. 'I felt sure you told her years ago.'

'I chose not to.'

'Why?'

'Because it was my prerogative. I felt it was best.'

'Well, I didn't know that. So it's not my fault.'

'I still don't understand . . . what made you decide you had the right to tell her?'

'When she hears about Hugh she starts crying. I never hear such crying. All I want to do is calm her down. I said it's sad, but you have another father because there's still Joshua.'

Kate sighed. For a moment she was unsure what to say. It was pointless being angry.

'Are you still there, Katerina?'

'I'm still here, Sofia.'

'Did I do wrong? Or maybe you did. You should've told her years ago.' After a pause she asked, 'Were you ever going to tell her?'

'In time.'

'I'm not sure that's true. You leave it all these years. Maybe because of Hugh?'

'He was a good father to her,' Kate said. 'She couldn't have had a better one.'

'But now he's gone. So there's no reason for her not to know. After all, the other is the real father . . . what do they call it? Biological?'

'Yes, biological. He donated his sperm,' Kate said, with a touch of bitterness, 'but doesn't even know she exists.'

'So whose fault is that?'

'Probably mine.' She felt deflated; the call had been pointless, a mistake achieving nothing. 'Never mind, Mama. Go back to sleep.'

'It's too late. Michel's up . . . he's in the kitchen, putting on the coffee already.'

'Sorry I woke you both. Give him my best wishes,' Kate said. She hung up, wondering how to deal with Juliet's perplexity and grief that was so close to anger.

They sat together late that night. Kate talked while Juliet listened about her mother's young life in the 1960s – barely twenty years before her own time of adolescence – but so very different. As she had not heard these intimate details before, she had never realised the polarity in their upbringing.

Kate spared herself nothing; she spoke candidly of things she'd kept buried for years; the shock of being left with a taciturn father who was almost a stranger, the insecurity of a new life as a foreigner, being teased at school until she learnt English, and then at the age of seventeen meeting Joshua on the beach. She admitted how easily she was seduced into losing her virginity below his grandparents' house, and how after that she fell completely in love and believed it was reciprocated.

'Trying to look back objectively, I suppose I was longing for some tenderness in my life, and so I was naïve, an absolute pushover.'

'Mum,' Juliet protested.

'I'm afraid I was, darling. I even thought his friends were my friends because they were polite; it took me a long time to find out a lot of them really didn't like me.'

'Why on earth wouldn't they like you?'

'Because I was a wog . . . that's what you were in those days if you came from almost anywhere except Britain. And my dad was just the chef at the local Greek caff. They were rich kids and he . . . Joshua . . . was their young Adonis. I don't think we used the word charisma then, but he had it in spades.' She hesitated, a frown shadowing her face. 'The former girlfriend he ran off with had been his sexual partner since they were sixteen. That's the sort of dumb Dora I was. I didn't know any of it until long afterwards.'

Juliet was silent for a moment, attempting to imagine what it must have been like. A different girlhood to the warm affectionate atmosphere she'd been brought up in. Not a world she would've liked to inhabit.

'Was the girlfriend the reason he ran away?'

'No.'

'Aren't you going to tell me? I need to know it all, Mum, before I meet him. I think I should meet him.'

'Of course.'

'If I can find him.'

'I'm sure you will. As to why he ran away, one of my friends wrote me a letter. I've always kept it, and I think it explains some things better than I can.' She went into the room she and Hugh had used as a study and returned a few moments later. 'It was written by Damien Raphael . . . he lives in England now.'

'I remember him!' Juliet exclaimed. 'We used to talk about him, sometimes, when I was a schoolkid,' she said as she took the typed sheets of paper. 'And I even went to see a play of his in London.'

'Was it good?'

'Terrific.'

'So is the letter,' Kate said. 'I think you should read it.'

It was warm and sunny the next morning, so they had breakfast in the garden. While Kate fed the kookaburra Juliet sat at the table and re-read the letter. She was glad her mother had kept it; there had been so many questions, so much bewilderment after her grandmother's disclosure. For much of the night after reading it the first time she had remained restlessly awake, trying to imagine what it had been like for Kate as a young schoolgirl being sidelined as a dago, a wog – terms that had never been applied to her – then at seventeen having a love affair and finding herself pregnant and unable to tell anyone, particularly her own father. And, to make it worse, being completely abandoned by Joshua; although to be fair, Juliet thought, no one had known of her pregnancy. But all that time living in a shabby room alone without any money except the little she earnt, and no friends. Not until two people had come to her aid: Mandy, and Hugh Forrester – the man she had grown up believing was her father. She still found herself unable to think of him as anything else. Her father, yet not truly her father.

'Coffee?' Kate said, crossing the lawn with a tray to rejoin her at the table. Juliet handed back the letter.

'I'm glad you let me read it. Damien was really a friend.'

'A friend of mine. Not Joshua's.'

'No.'

'So to be fair, you have to take that into account.' Kate poured the coffee, then handed Juliet a list of names and addresses. 'You might get a different opinion of him from some of these people.'

'Who are they?'

'A few of Joshua's circle from those days. I don't know where they are now, but this might help you to find him. I suggest you try Andy Scott at Collaroy first, if he still lives there. He was one of the nicer guys.'

'Thanks,' Juliet said, and leaned across the table to impulsively kiss her. 'I'll let you know what happens, and how I get on.'

'No, don't. Please don't do that,' Kate said quickly. She took a sip of coffee, realised it was too hot and hastily put it down, feeling as if she'd burnt her mouth. 'I know I should've told you years ago – it was wrong of me. The truth is that I was afraid; I mean it – afraid he'd try to win you away, be the walk-in glamorous dad who could afford presents or nice holidays and I couldn't possibly compete.'

She looked at her daughter across the table, seeing traces of him. The shapely retrousse nose, the way she moved sometimes, or a turn of the head. Not the facile smile or the occasional arrogance, thank God. 'I was selfish,' Kate admitted, and was reflective for a moment. 'But there was Hugh,' she continued quietly. 'It meant such a lot to him, people believing he was your father. Other things disappointed him in his life, but being your dad was never one of them. So I put it off. Year after year while you were growing up I lived with this duplicity, and I think if it hadn't been for your grandmother I might never have told you. But as she said in her own inimical way, Hugh's gone and so he can't be hurt any more.'

She saw Juliet's startled reaction to this, and reached across to take her hand.

'She wasn't being cruel, just . . . well, just typically Sofia. If you ever get to meet her, and I hope some day you will, you'll realise she's rather unique. She can be both infuriatingly impossible and quite endearing, sometimes even at the same moment.' Kate risked another sip of coffee. 'Forget all that. I'm trying to get around to asking something, darling. I want you to do me a favour.'

'What is it, Mum? To do with my . . . with Joshua?'

'Yes. Find him, get to know him; that's your right as his daughter. But leave me out of it. On the day you were born, I made up my mind never to see him again. Not out of anger or spite, but because if I was to have a new life I had to relinquish the past. Well, I've done that. He was the past, and it took an effort to obliterate him, let me tell you. But I did it, and until last night I've barely thought of him. And that's the way I want it to remain. Please?'

'I promise,' Juliet said, and came around the table to envelop her mother in a hug.

Often in the years that followed Kate would wonder whether they had met, but Juliet kept her promise and said nothing. It was soon after this that she found a job as a cadet reporter on a country paper in Victoria, and Kate's own life underwent a radical change.

It happened when Roger Montgomery resigned from the legal firm that had borne his name.

Deciding the big end of town and the jurisprudence they engaged in was no longer his kind of law, he resolved to specialise in immigration cases and asked Kate to join him. She was eager for such a challenge, and realising the salary would be minimal, made another trip to see her bank manager. With that settled, she had a bigger mortgage but enough cash in her account to feel more confident in the future: working to assist refugees whom she could understand and empathise with was exactly what she wanted, and it was without regret she gave up all previous ambitions, exchanging them for a modest desk over a sandwich shop.

Four years later Juliet was working in Auckland, where she became engaged to a young businessman who had been a former All Black rugby star. Determined to give her the kind of wedding she'd denied herself, Kate had persuaded them to be married in Australia and combed her address book to send out invitations.

In the process she came across and hesitated at Damien's name, remembering receiving the invitation to his own wedding. But she hadn't written to him in years. It would be a presumption. He'd become quite famous; she often read about him in the newspapers, and once saw a picture of a smart new house he'd bought somewhere in London, but she no longer knew where to contact him. She did hear that he and his wife had come to Australia on a visit to the wife's parents in the Barossa – there was no mention of children – but by the time she learnt of this the local press reported he was back in London to attend the opening night of his new stage play.

She crossed out the old address and thought it was a pity they'd lost touch, but doubted any longer if they would have anything in common.

PART 4

2001–2002

Chapter 19

It was November 25th, 2001. The night before Kate's fiftieth birthday, and a month since the sinking of the fishing boat known as SIEV X. Other news had overtaken the tragic drowning of three hundred and sixty-five people, almost half of them children, and all mention of it by now had virtually disappeared from the media.

The eve of her birthday brought a message from Athens. If the past decade had changed the methods of communication, Kate thought, the years had seen no variation in her mother. The email wished her love and happiness for tomorrow's big event, but the sentiments expressed were vintage Sofia. *The trouble with you being fifty,* she wrote, *is that it makes me so damned old. It's hard to imagine I'll soon be seventy, and I'm seriously considering the prospect of having a neck tuck and putting my age back ten years.*

'And she'll do it,' Kate told Roger, his wife Anna and Mandy, recounting some of Sofia's past behaviour, and making them laugh at what she had to admit seemed amusing in retrospect. It was a quiet dinner before tomorrow's celebratory party: a relaxed evening with her three closest friends, a contrast to the past stressful month when the amount of work and the flood of people besieging their tiny office had become an increasing problem.

It was impossible to turn anyone away. So many were in acute distress, still unsure if they had relatives on board the sunken boat. In their cramped space over the sandwich shop, she and Roger had been inundated with requests for help in obtaining names of the survivors. But as he was occupied with court attendance most of this work fell to Kate. Ever since the disaster she had spent much of her time seeking information and visiting detainees in Villawood.

She had begun to dread the drive out to the detention centre where the guards now seemed to be deliberately delaying entry procedures. At times it felt to her the more familiar the face the less cordial the attitude, let alone any show of compassion. The worst days were those when she had to tell fretful relatives there was simply no news; she could not verify if those they asked about were alive, or even if they'd been on the SIEV X, as there were no real passenger lists and the names of casualties had become virtually impossible to obtain. The tension this created, and the strain of being the messenger, was becoming intolerable.

There had been a flood of rumours since the tragedy. It was being claimed the smuggler Abu Quassey was just a figurehead; that highly placed Indonesian army officers were the real organisers, involved in a conspiracy to rid their country of 'troublesome' refugees. A staging hotel in Sumatra used to house asylum seekers was allegedly owned by a prominent army general.

Intelligence cables sent by the Australian Federal Police unit based in Jakarta were said to be missing. A claim by survivors that they had sighted two Australian ships that had made no attempt to rescue them was strongly denied by Naval Headquarters. So was a statement that air surveillance patrols had reported no word of the stricken vessel, even though they had been in the area at the time.

Innuendo was rife. There was even talk of a 'disruption program', a tactic used off the Malaysian coast during the period of the Vietnamese boat people in the 1970s, whereby small craft were deliberately sabotaged to halt a flood of refugees. The Foreign Minister was furious in his rebuttal. On radio he declared no sane person would believe an Australian government would stoop to such a thing. Nevertheless there were whispers . . . and as parliament was prorogued because of the impending federal election, these allegations could not be aired in the public forum.

Two weeks after the sinking finally came the election with a predicted result. The terrorist attack on America, together with the drama when the Norwegian ship *Tampa* rescued drowning asylum seekers and was forced by prime ministerial intervention to land them outside territorial waters – these events and the shrill determination to exploit the ensuing headlines had assured victory for the Howard government.

Even SIEV X with its drowned children had been a factor, Kate believed. She felt there was such a large number of people like Victor Henderson who had no shred of moral conscience about the fate of boat people. Her neighbour vilified them openly; others were more discreet and expressed their opinion at the ballot box. There were others still who demonstrated prejudice in a very different way.

The complaints about their office had been growing all year. The mood of the neighbourhood had grown so hostile it could no longer be ignored. The goodwill Kate had established among those in the quiet backstreet village of shops and apartment buildings near the university had run out. There was a time when she would always be greeted by a cheerful hello, by friendly smiles or waves;

now it was a combative stare, an indifferent shrug or an averted gaze.

The office was simply too small; the demand for help too pressing. A stream of new immigration laws and severe tightening of the old ones had caused this. The rights of refugees, in defiance of the United Nations charter, were being altered. A privative clause excluded all chance of an appeal. The courts were in the process of becoming a jungle, and there was a crucial shortage of lawyers either able or willing to take on these cases. The financial rewards were slight, the public odium considerable.

It was, they both realised, an ironic situation. Roger Montgomery had acquired a reputation as one of the solicitors of last resort. Because of his popularity their room above the sandwich shop was overcrowded every day; lines of anxious appellants grew longer and snaked out into the street, often obstructing entry to the shop below when people arrived to buy their lunch, and extending to block other doorways.

It had culminated with a brash young legal adviser for the building's owner arriving one afternoon with a demand for them to quit the premises. He introduced himself as Clayton West of Hawkins, Ainsley & West, and informed them that a clause in their lease authorised a seven-day termination of occupancy if the business caused an annoyance in the neighbourhood.

'Which cannot be in dispute,' he said, taking documents from his briefcase, 'because my client has a petition signed by every tenant in the street. They object to the crowds, and say the noisy babble of foreign tongues adversely affects their trade.'

'Noisy babble of foreign tongues?' Kate queried. 'It sounds unreal to me.'

'Unreal?' He was instantly combative.

'Made up, Mr West,' she was quick to retort. 'An Anglo phrase. Did Stefan the Czech watchmaker use that expression? Did Rico the Maltese plumber? Or Mr Mburu from Kenya at the dental clinic?'

'Don't play smart-arse games, Mrs Forrester. Even Mr Patel, the Indian owner of the sandwich shop downstairs, signed this, and those are the exact words he used. Some went further and complained that your clients are unruly and far from clean. If I may quote?' He read carefully from the petition. 'There's a strong stink of urine most of the time, and quite often a smell of shit . . .'

Kate was about to vigorously deny this when Roger intervened. 'That's a fucking lie,' he said heatedly.

'Temper, Mr Montgomery,' West reproved him. 'I don't think that's at all necessary in front of your assistant.'

'My office manager,' Roger icily corrected him, and only Kate, who had known him more than half her life, could tell he was enraged beyond discretion. 'She is a highly skilled person in the detection of those who tell fucking lies. Now take your bogus petition and get out of here.'

'Excuse me,' Clayton West said, 'but it's you who have to get out. My client, Dr Theophilus, believes the premises are being used as a centre for recruiting terrorists.'

'You're out of your tree, mate,' Roger said.

'*Theophilus*,' Kate interjected, seizing on the name. 'A Greek?'

'A loyal *Australian*, wherever he was born,' the lawyer retorted, 'a citizen of this country who detests illegal immigrants. He believes they should take their place in an orderly queue.'

'Tell the doctor,' Kate said, 'they come from places where there is no queue.'

'That's *their* problem. My client's concern is the misuse of his

253

building.' Clayton West turned his back on her and handed the document to Roger with a confident shrug that seemed to suggest the matter had already been decided. 'Here's your notice to quit within seven days.'

Roger ripped it in half and said he intended to appeal. And he would ring the local newspaper to say that if they wanted a story to send a reporter around. West laughed and told him the local paper already had the story – and the news of an appeal would put it right across page one.

As the lawyer had predicted, it was there the next day, front page in the mid-week edition of the district *Express Gazette*. A slanted and highly prejudicial story, in which the smell of urine and faeces was frequently mentioned. A prominent boxed centre-piece declared the well-known lawyer for these refugees had torn up the notice to quit and intended to appeal. This, the paper explained, while unlikely to succeed, was clearly designed as a delaying tactic, for the approach of Christmas meant the matter would likely be stood over until the New Year. Therefore the unfortunate shop owners and residents of the area would have to suffer further harassment and discomfort until the law could be implemented, because of the obstructionist tactics of this wayward solicitor.

Roger read it, frowned and absently scratched his head as if there were more important things on his mind. 'Garbage. Ignore it,' he said.

Kate nodded. There was no time for discussion because the office was again full, but she knew they couldn't ignore it. Even though the article was unfair, the shopkeepers were certainly not going to ignore it. She understood their feelings, and had even tried to work out a way to resolve the impasse. She was thinking of this as she drove twice around the block the following morning, searching for a parking place. An answer to the problem, like finding a vacant slot for her car, seemed elusive. Their clients were so dependent on Roger. We need larger premises but can't afford it, was her dismal summation, knowing their financial position this year was worse than ever.

Finally a truck pulled out, and she was able to park the car only a short walk from the shops. The street door beside the sandwich bar was usually locked until she or Roger arrived; today it had been carefully jemmied and forced open. Kate ran up the stairway to where the door to their office lay flat, smashed from its hinges. All the windows were broken, the walls defaced with vicious and lewd graffiti. She picked up the phone to call the police but the cable had been ripped from the wall and cut into pieces. An unmistakeable smell made her turn, which was when she saw the excreta that was smeared all over their computers and across both their desks.

By the time the police arrived Kate had swept up the broken glass and tried vainly to scrub off the offensive slogans. **DIRTY FUCKING TRAITORS** was the wording of one of the less crude messages, but there was no way she could obliterate any of it. She had tried buckets of hot water and bleach, but cleaning the desks was an equally impossible task, for their computer keyboards and all the files were smeared and ruined. Besides, as one of the policemen told her, she shouldn't have tried to clean anything: it was a crime scene and she may well have disposed of evidence.

'I'm sorry,' Kate said, feeling sick, and went to sit on the stairs to intercept clients and tell them the office was closed for the day, or perhaps longer.

Her mobile phone rang shortly afterwards and it was Roger, who had received the message she left for him at the Federal Magistrate's court. She told him not to come to the office, and that if the police allowed it she would do her best to clean the place. When she ended the call she saw Ahmed Patel, the Indian owner of the sandwich shop at the broken street door below, his dark liquid eyes fixed apologetically on her.

'I heard what was done,' he said. 'Such bad things to disturb our lives. Is there anything we can do to help?'

'No, thank you, Mr Patel,' she said, and knew he was waiting for a friendly word. Today, at this awful moment, she felt unable to offer it, despite the long time they'd known each other. She waited until he went away. Then she took her mobile again, dialled Mandy and asked if she could come to the office and bring her new digital camera.

The doctor's receptionist was adamant; his appointment schedule was full for the rest of the day. In fact it was entirely filled for several weeks to come, and as he did not see patients without a referral, there was no possibility of him seeing Mrs Forrester that day or any other.

'I'm not a patient,' Kate said, handing her a sealed envelope and asking it be given to the doctor between his appointments. The woman frowned, glanced at it curiously and was on the point of opening it when Kate pointed out it was a private communication, and the envelope said so. Ignoring the other's hostile stare she sat in a chair by the window.

'I can't promise he'll have time to waste,' the receptionist warned, and a steady stream of patients came and went during the next hour while Kate thumbed through glossy magazines that claimed to reveal the secret bedroom stories of the royal family and various Hollywood celebrities.

Soon tiring of these, she gazed out the window. The doctor's rooms were in South Elizabeth Street and looked down on the network of railway tracks leading into Central Station. Below her a suburban train went slowly past the signal boxes near the old disused mortuary station, and beyond it Kate could see the street where she'd lived when she was pregnant. The building with its maze of cheap cubicle accommodation was no longer there; in its place was a tall hotel with a pretentious neon sign that proclaimed it *The City Gateway*. This was rather undone by another sign offering cheap vacant rooms, day or night.

Not the most salubrious part of town, Kate mused, with its cluster of gun shops and porno parlours, but it had been a haven at a time in her life when she needed one. It was full of memories. Up the hill towards the park was the coffee shop where she and Mandy had met, and where Hugh had come daily for his long blacks. Recalling how he never took sugar but always vigorously stirred his coffee brought a sharp moment of grief. After more than a decade of widowhood, it could still happen.

It was finally the end of the working day. After the last of the doctor's many patients was dispatched, the receptionist told her he could now spare a few minutes, but only a few because he had an important dinner engagement. She clearly regarded the brevity of the appointment as a minor victory over this intruder who had tried to upset her schedule.

Kate tapped on his door and heard a deep voice impatiently telling her to enter. It did not auger well.

Dr Alexis Theophilus was a tall, powerfully built man. Even

sitting behind his desk this was apparent. He had a black moustache and dark hair, and reminded Kate of Anthony Quinn. But the irritation with which he surveyed her contained none of the charm Quinn had displayed in the film role of Zorba.

'You apparently work with Montgomery, the solicitor,' were his first words, 'and according to your note these photographs illustrate what was done to the office.'

'Yes,' Kate said.

'And why did you think I'd be interested in seeing pictures of my property looking filthy and desecrated in such a manner?'

'I thought it might show you the kind of prejudice we meet each day trying to help people.'

'Boat people,' he said, making it sound like an accusation.

'Why is that such a pejorative term?' Kate replied. 'I came here by boat. Half of this nation did; so did their families before them.'

'Not fishing boats. Not without visas or the correct papers.' He waited for an answer; when she failed to respond he nodded as if the point was made to his satisfaction, and gestured for her to sit down.

'We were lucky. The times were more compassionate,' she said, taking the chair in front of his desk. 'Even if school taught us what it was like to be a wog.' She watched him frown as if already regretting this conversation.

'That was long ago, Mrs Forrester. Things are far different now.'

'For us, perhaps. Not for newcomers . . . the boat people, that you detest.'

'*Detest?*' he snapped with renewed irritation. 'What the devil are you talking about?'

'Your lawyer said it. I'm quoting him.'

'Lawyers tend to grandstand. You should know that.'

'So you don't hate them?'

'Of course not,' he retorted heatedly. 'I may disapprove, or think them unwise to take such risks. But detest or hate them . . . certainly not!'

'I'm glad you don't.' Kate's quiet reply was in contrast to his outburst. 'People who feel that way are difficult for me to understand. Like a neighbour of mine . . . it's an awful thought, but he seemed pleased those children drowned on the SIEV X. So many kids and their parents, what was their crime? They were trying to escape from Saddam Hussein and the Taliban.'

'Mrs Forrester . . .' Theophilus tried to interject, but she persisted.

'Let me finish, please. This neighbour loathes Saddam, but doesn't want his victims to come here. I don't know where he thinks they could go, but his philosophy is clear . . . not in his backyard. If any children do reach our shores, he's happy they're locked up behind razor wire. Of course, he's never seen a child shut in a detention centre, bewildered and scared, not understanding why they're imprisoned, without toys, hope or affection. So I'm glad, Doctor, as a fellow Greek, that you're not like my neighbour.'

'I assure you, I'm not. Now tell me why you came here? Did you hope you'd get a sympathetic hearing from a fellow Greek?'

Kate shook her head. 'I thought that most unlikely. But I did hope you wouldn't be as intractable as your lawyer painted you. Do you truly believe our office is used to recruit terrorists?'

'Don't be absurd.'

'It sounded absurd when Mr West told us.'

'I'll have a word to Mr West,' the doctor promised.

'Meanwhile,' said Kate, 'without his help I thought we just

might be able to have a rational discussion about a way to solve this problem.'

'Did you indeed?' he replied, gazing at her. 'The problem, Mrs Forrester, is not easily solved. The problem is my tenants being annoyed and overrun by your clients. I own most of the buildings in that street.'

'I know you do. I looked up the land titles.'

'And I had someone look you up while you were kept waiting this afternoon. You were the office manager at Montgomery & Associates, who are now Sydney's biggest legal firm. Did they fire you?'

'No, I left by choice. You can have that checked if you wish.'

'I already have. Otherwise I wouldn't have bothered seeing you.'

'You're obviously wary of Greeks,' Kate said, risking a smile.

'"I fear Greeks even when they bring gifts." Do you happen to know who wrote that, Mrs Forrester?'

'Virgil did. When we gave the Trojans a horse. And how right he was about that!'

Dr Theophilus laughed as there was a brief knock and the receptionist looked in.

'Your dinner appointment, Doctor,' she reminded him, appearing surprised by the laughter. 'You'll be late.'

Bugger, Kate thought. The office praetorian guard, just when things were looking hopeful.

'Before you leave, Fiona,' Theophilus told her, 'phone my wife and say there's an emergency. I'm unavoidably detained.'

'But, Doctor . . .'

'It's a family dinner, not a meeting of the Medical Board. Tell her I'll be there for coffee.'

The receptionist compressed her lips as if such a lie was

anathema to her. When the door shut on her disapproving face, Theophilus smiled at Kate. Conspiracy, she decided, made him look more agreeable, though gifting him with the élan of Anthony Quinn was overdoing it somewhat.

'So you think we can solve our problem,' he said. 'And no Trojan horses?'

'No Trojan horses,' she agreed.

'There's a Greek restaurant in the Haymarket. Shall we try breaking bread, to see if it helps us with our discussions?'

The Poseidon Temple was dimly lit and half empty. They picked a table in a discreet corner, where Alex, as he requested she call him, gave Kate a précis of his life. He had come to Australia as a babe in arms in 1948, which she estimated made him a few years older than her. He was a consulting surgeon at the Royal Prince Alfred Hospital, with a wife and two adult children. As the evening progressed and he learnt she'd been a widow for some years, it became apparent he was more interested in a flirtation across the candlelit table than resolving the office problem. Over cheese, with Alex proposing another bottle of merlot or else a liqueur, she thought it was time to change the subject.

'If I talk to the shopkeepers and all the other tenants,' Kate said, 'and try to achieve some sort of rapport with them, will you withdraw the notice to quit?'

He made her wait while he raised his glass and studied the last of his wine, as if searching for an answer there.

'So it's cut to the chase time,' he finally said.

'I mustn't keep you from that promised coffee at home with your family,' Kate replied, softening it with a smile.

He finished the wine and gazed at her over the rim of the glass.

'You are a delightful woman, but I expect you've often been told that.'

A modest non-committal shrug seemed the best answer. He was fishing, but not for an early return to the family nest and his waterfront home in Mosman.

'And beautiful when you smile,' he added.

'The chase, Alex,' she reminded him. 'The notice to quit.'

'My solicitor would be unhappy if we withdrew.'

'He's a rather brash young man who'd soon get over it.'

'I expect he would,' Alex agreed. Clearly the discomfort of his legal eagle meant little to him. 'But of course, there are other offices. You'd soon find somewhere else.'

'Not as central,' Kate replied, avoiding the admission they could hardly find one as cheap. 'Yes, we could locate to another. But we'd lose touch with vulnerable people who depend on our help. We have mainly word-of-mouth contact with refugees and asylum seekers, and if we have to move many will assume they've been abandoned. After all, they're used to disillusion . . . and who can blame them? Half the world wants to pretend they don't exist.'

'You're obsessive about these people.'

These people! I hate that phrase, she thought. It was a description favoured by the immigration minister, and often heard in tirades on talkback radio. *You and I were these people once*, she almost told him, but knew it would not be well received, and creating discord now would be stupid.

'Perhaps I am fixated,' she agreed instead.

'Can I see you again?' he asked, without preamble.

It was hardly a surprise, but she'd hoped to avoid it.

'I thought there were to be no Trojan horses,' Kate said carefully. 'You have a wife and family.'

'My wife and I have an open marriage.'

'Alex, this is awfully difficult,' she told him, 'and I don't want to spoil what's been an enjoyable evening. But my partner and I don't have that sort of arrangement.'

'Partner?' He looked discomforted. 'You forgot to mention him.'

'Actually,' Kate murmured, 'it's not him, it's *her*.' She summoned a discreet smile. 'Maureen. That's my partner's name.'

It was like a Neighbourhood Watch meeting, Kate thought, or even a Christmas street party, with the road cordoned off and all the tenants and shop owners gathered. In addition there were dozens of occupants of the district's apartment blocks among the crowd, while others were looking down on the scene from their windows and balconies. If it was Christmas time there'd be booze and people arriving with food offerings on plates, instead of which they were gathered outside the sandwich shop and she was standing on an improvised rostrum trying desperately to think of what to say.

'I'm so glad everyone has turned up today,' she began nervously. Roger had organised a microphone, and she could hear her voice echo off buildings across the street, which was incredibly off-putting. What also caused discomfort was the large figure of Alex Theophilus standing in comparative anonymity at the rear of the crowd.

Maureen, she thought. Why that name? She didn't even know a Maureen; hadn't known one since her schooldays. She'd blurted it out to avoid a blunt and wounding refusal, to salve his pride and tactfully extricate herself from the move on her he'd been intending all evening. A moment of pure impulse, but it had worked. After a startled expression of . . . astonishment? Disappointment? Whatever his initial reaction, it had been instantly replaced by polite acceptance, as if to imply homophobia was anathema to him, and choice was every adult's right. Sexual pursuit was off the agenda. In the few minutes that elapsed between his signal for the bill and its arrival, the matter of the office had even made some progress.

If she could pacify the protesting neighbours, he might reconsider, he'd said. But he'd want clear proof of harmony being restored, which was why he was here now, waiting to be convinced. Waiting like all the expectant faces were waiting, gazing at her.

'Well, we've turned out like you asked, Kate,' a voice from the crowd called, 'so say something. What are you going to tell us?'

It was Stefan the watchmaker, and it brought a laugh that oddly freed her from vacillation. 'I'm not here to tell you anything, Stefan,' she replied. 'I'm here to ask you to let us stay. Roger and I have been working from this office for ten years, and we love it here. You've put up with us until now, but lately I'm sure you know things have become very unfair and tough for the people we try to help. They're boat people. They get abused and called names, and locked up with their children. Do you think that's fair?'

She waited for an answer, but there was none.

'Look, some of you are upset. It crowds the streets, interferes with your business and daily life, and you have every right to complain about that. But they mean no harm. They're not dishonest or disagreeable, not criminals or troublemakers, just folk looking for a new life, a new start, and I think there's a lot of us here who should know how that feels.' Her eyes swept the crowd, picking out many whom she knew were from Europe and parts of Asia, hoping for their understanding. 'So what I propose is this. If you agree to give us a fair go, I'll explain to our clients they have to make appointments in advance. That way we can ration the numbers, and not block access to your homes and your shops.'

They were listening intently, but she couldn't tell what they were thinking. She wished it was Roger with his lawyer's ability for oratory up here, but Roger had insisted it be her. She was the one best known to the people of the neighbourhood, he'd said. But what else could she say to convince them?

'If you can go along with that, the man who owns our leases is a decent, fair-minded person, and he's willing to withdraw the notice to quit. It would make me very happy if we could be friends again, the way we've been for so long. I do miss those morning greetings, the smiles and cheerful waves. I miss your companionship, the daily chat and the local gossip, and I especially miss the beaut sandwiches that Mr Patel makes, the best lunch special between here and Sydney Uni. So if I try, will you try – and can we all be mates again?'

There was a long moment of silence and she feared she'd failed. A woman in the front row shrugged; a man who worked in the delicatessen shook his head and started to turn away. Then all of a sudden a voice called out.

'Onya, Kate. We're with you.'

It was Drago Vjukic, a Yugoslav who owned the hardware shop. Reinforcing his opinion, his wife Stoika put her fingers to her lips to emit a piercing whistle. A wave of good-humoured laughter greeted this, followed by shouts of approval and applause, and the next moment she was surrounded by smiling faces and welcoming hands. In the background she glimpsed the doctor's nod of quiet approval, and as he moved off, unrecognised by others, he lifted his arm to her like a parting tribute.

Anna Montgomery enlisted their two sons, and they set to repainting the office. Mandy arrived with cleaning fluid that stripped the obscenities, while Roger and Kate salvaged what they could of their files, relieved that the dominant odour was now merely the smell of new paint. In between restoration they considered their change of fortune.

'So what did you say to convince the landlord?' Roger asked. 'I heard he was an awkward bugger.'

'Greeks are unpredictable,' Kate said.

'Just listen to her,' Mandy grinned. 'Two Greeks together by candlelight, that's what did it. Did he make a pass?' she asked, when they stopped for lunch. 'I heard he was a well-known pants man.'

'Settle down, Amanda,' Kate replied amid laughter, while they ate sandwiches supplied by Ahmed Patel who had firmly refused to accept payment. Tomorrow, he'd told them, it would be business as usual, but not today. Today was his shout.

Philanthropy seemed to be the vogue. Anna returned from the hardware store with paint that the owner insisted on donating. The goodwill thrilled Kate. A tiny community had changed its attitude. Of course it was too much to hope it would happen across society, but perhaps it was the start of something.

She enjoyed another of Mr Patel's delicious sandwiches. His shout indeed, she smiled. Today it seemed as if they were all Aussies.

~

It was a rare good moment in the past year, for there had not been many. A small victory among numerous defeats. The Pacific Solution was now being ruthlessly implemented. Refugees were isolated on Nauru, creating a feeling of being abandoned on the bleak atoll.

In the late summer of 2002 the war in Afghanistan was the main news topic of the day, but the presidential vow that Osama bin Laden would soon be captured or killed was beginning to sound like a broken record. In his speeches Bush began to turn attention increasingly towards Iraq. He accused them of hostility towards America and supporting terror, of plotting to develop anthrax and nerve gas and nuclear weapons.

'He sounds like he wants to go to war there as well,' said Kate. 'Let's hope we won't be talked into it.'

'We will,' Roger assured her. 'We've lined up for every bloody war since we were a colony. The Sudan, Crimea, the Boer War, World Wars One and Two, Korea, Malaya, Vietnam. Blow a bugle, Kate, and I'm afraid we're there, saluting.'

Meanwhile at the office Kate ensured they kept their promise to the residents, impressing clients with the need to make appointments. It settled problems in the neighbourhood, but meant she and Roger had to work longer hours to deal with the escalating number of cases. Those seeking aid showed no sign of diminishing; on the contrary – as the laws became more severe, their workload increased. Most days she didn't leave the office until long after dark, arriving home too exhausted to cook a proper meal, yet despite the fatigue unable to sleep well. And there were other, more personal stresses keeping her awake in the pre-dawn hours.

'You're a wreck,' Mandy informed her with customary candour, one night in The Mock Turtle when Kate had called in after work and was persuaded to stay for a meal. Mandy's staff was looking after the other tables, while she and Kate ate at a corner banquette.

'If you don't ease up, I predict a breakdown.'

'God, you are a comfort,' answered Kate.

'Well, someone's got to tell you. Roger's too absorbed with work to notice. Besides, when people ask how you are, you always say you feel fine. Even if you don't. C'mon, admit it – you do that every time.'

'Has it ever occurred to you, Mandy, when people ask how you are, the last thing they want to hear is the full medical agenda? They'd rather not know you've got flu or feel profoundly depressed.'

'Are you?' Mandy promptly asked.

'Am I what?'

'Profoundly depressed?'

'Not especially.'

'Convince me,' her best friend said.

'You are a pain in the arse sometimes,' Kate retorted, laughing.

'Skip the compliments, kitten. You're tired, you're worried, and I'm concerned. I'd suggest another bottle of our Reserve Pinot to get you pissed so you'll talk, but you might get arrested driving home. So tell me, please. You are depressed, aren't you?'

'Frustrated,' Kate said, and before this could be misinterpreted she hastily explained. 'Discouraged at how hard we try and how little we can help sometimes.'

'At least people like you are in there fighting.'

'Trying to fight. Sometimes it's a losing battle.'

'I've never heard you say that before.'

'I've often thought it,' Kate confessed. 'We do our best, but . . .' She shook her head in what seemed like a gesture of futility. 'There was a family deported back to Afghanistan recently. Wife, husband, two kids. Known to the Taliban as devout Christians. We tried to argue they were at risk but nobody would listen. Yesterday we got news the parents had been killed for the crime of listening to a religious service on the underground radio. The kids are in a state orphanage. The girl is fourteen – God help her in there. They were a nice quiet family who simply wanted to become citizens and live here.'

'Shit,' exclaimed Mandy. 'Why were they sent back?'

'Why indeed? Someone didn't believe they were in danger, or else didn't bloody care.'

She drove home carefully, feeling better for Mandy's outspoken concern. Theirs was a valued friendship; one she treasured. They had few secrets. Mandy knew of the other pressures that troubled her, the intimate ones. How even after so long she still deeply missed Hugh. Whatever the difficulties of her job, at least the days were fully occupied with work; the nights were sometimes distressingly interminable. The empty space in the bed . . . she still occasionally reached out half-drugged with sleep until remembering no one was there. Worst of all, the desolate loneliness when she wanted to confide some excitement to Hugh, and the bleak awareness that this was no longer possible.

They had been close friends as well as lovers, and the void in her life still caused moments of sudden pain. Almost thirteen years. There had been a brief unsuccessful affair; another even more fleeting; and although solicitous friends rarely stopped trying to match her at dinner parties with available men, she felt a wry regret that she was unable to respond to their well-meaning selections.

Mandy knew how Kate was beginning to dread being constantly paired with a series of widowers or divorcees.

'Grandchildren, that's the answer,' she'd declared, when they'd been cleaning up the office. 'The patter of tiny feet is what you need. When Jules has kids she can send them to you for school holidays, and the great thing about grandchildren is when you've had enough you can give them back.'

But that was months ago, and now it appeared there would be no patter of tiny feet. Kate thought of Juliet's imminent return from Auckland, and wondered exactly what had happened there. After a few years of what seemed to be a happy marriage it had ended abruptly, and she was yet to know why.

Chapter 20

The kookaburra swooped for his evening meal, and Juliet watched him fly back to the high branches of the gum tree where he nested. She had come to spend the weekend, and she and Kate were in the garden.

'He's lived in that tree since I was knee-high and we first moved here. Do you really think it's the same bird, Mum?'

'Of course it is, darling,' Kate said, 'that's why he knows exactly what time to turn up for his breakfast and dinner. Never a minute late for his tucker, that one.'

Juliet smiled at her mother's certitude. It was such a comfort to be home in Australia and able to spend time with her. They strolled back to the verandah, where a bottle of Sauvignon Blanc was waiting for them in a cooler. The house felt like a haven, but one she had seen little of in the past ten years. After Hugh's death she found a job as a cadet journalist on a provincial newspaper in Victoria, and later moved to Melbourne for a stint on a weekly magazine before what seemed like the ultimate breakthrough – applying for and obtaining a job on the New Zealand *Herald*.

But it was the time spent in Auckland that had finally made her become disenchanted with journalism. Working as a reporter, one regularly dispatched to cover riots, car crashes and crimes, she'd begun to realise there had to be better jobs than confronting victims or their relatives, trying to prevent a door being slammed on her while she requested answers to insensitive questions of the injured or bereaved.

So she'd abandoned the job. Being a copywriter in advertising was hardly exciting, but it was at least impersonal; there were no widows or mothers with wounded faces whom she had to interrogate on how they felt after awful tragedies. *Are you upset, Mrs Smith, that the gang who raped your daughter got off on a technicality?*

She had found it unbearable.

But the reason for her sudden departure from New Zealand had nothing to do with work; the failure of her marriage was what had brought her home. It was a scar in her memory, and one that would remain so. Paul Adams was twenty-seven, already the manager of a coastal shipping company. He was tall, blond, good-looking and by consensus the most eligible bachelor in town. She had met him at a party given by Linklater Pattersons, the advertising agency she'd joined after leaving newspapers. He was a client and, as a former All Black rugby star, a popular guest. She had fallen deeply in love with him, and for over three years believed they were happy. Until one afternoon, coming home from work early, she had found him in bed with his best friend, a front-row forward from his club days. She felt anger at first, but tarnished by embarrassment, was unable to confide this to anyone, even her mother.

As Kate poured the wine Juliet tried to stop thinking about the awful humiliation and her hurried flight from matrimony; instead she looked up to the red gum where the kookaburra had vanished into his nest.

'Dear old Kooka. If it is the same one he'd have to be at least twenty-something.'

'Easily. They live that long, provided they don't meet up with any wedge-tailed eagles. Did you know they stay with the same mate all their lives? Extraordinary and rather sweet, isn't it.'

'Unlike some of us,' Juliet said with a shrug, unable to prevent a swift glance at her mother.

'I didn't mean to revisit that, darling.' Kate was instantly apologetic for the unconscious gaffe. 'But now it's said, what actually happened? Would talking about it help?'

'Not especially, Mum.'

'Whatever.' Kate promptly changed the subject, for she'd been rebuffed before. 'How's the flat turning out?'

'Okay. It's comfortable enough. I might look for someone compatible to share, if I decide to stay there.'

'You could move back here if you want,' she suggested, but Juliet shook her head.

'I'm a bit old to be racing home to Mum. Besides, you and I are best friends when we don't share the same roof, Mama,' she replied, using a rare term of endearment from her childhood. They both sipped their wine and she added, 'Also, I love it here, but there are too many memories of Dad. Even all these years later, it still seems like he's everywhere in this house.'

'I feel it sometimes in the garden,' Kate said, 'among the trees and shrubs we planted together. Him digging, me busy giving out technical advice – as he did occasionally remind me. It was true, too.' She smiled wistfully at the recollection. 'But I don't mind the memories.'

'I do. I mind that he's not here, and that he died so young,' Juliet said. 'I miss him terribly.'

273

'You and me both, darling.'

She did not venture to ask whether her daughter had met Joshua, even though she could not help wondering whether she found him or not. There had never been a mention of it since the day long ago when Juliet had promised not to speak about it.

It was a warm night and they grilled chicken and made a salad, which they took outside to eat. During the meal Juliet talked about her job; she'd been able to transfer as a copywriter to the Sydney branch of the same firm, Linklater Patterson. Advertising would never be her first choice as a career but it did pay the rent. She still loved journalism, but felt frustrated that the kind of work she strived for in newspapers continued to elude her. As she seemed so unsettled, Kate raised a subject that had been on her mind for some time.

'When do you get your holidays?'

'Not till June. Worst time of the year for hols. Winter.'

'That's summer in Athens. Sofia often says how sad it is you never made the last stage of that trip to meet her. She's going to be seventy soon, though I doubt if she'll admit it. I wondered if you'd like to go and see her.'

'Mum, I'd love to,' Juliet said, 'I really would. But with the costs of moving back and bringing my furniture from Auckland, I just can't afford it this year.'

'Perhaps I could,' Kate suggested. 'If you'd like to go, I'll gladly pay for it.'

'But can *you* afford it?' When Kate smiled and nodded, Juliet was surprised but still uncertain. 'Are you sure? I thought you and Roger worked for peanuts?'

'We do, but I always have a bit put away for a rainy day.'

~

Sydney airport was crowded. It was entirely different from the place where eighteen-year-old Kate had farewelled her father so long ago. Upgraded before the 2000 Olympics, it was now an international air-traffic hub, no longer small and friendly where personal contact was possible until take-off. The overseas terminal was massive, a shopping mall of overpriced boutiques, souvenir shops and duty-free outlets. There were queues everywhere; queues for check-in, for the ever-more stringent security, and finally for immigration, where visitors lost sight of those they had come to farewell.

Kate had a last glimpse of Juliet, a final wave before the doors slid shut and hid her from view. She went back to the car park and drove straight to the appointment she'd made with Alistair Marshall to again increase her mortgage.

For the first time the bank manager showed some reserve in granting her request.

'You do realise,' he pointed out, 'while we know house prices are still rising, if perhaps more slowly, your loan rarely stops rising. Head office is tending to keep a watch on these transactions lately. There may come a day when we're unable to continue your particular method of fundraising.'

'All I'm doing is using my home for collateral,' Kate said, as if this was simple economics. 'I want to send ten thousand dollars to my daughter to enjoy herself, so if you incorporate that into your calculations, I'd be grateful.'

Alistair Chambers sighed. 'Is this necessary?'

'It is to me,' Kate said.

'You could always sell the house,' he suggested.

'And do what?' she asked.

'Buy a nice apartment, and actually have credit in the bank?

Money you could put on deposit and draw on. Instead of what you call your moveable mortgage.'

'But I'd miss our occasional meetings like this,' she said and laughed at his reaction. 'I realise if I'm too extravagant the bank might one day own my house, but until then nothing in the world could make me leave it. I can't imagine living anywhere else. So if it ever becomes yours, Mr Marshall' – she gave him a warm smile – 'warn head office they might need a bulldozer to shift me.'

Sofia Vassos stood waiting outside customs at Athens International airport, eagerly watching as the stream of passengers emerged. She had a photograph but it was years out of date, and she was literally taken by surprise when a smart young woman came through who looked so exactly like Katerina that for a moment she was confused. Then the young woman smiled, and came straight towards her.

'Hello, Grandma,' she said as they met and embraced.

'My darling girl,' her grandmother said, 'welcome to Athens. I hope you had a good flight, and would you do me a tremendous favour and call me Sofia?'

'Of course I will,' Juliet replied. 'No problems. It hardly seems right to call you anything else. You look far too young for a granny.'

Sofia peered at her through the glasses that had been recently prescribed by the local optometrist – a quite unnecessary aid, in her opinion – wondering if Juliet had been coached by her mother. But she seemed utterly sincere and had the loveliest smile, just like Katerina, so Sofia hugged her again and they walked arm-in-arm to the luggage carousel. When Juliet's suitcase had been retrieved they went out to the car park where Michel Doumani was waiting.

Juliet saw a handsome and smartly dressed elderly man. He

greeted her effusively, but appeared slightly awkward. It was strange to meet this grown-up daughter of the little girl aboard the ship so long ago. He was uncomfortably aware he had been the cause of what happened on that voyage, but he allowed none of this to show. He shook hands with Juliet, kissed her on both cheeks, stowed her case and opened the car door for her; meanwhile hoping her flight had been comfortable, and if she wasn't tired or feeling jet-lagged they thought they might take her to lunch at a little taverna by the beach that served seafood and was a favourite of theirs.

Juliet reassured him that she was not a bit jet-lagged, not tired; just excited to be here and meet them both at last. Sofia watched this with quiet content. Michel was relaxing, responding to her charm. He was rarely if ever at a loss, but at first had been oddly nervous about the arrival of this inherited granddaughter. He felt she might want to revisit the past – might even want to visit Cyprus and meet Andreas who still lived there. The idea did not bother Sofia at all if that was what Juliet wished to do – as long as she went alone. She had no desire to see her former husband, who would now be over seventy.

Not, she thought, that seventy was old. She was nearly that herself, although people refused to believe it, and Michel was seventy-four. But a fine looking seventy-four. She had been happy with him for over forty years, and that happiness had almost compensated for her impetuous act on the *Ottoman Star* in Sydney that had meant her losing Katerina. But here was Katerina's daughter, and she already felt a great rapport towards this lively and attractive young woman. And, best of all, Michel was now thoroughly at ease, chatting amiably with her. Over lunch Sofia decided she would ask about that return ticket, and find out how long Juliet could stay.

It must not be a fleeting visit. There was so much for her to see, and with them both recently retired on good superannuation and now able to afford it, there was such a lot they would enjoy showing her. Athens itself, of course, and all its wonders from the Acropolis to Piraeus . . . But so much else. Temples and marvellous old amphitheatres. Attica and the blood-red sunset at Cape Sounion, as well as Delphi, the Peloponnese, Corinth and Olympus – and if she stayed for the winter, there was skiing in the mountains!

Then there were the islands; the lyrical Greek Islands. They had friends on both Hydra and Mykonos. Not only there, they had friends in many parts of Europe who were always inviting them to stay. What could be better than to visit those friends in Paris, Switzerland, Italy – she and Michel with her lovely granddaughter . . .

They had no children of their own; it was the one thing that had been lacking in their lives. And perhaps in time . . . she stopped thinking of the future, sat back in the car and listened contentedly to Juliet and Michel getting acquainted.

Chapter 21

'A glorious summer' was the wording in Juliet's last email, but even nicer now they had left the heat of Athens and were touring Delphi and the Parnassus, full of antiquity and bacchanalian mythology. Sofia and Michel seemed intent on giving her a wonderful time, Kate thought, for there was no mention of plans yet to return home. That, she felt, was a good sign. And no email since then for several weeks – another good sign. If Juliet was so fully engaged and enjoying herself, it would not only do her a world of good, but give her time to think of the future without any pressure. The past had been such a patchwork of peaks and troughs. She had been unstable after Hugh's death, then a radiant bride before that too had ended in tears.

It had been a dazzling wedding. The house in The Crescent had been packed with guests, including many from Auckland. It had required a serious negotiation with Mr Marshall and his bank, but Kate had spared no expense because she wanted it to be a success. It seemed a great match; Juliet was happy and had married a young man she clearly loved. Being a popular former rugby star, the papers in New Zealand had made much of it. But less than four years later there were far different headlines; the marriage was over, and she wished she knew why.

Thinking of Juliet, she envied her the weather: a glorious summer in Greece, while she endured an unusually miserable winter in Australia. And this was easily the worst of it – a cold and wet afternoon as she left Villawood for what would be a difficult drive home after a dismal and wretched day. There was constant debate among those in detention centres over which time of year was the most unpleasant: summer's fierce heat or winter's gloom. The latter, it seemed, according to most opinion; 'a time of heartbreak and breakouts' were words that someone in a moment of angry cognition had spray-painted in large letters on a drab wall.

In the bitter cold of July and August the buildings were arctic. The open space where people tried to exercise and children played and kicked footballs (or sometimes empty tins, pretending they were footballs), was invariably windswept and became a muddy quagmire after rain. The eerie glow of orange floodlights added to a seasonal depression.

Kate had been visiting a man facing deportation to Jordan. Born there, he had been brought to Australia by his parents as a baby, but after a childhood of truancy and petty theft, and then a recurring adult criminal record, he had been stripped of his citizenship and was due to be sent back to his country of birth. The government seemed unconcerned that he knew nothing of Jordan since infancy, had no relatives in the country and could not speak the language. Kate had come to gather evidence that he would have no way to earn a living, and despite his life of crime the deportation was inhumane. In the few weeks remaining before he would be forcibly removed, Roger hoped to lodge an appeal on the grounds the action was morally wrong, and the man would be exiled to an existence where he might starve, or else have to beg for food in the streets.

It was during this that sirens began to sound, and news swept the centre that there had been a breakout. Security went into high alert. Gates were shut tight, inmates locked up and new visitors refused admission. Those already in the centre were told they'd be detained for questioning. A convoy of police cars began arriving to scour the neighbourhood. But it was soon established that the escape had been made by four young boys, and had taken place during the previous night and not detected until almost midday.

Despite this, all visitors were to be searched and interrogated, and no one was allowed to leave. When a lawyer working pro bono tried to protest at this he was yelled at, told to shut up or he'd be put into a cell. The behaviour of the Correction Management and the guards became intensely aggressive. Kate felt they were almost out of control, looking for scapegoats, eager to blame anyone for the lapse in security. When a media van arrived with television cameras, it was instantly suspected someone had smuggled in a mobile phone and alerted the press. She was rash enough to point out that their phones were prohibited, and was threatened by a guard who came so close that she could smell his stale breath, saying there were plenty of places where an extra mobile phone could be inserted. A full strip search, he added, looking suggestively at her, might be the best way to find it.

By midafternoon two of the escaped boys were found by police, hiding in a disused shed of an industrial area less than a kilometre away. They were brought back and handed over to the guards. Kate and the same lawyer glimpsed them both handcuffed and being escorted through a locked gate towards the high-security cells of the Management Unit. They were accompanied by angry guards with batons. The boys, barely old enough to be called teenagers, looked as though they had already been roughly handled.

PETER YELDHAM

'God help the poor little bastards,' the lawyer said.

Kate had a moment of claustrophobic terror. It was always an awful place; today it seemed positively evil. God wasn't going to help them, she thought; no one was going to stop what would happen when those guards had the boys securely locked in an isolation cell. After whatever punishment was going to be administered, they would then be confined there in solitary for days, a small concrete area with nothing to look at but the threatening razor wire above them.

Another of the runaways was accounted for an hour later. He tried to hitch a ride from a truck and was apparently injured when the driver refused to stop. News swept the centre that he'd been arrested and taken to hospital. For the remainder of the afternoon while the search intensified for the remaining boy, all the visitors were held like hostages, even though it was transparently evident they had nothing to do with the escapes.

It was becoming dark by the time all of them, including lawyers, caseworkers, volunteers from Oxfam and those from groups like the Bridge For Asylum Seekers, were finally released from interrogation and, in the words of one of the most hostile of the guards, told to get the fuck out of there.

Kate lined up with the others to collect her car keys and handbag, then drove away as quickly as she could. It had been an aggravating and wasted day. She had grave doubts if the man facing deportation, a misfit and a recidivist, would be granted an appeal, and she felt tired and frustrated.

The rain became heavier as she drove down Woodville Road, and approaching the junction of the Hume Highway she could see a stream of stationary cars. It looked very much like an accident had caused a major hold-up somewhere ahead, meaning a slow crawl home. She waited for the lights to change and went straight across the intersection, deciding to take the circular route along Henry Lawson Drive. The road was new to her but far easier; there was almost no traffic, and she could combat the dark and unfamiliar route by switching her headlights to full beam.

A sign identified a recreational area called SHORTLAND BRUSH, and through the gusting rain she glimpsed an artificial lake before driving deeper into the Mirambeena Regional Park. Her headlights revealed a succession of notices denoting picnic areas, playgrounds, a sports track and a number of public barbecue fireplaces. A truck approached on the lonely road and Kate lowered her lights, then flicked them to full again when it passed. As she did this the longer range of high beam revealed a faint movement ahead of her – something was emerging from bushes at the side of the road. Alarmed it might be an animal about to cross, she stamped on the brake.

Her car slid dangerously on the wet road, but to her relief held firm when she reached the gravelled edge. As it came to a halt she realised it was not a stray animal after all.

It was a child; he was frightened and dazzled by the headlights, he was drenched . . . and he was quite clearly Arabic.

The phone rang in the empty house until her voice said: 'This is Kate. Leave a message and I'll call you back ASAP.' Sitting at a table having her breakfast in a South Kensington coffee shop, Juliet spoke into her mobile phone: 'It's me, Ma, and I'm now in London where it's a warm and sunny morning. I've had this fab weather ever since I arrived here last week, and I've got some news. Nothing trivial like a new man in my life; more important than that. When I find an internet café I'll send you an email and tell you what good things have happened since I left Greece.'

Juliet thought it strange, after the wonderful time she'd spent with Sofia and Michel, including a fortnight sailing between the islands, that she preferred London. Perhaps it was the surprise news that had greeted her after she arrived. Or was it simply being on her own at last, instead of every day filled with enthusiastic suggestions of where to go and what to see, which she supposed was ungrateful of her for they had entertained her so well.

Perhaps it was just Sofia – *Grandmère*, as she kept thinking of her, but had not attempted to say the name aloud in her presence – *Grandmère* and a sneaking suspicion that she tried to avoid talk of a return to Australia whenever Juliet raised it, often subtly denigrating the place as if it had disappointed her. Juliet felt that a bit unjust, because according to family lore *Grandmère* had thoroughly enjoyed her time in an expensive hotel there, living in great style when Michel had been an executive in the shipping company and able to arrange such luxuries.

She put it out of her mind, for there were far more important things to think about. Thrilling, unbelievable things. Tonight she had a date with a sub-editor she'd met at *The Guardian*, but tomorrow she would go to an internet café in Gloucester Road, not far from her hotel room, to compose an email to her mother telling her all the news.

The boy was soaked and trapped in the glare of her headlights. Kate turned them off, leaving only the parking lights, and opened the passenger door. She called to him, but the rain was relentless, drowning her voice. She beckoned for him to come and take shelter.

Still he didn't move; immobile like a scared animal, but poised for flight.

'Please,' she called, but either he could not hear or did not understand English.

She got out of the car, hurrying to where he stood. She could tell he wanted to flee, but sensed he was wet and hungry and too exhausted to escape. Kate took his hand. His hair was matted, rivulets of rain ran down his face, and his dark brown eyes gazed at her fearfully. At first glance in the dim parking lights he appeared to be only ten years old. He was small and thin, shivering continually. She tried to indicate they should take shelter in the car, but he was tense and uncertain about trusting her. It needed a gesture, something to calm and reassure him.

'Wait,' she said, and stumbled back to the car, the wind blowing fierce rain into her eyes and making it difficult. On the rear seat was an old anorak which she retrieved and brought to him.

'For you. Put it on.'

She held it out for him it as he looked enquiringly at her, and when she nodded encouragingly he slid his arms into the sleeves. It was far too big for him, but she zipped it up, put the hood over his head, and took hold of his hand again. His face was hidden so Kate leaned down to make sure he could hear.

'Feel better?' When there was no reply she tried, 'Okay?'

It seemed a familiar word at last, for he nodded in response and this time allowed her to lead him to the car. She sat him in the front seat and hurried to the driver's side, climbed in behind the wheel, feeling chilled and soaking wet herself, while wondering what to do. Yet she knew the answer.

I have to take him back there, she thought, switching on the lights. There is simply no other option. She remembered the two other boys and the way they were handcuffed and handled roughly on the way to the high-security area. But what alternative was there? As she started the car and began to make the U-turn required to head back to the detention centre, she was made acutely aware of the boy's alarm. He cried out some words that she presumed were in Arabic; it could only be a plea, the way he gazed at her. He had pushed back the hood of the anorak and she could see his eyes. They were enlarged and frightened. He continually shook his head in mute appeal, then in English managed one beseeching word.

'No . . .'

'I have to,' Kate tried to tell him. 'It's a crime if I don't. And surely you have parents in there, or relatives – certainly someone who will wonder what's happened to you and be concerned?' Even while saying it she was aware he did not understand. She had completed the turn, and they were now temporarily halted on the opposite side of the road facing back towards Villawood.

'No,' he begged. Pushing back the sleeves of the anorak, he clasped his hands and held them out to her like a supplicant. He was still shivering, and his out-thrust hands in prayer mode were trembling.

Kate shook her head. 'I'm sorry,' she said. 'I don't want to send you back to that awful place. If it was my choice I'd take you home and give you a good meal. You must be hungry? Are you hungry?'

He looked baffled, unable to fathom what the stream of words meant, so she mimed the action of putting food into her mouth, and he nodded. Yes, he was hungry. He placed a hand on his stomach to emphasise it, as if any exchange between them might delay, might even alter her mind. He nodded again to emphasise his hunger. But it was his eyes that tormented her. Dark eyes, full of pleading and fear.

Please don't look at me like that, she wanted to say. 'They'll have to feed you, no matter what else happens,' was what she said instead, knowing he could not understand, but this time speaking for her own peace of mind, trying to rationalise the step she had to take.

If only she had not chosen this road to avoid the traffic . . . if only there had been no chaos on the Hume Highway . . . if only her light had not been on high beam. She felt angry with herself for the string of suppositions. It had happened and provisos of how it might have been avoided were futile and cowardly. She put the car into gear; it had to be done, there was no alternative. Indecision was only further tormenting him and causing her pain.

'No,' he whispered again, and this time it was accompanied by a sob as he tried to remove the anorak. The zip was stuck, but the jacket was big enough for him to pull over his head and struggle out of it. Then he ripped off his soaked T-shirt and turned his bare back towards Kate while uttering words that sounded frantic, gesturing her to look at it.

Kate was confused. She put out a tentative hand and felt what seemed like little ridges across his vertebrae. It was only when she switched on the car's interior light she could see what he had been attempting to show her. Livid scars disfigured the skin of the boy's back from his shoulderblades to his buttocks. He had been whipped. *Flogged* was the word that came into her horrified mind, and by the bruises and the rawness of the wounds, it had been a recent punishment.

~

Kate drove carefully. There was little traffic until after Bankstown airport when she began to be overtaken by long-haul trucks. Despite the rain they were speeding, passing far too close, dangerously so, their huge tyres sending up torrents of water that filled her windscreen. Shortly after this she heard the wail of a siren behind her, and in her driving mirror saw the menacing sight of a police car with all its lights flashing, rapidly closing the distance between them.

She hastily checked her speed; it was within the limit. Please God, she thought, not a faulty tail-light or some other reason to stop her and examine the car. Her heartbeat increased and she obediently slowed, ready to pull to the side of the road as the siren seemed to be demanding, but the patrol car went swiftly past and was lost to a bend ahead within moments. Perhaps he's going to nail one of the speeding trucks, she thought thankfully, and assuming she'd be safe from cop cars and heavy vehicles, she took the Milperra Road when she finally reached it.

It was a mistake; she realised that ten minutes later, when she saw the lights. There was a crash scene ahead, and what seemed like the same police car was stopped alongside a truck that had collided with a small sedan. In the blinding rain it was just possible to make out a uniformed figure with a torch waving her to slow down. She had a moment of panic. The boy seemed to be asleep; he had been ever since realising Kate was not heading back to the detention centre when she made the second U-turn. He had given her a look of heartfelt relief, then allowed himself to slide to the floor of the car where he pillowed his head on the passenger seat and had not moved since. Not even the siren had woken him; only the sudden slowing of the car now made him stir.

'Stay down,' she begged him, which only made him turn his

head sleepily and look up at her, wondering what was happening and trying to decipher what the urgency in her voice meant. They were almost at the crash scene when they heard the sound of another siren. The boy needed no telling; he ducked his head and huddled into a ball, out of sight. The lights of the other vehicle, an ambulance, appeared from the opposite direction. It was waved across the road in front of them by the drenched policeman as he signalled Kate to a full halt. She sat in an agony of apprehension only metres away from him, feeling a tightness in her chest. He moved to her side of the car and she had no choice but to open her window a fraction, trying to appear calm as he leaned down to speak, his voice almost inaudible in the drumming rain.

'Okay, ma'am. Drive carefully. No night to be out alone.'

'Thanks,' Kate said, closing the window with relief as he stepped back and she drove away. In the worsening conditions it would be at least another hour before she reached home.

'It's all right,' she said to the boy, and when he looked up she patted his shoulder to reassure him. In the glow of the instrument panel she glimpsed him nod in answer, then place his head on the seat as he had before. The next time she glanced down at him he looked asleep again. Exhausted, she thought; tired out from the long wakeful night and conveniently hidden from the sight of anyone in a vehicle that might draw alongside them when they reached the well-lit areas.

It seemed fortuitous until she began to realise it was nothing of the sort; this was a child who'd had to hide and escape before, from places far worse than this. At least everyone assumed they were worse. Yet the cruelty he carried like a testament had been meted out here in her own supposedly safe and civilised country.

While she drove she tried to imagine what could happen next.

She had crossed a line tonight, done something undreamt of, but had no regrets about her decision. It was utterly impossible to imagine taking this child back to the place where someone had inflicted such punishment, and where someone else, presumably a person in authority, had apparently allowed it to happen.

Chapter 22

When Kate reached home she was exhausted and the boy was now fully awake. There had been one other alarming incident, of all places in the road outside her house. By the time she drove across the Harbour Bridge the rain had eased to a drizzle and soon after this, as she passed over Munro Park and turned into The Crescent, it had stopped entirely. It was then that her headlights picked out a familiar figure striding along the middle of the road, and she recognised Victor Henderson. Clearly the rain had delayed his regular evening walk around the golf course until now, and she had a moment of anxiety that her passenger might sit up and be seen. So she tooted the horn to ensure Henderson stepped aside as she turned into her driveway.

She knew it had startled and probably provoked him. Most things did. She could see him in her rear-vision mirror, standing stock still beneath a streetlight and staring as she drove up the slope towards the house. Glaring, probably, she thought. Realising they must be at their destination, the boy began to sit up. Kate, noticing this almost too late, hissed a warning and put a hand on his shoulder to keep him down and out of sight.

They drove into the garage, and with a sigh of relief she used the remote control to close it. There was only the short ten-metre walk to the front door, but the porch light had automatically come on. She flicked the switch off in the garage, took the child by the hand, gestured with a finger to her lips to be silent, and they walked in the darkness towards the house. Kate could no longer see the street, or tell if the annoying Mr Henderson was still loitering there.

As soon as they were safely inside she helped him remove his wet clothes, ran him a bath, and while he was soaking in it she rang a number. The woman who answered was an Arabic speaker and a friend – the only person Kate could think of to trust. She desperately needed help to communicate with the boy.

'Can you cope tonight? I'll be there in the morning,' the voice on the phone said, and Kate had little choice but to assure her that she could manage till then.

After that she found a towelling dressing-gown that had belonged to Juliet when younger and wrapped him in it. Clean and comforted by the bath, he perched on a kitchen stool watching her intently while she prepared soup and heated bread rolls in the oven. Then they sat either side of the table for this hasty meal like two people who had known each other for some time, instead of strangers who had just met, unable to speak each other's language.

Kate looked at his shy smile and brown eyes that were no longer afraid, his small trusting face watching her every move, and wished she could keep him here in safety. But equally she knew this was impossible.

'That bloody woman,' Victor Henderson announced to his wife as he shut his front door, 'gave me a blast on the horn as if I was a nobody, and shot past me as if she was up to something.'

'Up to what?' asked his long-suffering wife, who knew if she didn't show interest it would mean trouble before bedtime.

'Up to something-no-fucking-good,' Henderson snapped. He had been in the military police for twenty years, and prided himself on knowing when a person was up to no good. There was an atmosphere, a look about them, a sniff of fear. His antennae could always pick it. And it was strange about the lights.

'What about them?' his wife asked, doing her best.

'The automatic light at their front door went on, like it always does,' he said. 'But it went straight off again, so it could only be that she turned it off in the garage and walked to the house in the dark. Now why would she do that unless she had something to hide?'

Margaret Henderson hadn't the least idea, but didn't like to say so. She thought Victor had 'a thing' about Mrs Forrester; maybe jealousy because she had the best block of land, or maybe because she was nice looking. Probably it was that – because he was sexual in an aggressive way and thought any woman fair game, particularly one without a partner, but there was no way in the world she would dare say anything like that.

'The body language,' Victor announced. 'It was a giveaway. You can always tell.'

What body language? his wife thought, if she was sitting in the car and it was dark anyway . . . She knew the trouble with Victor: after all this time he still resented not being in the army. Hated not being a military copper any more. Anything the slightest bit untoward and he'd make a mystery out of it, gnaw over it like a dog with a bone. She'd met and married him when he was a newly promoted captain on leave from Vietnam, with a smart uniform, a youthful swagger and a bunch of medals. Not knowing what he was really like.

She'd made a dreadful mistake, and grown afraid of her husband, as well as disliking him. Although hating him was a truer description. But she had no relatives and few close friends, and there was nowhere to go if she left him. She wouldn't tell him that either, but she felt sure he knew it.

In the middle of the night Kate woke and thought she heard a sound. She lay still and listened, then heard it again. She put on her dressing-gown and went across the hallway to the bedroom that had been Juliet's. Carefully opening the door she identified a sniffle from the small figure in the bed. He'd caught a cold from the hours spent in the rain, was her first reaction – but then she realised it was not that.

He was crying. Crying softly but relentlessly, as if his heart was broken. She switched on the light and saw the streaming tears. Sitting on the bed, she gathered him in her arms.

'What is it?' she asked, feeling helpless at their lack of verbal communication, as he clutched her tightly and now sobbed without restraint.

It was like a paroxysm of grief; Kate was shocked and confused by its intensity. She held him and tried to comfort him as best she could until the tears at last stopped, then she wiped his face, picked him up and carried him to her bedroom. She tucked him into her bed and climbed in the other side. When he saw this he snuggled eagerly into her arms and within a few moments was asleep. She heard his soft regular breathing, and felt his body relax. Kate lay awake for a long while wondering what could be done about him, how she must somehow contrive to stop him being sent back to Villawood, without having the faintest idea how this could be achieved.

She needed advice, and in such moments her thoughts invariably turned to Hugh. If he'd been with her in the car tonight, what would have happened? Would he have felt it too dangerous, warned her about the draconian law that imposed a long prison sentence on anyone helping escapees? Or would he have had a solution; it was this that kept eluding her as she finally fell asleep.

In the morning when she woke the boy was still wrapped in her arms, but his eyes were wide open and the first thing she saw was his contented face. It was like having a new and trusting child, but, told herself, she dare not think that way.

The boy's name was Omar and he was twelve years old. The friend Kate had telephoned the previous night arrived early. Rebecca Mannering was a softly spoken woman in her forties who had studied in Saudi Arabia, spent two years on an archaeological dig in Jordan and briefly worked as a nurse in Basra between the invasions of Iraq. She was fluent in the Gulf and Levantine dialects of Arabic, as well as Judaeo-Aramaic languages, and worked in the courts as an interpreter on refugee cases for Roger and other lawyers. She and Kate had frequent contact because of this and had become close friends; close enough to be trusted when Kate had called and asked for help.

Rebecca not only came to interpret but had brought a set of her son's clothes she hoped would fit Omar. Shorts, a T-shirt, a sweater, even shoes and socks. When she knelt down and addressed him in his own language he reacted excitedly at the sound of familiar words, and asked if he could please have another bath. It was a bubble bath this time; Kate found a packet tucked away in a cupboard and emptied it into the warm water, watching the way his eyes lit up as the bathwater foamed, and how he laughed and clapped his hands with sheer pleasure.

It was an enchanted moment, one that startled Kate with the feeling of emotion it engendered in her. She would've hugged him, but he jumped into the bath with a splash that brought Rebecca to see what had produced this joyful sound, and they watched him revelling in the soap suds. It was then that Rebecca saw the whip marks on his scarred back and could barely suppress a shocked exclamation.

'Should I ask how?' she murmured.

'Later,' Kate replied. 'But only if he wants to talk about it.'

The water was lukewarm before she could persuade him to leave the bubbles, accomplishing this by flourishing a king-sized towel, one that enveloped his skinny body almost twice. After this she gave him biscuits and lemonade, then dressed in his new clothes he talked freely to Rebecca and answered her questions, which in turn she interpreted for Kate. It was a heart-rending story of the kind they had both heard many times in the past few years, but told without any self-pity or poignancy – just the bare harsh facts.

His father had been killed at a bus stop outside their home in the city of Samarra by Saddam Hussein's elite guards. Shot while attempting to escape, the family had been told, but friends in the neighbourhood contested this; they said he wasn't escaping anywhere. Just waiting for a bus to the power station where he was a manager, and making the mistake of admonishing the guards for kicking a man they'd arrested.

A few months after this his elder brother, still angry at the father's murder and unwisely speaking of it in public, had been put in prison for dissent against the regime, and soon afterwards they heard he'd been hanged. It was then that his mother knew it was unsafe to stay, and hastily sold their home so they could finance their escape. She, along with Omar and his two sisters, had fled the country, taking the same route so many others had already travelled, to Indonesia where they survived for a year in limbo, and with almost the last of their money had found a people smuggler with a fishing boat. The mother and Omar survived, but both sisters died, drowned when the boat sank.

'The SEIV X?' Kate asked.

'No, the details were different,' Rebecca said. 'Omar and his mother survived by clinging to a scrap of driftwood all night until they were picked up by an Australian navy vessel; in the case of the SEIV there had been no naval ships in the vicinity to rescue survivors. From his description it seemed to have been a far smaller boat carrying only about twenty people, so its sinking had not made any headlines.'

Rebecca deduced that he'd been landed at what sounded like Port Hedland on the West Australian coast, but soon after his mother died as a result of the ordeal and, classified as an 'unaccompanied child', he'd been transferred to Villawood.

'But he was an orphan,' Kate said. 'How could he be kept in there?'

'You think it hasn't happened before?' Rebecca replied, who had been at Baxter and Woomera. 'The centres are full of people who shouldn't be there. Orphans, elderly people, all ages, all nationalities.'

'So for how long was he confined?' Kate wondered.

'About a year,' Rebecca estimated. 'He remembers last winter because it was so cold, then the bushfires and the heat of summer.'

A year! Kate thought, listening to Rebecca's soft voice and

the boy's answers. What kind of uncaring indifference made this possible? A small boy, an orphan, shouldn't have been there for a day, let alone a year.

Though she found it frustrating not being able to ask direct questions, through Rebecca's interpretation a picture was forming of a child lost in the bureaucratic morass, held in custody because he'd had no adult or lawyer to speak for him. Not knowing what was going to happen to him, why he was there or if he'd ever be released. The only friends he'd had in the world, he told Rebecca, were the other boys who were older and had organised the escape. He'd gone with them, but when they managed to cut the wire and crawl through during the night they'd said it was best to split up; four together would be too easy to recapture, and they'd left him on his own.

'So he just ran,' Rebecca said, 'ran as fast as he could for the rest of the night. He didn't know where he was running, so long as it was away from the detention centre. When he began to realise it was nearly daylight, he'd reached the park and he hid there.'

'All day in that pouring rain.' Kate tried to imagine his terror until hunger and cold had driven him back to the road where she'd found him.

Omar spoke again and Rebecca turned to Kate, translating his words with astonishment.

'He's some kid this, in view of what he's been through. He says it was lucky for him, the rain. He found a children's playground, deserted because of the weather. So he sat on a swing as he'd never been on one in his life before, then tried to keep warm by climbing the jungle bars and going up and down the slide.'

Kate saw Omar watching her. She tried to mime the roller-coaster motion of one person on a slippery slide, and he laughed. He came to where she sat, held out one of his hands and used the other, pretending to write on it. Then he looked at her expectantly.

'I know what you want,' she said, copying his mime. 'In the drawer behind you, Becky, there's a pad and pencil, even some crayons.'

'*Shukran,*' Omar said, thanking Rebecca, then spread himself on the floor and they watched him begin to draw. It took only a few minutes before he brought it to Kate for her inspection. It was a surprisingly good sketch of a tiny house, with the figure of a boy crouched inside it.

'Ah – I'd say that's a cubbyhouse' – Kate ruffled his hair affectionately – 'a cubby house at the playground. You sheltered in there.' She pointed at the figure in the drawing, then at Omar himself.

'*Na,am!*' He nodded, and rushed to show it to Rebecca. He spoke rapidly, indicating the drawing.

'What does *Na,am* mean?' Kate asked her.

'It means yes, you're right.' Rebecca confirmed. 'He's just told me it's a playhouse where he hid when the rain got heavy.'

Kate persuaded Rebecca to stay for lunch. She had already rung Roger to say she was indisposed and couldn't come to work that day. Omar brought his paper, the pencil and crayons to the kitchen table, and occupied himself busily drawing while Kate prepared a salad and the two women talked about the problem of what should be done.

'It's a tragic story,' Rebecca said, 'but it isn't likely to get him any special dispensation. We hear stories as bad every day.'

'Not quite as bad as this,' Kate said, 'if you take into account his age and those scars on his back. I think that makes it different.'

'It should,' the other agreed, 'but it won't. You know that.'

'So what's the answer?'

'I don't know the answer,' Rebecca replied.

Kate shook her head in disappointment. She sliced a mango to put in the salad bowl along with lettuce, tomatoes and red peppers, as well as slithers of apple and pear.

'Is that why everyone raves about your salads?' Rebecca pointed to the array of fruit it contained.

'The secret is, just chuck in everything,' Kate said, and asked her again what solution there was for Omar.

'Well, he has no family left, apart from cousins in Iraq, and he certainly can't go back there.' Rebecca was categorical about that.

'No. But he can't go back to Villawood either,' Kate replied with equal certainty, and there was an awkward pause while they both considered this statement. Omar lifted his head from his sketching and watched them, sensing this involved him and trying to gauge what was happening.

'You can't keep him, Kate . . .'

'I know. I just wish —'

'Don't wish.' Rebecca was explicit. 'The detention management are furious the media got hold of it. On news bulletins this morning they believe he may have had help. Because of the bad weather the police think he must still be in the area, unless someone gave him a lift. They'll have the names of everyone who was there yesterday, and you could even have the Federal cops turn up asking you questions.'

'In circumstances like this I'm more than willing to tell lies.'

'So am I. But be realistic. He can't be kept here indefinitely. What about your neighbours? Even the friendly ones might gossip.'

'I'm trying to be realistic. I do accept it's out of the question. I just want to know what's to become of him.'

'Have you said anything to Roger?'

'Not yet. Only that I needed today off.'

'I wouldn't tell him about this,' Rebecca advised.

'That's not the way we work. We never have secrets.'

'You should have one now. Or else you could put him in a very awkward position. An accessory, if the Federal Police got even a sniff of it . . .'

'Oh shit,' Kate said. 'I know that's sensible advice, but shit just the same.'

'Real shit,' her friend agreed, 'so we have to solve it. How about I make a phone call, and see what I can find out?'

'What sort of phone call?'

'Can I tell you that after I make it?'

Kate gestured to her telephone but Rebecca said the call had to be private, so she'd use her mobile out in the garden. Before she could leave, Omar spoke, and she translated his request.

'Omar asks could he have some more lemonade.' The boy added something and Rebecca smiled. 'And he wants to know if there's any chance of another bubble bath.'

Roger Montgomery was having a bad morning. A landlord in Fairfield, the owner of two rental properties, had informed his tenants he was doubling their rents, and as they were unable to pay, they had been evicted without notice. It was an event becoming too familiar to Roger: landlords were taking advantage of refugees with little experience of the law and the tight housing market. Four of the dispossessed, all refugee clients for whom he had won residential visas, had been waiting at the office when he arrived. Roger had a list of cases that would occupy him all day in court, so he intended to assign the task of finding them some emergency accommodation to Kate, but that idea had been put aside when she had called to say she was unable to work.

Trying to juggle court appearances while tackling the unscrupulous landlord had occupied him completely, and only the thought that Kate would be back to help tomorrow relieved the pressure. But now, having had a rushed sandwich from the shop downstairs for lunch, there was yet another call from her with the surprise news that a personal matter required Kate to take the rest of the week off.

Roger agreed; he had no option since she worked long hours for little salary and was rarely absent. But she had given no reason, which was quite unlike her, and he could not help wondering why.

Kate had set out lunch in the kitchen by the time Rebecca returned from the garden after her long phone call.

'I had to explain you're a friend and I trust you,' she said, apologetic about the need for privacy. 'I can't say much, except what you might've guessed by now. At certain times, when necessary, I'm a bit more than an interpreter.'

Kate looked at her with a feeling of sudden hope. Rebecca went on explaining as they sat at the kitchen table. Omar, fresh from his second bath of the day, was already there waiting.

'My contact – I can't mention names – will try to arrange a safe refuge. It's a matter of finding the most suitable people, then organising the necessary papers. There's just one slight problem.'

'What's that?' Kate asked.

'It takes time. At least a week.'

'A week? But in the meantime . . .'

'In the meantime I'm to tell you there's only one solution. He has to remain here.' She sensed Kate's sudden anxiety at this. 'It's impossible to move him anywhere else at such short notice. It could be dangerous, and bound to be upsetting for him, so there's no other option, Kate.'

'No,' Kate said, 'I can see that.'

'I wish I could stay to help you, but I've got a long list of cases and tribunal hearings. It could hardly be worse this week, a full workload every day.'

Kate nodded. Even while thinking of difficulties ahead, she fully understood the protracted hours interpreters had to work in the courts.

'Any problems you encounter, I can drop in at night to help, but only if it's urgent. My kids and Ben are not in the loop on this. The rule is we don't confide in anyone, even husbands.'

They became uneasily aware of Omar sitting with them, picking at his food and watching them, trying to divine what was being said.

'I'm sorry I haven't been able to tell you before,' Rebecca added, 'but this is what I've become involved in. The man I contacted is utterly reliable, but it's not easy to place a child. That's why he needs this extra time.'

'Are you sure he'll be able to find somewhere?'

'You can depend on it.'

It was reassurance, but with that came questions that troubled Kate about Omar's future.

'Will it be very far away?' Kate asked.

'We're never told where. It's safest not to know.'

'It could even be interstate, you mean?'

'Anywhere. Western Australia . . . Tassie . . .'

'So when he leaves . . .' Kate trailed off, not wanting to voice this.

'He'll go out of your life,' Rebecca confirmed, and gently added, 'it's the only way we can help people. You want him to be safe and free, that's how it's done. I was allowed to tell you this much, but I can't tell you any more.' She glanced at Omar. 'Let's change the subject. We're worrying him. You don't have to know the language to sense our concern, and this is one bright boy.'

Kate nodded, seeing his anxious gaze fixed on her. She rose from the table, patting his shoulder as she went past. Omar swivelled in his chair and watched her open the refrigerator and bring him a plate of jelly. Then she went to the freezer, and his eyes grew wide with expectation as she returned with a carton of ice-cream and a scoop.

'How's that, Omar?' She used the one word he knew. 'Okay?'

'Okay,' he answered with a big smile, and took a spoon to savour the first mouthful. He licked his lips and spoke to Rebecca.

'What did he say?' Kate asked.

'That it's delicious.'

Kate added a second scoop of ice-cream to his plate as Rebecca glanced at her watch and rose from the table. 'I've got to be on my way. Can you cope for a week?'

'I'll do my best,' Kate replied. 'Although I may run out of ice-cream,' she added, and when Rebecca translated this for Omar and they both laughed she realised how much easier it would if they could communicate. Even the simplest exchange was going to be a problem.

Rebecca collected her handbag, then spoke to the boy in Arabic.

'I've told him if you need to leave the house, he's to stay inside and not answer the door. If you have any worries, call my mobile. But as we never know these days whether Big Brother is listening, be discreet. Not too specific.'

'Are you serious?'

'I'm afraid so,' Rebecca said.

Kate walked to the door with her.

'I'm so grateful. I needed an interpreter so you were my obvious first thought. I didn't know you were in an asylum seekers' network.'

'After this you will have to try and forget it.'

'You can count on that, Becky.'

'I know I can. Otherwise I wouldn't have been allowed to help.'

'One thing still bothers me,' Kate said. 'I don't know if he spoke of this, but last night he cried. He was lying in the spare room sobbing his eyes out.'

'He told me.'

'I assume it was delayed trauma. So if it happens again . . .'

'I doubt if it will,' Rebecca answered. 'And it wasn't trauma,' she added.

'Then what? These were serious tears. Why?'

'Because he was happy,' was the unexpected reply.

'Happy?'

'He told me. He said he felt safe with you, and he hasn't felt safe with anyone since his mother died. Kids in there are distraught, so disturbed and plain bewildered at their treatment, that some sit silently and hardly ever talk. They won't allow anyone to get close to them; they reject even a friendly approach. You must have seen them.'

'I've seen a few,' Kate said, 'but this —'

'This is one stage further. Something awful happened in there.'

'Did he tell you who beat him like that?'

Rebecca shook her head. She looked back at Omar, still eating his ice-cream. 'A bad man, he said, wanted to do bad things.'

'Oh Christ,' Kate whispered.

'Maybe a guard, or . . . we'll never know. But the worst traumatised kids can't even laugh or cry any more. So it's good that he did cry. His tears were the first in a long time, because he'd found someone who cared.'

Kate stood at the door, watching her friend drive away, wondering how she could possibly live up to this kind of expectation. She felt a small hand slip into hers and looked down at Omar's anxious face.

'You and I have to learn how to talk to each other,' she said, and tried to think how they could manage that.

Chapter 23

By the time Kate tucked Omar into bed, she was almost ready for sleep herself. It had been a long time since she'd looked after a child, let alone one she was unable to converse with, and she felt compelled to be with him constantly. Yet as the afternoon went on she found instances of what seemed like communication between them.

She noticed it first when she said aloud that she thought she'd have a cup of tea. And perhaps she had also looked at the tea caddy or even the cups on the dresser, but whatever it was he must have been closely observing her, for he went across to the electric jug and switched it on.

'Thank you, Omar,' she said, clapping her hands in approval, and he smiled a happy smile. Then she brought a cup for each of them, and went through the process of how he liked his tea; a negative shake of the head to milk, but an enthusiastic nod to sugar. Three spoonfuls he signalled, holding up three fingers.

'That'll help your energy levels,' Kate said, and when he looked blank she adopted a physical pose with her arms flexed and fists clenched. That was when he copied her pose and raised another finger to request one more sugar. Making bridges without words began to seem like fun.

Later, when she went out to feed the kookaburra Omar was close by her side, rather nervously watching it fly down towards them, then laughing with great excitement as he saw it snatch the meat from her. Afterwards he'd tugged at her hand, anxious to hurry back into the house, where he took his pad and pencil and had drawn a sketch of the kookaburra poised to take the meat from her extended arm.

'Good,' she said, 'that's really good!' Finding a corkboard in the study on which to pin the drawing, Omar brought his earlier sketch and Kate pinned that up as well. She carried the board into the living room, and placed it in a prominent position on the rarely used old piano, sensing the pleasure this gave him.

While she prepared dinner she turned on the television, hoping to find a children's program, but he appeared disinterested until during the news there was a story on the continuing search by the United Nations for hidden weapons in Iraq. It contained footage of mosques and palaces in Baghdad, and he sat up intently, turning to Kate to gain her attention. She left the spaghetti she was cooking and came to watch. A moment later this changed to Saddam Hussein addressing a meeting, and Omar became agitated. He spoke some obviously angry words, then pointed two fingers in the shape of a pistol at Hussein, shouting 'Pow, pow', a child's universal simulated sound for gunfire.

Kate used the remote control and found him another channel. A soccer game was playing, and his face lit up. He spread himself on the floor in front of the screen, hands cradling his face to watch it. It kept him there until dinner was ready, but soon afterwards he was yawning, barely able to keep awake until she tempted him with another helping of ice-cream. When he was tucked in bed she kissed him goodnight, switched off the light, leaving the door open and the light on in the hall just outside his room.

It was then she remembered to check her phone messages of the past twenty-four hours. Among the calls was one from Juliet in London, saying she had exciting news and would send an email from an Internet café. In fact when Kate went to her computer, the email was already there.

Dear Mum,

Extraordinary things have happened on this side of the world, and I can't wait to tell you. I kept a diary all the time I was touring around Greece with Sofia and Michel, and as soon as I reached London I hired a laptop and put it down in an article. More or less just for fun, but it turned into something that felt good. Like 'Aussie girl meets her unconventional granny, and gets to know the country while they try to get to know each other.' I called it 'Greece with Grandmère.' Sofia might not forgive me, but it has a nice alliterative title.

So, I thought why not – and sent it off to my favourite newspaper here in England, *The Guardian*, and the big news is they've bought it! But the even bigger news is they asked if I can expand it and have commissioned two more articles.

Because of that I can afford to stay in England for another few months to write them, and I've had a few meals and made friends with one of the sub-editors, who says it's the way they trial people, and if I can come up with the goods he thinks there could be something more permanent, like regular freelance articles. I'm trying not to get too excited because I think he fancies me a bit, and maybe his scenario is wishful thinking. But of course I am excited, and my mind is teeming with lots of great ideas.

I did promise Sofia and Michel I'd go back to Greece, as they want to take me skiing, but that's cancelled now. Between us, I think she'd like to see me settle in Athens, as if after abandoning a daughter on the other side of the world she'd quite like to acquire a grand-daughter instead to make up for it. That's my private opinion, but don't start a family war by letting her know I said so. And don't worry, a new life in Greece won't tempt me. On the other hand, a few years in London might. It all depends how my next articles go. Cross your fingers that this will really get me back on track as a journalist, the kind I always wanted to be, and away from writing about soap, cosmetics and tampons for ever.

Fondest love, Juliet

That night Kate wrote a brief reply, saying her fingers were firmly crossed, even though it occurred to her that success for Juliet in England might mean some years before they'd see each other again. But the upbeat letter was a relief; she seemed so buoyant and optimistic; such a contrast to the unhappiness and negativity of the past year.

Impulsively she put in a P.S. I have a small friend staying with me for a few days, and am going to search for some of your old books like the *Famous Five* or the *Terrible Ten* and read to him at nights. As we don't speak the same language it should be an interesting experiment . . . Then, thinking of Rebecca's warning, she deleted this.

Yet it seemed needlessly circumspect. She knew there was a surfeit of new security laws, but surely on her own computer such protection was absurd . . . She almost hit the key to reinstate it, but in the end decided on caution.

~

When Kate went to the front gate the next morning to collect the newspaper, there was a paragraph that reported the third youth in the escape from Villawood had been treated in hospital and was now back in the detention centre. It was confidently expected the fourth would soon be back in custody.

The report concluded with a statement from Federal Police that anyone having knowledge of the missing youth should not approach him. The Centre Management confirmed he was a known troublemaker, and in the public interest the police were advising he might be dangerous.

Talk about spin, Kate thought, deliberately calling him a 'youth' to create the impression he could be a teenager. He's a little boy; small for his age. As for labelling him a troublemaker who could be dangerous, she angrily wondered if the Australian press had given up investigative journalism, and now printed whatever misrepresentation was handed to them by government outlets.

Omar was torn between joy and nervous excitement. He carried a strip of meat that Kate had given him, and she produced her camera as they went outside to feed the kookaburra again. This time Omar was to do the feeding; Kate gestured for him to stand and wait while she found a good angle, then signalled him to move closer.

He held out the meat, feeling increasingly anxious as the bird stayed on the ground, uneasy at the boy's presence and this change of routine. Kate snapped a shot of this, then kept clicking until the kookaburra decided his hunger outweighed timidity, and flew the last few metres to snatch the meat from Omar's outstretched hand. The boy's mouth opened in startled surprise, his eyes sparkled and his burst of laughter was joyfully infectious as the kookaburra flew up towards his hidden family, vanishing into the gum tree.

They went inside and she plugged the camera into her computer. Omar sat beside her, watching in silent wonder as the series of pictures appeared in a slide show, until Kate selected the one taken in the split second the food was grabbed from his hand.

That's the one! she thought. His face caught in a magic moment of elation and sheer delight. She found glossy photo paper and printed two copies, indicating to him they must let them dry.

After that she showed him how to hold the camera and what to press. She posed a short distance away smiling as he took her photo. When it was displayed on the screen he clapped his hands with pleasure at his achievement. Kate printed a copy and when it was dry gave it to him. Omar took it to the piano in the living room, and pinned it on the corkboard like a trophy.

In Villawood the blame was being assessed in an atmosphere of rising anger and urgency. Investigation had proved there had been a complete lack of security and no proper check before lights out that night; the four escapees had hidden in an equipment shed that should have been locked, and before dawn, with the aid of a stolen file, had managed to cut a hole in the razor wire. The guards at the time had already been found guilty of drinking while on duty and suspended without pay. In the meantime the three boys who had been recaptured were put in separate isolation cells, awaiting an interpreter. Two were Iranians, one a Palestinian. They'd been subjected to sleep deprivation, reduced rations and kept in a state of extreme anxiety for over forty-eight hours since their recapture.

The problem, according to Brian Benedict, the detention

centre's deputy assistant in charge of the investigation, was a matter of finding a suitable interpreter. He declared the choice of Rebecca Mannering, who was at the centre that day for another appointment, to be quite unsuitable. On being asked to delay her appointment and attend the interrogation of the escapees, she had refused until they'd been properly fed and allowed to rest.

'The woman's a well-known chardonnay-drinking bleeding-heart member of the loony left,' he fulminated to the senior administrator, claiming she had taken the side of detainees while working at Woomera, where she had made inflammatory statements to the press. He asked for someone else and was irritated to be told Ms Mannering was the best available, and since he had taken it on himself to treat the three boys like adult insurgents, he'd better resolve the matter and make peace with her before more shit hit the fan. There had been too many bad-news stories, and the immigration minister was complaining.

It was a disgruntled deputy assistant who was obliged to tell Rebecca the treatment of the boys was not of his making, and they would be fed and allowed a short rest before the interrogation.

'Not too short a rest,' she insisted, and it was midafternoon before an enquiry took place.

Rebecca's skill was at once apparent as the cross-examination began and she deftly switched between translations for the Iranians and then the Palestinian. She soon realised all three were telling carefully contrived and almost identical stories, but since the questioning was being recorded she had to faithfully interpret what was said.

Their answers were that the escape had been the sole idea of the Iraqi boy still at large, whom they only knew as Omar. He'd hatched the plan, having been told the guards on late duty were known to get drunk and be careless. He'd stolen a file from the tools of a visiting workman, which was used to cut the wire. Yes, they asserted, they were telling the truth. They had been foolish to listen to him, but he was very persuasive.

'I don't think I believe them,' Rebecca decided she had to risk telling Deputy Assistant Benedict and his group of interrogators.

'Why not?' she was asked.

She carefully phrased her reply. 'I've been told the boy was much younger than them,' she said. 'These three are tough and streetwise. In my opinion you should doubt their stories.'

'It's not your opinion we need, Ms Mannering,' Benedict replied with some satisfaction. 'You're an interpreter, nothing else. Just ask them, when they split up, where this scheming little bastard was heading.'

Rebecca remained impassive, concealing all trace of antipathy as she asked the question. Unfortunately, she thought, this time the three were telling the truth. The last they'd seen of him, Omar was running down Woodville Road in the rain.

'Where might he go from there?' Benedict asked his committee, no longer paying any attention to Rebecca. She saw one of them refer to a large-scale map of the district, and watched him trace his finger down Woodville Road to the main junction of the Hume Highway.

'He'd be scared of traffic on the main road, even late at night. So he'd most likely go this way. Towards Shortland Brush or Mirambeena Park. Both good places to hide, especially the next day in the rain.'

'Until some misguided Samaritan picked him up,' Benedict said, and noticing Rebecca was still waiting there, brusquely told her she could go.

'They've worked out where he went,' Rebecca said that night. She came to give Kate a special mobile phone. 'Use this if you have to call me for any reason. It's safe . . . Guaranteed secure by a tame Telstra technician.' Over a drink she outlined the day's interrogation, and how the blame had been put on Omar.

'Nobody will surely believe that!' Kate said, incredulous that the small boy she'd earlier tucked into bed could be thought such a conspirator.

'Benedict will,' Rebecca assured her. 'He's as thick as two planks. It's another reason we have to get Omar out of here as soon as possible.'

Kate had conflicting feelings about the prospect. 'Any word on that yet?'

'Not yet. Can you cope?'

'That's not the problem.'

'What is?' Rebecca asked.

'I think I'm going to miss him.'

Chapter 24

Roger had worked late and was about to leave the office when there was a knock at the door. It was the last thing he needed; it had been an arduous day, again emphasising just how much of the workload Kate took for him, although he knew it already.

'I'm sorry,' he called as a visitor entered, 'but the office is closed.'

'Federal Police. Sergeant Lance Wallace.' He was an extremely tall man, unusually thin, with a high forehead, and any remaining strands of his hair were deftly spread across his scalp. 'It's Mrs Forrester I wish to talk to. I believe she works here?'

'She does,' Roger said, 'but she's taken a week off. Can I help?'

'You could confirm whether she attended the Villawood Detention Centre two days ago.'

'She did,' Roger said, 'she went there to interview a client for me. I actually meant, can you tell me the reason for the enquiry?'

'That's a private matter for Mrs Forrester,' the sergeant answered. 'Is she to be found at her home address?'

'As far as I know,' Roger said, 'although I don't keep up with her daily movements.' He was trying not to be irritated by the other's manner. It seemed to come with his height – almost a head taller than Roger – and verged on the imperious.

'Is it her custom to take a week off?'

Roger frowned. There were civil ways to request information, and this man seemed determined to ignore normal procedure.

'I don't understand what you mean by that question.'

'It seems fairly straightforward, Mr Montgomery.' He glanced at a file he carried. 'You are Mr Montgomery?'

'Yes, I am . . . and I still don't know what you mean by your question. Kate Forrester manages this law office. She works long hours and no, it's not her *custom*, as you put it, to take a week off. But she felt like a break, which doesn't surprise me. So why the interrogation?'

'Hardly that. Just a simple enquiry, sir, which you have managed to answer, after all. And what time did she leave Villawood that day?'

'I haven't the remotest idea, Sergeant Wallace. I expect if you come back next week she'll be able to assist you. As you don't wish to tell me the reason why you're here, I really can't help you.'

The Federal Policeman had a cold stare that he used to effect before abruptly turning and leaving the office.

The next morning Kate drove along The Crescent and headed for Cammeray, where she turned east onto Military Road and Neutral Bay. It was not until they had passed through Mosman village that she tapped Omar on the shoulder, and he rose from hiding on the floor of the car and occupied the seat beside her. She indicated the seatbelt and slowed down in case he had any trouble with it, but he attached it around himself and smiled at her glance of approval.

He was excited, she could tell. So am I, she thought.

It was a risk, and she dreaded to think what Rebecca might say, but after four days in the house she could tell he was becoming restless and she had begun to run out of ideas on how to entertain him. Then she remembered picture books stored away in a trunk from Juliet's childhood that she had kept in a sentimental moment.

So it was with some pleasure that when she found them and gave the books to Omar he spent hours pouring over them. In particular a book of animals seemed to fascinate him. The next morning she found he had meticulously drawn lions and tigers as well as an elephant and a giraffe. It was seeing them pinned on the corkboard that gave her the idea.

She packed a picnic lunch, mimed a message that they were going out by car, and went down to the mailbox to check that no one was in the street. Reassured, she came back to be surprised he had changed into a clean T-shirt, after which she locked the house and accompanied him out to the garage. In the car she had no need to gesture for him to sit on the floor and keep out of sight, he had already taken up position there. And now he was sitting beside her, gazing at the mansions on Bradley's Head Road, a succession of fine old Victorian and Edwardian homes that these days were sometimes divided into apartments, but still gave off an aura of past grandeur.

When the road ended she turned into a car park. Omar reached for the picnic basket, then they locked the car and went to the ticket booth.

'One adult, and my nephew who's visiting Sydney,' Kate said, and the woman gave them the tickets, smiled and wished the boy and his aunt a nice day. They went through the turnstile and entered the zoo.

—

'On our list there are still four cars to be checked that left the Centre late that afternoon,' Sergeant Wallace said, 'and I've eliminated two of them. It leaves a lawyer who was in a meeting with the committee, so he's hardly in the frame, and a caseworker on a legal visit.'

'Who's that?' Brian Benedict asked.

'Mrs Forrester. Kate Forrester, attached to Roger Montgomery.'

'Attached,' Benedict said with a salacious grin, 'does that mean they're fucking?'

'Colleagues,' Wallace retorted, who was rather straitlaced and thought the deputy assistant manifestly vulgar.

'I've seen her around the place.' Benedict was intent on prurience. 'I wouldn't half mind giving her one.' He made a rigid fist and shrugged when Wallace looked unimpressed and turned away. 'So where are you going?'

'To find her and check her out. Where the hell do you think?'

They went slowly down the winding pathways, past the aviaries with brightly beautiful rosellas and parrots, lyrebirds with tails like oriental fans, robins, fairy wrens and a black-faced cuckoo-shrike. 'Which is neither a full cuckoo or a full shrike' said the notice on the wire enclosure, and Kate enjoyed the description, wishing Omar could read it.

He kept darting forward to gaze at the birds, and then move back to grip Kate's hand. She was carrying the picnic basket, and frequently put it down to use her camera and capture moments of him mesmerised by the range of animals. When they passed the laughing kookaburras, one was in full voice and Omar stood and listened to it, then looked up at Kate open-mouthed, as if to say their kooka didn't make a noise like that.

I understand you perfectly, she thought, and knew if he was free and able to stay with her they would soon be having chats about all manner of things. She had a moment of regret she would never be able to spend that kind of time with him.

At the monkey enclosure he was at his most vivacious, laughing in sheer excitement at their antics as they swung on branches and scratched themselves. A middle-aged couple kept watching this interchange between the boy and the chattering primate with smiling interest.

'Lovely to see such enjoyment,' the woman said to Kate, and the man patted Omar on the arm and handed him the remnants of a bag of peanuts to feed them. When he looked in confusion to Kate, she quickly retrieved the bag from him and apologetically gave it back to the man.

'I promised his mother he wouldn't feed the animals,' she said, 'she's a friend from overseas, and rather strict in her views.'

'Well, she's right,' the woman said, pointing to a sign requesting the public not to feed the animals. 'What's the boy's name?' she asked.

'Omar,' Kate said, unable to avoid answering. She was anxious not to linger with the congenial couple before there were more questions.

'Where's he from?' the man asked.

Hong Kong was the first name she thought of, and it was said before she could think of the consequences.

'He doesn't look Chinese.' They were appraising him, still affable but curious now.

'No,' Kate said, hurriedly trying to improvise her way out of the blunder. 'I mean that's where they've flown from. The family live in Dubai, but they're just here for a visit. He doesn't speak English yet.' She gave a quick glance at her watch. 'We have to meet the parents in an hour, and he wants to see everything. We better get weaving.'

'Well, enjoy the rest of it,' the man said. 'Nice to see a young bloke having a good time at our zoo. Even better to meet one who came through the front door, not like that mob of boat people.'

Kate waved and steered Omar away. When he abruptly stopped at the orangutans, Kate could just hear the couple as they moved off.

'You and your boat people,' the woman chided him, 'of course he's not one of them. But I meant to ask her what language they use if he can't speak any English.'

Whew, Kate thought; protect me from inquisitive strangers. As they moved on to gorillas and grey gibbons she tried to devise a more sensible reply in case they had another friendly encounter.

Roger phoned and heard Kate's answering system. He left a message that it was in regard to the mental state of the Jordanian recidivist she'd seen the day of the escapes, for the Immigration Department had refused to reconsider, and he would be on a plane to Amman unless they could pull something out of the hat. It seemed the iniquity of deporting a man to a country he'd left as a baby, where he had no hope of earning a living, was not on the conscience of the department, so the only chance for their client was to have him committed.

'Not a nice outcome,' he told her machine, 'but we live in insensitive times, Kate. On a more personal note, I have to say I miss you. The office becomes hard to manage, frantic queues all down the stairs again and along the street. The natives, meaning our local shopkeepers, are restless. Anna says I'm lucky you only want a week off, and thinks we should take regular holidays like normal people. Which is all very well for my wife the pathologist, as we all know there's money in medicine, and not in our kind of law.

'I'm sorry to rabbit on, Kate. I'm probably using up half your tape. A cop came to see you yesterday, a Federal Policeman, who wouldn't confide in me but I think it's about the detention centre. Not a very agreeable sort of cop, I thought, but I daresay he has to keep us safe from kids absconding, although probably the poor little bugger is back inside by now. And on that sour note it's over and out. Ring me. Anna wants you to come to dinner tonight if you can. Short notice but here's hoping.'

He hung up, and could not help speculating on her unexpected request for a break. Maybe she'd met someone. That would be good, he thought. No partner all these years since Hugh. A couple of fleeting affairs, according to Anna, who said Kate had settled for living alone.

A bloody shame, he thought.

Omar looked longingly at the harnessed elephant, with children strapped in seats along his flanks, as it passed them. Kate felt sure he would love it, but feared for what might happen with him stranded amid a bunch of cheerful and curious children. She felt relieved when he gave a tiny shake of his head, and they moved on to the pygmy hippopotamus, then the pandas and a snow leopard.

She thought again how instinctively they communicated, and how easy it would be to teach him English. She'd begun to wonder why he had never learnt even a few words, and remembered Rebecca's remark about the pain and confusion of some children. Perhaps in addition to not laughing or crying, some had become determined never to understand the orders they were given. There were a lot of psychologists and even volunteer visitors and caseworkers who must be studying this problem.

Kate was eager to pass the snakes, but Omar was rapt. He pointed at the sleek head and olive-coloured scales of one who lay coiled on the ground like rope. *Oxyuranus scutellatus*, said the sign, *Coastal Taipan*.

'That's not for taking home as a pet, my darling,' Kate could not resist saying aloud, 'that's the most dangerous snake in the zoo.'

'Just about,' said a grizzled man, wearing a suit and tie and an old akubra hat that spoke of outback acres, 'though I'd also watch out for the King Browns, little mate.' He grinned and doffed the hat at Kate. 'Mind you, the Egyptian cobra can do a bit of damage. And the Mulga.'

'I'm taking him to see the pelicans.' Kate smiled, tugging Omar away from the reptilian zone with its allure of dragons, crocodiles and other frightening amphibians.

They continued to zigzag their way down the sloping pathways of the zoo, frequently catching glimpses of the water, and once, when the trees allowed, seeing the great sweeping panorama of the harbour and the city towers beyond. Kate held Omar as high as she could lift him so he could view the dazzling sight below. It was the harbourside position that gave Taronga Park Zoo its fame. There were ferries plying back and forth towards the Quay, and a distant yacht race with myriad sails on the sunlit water had an impressionist eloquence like a McCubbin painting.

It's such a long time, Kate thought, since I stood here and saw this view. Juliet's eighth . . . no, her ninth birthday, and Hugh picked her up and put her on his shoulders to show her this sight, and then we all went for a ride on a ferry.

Which seemed the next rational thing when they reached the lower exit to the zoo and the harbour terminal as a ferry was approaching. Kate knelt beside Omar and pointed to it. His face lit up, the soft brown eyes widened and appeared to be asking if this was really possible. Dreams were unfolding today, way beyond his wildest imagination.

Kate took his hand. They went to buy tickets for the trip across to the harbour to Circular Quay and back again.

Driving home, she was tired but utterly fulfilled. Omar's happy face made her feel as if it had been one of the best days of her life. They had stood on the steps of the Opera House, walked up Macquarie Street to the Botanic Gardens, then returned to the famous fish shop opposite Circular Quay, purchased a bundle of fish and chips each, and eaten them on the ferry while returning to the zoo. The picnic basket she had so meticulously prepared that morning was ignored; still carried unopened when they took the sky safari chair lift back to the car park. And the aerial trip above the zoo had its own wonder for Omar, because he could see the entire harbour from the Bridge to Watson's Bay, a gorgeous panorama of limpid blue and through it, like an unexpected bonus to the day, a stately passenger ship negotiating its way towards the overseas terminal.

When they drove out of the car park Omar slid from the seat and adopted his concealed position. It was a slow trip back through heavy traffic, and by the time they came down the winding road from Cammeray and into The Crescent it was late afternoon. The sun was low in the west, distracting her when she headed up her own driveway, and it was only at the last moment that she saw two cars parked there, and two people waiting. One of them was Roger Montgomery; the other a very tall thin man who turned with ill-concealed impatience at the sight of her arrival.

Thank God for Omar still huddling out of sight, she thought, as she ignored the tall man's signal to stop, opened her garage door with the remote control and drove in, closing it behind her. She just had time to gesture the boy to stay there, warning him to silence with urgent fingers to her lips, before she hurriedly emerged from the side door to confront at least one unwelcome visitor.

Chapter 25

Roger moved quickly to greet her with a kiss on the cheek and a hurried apology. 'Sorry to drop in, Kate. I arrived a few moments ago to find Sergeant Wallace of the Federal Police here, also waiting —'

'No need for that, thank you,' Wallace interrupted him brusquely. 'I'm quite able to introduce myself.' He produced his I.D. for Kate to inspect. 'I need to ask you some questions, Mrs Forrester.'

'Well,' Kate said, looking from one to the other and trying to appear composed, 'perhaps we'd all better go inside.'

She unlocked the front door. 'Did you get either of my messages?' Roger asked her as they went into the house.

'No, I've been out all day.'

'Anna was hoping you'd come to dinner. Tonight, if you're free? That's why I stopped off on the way home.'

'Sorry, Dodger, not tonight. I've had a rather full day.' She turned to the policeman. 'Look, I really need to freshen up. Could you come back in half an hour?'

'It would be more satisfactory,' Wallace informed her, 'if we had our interview now.'

'Well, if it won't take long,' Kate said, starting to feel anxious.

'That depends on you, Mrs Forrester. Perhaps Mr Montgomery can say whatever he wishes to say, and then leave us?'

'I don't think that's necessary.' Roger deliberately removed his overcoat, hanging it on the hall stand. 'I'm not accustomed to being told to leave a friend's house by anyone. And as she's not only a friend but my associate and I'm also her lawyer, I'd prefer to stay.'

'I can't think why you're taking this attitude, Mr Montgomery.'

'It's no attitude, Sergeant.' Roger seemed relaxed and totally unfazed, as he followed Kate into the living room. 'You ask your questions. I'll ask Kate if there's any chance of a beer.'

'Usual place, Roger,' she said, then felt it obligatory to include the police officer. 'I don't suppose . . .'

'No, thank you, Mrs Forrester,' he answered so curtly she knew he was thoroughly annoyed. She was unsure what game Roger was playing, but he and the sergeant clearly disliked each other. It was reassuring to have him there, but not if it prolonged the police visit. She just had to pray Omar would remain in the car, because otherwise . . .

'I'm sorry,' she said, realising the other had spoken.

'I said this is pure routine, madam. I hope you understand that?'

'I imagine so. Would you care to sit down?' she asked.

'No, thank you. I prefer to stand.'

Kate sat in an armchair. Roger came back from the kitchen with a beer. He went to lean against the piano by the row of casement windows, drinking from the bottle as he watched them. Wallace tried to ignore him.

'We're checking on people who were at Villawood on Monday, the day of the escape, and you may be able to assist us.'

'Assist?' She managed to look suitably puzzled. 'But the escapes were the previous night. I thought it was all resolved.'

'It's the time of your departure that afternoon we're interested in. Can you tell me what time you left.'

'Quite late. We were kept there to answer questions.'

'Five twenty-five,' Wallace said, referring to notes on a paper he took from his pocket. 'That was recorded on our exit scanner.'

'If you say so,' Kate replied. 'It was getting dark, so it must've been about then.'

'What road did you take on the way home?'

'There was heavy traffic. I took a detour though the Mirambeena Park.' She saw him glance at his notes and nod. She'd had a feeling the policeman at the crash site might have routinely taken the car number, so the truth was safest.

'It's the area we believe the escapee was hiding.'

'I suppose he could've been.'

'But you didn't see him?'

'No,' Kate replied, looking directly at him. 'How could I see anything? It was a difficult drive in heavy rain, and hard to even see the road, let alone anything else.'

'So you saw no one?'

Kate shook her head and shrugged as if this was repetitive, and in doing this glimpsed the corkboard still on the piano, with her photo and Omar's crayon sketches pinned on it. She saw Roger follow her gaze, lower his beer bottle and casually pick up the board.

'Mrs Forrester?'

'Sorry, I thought I'd answered. I saw nothing, except a police car at a smash, and a wet cop in the rain who told me to drive carefully.' Roger now sat on the piano stool, and the corkboard was out of sight. The relief emboldened her. 'Why all this, Sergeant? Surely they've been recaptured by now.'

'All but one.' Wallace turned to see what had diverted her. Roger, still perched on the piano stool, raised the beer bottle to him.

'Finished with my client?' he asked.

'I'm required to carry out instructions,' Wallace said, tight-lipped. 'And since Mrs Forrester has not yet been cleared, my orders were to interrogate her. She was one of the last to leave, and she did drive home along the route taken by this troublemaker.'

'Troublemaker? A small boy,' Kate said impulsively, and saw from the expression on Roger's face that he wished she hadn't spoken.

'How did you know that?' Wallace rapped out the question.

'In the paper,' she said unthinkingly, then realised her mistake. 'Or did I hear it at the detention centre? There was a lot of talk while we were there, so that was probably it.'

'It most certainly was not in the papers.' The federal officer was adamant. 'The centre kept the ages of all the escapees out of the news.'

'Why was that, Sergeant?'

'Policy, Mrs Forrester.'

'Of course. The policy of not reminding the public that they imprison children.'

He disdained to reply to this. Roger got suddenly to his feet.

'I'm afraid my client is tired, Sergeant Wallace. She's given you what answers she can, and now you're unduly harassing her.'

'I rather thought she was attacking me, or perhaps the Villawood management, Mr Montgomery.'

'I'm sure we both realise that refugee advocates and those who visit the detention centres have their own private views on the place and what occurs there,' Roger said in his most engaging and reasonable manner.

'But we have to deal with these people,' Wallace replied, trying to match his equanimity.

'*These people*,' Kate said, unable to prevent herself. 'I do have a problem with that phrase.' As they both turned to look at her, Roger in warning and the sergeant in perplexity, she added: 'It's a description I remember when I was *these people*. It applies to any minority, Sergeant Wallace. Me when I was a migrant, to the Vietnamese and every other kind of refugee since then . . . it's intolerant and discriminatory —'

'Kate!' It was Roger, angrily trying to make her shut up, and she suddenly realised the tension had unbalanced her like a delayed attack of shock. There was a little boy hiding in the car outside after a joyous day who was totally dependant on her, her long-time friend Roger, who knew something was going on and was anxious not to hear more, and the tall, half-bald Federal cop, who was only doing what he'd been told to do.

'I'm awfully sorry,' she said.

'Well, so am I if I upset you,' Wallace said. 'I just follow orders. It might seem as if I'm being officious, but it's my job. I know it's one small boy, but I'm told he must be found. Sometimes you people are inclined to forget that he did come from a country where children are often recruited as suicide bombers.'

When his car drove out of sight, Roger watched it from the windows, and Kate returned from the front door. She wanted to reassure Omar who was still in the garage, but had to hope he would wait for the second vehicle to leave. In the meantime she wondered what she could possibly say to Roger as he handed her the corkboard.

'Dodger —' She started to frame an apology, but he held up a hand to prevent her.

'You obviously can't join Anna's dinner party tonight.'

'No, I can't.'

'When?'

'Next week,' Kate said.

'And by then . . .'

'By then I'll be able to come to dinner.'

'I'll tell her.' He paused. 'Now – can I tell *you* something, Kate?'

'I expect you will.'

'I did call here to ask about dinner tonight. Then I saw the Federal cop waiting, and thought I should stick around. Do you know why?'

She shook her head, although she felt sure she did.

'Because I thought it impossible, but one part of my brain said you were an impulsive romantic . . . who might just have been insane enough, or soft enough, to have jeopardised your life and our ten . . . no, eleven-year-crusade to do something for our clients. Remember them? The poor bastards who flee from the fucking Taliban or Al Quaeda in fear of their lives, forced to risk horrifying journeys in leaky boats. And if they somehow survive this and get here, what does our country offer them in the way of shelter? Razor wire and years of being treated as criminals. Or worse – because even hardened crims have a trial and a set jail term, whereas our clients are locked away without a charge; they can be handcuffed, sedated, kept in solitary, shipped to Nauru, driven to despair or insanity, and most people neither know nor care. That's what we try to fight, Kate, and any quixotic gesture that endangers this disturbs me more than I can say.'

She had seen him being passionate in court, but had never had his hard-edged rhetoric directed at her. There was no point in protesting her innocence; the corkboard she held was an admission of guilt.

'Shall I try to explain?'

'No. Please don't say a word.'

He was right, of course. Right not to be told anything, right about her impulsiveness. But he had grown up in an affluent environment, an Anglo who had never had to listen to epithets like dago or wop or reffo, or ever gone to school terrified about what would be said in the eleven o'clock break or the lunch hour. And yet nobody had been closer to her since the day she joined his father's firm as a lowly clerk. And few people in her life were more important than Roger and his wife Anna.

'Tell Anna I can't come to dinner tonight or the rest of this week,' she said. 'But next week, would that be convenient? And if it is, we'll talk of other things. I'd like to tell you about what's happened to Juliet, soon to be a columnist for *The Guardian* newspaper in England.'

'That sounds like tremendous news.' Roger looked pleased. And after a moment said quietly, 'You take care, Kate.'

She stood in the driveway and watched him drive away. Then she went into the garage. Omar sat curled on the floor of the car, his head resting on the front passenger seat, fast asleep.

The kookaburra was perched on the clothesline outside his window, waiting to be fed. Omar pushed his face through the bedroom curtains, propped his elbows on the windowsill to support his chin in his hands and watched the bird thoughtfully for a while, wondering if he ever laughed like the noisy one at the zoo. It had been the most wonderful day yesterday, all the animals and the ferry ride, and the boats they'd waved to on the harbour. It nearly made him want to cry, it was so nice.

He had woken early and already been to the bathroom. He thought she must still be asleep, because the door to her bedroom was shut. An idea came to him. He knew the paper was delivered early each day by a man in a car who drove past the house and threw it wrapped in plastic stuff to stop it getting wet. He decided to surprise Kate. That was her name. He could spell it in letters, but saying it was different. Kay-et. Kay-t. Kayt, he practised saying it softly aloud. That's what he'd do, fetch the paper and surprise her by putting it outside her bedroom door. And then, after she'd read it and they had breakfast, she'd show him some of the pictures she'd taken at the zoo.

He dressed and tiptoed through the house, slipped out the front door, leaving it open, and went down the sloping garden towards the road. Everywhere was quiet, which was good, because the other lady – Becky – had told him it was important not to let anyone else see him. He looked for the newspaper, not able to find it at first, until he realised it was stuck in the middle of some bushes near the letterbox. He crawled in there to recover it, and while stretching out to reach it he began to hear footsteps.

Quick footsteps, like a man walking fast. Almost like the noise of a soldier marching. They came close and stopped. He could see a man standing near Kayt's letterbox. He'd just stopped there, looking. But looking at what? He seemed to be looking at the house, then he came closer and opened her mail box. But he wasn't a postman, so why was he doing that? Was he a robber, going to steal something from Kayt?

Omar thought he must try to warn her, but first he reached for the newspaper, and it was the rustle of the bushes that caused the man to turn and see him. They were only a few feet apart.

'Bloody hell,' Victor Henderson said, 'who are you?'

Omar was frozen. He'd been seen; Becky had said it was very important not to be seen, but this was someone doing bad things against Kayt. He shouted and gestured at the man to go away.

'Jesus Christ, you're a fucking Arab!'

As the man tried to reach out to grab him Omar jumped back, turned and ran as fast as he could up the slope of the garden and into the house.

Henderson saw him enter and heard the door slam. He turned to run back along The Crescent towards his own house.

Kate heard the front door slam, and was half out of bed when Omar rushed into her bedroom with the newspaper.

'That's a lovely surprise,' she said, then realised he was breathless and distressed. 'What is it, Omar? What's the matter?'

He gasped out words in Arabic, pointing, trying to tell her. Then he beckoned her, and ran out to the casement windows that faced down towards the street. Kate followed him, as he pointed again, spoke some more in his own language, trying desperately to explain.

She was baffled by his increasing agitation. He ran to get the drawing pad and a pencil, and drew a letterbox. She gazed at it, puzzled.

'Something in the letterbox?'

Omar knew she didn't understand. So he started to try and draw the man. The main thing he could remember was a thin moustache, so he drew this.

'Oh my God,' Kate said, and mimed the way Victor Henderson marched with a strut, moving her arms up and down.

He nodded.

'He saw you?'

When he looked puzzled she put her hands to her eyes like a pair of binoculars.

Omar nodded again, pointing to himself.

'Oh shit,' Kate said, and snatched up the phone, then remembering just in time to use the mobile Rebecca had given her.

Margaret Henderson had settled with the newspaper, looking forward to a peaceful hour before her husband came back from his walk, when she heard the door slam.

'Is that you?' she said, upset at the loss of her quality time.

'Well, it's not likely to be a lover, is it? Not the way you look in the morning.' He found the telephone book and started to search for a number. 'I told you, didn't I? I said a few days ago she was up to no fucking good. The old antennae. But you wouldn't believe me.'

'Believe what? Who's up to no good? What are you talking about, Victor?'

'She's got an Arab kid with her. He's there in her house, so don't try to tell me the old antennae's a load of bullshit. I've got the bitch.'

'*Who*?'

'Don't fucking shout, Margaret. Missus fucking Forrester, that's who. Lady Muck who works for that lawyer trying to flood the place with rag heads. Boat people. Muslims. Understand now? There's a little reffo bastard in her house, and I've got a fair idea who it is.'

'What are you doing, Victor?'

'My civic duty, you daft cow. Calling the Federal Police, of course. What else would I do?'

The phone rang, and just when Kate was in despair and about to hang up, Rebecca answered.

'Becky, can we talk?'

'With care. Something wrong?'

'*Mayday*, if you know that one. Bad news. Shit hitting the fan.'

'Can you get out of the house and bring the problem here?'

'The sooner the better, I think.'

'Right, I'll be here. Don't come into the house. When I see your car I'll be ready. Just follow me after that. Okay?'

'Be with you in twenty minutes,' Kate said. She hung up and started to get dressed.

'What sort of a fucking police force are they?' Victor Henderson raged. 'Useless bloody keystone kops. Are these the people we rely on to keep law and order?'

'It's no use shouting at me, Victor,' his wife said. 'I'm sure they'll put someone on in a minute so you can explain.'

'They should be on their way here! Fucking idiots!' He suddenly reacted as he heard a voice ask could he kindly give his name, and state the details again. 'But I've already told two people —' Henderson started to say.

'Now tell me. I'm Sergeant Lance Wallace, Federal Police. Just explain calmly, and try not to shout or become abusive. Your name?'

'Victor Henderson.'

'Right, Mr Henderson —'

'It's Captain Henderson, actually. Australian Military Forces, Retired.'

'Thank you. Address?'

'Look, Sergeant, the kid won't be there if you go on much longer. The woman's name is Mrs Kate Forrester, and I'm trying to tell you —'

'Forrester? Did you say Forrester?'

'Yes. I already told the switchboard operator —'

'Just be quiet a moment, Mr Henderson. Forrester, The Crescent, Northbridge? Is that who you mean?'

'Yes!'

'Why the hell didn't you say so sooner?'

'I tried to —' Victor Henderson looked at the phone in his hand, astonished and affronted. 'The bastard hung up on me.'

Margaret Henderson tried not to show her satisfaction as he slammed down the phone.

'He fucking hung up on me!'

'Well . . . you've done your civic duty, Victor. You can go off and enjoy your walk now.'

'Don't be bloody stupid. I'm going to make sure that bitch can't make a run for it!'

'And how will you manage that?' she asked.

'Take our car, of course. Block her driveway.'

'You said the battery's flat.'

'I said for you to get a new one. I told you, remember?'

'And I intend to. Later today.'

Henderson looked at her with hatred. He snatched the car keys and went into the garage. She heard him trying the engine, heard it wheeze and fail to start. He started shouting abuse at it, at her, at everyone, or so it seemed. When she looked from their front window he was running down the road and around the corner towards the Forrester house.

Omar was securely crouched in the car so no one could see him as Kate reversed out of the garage and drove down towards the street. When she paused there to check on traffic, she saw Henderson making his way back. He was running, gesticulating and yelling at her, but too far away for her to hear what was being said.

She reached down to ruffle Omar's hair, reassuring him all was well, then drove swiftly off. In her driving mirror she could see the figure of Henderson start to diminish into the distance, then come to an exhausted and frustrated halt.

She went through the back streets skirting Neutral Bay, headed for the Spit Bridge, and less than fifteen minutes later was outside Rebecca's home in Clontarf.

Rebecca was parked by the gate waiting for them; she gave a quick wave of acknowledgement and drove off in her Volkswagen. Kate followed her, not knowing where they were going until they went past Fairlight, came down the hill and she saw the pine trees fringing Manly Beach in the distance.

Chapter 26

The man they came to see lived in an old block of red-brick units on a hill above the Manly Oval. It was a ground-floor apartment with its own side entrance and, after they had both found parking spaces, Rebecca led the way there and rang the bell. Although the sense of urgency was gone, Kate still felt shaken by the narrowness of their escape. She held Omar's hand tightly and felt his responding grip as they went inside.

Graeme Edwards looked like an elderly schoolteacher or a retired librarian. He was a quiet man in his early sixties who spoke a smattering of Arabic, just enough to welcome Omar and make him feel relaxed. It was important, for the boy was tense and scared, unsure what would happen to him now, clinging to Kate and plainly upset at realising he could no longer remain with her.

'Some tea, I think, while we all settle down and try to get our breath back,' Edwards said, leaving them in a small living room that felt overcrowded with large lounge chairs while he went to make it.

Kate quickly explained to Rebecca the sequence of events, and told her but for Omar's quick thinking in alerting her they might have been trapped in the house by her neighbour.

'Do you think he called the police?' Rebecca asked her.

'Sure to by now, if he hadn't already.'

'Should you get back there, in case they turn up?'

'I can't stop them turning up,' Kate said, 'but if I'm not there they'll have to wait.' She gave Rebecca back the mobile phone. 'Better get rid of that for me. I just want to stay and make sure Omar's got somewhere safe to go.' She felt strangely reckless, as if whatever die was cast, it was less important than her leaving Omar insecure and fretting.

'Kate, I'm worried about you.' Rebecca was frowning, troubled by the thought of the police.

'Well, don't be. Talk to Omar. Tell him the one thing that won't happen to him now is being sent back there. Please, Becky.'

Rebecca moved to the chair beside her, where Omar was now perched on Kate's knee. Kate watched her talk to him, then listen as he replied, after which a voluble conversation ensued. She wished she could understand a word of this busy exchange, then Rebecca said something that sounded like a word of astonishment and turned to gaze at her.

'What?' Kate asked her.

'*He says you took him to the zoo!*'

'If I could speak to him, I'd have said don't mention that.'

'The zoo, Kate?'

'So? I just thought he should have a good time, see the animals, go on a ferry, be like an ordinary kid for one day of his life . . .'

'Oh God,' Rebecca said. 'You're quite mad . . . but it's the loveliest thing I've heard in ages.' She seemed overcome, on the verge of tears.

'I told the lady at the booth I was his auntie. And two people said what a nice boy he was, and how good to meet one who came in the front door, and not on a leaky boat.' Kate laughed at the memory. 'Because I told her the family had flown here from Hong Kong.'

'You idiot,' she said affectionately. 'It gets madder and better.' Rebecca's eyes were moist.

Omar was clearly puzzled, looking at their laughter and tears, till Kate put her arms around him so tightly that he seemed to know it was goodbye. She placed him back on his feet and stood up as Graeme Edwards came in with a tea tray.

'Kate, you're not staying?'

'I've got things back at the house I ought to get rid of,' she said. 'But can you tell me where he's going?'

'I can't do that. But I can show you this,' Edwards said, putting down the tray and producing a folder of snapshots. 'He wasn't expected by the folk until this weekend, but I've spoken to them and all's well.'

He opened the folder. There were photos of a farmhouse and a middle-aged couple who owned it. In addition there were pictures of animals, a baby lamb, a cow being milked, a labrador dog and several horses, including a tiny foal. Kate knelt and showed them to Omar. She watched as he thumbed through them and began to smile.

'Yes?' she said softly, and he nodded in response.

'Yes,' he whispered. The smile grew as he looked at the horses again, then put his arms around her and hugged her until she felt quite breathless.

Still on her knees with Omar holding her, she looked to Edwards. 'Will he be safe? If those two suddenly acquire a child, won't there be questions asked?'

'There's a prepared cover story, Kate. One that will fit with their circumstances. If he can arrive openly with a believable background there are hardly ever any questions. That's why this is more important than most placements. It's vital a child is accepted, able to go to school and become part of the community.'

'And you can't tell me where?'

'No.' He shook his head.

'Not even which state?'

'Nothing. I wish I could, Kate, but I do promise you he'll be cared for and loved.'

'As long as he is, then nothing else matters.' She suddenly felt on the verge of tears herself, and had to get away.

She picked up Omar and kissed him while stroking his cheek with a soft touch of her hand. She wanted to say so much, to tell him how happy she'd been in the days they'd spent together, but perhaps he already knew without words from her.

'Goodbye,' she whispered to him. 'God bless.'

She handed him to Rebecca, nodded to Graeme Edwards, and left before she made a fool of herself. Her car was across the street. She went and sat in it, wiped her eyes, blew her nose and told herself to settle down and try to remember she was fifty years old.

Then she slowly drove home.

They were waiting for her outside the house. Two cars, Sergeant Lance Wallace and four other men whom she knew would also be Federal Police. In the garden, as if he'd come to gloat, was Victor Henderson.

'Mrs Forrester,' Wallace said, 'where's the boy?'

'What boy?' she replied, and before he could answer she asked if they had a warrant.

'Of course,' he told her, and produced it.

'And does that person' – she turned to indicate Henderson – 'does he have a right to be here? Or is he trespassing?'

'C'mon, Mrs Forrester —'

'I'm serious, Sergeant. If you know the law, I suggest you tell him this could invalidate your warrant.'

'Rubbish. You're wasting my time,' Wallace told her.

'Please tell him to leave. I won't open the house until he goes, and if you break down the door that will be used by me in court.'

Sergeant Wallace came close and stared at her. 'You're a stupid woman,' he said softly, so none of the others could hear. 'You've got no chance, Mrs Forrester. He's a prosecution witness.'

'If he is, then you make my point. A crown witness, who stands gloating while you break in? There are neighbours next door, if you care to look around, who are observing this. Friendly neighbours.'

'Fuck it,' said Lance Wallace, who rarely swore, and turned to his men. 'Get rid of that bastard. Piss him off home.'

Kate watched as two police officers went to confront Henderson. There were angry protests until they took him by the arms and escorted him to the front gate. Kate watched until he was out of sight. She turned back to Sergeant Wallace.

'Satisfied?' he asked.

'If you had a neighbour like that,' she said, 'would you like him in your front garden?'

Wallace shrugged, as if it was immaterial. 'May we go in now?'

Kate opened her handbag and gave him the key. She went and sat at the garden table as they entered the house. She could see their figures as they moved through the rooms, heard the raised voices of success as they found what she knew they would find.

I should have spent time hoovering the place, she thought. It was an expression she'd heard in a crime film . . . cleaning out the evidence or hoovering the 'joint', since it was an American film. But there wasn't time. I had to get Omar away, or there would've been no new life for him, wherever that life might be.

She saw Wallace come out, his hands full of evidence.

The corkboard and the drawings. Well, perhaps not compelling proof. But the photo she'd taken of him and printed, the one with the kookaburra that she'd hidden in a drawer. That was undeniable, convincing enough to make even the sergeant look pleased.

There was a long drawn-out process after she was taken into custody. At one stage a more senior officer took over. She faced him across a table in an interrogation room. It was made clear to her that she could help her own case by helping them.

'All we need are the names of your accomplices,' she was told.

'Accomplices?' Kate said. 'I think you must have been watching too much television.'

He continued to study her, letting this go unanswered as if well accustomed to pointless denials.

'This morning you took the boy from your house after our witness saw him. You took him to people who helped you. Just the names, Mrs Forrester. After all, why should you be the one to take all the blame?'

'I can do nothing that will help you recover him.'

'You're being foolish. Those people are breaking the law of the land, and you're protecting them.'

'I'm protecting a twelve-year-old child, who should never have been put behind razor wire. The law you talk of decided he should be locked up.'

'Perhaps there's a need to re-examine that. Once he's apprehended, a possible inquiry —'

'Please,' she said, shaking her head in dismissal of this fiction. 'We have an open-and-shut case.'

'I'm aware of that,' Kate said. 'But you won't need it. I intend to plead guilty. I picked him up that night in the teeming rain. He was wet and afraid, and he'd been ill-treated. I kept him in my house. There are no "accomplices". No names.'

She was charged, fingerprinted and bail was refused. Under the recent security laws, she was told, they could prevent her the normal judicial process. Communication with a lawyer or anyone else could be made very difficult. But that was entirely up to her. As a whistleblower she would place herself in a quite different position. She might even be granted immunity.

There are still no names, she told them.

In London over two months later, it was early November, wet and gusty. A premature winter's day. Steady rain was falling, swept by a cold north wind. A young woman got off a bus, huddled into a light raincoat and wishing it was a Driza-bone or a ski jacket as she approached a house in Chiswick. A substantial house, with a high walled garden. There was an agent's For Sale sign with the word SOLD pasted across it. She tried the heavy street gate that opened and walked to the front door. She could see no curtains framing the windows, or any evidence of furniture inside. Unsure if the bell would still work, she used the brass doorknocker. There was a long delay and still no answer when she tried again.

She walked around the house and peered in. The rooms were all empty. A wasted journey, she thought. She looked through windows into the largest room. It was lined with bookshelves holding no books. No furniture. A mahogany floor with evidence on the dark wood where carpets or rugs had been removed. She was about to turn away, try to find a pub or a coffee shop, somewhere warm and dry, when she sensed a movement and heard a sound from inside. A man came into the room. A man wearing jeans and a flannel shirt with a floppy jumper. She rapped on the window.

He turned and stared. She rapped again, and found a tissue to wipe away the rain on the glass so she could see him more clearly. He seemed about the right age, in his early fifties. No trace of grey in his red hair. He frowned and came across to the window, gazing at her. She indicated the rain, spread her hands in a mute appeal against the cold and waited.

He undid the window lock and opened it.

'If you're from another hopeful estate agent, it's sold.'

'I'm a journalist.'

'Christ, that's worse.' But he stared at her thoughtfully. An Australian accent, soft, like one he remembered.

'My editor said you'd smartly show me the door. But he didn't know you'd sold the door, along with the rest of the place.' She saw it made him smile and then look at her again, more carefully. 'Whereas my mother,' she continued, 'once told me you used to be a friend, so I thought it was worth a shot.'

'Good God,' he said. 'Is this why I thought I knew you?'

'Well, they say I look a bit like her,' Juliet Forrester said. 'Any chance of coming in out of the rain?'

PART 5

DAMIEN

Chapter 27

When the doorknocker sounded in the empty house, I thought it might be the removalists, coming back because they'd forgotten something. But the furniture was all gone, the rooms were deserted waiting for new owners, and I was alone. There was a second knock. I had no intention of answering it, because it could not be good news; it could not, in fact, be news of any kind that would be welcome. Probably another bloody agent. So I ignored it, and whoever had been there seemed to give up and go away.

I walked through the house for one last time, the awful emptiness and echo of my own footsteps making it feel as if I'd ventured onto the *Marie Celeste*. The living room, once a centrepiece of our lives, was bleak and sad; the bookshelves bare, the rugs and furniture removed, as if the room had never contained the baby grand or a Victorian chaise, let alone the armoire desk and Jacobean cabinet; treasures we'd so lovingly collected at country auctions. Now they were all in store, or else with Ingrid in her Kensington mews cottage. The walls looked naked and shabby without paintings, most of it the cherished work of artist friends, one an early Russell Drysdale picked up in a sale by a fluke.

It was time to go. Lock up and leave. And then I heard a tapping on the window. A figure was outside, made difficult to recognise by the rain-smeared windows. An unexpected guest when the time for guests was long gone. But a persistent one, for she tapped again. It was a woman trying to use a tissue to wipe a clear spot on the glass. I unlatched and opened the window.

A *young* woman I could see now, rather wet and windblown, wearing a tan raincoat that was not much protection against the weather. She had dark silky hair and distinctive deep-blue eyes. Not quite as young as I first thought, probably in her late twenties or early thirties. When she spoke she had a slight Australian accent, and the voice along with the colour of the eyes reminded me of . . .

But I had to be wrong. It was just an illusion; I could not possibly know this woman; I was thinking of someone else. Then she told me her mother was a friend, and there was no longer any chance of a mistake. I felt as if I was nineteen again, standing amid a noisy crowd. A New Year's Eve party to celebrate the arrival of 1968, the first time I saw her, at a beach house in Narrabeen.

That was when Juliet Forrester reminded me it was raining, and was there any chance of coming inside so she could interview me. It turned out she was a journalist for *The Guardian*, and seemed unwilling to take no for an answer.

There was nothing in the house. No seats to sit on, no cups to drink from. No tea or coffee. If Juliet had come for an interview, the saga of the end of my marriage had already been the subject of too much interest in the British tabloids, with all the usual distortions. I dreaded another version.

Still, she was Kate's daughter, so I locked the front door, left the keys in the mail box as arranged with the agent, and we ran for my car.

The nearest pub, we'd decided, and headed for the Fox and Dragon two streets away. The rain was now stronger, the windscreen wipers barely coping, but I pulled up as near the entrance as I could, asked her to grab a table in the saloon bar and order me a whisky.

'It's my shout,' I called, but she was off and running, the light Aussie raincoat no match for the storm being blown across Britain from the Hebrides. Almost dark by now, it promised to be one of those ferocious nights where people stay home, television screens glow and ratings break records, no matter what the program.

By the time I found parking, Juliet was warming herself in front of a fire, and a decent-sized whisky was waiting at a corner table, along with a glass of house red for her. We sat and talked and she filled in the long gap since Kate and I lost touch, when I learnt for the first time of Hugh Forrester's death and Kate's life in the years since then.

'Your mother had a big office with a view when we last wrote.'

'She swapped it for pro bono work over a sandwich shop,' Juliet said, 'trying to free people from detention centres. She's very anti the way we're treating refugees.'

It sounded like the Kate I remembered. How was she, I asked, and Juliet said fine, as far as she knew, but busy because she hadn't heard from her recently.

'Not even an email. But that's my mum when she gets obsessive about cases,' she said affectionately. 'I've booked a trip home to spend a few weeks at Christmas with her.'

We sipped our drinks and I asked her how she'd got her break with *The Guardian*. Not an easy market to crack, with an oversupply of media graduates. She told me of her travels with Sofia Vassos that led to 'Greece with Grandmère'. And although the newspaper had given her a short-term contract, she felt she still needed to prove herself, so could she please turn on her mini-recorder and start to interview me?

'Before you do,' I said, 'the media's already given me a hard time. Pictures of Ingrid in her new home with new partner on too many front pages. The British press decided it was either a clash of egos, a fight over money, or arguments about our failure to have kids. A neighbour even fronted up to claim we threw things at each other and shouted obscenities. None of it was true. Not one thing.' I took a large swallow of my whisky, and wished I'd settled for a glass of wine like her. I noticed the tiny recorder had not yet been switched on.

'The truth is, we were going through one of those sporadic marital moments. Not the seven-year itch, or the fourteen-year irritation – this was the twenty-year stocktake, when you stop to wonder what it's going to be like for the next twenty. I'd written a screenplay to be shot in Spain. The main role was perfect for Ingrid. Time apart, we both thought, would be good for us.' I looked across at her and the recorder. 'Do you want to turn that thing on?'

'Not yet,' she said. 'Tell me the rest.'

'It's a short ironic story. The actor they cast opposite her was a graduate from the soap-opera school of acting. But he was great in the love scenes. Very sexy. That's where the irony comes in. They were both so good that I wrote extra love scenes, and they enjoyed them so much they kept playing the roles long after the cameras stopped turning.'

'Crikey!' said Juliet.

I laughed. I hadn't heard that word used since I was a kid.

'So that's how the cuckoo got into my nest. Your editor might give you brownie points for that true confession.'

'He might. But if there are points to be had,' she said, 'I'd rather earn them writing a different kind of story. This one's about the kid from Sydney whose Italian dad tried to make him become a bank teller, and whose eccentric aunt and uncle took your side and started a family feud.'

'That's never been in the papers,' I said, startled.

'Source material from my mum, reminiscing about the days when you two were trying to stop the Vietnam War. She once met Angelo and Fanny and said they were gorgeous people. It was the rest of your family who were nuts – present company excepted.'

I laughed, liking her and her cheeky grin. She was another kid from Sydney, and I knew how tough the journey could be.

'Have you got plenty of tape?' I asked.

'Heaps.' She switched on the recorder, put it in front of me, and I found myself telling her things about my early life and dysfunctional family that I'd never told any journalist before.

It was cold and dark when we left the pub. The rain was still bucketing down, so I asked if I could drop her home. There was no way in the world she'd get a taxi on a night like this. We ran for the car, and when I drove off she gave me an address in Old Brompton Road.

'A big block of flats on the corner of Redcliffe Gardens,' she told me, and when I laughed she asked me why.

'You have to mean Coleherne Court.'

'That's right.'

'I used to live there.'

Juliet turned and gaped at me. 'For a big city this is a small world, and steadily getting smaller,' she said, then after a pause suddenly asked, 'did you live there when you and Mum were writing to each other?'

'Part of the time. Yes.' I remembered because she had bought a painting, a wedding present, and sent it to me there.

'That's strange.' Juliet sounded troubled.

I turned to glance at her. 'What's strange?'

'It's a new address for me. I told her in an email I'd moved here a few weeks ago. She would certainly remember you'd lived in the same block. So it's odd she hasn't written back or, being Mum, rung up to share that news with me.'

'You think something's wrong?'

'I don't know. I just assumed she was busy at work. But now I'm starting to wonder.'

'Away on a holiday?' I suggested.

'Not without letting me know.'

'You think she's ill?'

'Mandy would've rung up, for sure. Mandy's her best friend.'

'Don't worry too much. There'll be a simple explanation.'

'Has to be. I'll ring tonight. I'd like to tell her about the interview; it'll be a nice surprise.' The thought of this seemed to cheer her, and she wanted to thank me for the afternoon I'd spent. She felt hopeful that it was going to please her editor.

Her enthusiasm was infectious. As we pulled up outside Coleherne Court I gave her my new address and said I'd look forward to reading her story. The rain had eased and the block of mansion flats with its private two-acre garden was a familiar sight. I'd once owned a lease on one; Juliet told me they were now selling for over a million pounds, and I thought ruefully of how I'd sold mine long before such stratospheric prices. She was sharing one of the smaller rented apartments with a sub-editor friend. From the fond way she spoke of him I got the feeling they were on the way to becoming slightly more than friends.

'Maybe I should write a piece about this block and all the people who have lived here,' Juliet said, pointing at the corner flat that we both knew Princess Diana had once occupied before her marriage. 'Where were you, Damien?'

'Further along. Opposite a fashionable street of very expensive houses that were locally known as Crap Alley.'

She laughed. 'Seriously?'

'Very seriously. All the local dog owners used to walk their pets there at night to do "jobbies", and the rich and famous had to be careful where they trod the next morning.'

She was still laughing when she kissed me on the cheek, thanked me for the interview, as well as the ride home and the story of Crap Alley. About to get out of the car she turned and asked me, 'Do you ever think of going back to Aussie, Damien?'

'Only for a visit. Next year is Uncle Angelo's ninetieth birthday. It's a command performance, and I'll be there for that.'

I watched her cross the road, thinking how she even walked like Kate. I hoped her concern was unwarranted, and there would be a simple explanation for the failure to keep in touch.

'My love to your mum when you talk to her,' I called, and she acknowledged it with a wave before going inside.

She sent a copy of the article a week later. It was written with both fun and affection, charming depictions of my aunt and uncle, and even a sympathetic portrayal of the bemused and mostly confused pubescent that was me. It came with a note.

Editor seems pleased. Hope you are. Have only been able to get Kate's answering machine no matter how often I try, so I rang Mandy.

Apparently Mum's been working too hard and on doctor's orders is now away on a holiday. All a bit strange, because it's so unlike her not to have told me. I don't know why I'm so worried but I am.

It was almost a year later before I found out the truth. I left London in the winter as a new play of mine was to start an American tour. We began in Boston, where the play was to rehearse and open, hopefully the prelude to a Broadway transfer. By the time it had toured all the way down the east coast to Washington, finally managing to open in New York, it was summer, and I was exhausted by months of rewriting and the demands of a difficult producer.

I fled New York, where the critics were only lukewarm, and spent a month in the heat of Barbados, where the beach was more restful, before returning to London. Because of occasional echoes of my divorce in the British papers, I'd cut some ties in England and changed my email address. It was only when I arrived back that I found various messages from Juliet, written regularly until she had given up.

I don't know where the hell you are, she had written in a plaintive note, *but my mother is in prison. When you get back from whatever part of the planet you've been visiting, maybe you could call me?*

In a state of shock and disbelief I called her phone number at Coleherne Court, and a new tenant answered who said Juliet was in South Africa.

I asked how I could contact her, and was told her boyfriend was still working at *The Guardian*. So I rang him.

'She's in South Africa,' he told me. I said that I'd heard this and asked what she was doing there.

'Interviewing Nelson Mandela,' he replied, as if I'd asked a really stupid question.

Chapter 28

The plane flew high above the inland, over clay pans and a parched vista of red earth and spinifex. Just when it seemed as if nothing could survive down there, I glimpsed sunlight reflecting off the galvanised roof of an isolated homestead with a tiny patch of green lawn, a cluster of tin sheds and symmetrical stockyards. Remote, hundreds of kilometres from anywhere, it looked forlorn yet curiously courageous: the green lawn suggested domestic pride, the cattle yards a dogged sense of order. Looking at it I was reminded of my schooldays when I read Ernestine Hill's book *The Great Australian Loneliness* and, captivated by her depiction of the country's immensity and romance, was torn between an adventurous life as a jackeroo and a long-kept secret wish to become a writer.

Why a writer? My parents, aghast at what they considered a curious choice, had asked the same question. A writer – for heaven's sake! Australia produced sheep, not literary giants – apart from Patrick White, whom most had heard of but few had read. Be a jackeroo, I was advised. Look at Sir Sidney Kidman, who had started out as a station hand and ended up owning an empire the size of New Zealand. Or, if that no longer appealed, be an accountant; I could join my father's accountancy firm in the suburb of Chatswood, become a junior partner and in due course take over the practice.

As Juliet Forrester had written, my bookish ambition had sparked a family conflict; support from Uncle Angelo and Aunt Fanny had infuriated my father. In his opinion they were dangerous dissidents. To me they were quirky and endearing in a way that distinguished them from the drab society that was Australia in those insular years. Distance and the cost of travel kept us pinioned in our own backyard, where explicit novels were banned and radical new plays closed by police order. In this suffocating landscape my uncle and aunt had been a breath of invigorating air.

Thinking of the past and my youth led me to thoughts of summer holidays, parties on the beach, barbecues at the Collaroy basin, and from there to names like Joshua Maitland, Toby Robinson, Noelene, and of course to Kate Vassos. I used to fantasise about her, but it was totally one-sided. She was hopelessly committed to bloody Joshua, who in the end let her down so badly. I always dreaded that he would.

I could never tell Kate, until I wrote her the letter, just how much I feared their relationship would end in tears. I used to vainly wish it had been me sunbaking on the beach when she appeared that day. But in sensible moments I knew it might not have had the same result; I did not have Joshua's charisma, or his looks. Or his reputation, fostered when we were all at school together, of having been to bed with more women than the rest of the sixth form put together. It was notorious schoolboy smut that both thrilled and scandalised the sex-starved boarders, a standing built entirely on his propensity to boast of his conquests. After he met Kate I detested the thought of him regaling his cronies about intimacies with her. He never spoke of it to me, but by then I was hardly a crony.

Where was Joshua after so long, I wondered? Where were Toby and Noelene? The years had wrought many changes. My own parents were dead, soon after them Aunt Fanny, and now the only one left was Uncle Angelo, indomitable, living alone in the Buckingham Avenue house where he was about to be ninety, and apparently playing the Brahms concerto every night to his dead wife as if it were a requiem.

I slept for a while as we crossed the continent, and on waking began to wonder what my life would have been like had there been no Joshua Maitland. If on the day I'd helped Kate from the stampede at the protest march we'd simply gone home together, not to my home or hers but to Buckingham Avenue, where Aunt Fanny would have welcomed us and watched us go upstairs to the spare room that I called my own, and there we could have made wild and tender love, like nothing in my life before or since . . .

'Excuse me, sir.' It was a member of the cabin crew reminding me to fasten my seat belt, for we were making our final approach to Kingsford Smith Airport and the sign was already switched on.

As we landed with a slight bump and the jet engines reverberated, I wondered if I'd be able to see Kate, in whatever prison she was being held.

We arrived late in Sydney because of a slow start; at Heathrow someone had left a parcel on an Arab airline desk, bringing instant alarm and chaos to the London terminal, and it was three hours before the bomb squad diffused the suspect object and found it was a birthday present to one of the flight attendants, a Minolta

Dimage. The delay was exacerbated at Singapore, and we reached
Sydney long after the scheduled time. Because of this I tried to call
Angelo, but the phone seemed out of order. Waiting in the customs
queue I dialled enquiries and was puzzled when told the number
was disconnected and no longer available.

I collected the car I'd hired at the airport, and only got lost once
on the intricate new network of tolls, tunnels and motorways to
the city. So much was new since my last visit before the Olympic
Games, but the Pacific Highway to the North Shore was still familiar
territory, and at Pymble I took a short cut on the road to Bobbin
Head and Buckingham Avenue.

From a distance the house looked as imposing and unique as
ever, so what I saw on arrival came as a shock. Unlike Uncle Angelo,
still erect, his hearing and memory unimpaired, time had not treated
the place well. The ornate entry gates were lying off their hinges,
there were slates missing from the roof and badly broken gutters.
The garden was almost completely overgrown, and what had been
a proud display of flowering shrubs and roses was now a tangle of
blackberries. The once immaculate lawn was brown and matted
with weeds, the garage where the chickens had nested was now
empty, and the shed that had housed the old Packard had collapsed.
A litter of rusty galvanised iron sheets and termite-infested timber
still lay in an untidy heap where it had fallen.

Angelo greeted me with the usual bear hug.

'My dear boy.' He still had a fine resonant voice; if not for the
violin he could have been a Shakespearian actor or a baritone.
'I was so looking forward to your arrival. When the plane was late
I began to fear the worst.'

I told him about the panic over the birthday present and he
laughed for a time, then shook his head. 'The war against terror,'

he said, 'the glib phrase of that idiotic man Bush, is now a war against ourselves. We are afraid of our own shadows, and of birthday presents.'

After I took the luggage up to my old room, he suggested a stroll before the daylight faded. I saw the disrepair, but he made no comment; it seemed strange he appeared unaware or uncaring about the sad state of the property. Until we reached the shed.

'Sold the old banger,' he said. 'Nearly as old as me and still going strong. Got a thousand dollars from a used-car dealer.'

'You probably made his day, Angelo.' I reflected on the well-kept antique Packard, a vintage treasure that would have grown more valuable with each passing year.

'You think the bugger robbed me?' he asked.

'Maybe,' I said, trying to be tactful.

'I wanted to get rid of it, Damien. Fanny used to love riding in it, remember? When she'd gone, the very sight of it used to make me sad. And I'm too old to drive. I'd have paid the bloke to take it away.'

'Well then, he didn't rob you,' I agreed, which made my uncle smile and pat my arm affectionately.

'We have lots to talk about,' he said as we strolled back towards the house. 'But first things first. There's a bottle of French fizz, a decent vintage, that's been waiting impatiently for your return. So I suggest we put a dent in it before we make any decisions about dinner.'

The living room was still vast, the chandelier huge above our heads, but I felt the lack of my aunt dancing down the stairs and taking me in her arms.

'It feels lonely,' I said, and he knew exactly what I meant.

'It's as lonely as hell. Every day I think of so many things I want to tell her, and I turn to do so but she's no longer there. She was the love of my life, Damien, and she's gone. I find it difficult to believe.'

He emptied his champagne glass and immediately poured himself another. He gestured to me, but I shook my head.

'The house, the garden – they're a heap of shit. You were tactful enough not to say so, but I could tell what you were thinking. It's all a heap of shit, because it was her house – I bought it for her, to impress her so she'd marry me, and now it's a millstone.' He suddenly surprised me by laughing, and I wondered if he was drunk. But he wasn't.

'It's your millstone, my boy. There's no one I want to leave it to except you. No one else Fanny would've allowed to inherit except you. She was so proud of you; we both were. So next week I'm ninety, and I have a reservation in a decent sort of old folks' home down the road. No, don't make gestures of dissent: this place has already been transferred into your name, and you can either sell it and go back to London or live in it as Fanny always hoped. Your decision, Damien. Unfortunately you'll have to spend a few bucks fixing things up. I wish I could've handed it over in better shape, but I've run out of funds. My darling girl,' he said, on the verge of tears, 'is no longer here to win another lottery for us.'

'It used to irritate the hell out of my father,' I reminded him, and made him smile.

We finished the French champagne, then he went down to the cellar and returned with a large bottle of red wine. Without saying a word he gave it to me to open.

'Jesus Christ, Angelo, this is a magnum of St Henri, 1986.'

'So open it, Damien.'

'But it's worth a bloody fortune.'

'All the more reason to open it. Do we want to sell it? Put it in a garage sale or an auction? Of course we don't. We want to drink to your aunt. So open the blessed thing.'

I opened it. Of course he was right. We drank to Fanny, to her memory, her joyous sense of fun that had filled this house with such delight. We got completely pissed and never even remembered that we hadn't eaten dinner.

I had a hangover in the morning. Uncle Angelo had already been for a walk to buy groceries, and had cooked himself bacon and eggs by the time I managed to negotiate my way downstairs.

'You're not supposed to feel crook after good wine,' he said.

'I think it's jet lag,' I replied.

'Sit down and I'll make you a Spanish omelette,' he told me.

'Please God, no,' I answered, whereupon he roared with laughter and said I was anaemic from those low winter clouds in England that prevented any sunshine, and did I realise that we'd celebrated last night with a bottle worth about three thousand bucks? And before I could even register this, let alone express dismay at it, he said it was a night he'd been waiting for, because Fanny was worth it – every cent.

Which, of course, she was. And even if I did have a terrible headache, it made me happy to have been a part of it.

I told Angelo what little I knew about Kate being tried in a closed court and her custodial sentence, details I'd garnered from Juliet when at last I'd been able to make contact with her by phone. At the time, she was on board a train to Budapest; another article, this one about the great days of the Orient Express.

'I'm here under protest,' she'd told me. 'I should be at home – it's where I want to be – but Mum said she'd never forgive herself or me if I chucked it all to become a prison visitor.'

'I don't think any of us would forgive you. I'll tell Kate your next assignment might be an interview with the Pope.'

At least I left her laughing, with just time to say she thought her mum had been moved from her original prison, but wasn't sure where to. I promised to find out and to let her know, then we lost the call as the train went into the Simplon tunnel.

Angelo admitted he knew little about the case, for he rarely read the papers these days, couldn't stand the radio shock-jocks, and hardly ever looked at the nightly television news either.

'But I remember her,' he said. 'She came to the ship to see you off. She was the loveliest creature. We wished she'd been your girl.'

'Someone else's,' I answered.

'Are you going to try and see her?'

'If I can. First of all I have to find her, Angelo.'

'I think,' he said, 'it's always a good idea to start by looking in the phone book.'

Reminded about his own telephone, I told him of the attempt to call from the airport. 'It must be out of order.'

'No, I told them to cut it off. The friends who used to ring me up are dead. The only calls I was getting were charities, or someone in Bombay trying to offer me new money-saving phone deals. In the end it seemed easier to cancel the line.'

It was fortunate he'd kept his directory, as it contained an entry for *K Forrester, 2 The Crescent, Northbridge*. I knew she wouldn't be there, but I had to start somewhere.

I drove there the following day. Kate had once sent me a photo of the house, but this wasn't the same place. I remembered a luxuriant garden and a sprawling weatherboard bungalow. None of this remained. Instead there were four small houses in various stages of construction. I asked if anyone working there knew how to contact the former owner.

'She's in the slammer,' a carpenter said. 'Got a few years so I s'pose she's still in there. No idea which nick, though.'

No one else knew either, but an electrician installing underground cables gave me the name of the developer, Henry Miller Constructions Pty Ltd, and the address of his city office. When I found my way there it was clearly the listed address of a great many other firms as well, just one tiny room and a lone secretary busy taking all their messages.

'He's in Bali,' she said when I asked to see Mr Miller, and she referred me to another Mr Miller, a real estate agent. 'He's in Crows Nest.' She handed me a card and told me they were brothers, and she knew nothing about their business but that this Mr Miller was the one to see. The other one spent most of his time surfing.

So eventually I ended up in the offices of H. Miller & Associates, enduring an interminable wait while the agent was occupied with a series of phone calls.

'Sorry,' the attractive red-headed receptionist said. 'He lives on the blower. The only man I know who carries two mobile phones with him if he's out of the office. Were you here about buying or selling?'

'Neither,' I replied. 'A personal matter.'

She gave me a careful look. 'Not from the tax office, are you?'

'Not me.'

'Just wondering.' She smiled. 'They've been after his brother. He has holidays in Bali and claims it on expenses. Supposed to be building a luxury hotel; we call it the Mystic Palace because it doesn't exist.'

She broke off abruptly as the instrument on her desk showed the latest call was terminated. The estate agent came to the door. He was a thickset man, wearing an open-necked shirt and bright-red braces.

'Mr Raphael, on a personal matter,' the secretary announced.

'Howie Miller,' the agent introduced himself, looking cautious. His handshake was moist, and I noticed sweat patches on his shirt. After showing me in he left his office door ajar, as though I wouldn't be staying long.

'Nothing to do with your brother,' I said.

'Why, what's he done now?'

'I've no idea. I think he's in Bali.'

'He's an idle bastard,' Howie Miller said. 'What do you want to see me about? I'm a busy man.'

'I'm trying to find out how to contact Kate Forrester.'

'Oh . . . her.'

'I was told you might be able to help,' I said.

'She was a lot of trouble, that woman.'

'You mean politically?' I sensed I was on delicate ground.

'I mean in every possible way. She wouldn't sell, not for years. Well, I got the place in the end, but she cost me two houses. I could've put six villas in there, but she rigged it so there was a limit of four.'

'You mean when she sold to you?'

'She didn't sell. Well, not willingly. The bank forced the sale.'

'Her bank?'

'That's right. When she went to jail she was into them for most of what the place was worth. Some friendly bank manager had let her keep re-mortgaging whenever she needed a few quid. He got fired, and I got a whisper they wanted a quick sale so I got in first. But four flamin' villas . . . She'd persuaded the fucking manager to put a clause in the mortgage document, and the bank said take it, or if you want more, take us to court. Well, you don't take a bank to court, unless you've got a hole in the head. Four bloody villas . . . it shoulda been six.'

'I daresay the sale price was adjusted accordingly?'

'What's that got to do with you?' He was beginning to sound testy, and I knew my last comment was a blunder.

'Nothing at all. Mr Miller, I'm trying to find her. I was told you might be able to help.'

'Well, you were told wrong. I wouldn't have a clue if she's in jail or where she is, and to be honest I don't give a tuppenny stuff.'

The phone rang then, and he picked it up and asked his caller to hold before turning to me. 'Important call, this one. Sorry.' He seemed indifferent as I nodded and went out, closing his office door.

'He's a miserable bugger.' The red-head, who had overheard our conversation, wrote a name on a slip of paper and gave it to me. 'That's from the sale file. It might help. If it does, tell her people like me were on her side, will you?'

Chapter 29

Mandy Pollard was a plump cheerful woman with lively blue eyes behind a pair of large trendy glasses. She lived in an apartment overlooking the Garden Island naval base in Potts Point, a place I eventually found with the assistance of Gregory's street directory, having twice taken wrong turns and arriving for our eleven o'clock appointment a few minutes before noon. I started to apologise for my tardiness, but she was unfazed, dismissing it with a smile.

'Kate said you'd get lost.' She asked if I'd have tea, coffee or a beer, and said personally she'd have a cold tinnie.

'You've talked to her?' It was welcome news after my lack of success so far.

'Half an hour ago. A beer, or is it too early?'

'But where is she?'

'Hang on, Damien; first things first. Beer, or are you on London time and want a cuppa?'

'A beer,' I said, 'sounds particularly grouse.'

She shook with laughter.

'What's funny?' I asked.

'Your English accent, combined with the word grouse.'

'Do I have an English accent?'

'I should say so, *old chap*. Didn't you know?'

'I'm always told different things. When I come home, friends say I sound like a Pom. In London I'm told I sound like a bloody Aussie. Please, Mandy . . . where's Kate?'

'Prince of Wales Hospital.'

I stared at her, feeling baffled and trying to absorb this news.

'I thought she was in prison,' I said. 'Juliet told me she was. She was upset you kept it from her for months.'

Mandy nodded. 'I didn't want to, but Kate said we must. She was trying not to distress her or divert her focus from the job on *The Guardian*. I still haven't told Jules she's ill and in hospital. Orders from Kate. She said not yet.'

The shock of these revelations was beginning to distress me.

'What sort of illness? Can I see her?'

'Tomorrow,' she replied, avoiding an answer to the first question, and giving me a can of Fosters.

'Is she okay?'

She was silent for a moment, then shook her head. 'Not really.'

'Please, Mandy, for Christ's sake, tell me. What the hell is it?'

'She's having a lot more tests.'

'Tests for what?' I felt as if it was a conspiracy to keep me from knowing. 'Mandy, be fair. Tell me what the fuck is going on.'

'They're still assessing how bad it is,' she finally admitted with great reluctance. 'We can try talking to the oncologist.'

'Oncologist? But that's —'

'Cancer,' she said. 'Breast cancer.'

'Shit.'

'Shit indeed. Sit and relax. There's rather a lot to tell you.'

~

There was a lot, and that night I was awake for a long time thinking over what I'd learnt during the afternoon with Mandy Pollard. She had rung the hospital and discussed it with Kate while I was still making wrong turns in the unfamiliar traffic, and they'd agreed I should be told everything. Kate just wanted me to know the truth about her life, because she said there'd been too much deception between us ever since her pregnancy with Juliet, and as Mandy was the one friend she'd never had to deceive, who better to tell it.

'But of course that's not quite true,' Mandy said to me. 'I was kept out of the picture when she helped the Iraqi boy. It came as a complete shock to her friends. The Federal Police claimed she must have helped a great many others. The press got stuck in. The radio ratbags . . .' She gave a shudder. 'Horrible. This country was so gung-ho after 9/11. "Criminal behaviour aiding illegal alien escapees", one bloody newspaper called it, although whether the judge said anything like that no one knows. But she pleaded guilty and didn't want to be represented, not even by Roger, so some people said she was lucky to just get four years.' She sounded angry. 'Lucky!'

'Why not be represented by Roger?' I asked. 'After all, she worked with him.'

'That was why.'

'What do you mean?'

'She was determined he mustn't be involved. She didn't want him tainted – that was her word – she wanted him to go on being there for refugees, because there were so few lawyers for that kind of work, and he was one of the best.'

'She seems to have been worried about everyone else. Roger, Juliet – everyone but herself.' Mandy nodded. I felt helpless, able only to bombard her with questions. 'So does she have to go back to prison, if she gets through this?'

'Almost certainly. The rumour is the government was furious her sentence was only four years. They wanted a punitive term.'

'Wasn't that punitive?' I asked.

'Not to the Attorney-General. It was actually four with a non-parole period of two, but parole depends on so many things. I think they'll try to see that she serves the rest.'

'What – the whole four years?' I was stunned at the savagery of this.

'If she's well enough and they can swing it, the bastards wouldn't give a stuff.'

Mandy was so upset, I wondered if she'd told me the full extent of Kate's condition. She made some sandwiches, and we had another cold tinnie. I asked a few questions.

'How many escapees did she admit to helping?'

'Only the boy. But they accused her of many more; they said she was in a network hiding dozens of refugees, and condemned her for refusing to name the other criminals involved. You have to realise, Damien, last year was a horrible time. After the *Tampa* and the SEIV X, it felt as if anyone who didn't denigrate asylum seekers was a traitor. And Kate played into their hands. She was on the record as stating there are thousands who regularly arrive by plane and overstay their visas for months; even years. Some just settle, blend into the landscape of all the European faces. They're never hunted and put in cages.'

'Mandy,' I said, 'facts and figures. If they accused her of more, did they have any evidence?'

She shook her head, dismissing the prospect. 'If you believe her, and I do . . . just that one little boy. She was very proud of helping him. Refused to deny it,' Mandy said fondly, 'but that's our Kate.

Impetuous, sometimes crazy, but if we had more like her we mightn't be so ashamed of what's been happening in our country.'

I nodded, thinking about this. Mandy was studying me.

'What?' I asked her.

'She trusts people. Can she really trust you?'

'I hope so,' I said.

'This is about Juliet.' She looked at me again, and went on with what she'd chosen to say. 'She's Joshua's child.'

'I did wonder, Mandy.'

'Kate said she thought you might've had an inkling.'

'Does Juliet know about her father?'

'Oh, yes. Dear old grandma in Athens told her, after Hugh died.'

'And what happened? Has she seen him . . . Joshua?'

'Yes. Ages ago. Kate asked never to be told, so she still doesn't know. But Jules told me. She needed to tell someone.'

'Do you feel you want to tell me?'

'I think so.' She hesitated, then to give herself some time to consider it, suggested we had another cold tinnie.

'You have a tinnie,' I replied. 'Any chance of an even modest sort of white wine?'

'Thank God,' she laughed. 'I was trying to be sociable. Kate said you only drank beer.'

'Kate's thirty years out of date. I'd kill for a chardonnay.'

'Bloody oath, mate, so would I,' Mandy said with a relieved grin as she rose and went to the kitchen for a bottle and wine glasses. 'My bladder feels under less stress already.'

So we exchanged tinnies for a Margaret River, and Mandy told me about Juliet and her biological father.

'This was long ago, when she was still a cadet reporter. She had

372

a list of names Kate gave her, which helped her find him. It turned out Joshua had moved to Melbourne where he was a partner in a wine bar. He and a thirty-year-old blonde from St Kilda. Jules got the impression the blonde put up the money.'

'Sounds about right.'

She smiled. 'Of course, you knew him.'

'From the age of nine. Did they meet?'

'That was Juliet's intention. She went to Melbourne, to the wine bar for the big moment . . . You know, the classic intro: "I expect you don't realise this, but I'm your daughter." And then she saw him working the room. I gather he was good at that sort of thing.'

'The best,' I said, experiencing a moment of jealousy.

'So he stopped at each table that had a pretty young girl . . . did the chat, the hand kiss, the flirtation . . . Girls about the same age as herself, Jules realised, and by now he wasn't the young and handsome guy she'd heard about from grandma . . . He looked more like Dorian Gray.'

I laughed; I couldn't help it, and it made Mandy pause for a moment.

'Truly, that's what she said. So when he was two tables away, she thought, If he drools over me, I'm going to be sick.'

'What happened?'

'She got up and fled the joint. Deciding that for her Hugh was the father she'd grown up with and known, and he was the one who mattered. Never said a word to her mum then or since, and swore me to secrecy.' She looked contrite. 'I shouldn't really have told you.'

'I'm glad you did. It's a pity we can never tell Kate all that,' I said, and raised my glass to her. 'Dorian Gray! I think you've made my day.'

~

By the time we went to the hospital the following morning, I knew almost everything. The intervening years had been encapsulated in an afternoon. Among other things I learnt from Mandy was how often Kate staved off financial disasters; for instance, when she gave up her well-paid job to look after Hugh, then later supplemented her salary so she could work with Roger Montgomery, and how she provided Juliet with a big wedding by regularly extending her mortgage on the house.

'She acted like there was no tomorrow,' Mandy said affectionately. 'It caught up with her in the end, but only because she was in the nick and couldn't make repayments.' She shook her head and sighed. 'Mind you, she was no genius with money, our Kate. She was devastated to learn that awful estate agent finally got hold of it.'

'Does she know he's furious, bitching about the number of houses she prevented him building?'

'I'm sure she'd like to know. Tell her. She needs a smile or two.'

We reached the fourth floor and Mandy led me towards a small private room. She pointed to the door, signalling that she'd wait for our appointment with the oncologist, and I went in to see what Kate Forrester looked like after all these years.

She was thin and gaunt. At first I thought she was asleep, then a hand stretched out to hold mine, and that was the moment when I knew why I'd come home. Not only to celebrate Angelo's ninetieth birthday; but because of this woman who once begged me not to give in to my father's wishes, and had been somewhere deep in my heart ever since.

Chapter 30

The oncologist had been famous in another career before taking up medicine. I recalled seeing him on television playing at Cardiff Arms Park as a halfback in a Welsh rugby team that won the Five Nations Trophy; then after retiring from the game and working as a resident doctor in a London hospital, he had emigrated to Australia.

He told us that Kate had complained of continual fatigue during the first year in jail, but had received scant sympathy until a visiting locum became concerned and ordered an X-ray. This showed an abnormality that required further analysis, and eventually an ultrasound revealed a tumour.

'The diagnosis came as a great shock to her. There'd been no pain, and she thought the tiredness and general low energy was stress-related. The prison authorities, who to say the least had been dilatory until then, called in a specialist who prescribed chemotherapy in an attempt to shrink the tumour. It is sometimes done with success before surgery, but in this case it was the wrong choice. Chemo, I'm sure you know, often makes patients ill, but with Mrs Forrester it caused a serious allergic reaction. When this happened she was transferred here to my care and we stopped the treatment. I believe the authorities wanted her put in a ward, but I insisted on a private room. She needed it after that traumatic time in jail.'

The doctor's name was Owen Griffith-Jones, and his Welsh accent was musical and hypnotic. Mandy and I were in his consulting room on the second floor of the hospital's medical centre, and from the window there was a distant view of the campus belonging to the University of New South Wales. He had told his secretary to block all calls, although there was a full waiting room outside, but he was determined to explain it to us in complete detail.

In his candid opinion – he assumed we did want a candid opinion or we wouldn't be here – Kate would not see another summer unless the cancer was surgically tackled. He made it sound like a rugby manoeuvre, but I began to have faith in his pronouncements and to trust him.

I found out later he greatly admired what Kate had been doing, but that was after I discovered he visited the Villawood centre himself, not in a professional capacity, but as a sympathetic volunteer who went to talk to children and their parents, taking books and toys there on the weekends. It had begun to surprise me the way I kept encountering people who endorsed what she'd done. While the media had vilified her and an authoritarian government had locked her up, it was a relief to discover that not all people were like her military neighbour or the odious Howard Miller.

There was good news and bad news, Griffith-Jones told us. The ultrasound showed a tumour only in the left breast. But the size of it, four centimetres, was a slight concern, for it was in the medium to high range, and there was always the possibility the cancer might have spread into the lymph glands. The surgeon he'd enlisted proposed a modified radical mastectomy, and we could meet with him and he'd explain what this entailed.

'Now the bad news,' he said. 'Someone has to persuade Kate to have this surgery.'

'She doesn't want it?' I asked.

'She's unsure. She thinks it might only be playing for time. I've tried to assure her if we felt that, we wouldn't be operating.'

'Playing for time? Did she use those words?'

He hesitated. 'Yes, she did.'

'You mean a short life span?'

'We have to assume that's what she meant.'

'That doesn't sound like the Kate I knew.'

'Of course not. How could it be?' He was impatient, the Welsh accent no longer so lyrical. 'She's profoundly depressed, Mr Raphael, with good reason. Her world has collapsed. If you think about it, cancer is just one of the afflictions overwhelming her now. She's homeless, penniless, and faces returning to prison soon. She's had fourteen months there and found it threatening and disturbing.' He glanced at Mandy. 'You were a regular visitor, I understand, so you won't be surprised.'

When Mandy nodded agreement, his gaze turned once again to me, his voice more moderate this time.

'The Mulawa Correctional Centre; an odd choice, it seems to me, but someone in authority decided on a high-security female prison. The criminal population there labelled her an enemy of the state. The worst of the worst, amid the thieves and murderers. She came in for a lot of hateful abuse; she was spat at, called vicious names. She dreads being sent back there but knows it's inevitable.' He shrugged. 'Her best hope would be if she were allowed home, but she no longer has one. Nor a career. She doesn't have a lot going for her, does she? I think the future has become too difficult, and she's just stopped caring about it.'

I stared at him, then at Mandy, and realised the doctor was saying the things Mandy had found too difficult to talk about.

'When do you and the surgeon want an answer?'

'Would it shock you if I said before next week?'

'You mean this week?'

He nodded. 'That would be best.'

'Does that mean it's urgent? Desperate?'

'No. It means it's sensible. The sooner the better.'

'And then what?'

'You should ask the surgeon, but he'll say that will depend on how invasive the cancer is. If there's malignant tissue that hasn't shown up so far, it might be necessary to also remove the right breast.'

'Does she know that?'

'Yes,' he said reluctantly. 'I realise it added to her depression, but she had to be told. Full disclosure is the doctor's dilemma today, Mr Raphael. We have to explain the best and worst prognosis. It might be a bloody sight easier for us and the patient if we didn't.'

I stayed at the hospital late that night, while Mandy went home to Potts Point. Dr Griffith-Jones – who told me to call him Owen – said the rules were elastic in the private wing, and if I could stand the tucker I could request a meal from the trolley when they brought Kate's dinner. Or else there was a canteen downstairs.

'Tucker.' I grinned at the Welsh way he pronounced it, and asked how long he'd been in Australia.

'Twenty years,' he replied. 'I came for a holiday, met a girl at a party, decided this country was better than Wales and now we've got three kids and live in Coogee.'

'That's how it should be,' I said. 'A world without barriers and rigid borders.'

'If only.'

He asked when I intended going back to England, and I said it was an open return ticket. But not before Kate had her operation and was hopefully on the way to recovery.

'So persuade her,' he said as we shook hands, 'and you can book a flight next month to see the rugby test at Twickenham. Kate realises you're only here on a visit, but I think it would help if you were here until she started to recover. If you can spare the time.'

It was quiet in the hospital's private wing. The doors of each room were always left half open to enable the nurses to look in and check their patients, but it grew even quieter as visitors left and the hum of the lift was no longer audible. Sitting in a chair near her bed, I thought it was about nine o'clock when I heard Kate's soft voice.

'Damien . . . ?'

I opened my eyes and saw a young African nurse adjusting Kate's pillows, and both of them were smiling at me.

'Did I miss something?' I said.

'About an hour,' Kate answered.

'What?' I looked at my watch; the small hand no longer indicated nine. It was a few minutes to ten o'clock. 'Jet lag,' I said instantly, and the nurse giggled, saying if I intended to stay the night she'd fetch a blanket.

'I'm sorry,' I said, as we heard the squeak of her shoes in retreat towards the nurses' station. 'I had a huge piss-up with Uncle Angelo, and I don't think I've quite recovered. Beware of ninety-year-old relatives with a good grog cellar.'

'How is he?' She tried to get comfortable on the newly arranged pillows, and I moved to shift them for her.

'Is that better?'

'Yes.' She smiled. 'She's a sweet girl, but always gets the pillows wrong. So, we were talking of Angelo. Does he have a hangover?'

'Him? No chance.' I told her about the next morning and his offer to cook me breakfast. 'He sent his love.'

'I remember him the day I came to see you off. He and your aunt were so nice to me.'

'I'm not surprised. For years they kept writing to say that I was a fool.'

'Why?'

'They seemed to feel I should've asked you to marry me.'

There was a slight pause. 'They didn't really say that.'

'They did. Lately I've come to agree with them.'

It was a strange moment. The room was in semi-darkness and the reflected light from the corridor caught her face; I thought it was a smile that dismissed my words as an attempt to be kind.

'You've just had a divorce,' she said quietly. 'You don't need another entanglement.'

'Why do you think I'm sitting here so late at night?'

'Because you fell asleep, darling.'

She made me laugh. And my laughter had an effect; it enlivened her face so for a moment in the soft light she looked younger, like the girl I had seen crossing the lawn at my cousin's house on Fisherman's Beach more than thirty years earlier.

'Kate,' I said, and stopped, while trying to sort out my words. 'Can I call you Katie again, like I used to?' She nodded. 'Can I also tell you I love you?' She said nothing; just gazed at me. 'I've loved you since I was nineteen and you were seventeen. That's a hell of a long time ago.'

'It is,' she said.

'The oncologist says you're unsure about an operation.'

'I'm unsure about everything, Damien. Will it prolong my life so I can serve the rest of my time in that dreadful place?'

'I talked to Roger today. Met him for the first time and liked him. He says the government will look ugly if they try to enforce it. Sending a cancer patient back to prison for the rest of their term would be for no reason except more punishment.'

'Roger's an optimist. I'm a terrorist-related offender, and they don't mind looking ugly. It wins votes.' She tried to shift her pillows again, and I did it for her. 'Thanks,' she said, 'it's really the bed that's uncomfortable. A bit like sleeping on an ironing board.'

'You could be out of here after the operation. No more ironing board.'

'They have ironing boards in jail.'

'Owen, the oncologist, says they'd keep you here for radiotherapy. And just in case that wasn't necessary, they'd keep you here anyway, for as long as possible.'

'You've had a busy day, talking to so many people. No wonder you fell asleep on me.' I smiled, for this seemed more positive, until she went on. 'But even if Roger is right, and the surgeon's right, and my dear Welsh oncologist . . . even if the lot of them are right . . .' She shook her head almost despairingly. 'I keep on asking myself, what's it for? What's it really for, Damien?'

'For me,' I said quietly.

In the dim light I couldn't see her expression. She seemed to be staring at me.

'I don't want to go back to London, Kate. I've realised that in the past few days. I want to move back home. My uncle's put the house in my name, and I'd enjoy living there, restoring it to what it used to be. But I could only enjoy it if you were there with me.'

There was no reply.

'Kate? Katie?'

'Yes,' she said.

'Do you mean yes, you heard? Or yes, you'll come and live with me?'

'Have you got a handkerchief,' came a small voice, 'because I think I'm about to bawl my eyes out.'

I found a tissue; it was the best I could do, and I sat on the bed with my arms around her until the tears were over. We heard the African nurse's footsteps advancing; they slowed at the door and then stopped as she peered in.

'You take good care of my patient.' Her voice was full of cheerful merriment.

'I'll try to,' I said. 'If she'll take care of me.'

Chapter 31

There was a warning shout from the rooftop and a container full of broken slates was lowered to a waiting skip, then emptied with a noisy clatter. A pallet with another batch was hoisted to where the team were waiting, while other men on long ladders were replacing guttering. The old house echoed with the spate of activity.

'Wonderful resonance, all this toil taking place,' my uncle said. 'There's nothing I like better than hearing the sound of other people working. Always have done, my boy. It used to infuriate your father.'

'I know. It was a favourite pastime for you and Fanny, stirring him up.'

He laughed. 'We were a pair of mischievous buggers. But he was so . . . what's the word?'

'Serious?'

'Seriously up-himself, I would've said. Poor chap, he couldn't help it. He thought that adding columns of figures was a contribution to society. Even tried to turn you into a number-cruncher.'

It was his visit first since moving to his new home, anxious to see the start of the renovations. Sitting outside in a cane chair I'd brought down from the upstairs verandah, he looked fit and debonair in white cotton trousers, Prada loafers, a royal blue silk shirt and wide straw hat to keep off the sun. For all the world like an Edwardian gentleman who had strayed in from a previous century.

His ninetieth birthday had been celebrated at the retirement village which, despite my initial concerns, was a delight. Waratah Gardens was landscaped amid ornamental lakes and set in natural bushland. Angelo had acquired a compact small apartment, and after only a few days in residence appeared to have gathered a surprisingly large number of close friends. It was meant to be a quiet evening, but he had brought out his violin, and towards midnight sat on the dining table surrounded by his new circle, all singing lustily while he played 'Waltzing Matilda' and 'Click Go the Shears'. I wondered if Waratah Gardens was ever going to be quite the same again.

Two days later I drove him to Randwick to see Kate in hospital. It was only her third day after the operation. Each daily visit – I tried to reassure myself this was not wishful thinking – there seemed to be a small improvement in her spirits.

I'd spent the afternoon in her room after she was taken down to surgery, wanting to be there when she returned from the recovery ward. Then I sat with her much of the night while she slept in snatches, woke and in hazy murmurs spoke of times past and distant memories, the barbecue at Fisherman's Beach, the chaos of the Vietnam War protest march, the years of letters between us that had eventually become Christmas cards, and in between this, under the influence of sedative medication, started talking about a child called Omar whom she'd wanted to adopt.

But when I brought Angelo to see her she was wide awake and freshly made up by her favourite nurse. She looked wonderful, and my uncle was instantly infatuated. It almost turned into another celebration of his birthday when he insisted we bring a bottle of his favourite tipple.

'French fizz, Katerina.' He loved the sound of her full name, and the way it rolled off his tongue made her smile. The smile enchanted him. 'Do you the world of good, all the best doctors say so.'

'They must be those doctors who own vineyards, Angelo.' She sat up in bed, no longer so dependent on the pillows. 'My Welsh wizard says no grog until I can walk unaided. Ten lengths of the hospital corridor without a helping hand or a frame.'

'Hard taskmasters, the Welsh,' he asserted. 'Can Damien and I open the champers and have a modest sip to your health?'

'I'd be honoured,' she said, and finding a teaspoon in the room he insisted she should have at least one millimetre of champagne. When he handed it to her she licked the spoon and pronounced it a very good year.

I loved the byplay between them, the two people I cared for most in the world, and after toasts to her beauty and courage, and the hope she was going to be the chatelaine of his former house, which she would endow with charm and grace, I took him home to his new abode.

The next time he came to visit me the roof was repaired. We walked through the garden to view the progress that was taking place. I'd found a local handyman to get rid of the blackberries, dig up the beds and plant flowers and new shrubs, while behind the house a truck was loading the remnants of the former garage and lean-to.

'Why did you put the chickens in the garage, instead of putting the Packard in there?' I asked him.

'I haven't the faintest,' he answered, until a thought occurred.

'Maybe it was the foxes: they weren't interested in cars, but it would've been like the Valentine's Day massacre if they'd got to the chooks.'

It seemed to answer the question that had always puzzled me. Inside the house a painter was decorating the living room, and a plumber was putting new washers in dripping taps. Angelo said Aunt Fanny would be pleased at what was happening.

'How long before Kate can leave hospital and come home here?' he asked.

'Depends,' I said.

'I thought it was all settled.'

'It's settled we'll live together, and that we love each other. But it depends on the Department of Justice.'

'That's bad news. They're a mob of bastards,' Angelo said.

'They are,' I agreed. 'But they're the bastards we have to deal with. Unless we get awfully lucky.'

'How?'

'Roger's made an application to the Supreme Court for a late appeal.'

'On what grounds?'

'He seems to think there might've been an error in the sentence, but I doubt if it'll be allowed.'

'What happens if it isn't?' When I tried to avoid answering he said, 'She'd have to go back to prison, wouldn't she?'

'Yes.'

'For how long?'

'That's the worst part. At least ten months . . . but if there was no parole it could be almost three years.' I hated even speculating on this, dreading to think what it might do to Kate emotionally.

'That's barbaric,' he said. 'And grossly unfair.'

'You and I think so, Angelo, but we may be in the minority.'

'Unfair. She belongs here. Like you do. Took an awful long time, but it was always what we wished for.'

I didn't question this. He was a man who spoke the simple truth, and I could so easily imagine he and Fanny the day after Kate came to see me off to England, hoping for a happy ending that for all those years had never looked like taking place. My only regret was Fanny not being here to witness it.

We longed for news about if or when an appeal might be heard, but there was none. The lack of any word made us both tense. A week passed, and then another. Kate was now on the way to recovery; the morphine drip to control the pain had been removed, sedatives reduced, the network of tubes that had monitored her heartbeat and blood pressure now just a memory.

The surgeon was pleased; his decision to proceed with a mastectomy had been justified, he told her, and lymph nodes from beneath the armpit had been sectioned without an additional cut or further scarring. These had been tested and showed no sign of metastasis, confirming the cancer had not spread.

'I believe there'll be no problem,' he told her, 'although you must have check-ups every six months for the next few years. Someone will come and talk to you about an external prosthesis that can be worn inside a bra. It'll help with posture and balance, and avoids stress on the back.'

'And looks better from the front,' Kate added.

She was walking regularly along the hospital corridor and working daily with the physiotherapist. In the normal course of events she should have been discharged by now. That she was still in hospital was due to the intransigence of Owen Griffith-Jones, who was determined to keep her from being returned to prison as long as possible. He declared her recovery was not yet complete, and she was unfit to be moved, least of all back to a cell at the correction centre where she'd previously suffered such neglect. Besides, he was monitoring her condition to decide if radiation therapy was required, in which case he would prefer her to remain. Like us, he hoped he could prevent a transfer back behind bars before her case was given consideration, but it was a delaying tactic that could not last much longer.

The lack of decision about the appeal was weighing on Kate's mind, but outwardly she professed to be sanguine.

'Now I'm better I'll be able to put up with it, darling, especially knowing you'll be waiting for me. As well as being my favourite prison visitor,' she added, trying to sound optimistic. 'It's only another ten months – if I get parole. That's not a lifetime.'

'It feels like a lifetime to me.' I avoided saying I dreaded the effect a return to maximum security at Malawi might have on her.

Work on the house was proceeding rapidly, and the place began to look again like it did when I was a boy. I bought instant blooms to brighten the newly dug gardens, had the gates mended and more painters moved in. Most days I drove to the hospital, and had so many meals there that I grew almost as sick of the food as Kate. I promised her lavish meals in romantic restaurants, starting with a slap-up dinner at Mandy's restaurant The Mock Turtle. Neither of us mentioned there might be a delay before that could take place. In fact, we'd begun to talk rather less about the future.

We were halfway through attempting to eat a meal, which the

hospital insisted was lamb casserole, when Roger Montgomery arrived. He kissed Kate who said he looked hungry and generously offered him her lunch. Roger grinned and said no chance; she'd tried that the last time he visited.

'It's probably the same old meal, heated up,' Kate replied.

Roger had news, too astonishing to report by phone, he announced, and had therefore come to tell us personally. The Supreme Court had agreed that, because of the circumstances, they would hear his submission on *Forrester v The Queen*.

'Roger!' Kate put her meal aside, her excitement immediate and infectious. 'How did you do that?'

'I managed to get a copy of the sentencing statement.' He opened his bulky briefcase and searched for a document. 'Now, listen carefully. This is what the judge said: "You have pleaded guilty to hiding and providing shelter for escapees and unlawful persons thus committing terrorism offences under the Criminal Code Act of 1995". But in fact you didn't!'

'But I did plead guilty,' Kate reminded him.

'Yes. You pleaded guilty to hiding and providing shelter for *one twelve-year-old boy. One escapee.* There was some carelessness in that closed court. Lack of public scrutiny, perhaps.' He thrust the document back into his case with a triumphant gesture. 'You know me, Kate; I'm never unduly optimistic, but this time I think we might actually have them by the balls.'

Unlike her original trial, the appeal against the sentencing process was not held in camera. Because there was no media announcement, it did not attract any attention; the court was almost empty apart from the lawyers, officials and three judges, while I was the sole occupant of the public gallery. Kate was not there; on legal advice she had remained in the hospital. In Roger's words: 'You're looking so well and happy, they might think you're fit enough to do the rest of the time.'

His statement to the bench was short and to the point. He made no plea for clemency because of her illness, nor any mention of parole or that she might in fact be entitled to it for good behaviour. Just that the trial judge had made a simple error in the sentencing process. There were no multiple escapees. That was an assumption by the Prosecution, no doubt based on advice from the Federal Police, and perhaps swayed by the media coverage of certain newspapers and radio personalities.

It had gone unanswered, because the accused had no legal representation. This was admittedly by her own choice, he told the justices, because of her wish to plead guilty, but she pleaded her guilt only to hiding *one* twelve-year-old malnourished orphan refugee.

I admired the way Roger managed to slip the emotive words into his prescribed statement. It was as if he was asking, Did such a child pose a threat to the Australian nation? Was a cold and hungry orphan an enemy of the state? And perhaps – if their Honours were of a mind to wonder – were we in danger of becoming absurd in the eyes of the civilised world?

None of this, of course, was stated. But it felt there to me, inherent between the lines. It may have felt so to their Honours as well, or perhaps they simply ruled on the law as found in the relevant section of the Criminal Appeal Act. Or did they, when allowing the appeal and directing the applicant be freed, perhaps think a woman who risked her liberty to save a boy from brutality might, in more rational times, be considered a Samaritan?

The trouble with judges, I said to Roger as we left to break the news to Kate, is they would never admit to such a sentimental verdict.

Roger, whistling to hail a cab, said, 'The law is often an ass, Damien, but thank Christ, not today.'

She was discharged from hospital and we went home to the house I was always happiest in when growing up. I stopped a short way down Buckingham Avenue so she could get a long-distance view of it, wondering what her first reaction might be.

'Do you think it looks like it belongs on the Yorkshire Moors?' I asked her. 'Or perhaps to Miss Cavendish in *Great Expectations*?'

'I think it's gorgeous,' she said, pointing towards the attic, the folly on the top floor beside the chimney pots. 'Is that the room where Angelo used to be banished, to play his violin?'

'That's it.'

She smiled, as if promising herself an early visit to it. 'My darling,' she said, 'I think we're going to be awfully happy here.'

I put my arm around her, and she leant against me. I could feel her skin through the thin summer dress. Smooth soft skin. She was no longer gaunt or exhausted; silky dark hair framed her face and her dark-blue eyes were vibrant. She looked like a lively thirty-year-old, and I felt filled with longing. We had so many years to make up.

There was a very private housewarming the following month. Just a few old friends, and some new ones. Mandy, Roger, his wife Anna, Rebecca Mannering, Owen Griffith-Jones, as well as Akeyo, the African nurse who came from Kenya, and of course Uncle Angelo with his violin. He played part of the Concerto in D major, as well as 'Farewell to Old England Forever' and 'The Wild Colonial Boy', before making a gracious speech about how the house had been waiting for our arrival. And how it would be alive again, the way it used to be, full of love and miracles.

Epilogue

Easter 2004 came. It was the anniversary of the invasion of Iraq, and would soon be twelve months since George W. Bush, in his flack jacket as commander-in-chief, had stepped onto an aircraft carrier that bore the promise *Mission Accomplished*. At the time we almost believed it, like we'd almost believed him about the weapons of mass destruction.

Later that year in Australia, the government tried to fast-track new and tougher anti-terrorism laws. The Federal Attorney-General proposed powers to detain and strip-search children as young as twelve, but these were blocked in the Senate. Australians were encouraged to watch out for any unusual activity, and report it to ASIO or the Federal Police. We learnt a national security hotline had been installed for citizens to inform on each other. A 'ringing success', declared the Attorney-General, announcing it had received 42,000 calls in the past two years.

Kate and I saw these things on the television news, and if we hadn't been so much in love it would have been an awful and depressing year. But our own news was brilliant. She had had two check-ups, and both were clear. From now on the examinations would be only annually. That was the best thing that happened.

Soon after Easter there was a flying visit from Juliet and her sub-editor. They told us they were getting married right after Juliet's next assignment, which was an interview in America.

'Who is it this time?' I asked the husband-to-be.

'Tiger Woods,' he said, as if I should've known.

I began work on a new play. Kate unobtrusively went back to the office above the sandwich shop to assist Roger, though at reduced hours.

In the spring I received a welcome phone call, and the following weekend suggested to Kate we have a few days in the Hunter Valley and visit the vineyards. We went via Wollombi along the Broke Road. The recent rain had broken a drought and made the countryside look as green as Ireland. We called on Jim and Philippa Davern, friends who owned the Wandin Valley vineyard at Pokolbin, spent the night with them and next morning headed north to Gloucester and the Barrington Tops. It was another lovely day, perfect for relaxing and finding new places to visit together.

'We've got lots of time.' I checked the map and showed her. 'How about we turn at Murrurundi and go to Mudgee and Gulgong?'

'Fine,' she answered. 'Gulgong? Isn't that where Henry Lawson grew up?'

'It's one of the towns that claims him as a native son. They also have an opera house where Nellie Melba sang.'

'Is this a history weekend, Damien?'

I laughed and we drove through wheat fields and more and more vineyards. The wine industry was thriving in every state. I remembered when I first went overseas, Australian wine was trying to recover after years of being sold in bulk under the label *Emu* and being ridiculed as cheap plonk. Now it was a firm favourite on the shelves of most supermarkets in Europe.

We crossed a creek and looked down on a modest homestead. I stopped the car and Kate turned to me.

'Where are we, darling?'

'Have you ever seen this place before?'

'No,' she said, mystified, turning to look again. 'I don't think so . . .' Her puzzled face changed to gradual recognition. 'But it can't be. I mean, it's not possible . . .'

In the distance a figure was emerging from the farmhouse. A small figure, waving.

'Damien, it can't be,' Kate repeated.

'They told me to be here at three o'clock.'

'Oh God,' she whispered, 'it can't be, but it is.' She turned to me, her lovely eyes full of questions. 'How?'

'I begged Roger to help,' I said. 'It took a long time, but he told me to talk to Rebecca, and she introduced me to Graeme Edwards.'

The boy was running up the hill towards us. Kate got out of the car and called to him.

'Omar!'

'Kate!' he shouted. 'Missus Kate!'

She ran towards him, and they met in a fierce hug that made me wince. But she seemed oblivious to any pain their collision may have caused. She knelt beside him, crying and cupping his face in her hands as they gazed at each other. I got out of the car and cautiously approached them.

'You've got taller,' Kate said. 'Do you understand "taller"?'

'Of course,' Omar said with a broad grin. 'I go to school, Kate. I can speak heaps of Australian English.'

'You certainly can,' she replied, hugging him joyfully again.

~

We met the farmer and his wife. They had a son who'd been killed in a road accident when working in Jordan. Omar, to their neighbours and the rest of the district, was the child he'd had with a local girl whom they had adopted. I wasn't sure if the story would stand up to close scrutiny, but the boy was so appealing that nobody would wish to doubt it or him.

We had afternoon tea together, and Kate accepted the fact that Omar loved them and was happy here. He showed us the horse he rode and the cows he helped to milk, and it was hard to imagine this enchanting and happy child had ever been caged and ill-treated. He walked back to the car with us, and waved as we drove away.

'See you in the next school holidays!' he called. 'Don't forget.'

'No chance of that, Omar,' Kate called back. 'We won't forget.'

She waved until the boy and the farmhouse were lost in the distance, and we turned east and headed for home.

Author's Note

'The enemy of my enemy is my friend', according to the old proverb, but that was not the case in Australia during the first years of this century. We were preparing for war against Saddam Hussein while imprisoning those who fled from his brutality. It was a time of political opportunism, redeemed only by minorities; a few dissenting Federal parliamentarians, a group of human rights lawyers and, most importantly, those who went to visit, comfort and try to assist asylum seekers in detention centres. They gave their time and their friendship, and helped to atone for what was happening in Canberra.

The compulsion to write this book began in 2001, the day I saw a photo in the *Sydney Morning Herald* of three heartbreakingly beautiful Iraqi girls, sisters aged six, seven and nine, who drowned on an Indonesian fishing vessel. I kept the photograph and a mass of newspaper reports documenting that insensitive time until I began to write this novel two years ago. Among the articles were those by David Marr and Marian Wilkinson, Nikki Barrowclough, Kelly Burke, Margo Kingston, Lindsay Murdoch, Andrew Clennell and Cynthia Banham.

AUTHOR'S NOTE

I am greatly indebted to Kate Maclurcan, refugee advocate with the Bridge for Asylum Seekers Foundation, and also to Isobel Bishop. Both were generous with their time and help. My thanks also to Don Maclurcan for the insight provided by his case study *The Sinking of the SEIV X*. The illuminating book *Acting from the Heart*, edited by Sarah Mares and Louise Newman, was an inspiration – filled with stories from both sides of the razor wire by journalists like Ngareta Rossell and Jacquie Everitt, as well as over fifty visitors to detention centres.

My gratitude to Jon Cleary, a friend of many years, for permission to quote from his book *The High Commissioner*, and to my cousin John Clements for his vivid recollection of our own unique and endearing Italian relatives. Thanks also to Alfred Bell, Paul Power and the Refugee Council of Australia, Bruce Gee for his helpful research and Bryce Courtenay for arranging it. My sincere gratitude to family members: Bruce Yeldham, my granddaughter Olivia Cawthorne and grandson Peter Yeldham.

To designer Marina Messiha and publisher Rachel Scully, I was thrilled with the book's appearance, and look forward to what I hope will be a long association. Once again I had the pleasure of working with Saskia Adams, an editor whose enthusiasm and creative ideas make each novel a meaningful and enjoyable collaboration.

Finally, to Ali Watts of Penguin Australia. This book began with you, and for that and much more over the course of six novels since we first began to work together, my grateful thanks and best wishes for the future.

This is a work of fiction, but the events of that time were fact and remain a shameful testament to political expediency. To all those who gave me information and assistance, if there are mistakes in legal details or any other inaccuracies, the errors are mine.

Peter Yeldham
pyeldham@bigpond.net.au

Also by Peter Yeldham

Barbed Wire and Roses

The First World War, everyone said in 1914, would be over by Christmas, and Stephen Conway rushes to enlist. Leaving behind a new wife and a baby on the way, he soon finds himself in the trenches of Gallipoli. Four horrific years later, Stephen is the only survivor of his platoon. Shell-shocked and disillusioned, during the heat of battle on the blood-stained fields of France, he mysteriously disappears.

More than eighty years later, Stephen's grandson Patrick finds a diary that leads him to Britain and France on a journey to discover what really happened. It is a journey during which he unexpectedly finds love, and the truth about his grandfather's fate that is even stranger and more shocking than he imagined.

Based on true events, this is an unforgettable novel of courage and survival from a master storyteller.

'Five stars. A heart-wrenching account of our young Anzacs.'
ADELAIDE ADVERTISER

'A gripping tale of romance and mystery.'
WEEKLY TIMES

The Murrumbidgee Kid

Belle Carson longs for her young son, Teddy, to achieve the success that eluded her on the stage and screen. Determined to pursue this dream, she abandons her devoted husband and their Murrumbidgee River home for a more vibrant city life. But Belle's obsession leads her and Teddy – whom the press christens 'the Murrumbidgee Kid' – into a world where nothing is safe or familiar. And from her carefully hidden past a threat soon emerges to make their precarious lives even more vulnerable . . .

From rural Gundagai to the bright lights and shady underbelly of 1930s Sydney, this is a beautifully written and absorbing story about an unconventional family's coming-of-age.

'A strong and entertaining story.'
THE AGE

A Bitter Harvest

Senator William Patterson, wealthy and influential, hides a scandal from his past that could ruin him. Stefan Muller, a young penniless immigrant, seeks a promised new life in a land that does not welcome him. When the senator's cherished daughter Elizabeth falls in love with the impoverished Stefan, it creates a family conflict that threatens to destroy them.

From a tumultuous and vibrant Sydney to the lyrical landscape of the Barossa Valley, *A Bitter Harvest* is an epic saga of prejudice, political turmoil and lasting love from one of Australia's favourite storytellers.

'*An epic read and totally absorbing.*'
SUN-HERALD

'*Mixing fact and fiction, Yeldham takes his readers on a fascinating journey into the past.*'
BRISBANE NEWS

The Currency Lads

Daniel Johnson and Matthew Conway are currency lads – born and bred in the new land now being called Australia. Closer than brothers, they harbour a secret that binds them for life. But change is coming. When the British government resolves to turn back the clock and renew convict transportation, Daniel and Matthew find themselves on opposite sides of a fierce conflict that threatens to tear their friendship apart.

Set in the bustling maritime world of 1830s Sydney, and spanning two decades, this is an unforgettable novel of loyalty and love that captures the spirit and energy of early Australia.

'A ripping great yarn, featuring characters
with depth and storylines to match.'
WEEKENDER

'Combines the facts of a turbulent part of Australia's history
with a moving and often riveting fictional narrative.'
GOLD COAST BULLETIN

Against the Tide

They came from the ruins of the war in Europe: Sarah Wiseman, the survivor of a German concentration camp, Michael and Helen Francis, a brother and sister fleeing from the Russians in Budapest, and Neil Latham, the young English soldier who broke the rules to help them all survive. The four arrive in Australia seeking a new start in the lucky country.

But life in post-war Sydney, amid the gangs and corruption, and in the high country of Australia's Snowy Mountain Scheme, is hardly an idyllic existence. And the past, left so far behind, threatens to jeopardise all their futures in unexpected and terrifying ways. It seems only a matter of time before buried secrets will be revealed…

A compelling saga of friendship, love and survival.

Land of Dreams

Sam Delon is a young Frenchman born and raised in Japan. Florence Carter has led a quiet and lonely life in her native Australia. One meeting on a Sydney beach is enough to create a lasting bond between the unlikely pair – and enough to share a secret with the potential to transform Sam's life.

When Japan attacks Pearl Harbor, Sam becomes an enemy in his own country and exists under the relentless scrutiny of the military police, sustained only by the knowledge he shares with Florence. They risk everything to stay in touch – but as the bombs drop on Darwin and Tokyo, their commitment to each other is pushed to the limit.

A wartime story of love, courage and the ties that bind.

'Yeldham is a strong and skilful teller of stories.'
WEST AUSTRALIAN

'With Peter Yeldham, Australian historical fiction would seem to be in good hands.'
GOLD COAST BULLETIN